I used

Somebody found out that I still was. I got him right in the breadbasket. With plenty of *Oomph!* Because the recoil was enough to throw me back a step and spin me halfway around.

The villain folded up around the blunt quarrel, out of action. Unfortunately, he was not alone. His friends did not give me the time to crank the crossbow back to full tension. A shortcoming of the instrument that I would have to mention to Playmate.

Two shimmering forms came through the hole in the wall, unremarkable street people who flashed silver every few seconds. The one I had shot lay folded up like a hairpin outside, entirely silver now. Another silvery figure ministered to it, briefly flashing into the form of a bum every ten seconds. Only the fallen one didn't shimmer like I was seeing it through a lot of hot air. My bolt must have disrupted a serious compound illusion sorcery. . . .

ANGRY LEAD SKIES

"Cook brings a dose of gritty realism to fantasy."
—*Library Journal*

ANGRY LEAD SKIES

Glen Cook

From the Files of Garrett, P.I.

A ROC BOOK

ROC
Published by New American Library, a division of
Penguin Putnam Inc., 375 Hudson Street,
New York, New York 10014, U.S.A.
Penguin Books Ltd, 80 Strand,
London WC2R 0RL, England
Penguin Books Australia Ltd, Ringwood,
Victoria, Australia
Penguin Books Canada Ltd, 10 Alcorn Avenue,
Toronto, Ontario, Canada M4V 3B2
Penguin Books (N.Z.) Ltd, 182–190 Wairau Road,
Auckland 10, New Zealand

Penguin Books Ltd, Registered Offices:
Harmondsworth, Middlesex, England

First published by Roc, an imprint of New American Library,
a division of Penguin Putnam Inc.

First Printing, April 2002
10 9 8 7 6 5 4 3 2

1

Mom was too embarrassed to tell the truth. She never said a word. But I'm not entirely stupid. I figured it out on my own.

I was born under an evil star. Maybe an evil galaxy. With zigging mad lights quarreling all over angry lead skies.

The planets had to've been so cruelly misaligned that no equally malignant conjunction will be possible for another hundred lifetimes.

I have a feeling, though, that my partner will be there to gloat when those celestial maladroits again foregather to conspire.

Grumbling, head aching, empty mug in shaky hand, I stomped toward the front door. Some soon-to-be sporting an iron hook for a hand pest refused to stop bruising the oak with his knuckles.

The air shivered with amusement that only rendered me more glum.

Anything my partner found entertaining was bound to be unpleasant for me.

In the small front room the Goddamn Parrot harangued himself in his sleep, his language fit to pinken the cheeks of amazons.

I had to preserve the woodwork personally because Dean was out visiting his gaggle of homely nieces. And the Dead Man won't get off his can and answer no matter what the circumstances might be. He's had a severe attitude problem for about four hundred years. He figures just because somebody stuck a knife in him back then he doesn't have to do anything for himself anymore.

I peeked through the peephole.

I cussed some. Which always makes me feel better when that old devil sixth sense tells me that things are about to stop going my way.

Nowhere in sight, for as far as my eagle eye could see, was there even one tasty morsel of femininity.

I was so disappointed I grumbled, "But it always starts with a girl." My seventh and eighth senses started perking. They couldn't find a girl, either.

Then my natural optimism kicked in. There wasn't a girl around! There wasn't a girl around! There wasn't anybody out there but my old pal Playmate and a skinny gink who had to be a foreigner because there was no way a Karentine of his type could have survived the war in the Cantard.

No girl meant no trouble. No girl meant nothing starting. No girl meant not having to go to work. All was right with the world after all. I could deal with this in about ten minutes, then draw a beer and get back to plotting my revenge on Morley Dotes for having stuck me with the Goddamn Parrot.

Another ghost of amusement tinkled through the stale air. It reminded me that the impossible is only barely less likely than the normal around here.

It was time to air the place out.

Then I made my big mistake.

I opened the door.

2

Playmate isn't really nine feet tall. He just seems to fill up that much space. Though he did stoop getting through the doorway. And his shoulders were almost too wide to make it. And there wasn't an ounce of fat on the not really nine feet of him.

Playmate owns a stable. He does the work himself, including all the blacksmithery and most of the pitchfork management. He looks scary but he's a sweetheart. His great dream is to get into the ministry racket. His great sorrow is the fact that TunFaire is a city already hagridden by a backbreaking oversupply of priests and religions.

"Hey, Garrett," he said. Repartee isn't his main talent. But he does have a sharp eye.

That's me. Garrett. Six feet and change inches of the handsomest, most endearing former Marine you'd ever hope to meet. The super kind of fellow who can dance and drink the night away and still retain the skill and coordination to open a door and let a friend in at barely the crack of noon the next day. "That's not your usual homily, buddy." I've had a listen or two on occasions when I wasn't fast enough or sly enough to produce a convincing excuse for missing one of his ministerial guest appearances or amateur night sermons at some decrepit storefront church.

Playmate favored me with a sneer. He's got a talent for that which exceeds mine with the one raised eyebrow. The right side of his upper lip rises up and twists and begins to shimmy and quiver like a belly dancer's fanny. "I save the good sermons for people whose characters would appear to offer some teeny little hint of a possibility that there's still hope for their salvation."

Over in the small front room the Goddamn Parrot cackled like he was trying to lay a porcupine egg. And that amusement stuff was polluting the psychic atmosphere again.

The dark planets were shagging their heinies into line.

Playmate preempted my opportunity to deploy one of my belated but brilliantly lethal rejoinders. "This is my friend Cypres Prose, Garrett." Cypres Prose was a whisper more than five feet tall. He had wild blond hair, crazy blue eyes, a million freckles, and a permanent case of the fidgets. He scratched. He twitched. His head kept twisting on his neck. "He invents things. After what happened this morning I promised you'd help him."

"Why, thank you, Playmate. And I'm glad you came over because I promised the Metropolitan that you'd swing by the Dream Quarter to help put up decorations for the Feast of the Immaculate Deception."

Playmate glowered. He has serious problems with the Orthodox Rite. I gave him a look at my own second-team sneer. It don't dance. "*You* promised him? For me? That's what friends are for, eh?"

"Uh, all right. Maybe I overstepped." His tone said he didn't think that for a second. "Sorry."

"You're sorry? Oh. That's good. That makes everything all right, then. You're not presuming on my friendship the way Morley Dotes or Winger or Saucerhead Tharpe might." I would never presume on *them*. Not me. No way.

The scrawny little dink behind Playmate kept trying to peek around him. He never stopped talking. He strengthened his case constantly with remarks like, "Is that him, Play? He ain't much. From the way you talked I thought he was gonna be ten feet tall."

I said, "I am, kid. But I'm not on duty right now." Cypres Prose had a nasal edge on a cracking soprano voice that I found extremely irritating. I wanted to clout him upside the head and tell him to speak Karentine like a man.

Oh, boy! After closer appraisal I saw that Prose wasn't as old as I'd thought.

Now I knew how he'd survived the Cantard. By being too young to have gone.

Playmate put on a big-eyed, pleading face. "He's as bright as the sun, Garrett, but not real long on social skills."

The boy managed to wriggle past Playmate's brown bulk. Ah, this child was definitely the sort who got himself pounded regularly because he just couldn't get his brilliance wrapped around the notion of keeping his mouth shut. He just naturally had to tell large, slow-witted, overmuscled, swift-tempered types that they were wrong. About whatever it was they were wrong about. What would not matter.

I observed, "And the truth shall bring you great pain."

"You understand." Playmate sighed.

"But don't hardly sympathize." I grabbed the kid as he tried to weasel his million freckles into the small front room. "Not with somebody who just can't make the connection between cause and effect where people are concerned." I shifted my grip, brought the kid's right arm up behind his back. Eventually he recognized a connection between pain and not holding still.

The Goddamn Parrot decided this was the ideal moment to begin preaching, "I know a girl who lives in a shack . . ."

Playmate's friend turned red.

I said, "Why don't we go into my office?" My office is a custodian's closet with delusions of grandeur. Playmate is big enough to clog the doorway all by himself. We could manage the kid in there. If I dragged him inside first.

In passing I noted that my partner had no obvious, immediate interest in participating—beyond being amused at my expense. Same old story. Everybody takes advantage of Mama Garrett's favorite boy.

"In there, Kip!" Playmate is a paragon of patience. This kid, though, was taking him to his limit. He laid a huge hand on the boy's shoulder, pinched. That would smart. Playmate can squeeze chunks of granite into gravel. I turned loose, went and got behind my desk. I like to think I look good back there.

Playmate set Cypres Prose in the client's chair. He stood behind the kid, one hand always on the boy's shoulder, as though the kid might get away if he wasn't restrained every second. For the time being, though, the boy was focused. Totally.

He had discovered Eleanor.

She's the central figure in the painting that hangs behind my desk. That portrays a terrified woman fleeing from a looming, shadowy manor house that has a lamp burning in one high window. The surrounding darkness reeks of evil menace. The painting has a lot of dark magic in it. Once upon a time it had a whole lot more. It helped nail Eleanor's killer.

At one time, if you were evil enough, you might see your own face portrayed in the shadowy margins.

Eleanor had poleaxed my young visitor. She startles everyone at first glimpse but this reaction was exceptional.

"I take it he has a touch of paranormal talent."

Playmate nodded, showed me an acre of white teeth, mouthed the words, "There might be a wizard in the woodpile somewhere."

I raised an eyebrow now.

Playmate mouthed, "Father unknown."

"Ah." Our lords from the Hill do get around. Often playing no more fairly than the randier gods in some of the less upright pantheons. Offspring produced without benefit of wedlock are not entirely uncommon. Not infrequently those reveal signs of having received the parental gift.

I asked, "Am I going to grow a beard before I find out what's on your mind?" I heard a thump from upstairs. Katie must be awake. She would boggle the boy, too.

"All right. Like I told you, this's Cypres Prose. Kip for short. I've know him since he was this high. He's always hung around the stable. He adores horses. Lately he's been inventing things."

Another black mark behind the kid's name. Horses are the angels of darkness. And they're clever enough to fool almost everybody else into thinking that they're good for something.

"And this matters to me because?"

That air of amused presence became more noticeable. Kip definitely felt it. His eyes got big. He lost interest in Eleanor. He peered around nervously. He told Playmate,

"I think they're here! I feel . . . something." He frowned. "But this's different. This's something old and earthy, like a troll."

"Ha!" I chuckled. "More like a troll's ugly, illegitimate uncle." Nobody had compared the Dead Man to a troll before—except possibly in reference to his social attitudes.

I felt him starting to steam up.

The boy getting the Dead Man's goat should've told me something but instead left me a tad open-minded at a time when my finances didn't at all require me looking at work. Money had been accumulating faster than I could waste it. "I'll give you five minutes, Playmate. Talk to me."

3

Playmate said, "It would be better if Kip explained."

"But can he pay attention long enough to do it? Somebody *please* tell me something." Patience is not one of my virtues when I've got a sneaking suspicion that somebody wants me to work.

Kip opened and closed his mouth several times. He was trying but he'd become distracted again.

I sighed. Playmate did, too. "He lives in his own reality, Garrett."

"So it would seem. You know him. Long time know him, yes yes. You tell me, Horsepooperscoopinman. He invents things, yes yes? You're here, yes yes. Why?"

"Somebody—and I have a feeling it might actually be more than one somebody—has been following him around. He claims they've been trying to dig around inside his head. Then this morning somebody tried to kidnap him."

I looked at Kip. I looked at Playmate. I looked at Kip again. Heroic me, I managed to keep a straight face. But only because I deal with these problems myself on a regular basis. Particularly threats of mental vandalism and larceny.

Another cascade of remote amusement. Kip jerked in his chair.

I suggested, "Tell me why anybody would bother."

Playmate shrugged. He seemed a little embarrassed, no longer sure seeing me was the best idea. "Because he invents things? That's what he thinks."

"So what's he invent?"

"Ideas, mostly. Lots of ideas for devices and mechanisms

that look like they'd work just fine if we could get the right tools and the proper materials to build them. We've been trying to put a couple of the simpler ones together. In practical terms he's mainly made little things of not much value. Like a writing stick that doesn't crumble in your fingers like charcoal can but that doesn't have to be dipped in an inkwell or water every few seconds. Eliminates the problems you have with wet ink. And there was a marvellous tool sharpener. And a new style bit that isn't nearly as hard on a horse's mouth. I'm already using that one and it's been selling pretty well. And he has all sorts of ideas for complicated engines, most of which I just don't understand."

Kip's head bobbed a little, agreeing with Playmate but about what I have no idea.

"What about family?"

Playmate winced. That wasn't a question with which he was comfortable. Not in front of the kid, anyway. "Kip is the youngest of three. He has a sister and a brother. His sister Cassie is the oldest. She has four years on his brother Rhafi, who has a couple on Kip. His mother is . . . unusual." He tapped his temple. "Their father is missing." He held up two, then three fingers to indicate that multiple fathers had to be considered. Possibly Cypres wasn't aware. In such matters, sometimes, mothers can be less than forthcoming.

"The war?"

Playmate shook his head. He rested both of his hands solidly on Kip's shoulders. It was impossible for that kid to sit still. He had begun rifling through the stuff on my desk, reading snippets. He could read. That was not common amongst youngsters. I was willing to bet his literacy was Playmate's fault.

I pulled my inkwell out of harm's way while thinking that eliminating wet ink might be an amazingly wonderful trick. When I get going I get the stuff all over the place.

The boy said, "There are more of them all the time, you know. They're looking for Lastyr and Noodiss. They've hired a man named Bic Gonlit to help them."

"Garrett?" Playmate demanded. "What?"

"I know Bic Gonlit. Know of him, anyway."

"And? You look puzzled."

"Only because I am. Bic Gonlit is a bounty hunter. He specializes in bringing them back alive. Why would he be interested in Kip?"

Kip's tone told me he wondered why everyone else in this world had to be so thick. "He's not looking for me. They don't care about me. They want Lastyr and Noodiss. They're only bothering with me because they think I know where those two are."

"And do you?" Lastyr and Noodiss?

"No." Not entirely convincingly, I thought.

Those names didn't fit any recognizable slot. Not quite elvish. Maybe upcountry dwarfish. Possibly ogreish, if they represented nicknames. Noodiss sounded like something scatological in ogre dialect.

"Who are they?"

Kip said, "You can't tell them from real people. They make you think you're looking at real people. Unless you look at their eyes. They can't disguise their eyes."

Who can't? "What the hell is he talking about, Play?"

"I'm not sure, Garrett. I can't get any more sense out of him than that. That's why I brought him to you."

"Thanks. Your confidence makes me feel warm and fuzzy all over."

Playmate ignored my sarcasm. He knew me too well. "I thought he was mental, too, at first. This's been going on for a while. And I never saw anything to convince me that he wasn't making up another one of his stories. But then somebody broke into his flat. While some of his family were there. Which is weird, because the Proses don't have a pot to pee in. Then, next day, this morning, they came to the stable. Three of them. Three strange, shiny women. I've been letting Kip use a corner of the smithy for a workshop. He does his projects there. They tried to drag him off."

"You didn't let them?"

"Of course I didn't let them." He was offended because I'd even asked. "Though it wasn't all me. They seemed extremely distracted by the horses. Afraid of them, even."

"That just sounds like basic common sense to me."

"You shouldn't joke that way, Garrett." Playmate just will not believe the truth about horses.

"These guys know horses mean trouble and they've got a beef with this kid and those things are somehow a surprise to you?"

Some people view the world through a whole different set of spectacles.

Playmate chose not to pursue the debate. "Their eyes *were* weird, Garrett. Almost like holes. Or like there were little patches of fog right there hiding them when they looked straight at you."

I tried to imagine the encounter. Playmate abhors violence, yet, for a nonviolent idealist, he can be totally convincing in any argument that steps on a banana peel and slides off the intellectual plane. Playmate has sense enough to understand that not everyone shares his views. There are some people that need hammering and others that just plain need killing. There are people out there even a mother couldn't love.

"These visitors some new kind of breed?" All the races infesting TunFaire seem capable of interbreeding. Often the mechanics aren't easy to visualize but the results are out there on the street. At times nature takes a very strange turn. And some of the strangest are among my friends.

Kip shook his head. Playmate told me, "Give me a sheet of paper. I'll draw you a picture." He produced a small, polished cherrywood box with silver fittings. When opened it revealed a battery of artist's tools. He took out a couple of sticks I decided had to be Kip's inventions.

"Another unsuspected talent." I pushed over a torn sheet of paper. I'd only just started using its back side.

I recalled seeing charcoal drawings around Playmate's place but I never wondered enough about them to make a direct connection.

This detecting business requires great curiosity and attention to the tiniest details.

I was amazed once Playmate got started. "You're in the wrong racket, Play."

"Not much call for this kind of thing, Garrett." His hand

moved swiftly and confidently. "Maybe in a carnival." He was a lefty, of course. They always are. The guy who did Eleanor probably had two left hands.

The portrait took shape rapidly.

"The original must've been one ugly critter." It had a head like a bottom-up pear. It had a mouth so small it was fit to eat nothing but soup. No ears were evident but Playmate was still drawing.

His hand moved slower and slower. A frown creased his forehead. Pinhead sweat beads appeared. He strained mightily to get his hand to do something it didn't want to do.

He gasped, "Less call than there is for new preachers."

"What's wrong?"

"This won't come out like what I saw. I wanted to draw the woman in charge. A small woman, average-looking with ginger hair. Cut off straight above her eyes and straight all the way around the rest, two inches down from where her ears should've been."

The thing he had drawn owned no ears.

He was drawing something that wasn't human. Its head was shaped something like an inverted pear. Its eyes were oversize, bulgy, teardrops shaped, evidently without pupils. He did not put in a nose. Instead, there were slits, unconnected, forming an inverted Y.

I observed, "There isn't any nose. And what about ears?"

"I thought they were hidden under her hair. I guess . . . not. There're these dark, bruise-looking patches down here, practically on the neck. Maybe they do the same job."

That *was* weird. I couldn't think of a race that didn't have ears of some kind. In fact, most races have ears that make our human ones look like afterthoughts. Great hairy, pointy, or dangly things all covered with scales and warts.

"Old Bones, you've got to help us out here. Why can't Play draw what he really saw?"

Grumpy atmospherics. Kip squeaked. The Dead Man observed, *Mr. Playmate appears to be reproducing what was actually in front of him rather than what he believes he saw. It is possible he was gulled by some illusion. The illustration does resemble the boy's recollections of his elven acquaintances.*

"Wonderful. Play, I'll bet Colonel Block wishes he had somebody who could draw pictures like this of the villains he wants to catch."

"The Guard can go on wishing. You know I'm a simple man, Garrett. Not greedy at all. But I do have to point out that a second-rate stable operator like myself still makes a better living than the best-paid honest policeman."

"Most everything pays better than being honest. You want to work for Block and Relway, you'd better have a bone-deep law and order calling. Now what?"

Kip was making noises. He wasn't as impressed with the sketch as I was. "The eyes aren't right, Play."

"They wouldn't be, would they?" Playmate growled. "Since whenever they look straight at you they go all smoky. And they aren't eyes like ours, anyway. They don't have any eyelids."

"It's not that. It's their shape. They're bulgier. . . ."

Garrett!

The kid jumped, squealed, went paper pale in an instant, scattered the documents on my desk. He moaned, "They're here! They're trying to get into my head again!" He tried to jump past Playmate.

"Hang on to him!" I said. "That's just old Chuckles deciding to pick on me for a minute."

Old Chuckles demurred. He sent, *The young man is entirely correct, Garrett. There is an unknown creature in the alleyway out back trying to look into the house. I am confusing it and blocking it but that is extremely difficult. The work requires most of the attention of most of my minds.*

The Dead Man belongs to a rare species known as Loghyr. They have that knack. Of having multiple minds capable of parallel and independent function. I've heard that some develop multiple personalities. I can't imagine. Old Bones is a complete horror show being just one of himself.

Simultaneous shrieks sounded upstairs and in the small front room. I don't know what Katie's problem was but it was audibly obvious that the Goddamn Parrot had decided

14   *Glen Cook*

to focus his powers of persuasion on convincing the world that he was about as sane as a drunken butterfly.

The creature is now confused by what I have done. Which is to connect it to a couple of marginally sensitive but completely empty minds. Perhaps it will become equally lost.

"That's no way to talk about my girlfriend."

The Dead Man was able to make the air sneer. And I suppose he had a point. Nature endowed Katie with countless delicious attributes. At first glance excessive intellect doesn't appear to be one of those. But, actually, bimbo is a survival strategy that she has let get out of control.

The kid began babbling soft nonsense not unlike that of yon inebriated megamouth. It sounded suspiciously like some of the nonsense Katie whispered when she was about half-asleep and purring. I asked Playmate, "Kip have a history with booze or drugs?" The kid was now not speaking any form of Karentine I recognized. My place isn't the neighborhood ranting ground for any of those cults that specialize in speaking in tongues.

Even so, soon every fourth word out of Kip's mouth sounded vaguely familiar. They may even have been real words—completely out of context.

"No. Never. He doesn't have that kind of imagination. But this's exactly the way he got when those elves came looking for him."

"Elves? What elves? Are we suddenly starting to get somewhere?"

"No. I just feel more comfortable calling them elves. Say they were elf-sized but they weren't like any elves that we know. They were female. You ever see a female elf who didn't look like the devil's disciple?"

Not my choice of descriptives but I knew what he meant. Even the ugly elf girls are pretty enough and wicked enough to melt your spine with a wink and a smile and a wiggle if the fancy takes them. "No. Never have."

"These girls . . . weren't. They were almost asexual."

"How did you know?"

Garrett! I do not enjoy such an oversufficiency of mindspace that I can waste any following your digressions. Save that for later. The creature is in the alley. It is confused. It

*can be captured. Will you please see to that and cease this
passing the time of day with Mr. Playmate?*

"Play, my sedentary sidekick tells me one of your elves
is skulking around in the alley out back. Why don't we go
invite him to the party? We can smack him around a little
to break his concentration. Old Bones can ransack his mind
while he's distracted. Which means I'll be able to find out
what this's all about and you'll find out if there's any real
reason for you to worry."

Damn! That wasn't the best word to use. Playmate wor-
ries. All the time. And his worry-to-success equation is an
inverse proportion. He only gives up worrying and fussing
when things get truly awful.

Garrett!

"All right!" He's so damned lazy he can't be bothered
to die but he expects me to scurry like bees getting ready
for winter. And sees no inconsistency. "All right. Here's
the official plan, Play."

4

Playmate's job was to come into the alley from its Wizard's Reach end. Being younger and more athletic I took the longer way around so I could close in from the other direction. I trotted west on Macunado, then ducked into a narrow, fetid breezeway, where I kicked up a covey of pixies who were living under an overturned basket. Poor, new immigrants, obviously. I knew before I saw their ragged country costumes. "You folks better find yourselves someplace where you won't have to fight off the cats and dogs and rats." Though TunFaire's dogs and cats do, mostly, know better than to bother little people. But rats, while cunning, aren't always real bright. And as for the others, hunger has a way of overwhelming even the most pointed of past lessons.

These little folk thanked me for my concern by swarming around me, cursing in tiny voices while threatening to stick me with teensy poisoned rapiers.

When I entered the breezeway the Goddamned Parrot was a passenger on my shoulder. He was behaving. But once I started leaping and swatting at those damned mosquitoes he flapped toward a perch high above, whence he spouted gratuitous advice. To the pixies: "Stay to his left! He doesn't see as well on that side. . . . Awk!"

The racket had attracted the interest of one of those leather-winged flying lizards that sometimes nap up on the rooftops between pigeon snacks. They aren't common anymore, mostly because they have trouble outthinking large rocks. They make rats and pigeons look like shining intellectuals. They are very slow learners.

This one looked particularly shopworn. The trailing edges of its wings were tattered. It had patches of mold on its chest.

When it looked at the Goddamn Parrot it saw the answer to all its prayers.

It was the scruffiest flying lizard I'd ever seen but it still looked like the answer to a prayer or two of my own. Life would be so much simpler if I got rid of the chicken in the clown suit—as long as I could manage it in some way that wouldn't aggravate the Dead Man or Morley Dotes. Morley had gifted me with the jabbering vulture, accompanied by a strong suggestion that no harm should come to the monster, at my hand or through my negligence.

The pixies lost interest in me the moment the lizard started trying to get into the breezeway. They knew a real threat when they smelled one. A chorus of squeals preceded a general surge of the flock toward the scrofulous flyer.

The Goddamn Parrot dropped back down to my shoulder. He was shaking. For once in his sorry existence he was fresh out of smart-ass remarks.

As I got out of there the pixies proved that they'd been playing with me all along. As I left the breezeway a matron zipped over to ask which cuts interested me. "They's good eatin' on them things, Big'un. The giblets is real tasty when they's grilled."

"You people keep the whole thing. I brought my lunch." I jerked a thumb at my shoulder ornament.

"Ooh. . . . Pretty," one small voiced piped.

Another wanted to know, "Kin we have some of the feathers?"

I sensed a once-in-a-lifetime opportunity.

Something came over me. My jaw locked up. I couldn't mouth the offer I make almost every day, as many as a dozen times. I wanted to shriek.

I couldn't turn loose of the dodo in the clown suit!

The air seemed to tinkle and sparkle with invisible chuckles.

So! Old Bones wasn't quite as preoccupied elsewhere as he wanted me to think. I should've gotten suspicious when the painted jungle buzzard demonstrated such exceptional manners.

Interesting. The Dead Man hadn't ever before touched me directly this far from the house. Maybe he *was* distracted. Maybe distracted so much that he couldn't be as careful keeping the full range of his abilities concealed. Or maybe he just liked the Goddamn Parrot too much to let him go.

Wish I had time to experiment.

After our initial divergence of viewpoint the pixies and I went our ways on friendly terms. Meaning they were too busy harvesting everything but the flyer's squeak to waste time tormenting a Big'un. Though a couple of youngsters did follow me, mainly to get out of doing chores.

I headed east, down the alley, afraid my delays might have allowed my quarry to give me the slip. Though if I'd thought I would've realized that my foul-beaked companion would've been barking like the wolf at the end of the world if the Dead Man had suffered a moment's disappointment.

Something buzzed behind my ear. Not the family bird-brain, who was on patrol now, or, more likely, hitting on some nitwitted pigeon. I started to swat the sound, held up just in time. A pixie girl, definitely a little inexperienced, unwittingly drifted forward far enough to be seen from the corner of my eye.

One key to success in my racket is making friends. Lots of friends. In as broad a range of stations, races, and professions as is possible. A pixie ally would be a huge resource.

I started sweet-talking.

No telling what I might have accomplished if Fate hadn't decided to roll my bones.

The pixies let out startled shrieks at the same moment that the Goddamn Parrot barked my name.

5

I got about a tenth of second's glimpse of a man who fit his name perfectly. Unusual. He was all rounds. He had a round head with dwindling thickets of hair sagging to the south, leaving a blinding shine behind. He had a round mouth with puffy, round lips, round eyes, and a nose that was almost round as a hog's snoot. He had a round body, too. I didn't get a good look at his feet.

The whole globular package didn't stand but maybe five inches over five feet tall.

This was Bic Gonlit. Bounty hunter. A man you'd peg as an apple-cheeked little baker addicted to his own products. Or a guy who cracked feeble jokes in place of real entertainment in some dive harboring upwardly mobile aspirations toward the lower lower class. He was a man who had to wear elevator boots to get up enough altitude to cork a big, handsome boy like me.

Had to be the boots. He was known for the boots. Legend said he had had them specially made by a dwarfish cobbler in a sleazy little shop off Bleak on the southern edge of the Tenderloin. So rumor would have it, because the boots had been made into Gonlit's signature inside the TunFaire underworld.

Or maybe he'd brought a ladder, since ordinarily he was way shorter than me. The boots only made him two inches taller.

I didn't get a real gander at the infamous boots. I didn't see any ladder, either. I did get a vague glimpse of what looked like an overweight donkey behind my assailant, then

an outstanding look at an upwardly rushing alley surface
after Gonlit leaped up and whacked me across the back of
my skull. The one tap turned my bones to jelly. I sagged
into the muck like a candle left out in the summer sun.
The Goddamn Parrot and the pixie girl cheered me on. Or
jeered me. Or something. They made a lot of noise. I think
the donkey started laughing.

Playmate was fanning me when I opened my eyes, hoping
for some blond angel of mercy. Good friend that he is, he
had dragged me into the shade and propped me against a
wall, all before anyone found me and explored my pockets
for hidden treasure. I made a crippled kitten sort of sound
to express my appreciation and ask when the angel would
arrive.

Playmate said, "I wouldn't move around, was I you."

"I am me. And I don't plan to even breathe hard. My
head! And I didn't drink a drop." This morning. "I've got
to get ahold of a war-surplus helmet. One of the kind with
that big-ass spike on top."

"You'd still have to remember to wear it. What happened?"

"I was going to ask you."

"I don't know. I heard your bird screaming. Made me
suspect that you'd found yourself on the short end again.
You've got a talent for that. I charged up here. Behold!
You really were in trouble. A roly-poly little bald guy who
looked a lot like Bic Gonlit was strutting around you measuring you for a hearty whack with the great hairy club he
was packing."

"It was Bic Gonlit. I caught a glimpse before the lights
went out. He must've been wearing his extra special tall
boots, though."

"This isn't his normal style, Garrett."

"You know him?" I for sure wanted to know him better
than I did now. What little I did know was hearsay. He
was a bounty hunter who brought them in alive. He had
quirks and unusual personal habits and magic boots. I'd
seen him just often enough to recognize him. "You failed
to mention that when the name came up before."

"I didn't need to mention it. Kip told you all you needed. Then. I only know his reputation, anyway. Which doesn't include murder. He grew up in my part of town. He'd be a little older than me. He's supposed to have a big taste for fine food and good wine. Including the TunFaire Gold when he can get it. But if that really was him he's sure gone downhill since the last time I saw him."

"That was him. Or his evil twin. Maybe he's been eating so high he's had to expand his repertoire."

"He wouldn't just bushwhack a guy."

"Why the hell not?" Could Playmate be that naive? Even I would bushwhack a guy fifteen inches taller and fifteen years younger than me, not to mention fifteen stone lighter. Assuming that I was adequately motivated.

The quality and the nature of the motivation is what's worth debating.

On reflection Playmate decided he had no ready answer. I asked, "Where is he now?"

"He took off when he saw me coming. Jumped on a burro not much bigger than him and rode off, covering his face."

"Think he recognized you?"

"I expect that's why he bothered to hide his face. I mean, how many people of my size and coloring are there? And how many of those are likely to be caught hanging around with you?"

If Bic Gonlit knew who we were he was about to become scarcer than lizard hair. "Good points. I wonder. Did he know whose head he was bopping before he tried to brain me?" I have a reputation, partly for lacking humor about things like headbashing when it's my melon involved, partly for having acquired a number of close friends whose responses would be unpredictable if something unpleasant happened to me that wasn't my own fault. Some might start sharpening their teeth.

It's hard to imagine it being my own fault, but, in the laws of obligatory revenge there *are* exit codicils about "He asked for it," and "He needed it."

Playmate might be one of those friends. My partner is, definitely. I like to believe that Saucerhead Tharpe and

Morley Dotes are others, along with several powerful, wealthy family chieftains I've helped in my time. Those include the beermaking Weiders, the shoemaking Tates, and the we-don't-talk-about-what-we-do Contagues.

The Contagues would be the real worry for any villain, though the least likely avengers. The Contagues captain the Outfit, the Syndicate, the Commission, the central committee of the city's organized crime. Their strength and reach and savagery when roused are legendary. Even our wizardly overlords on the Hill concern themselves about needlessly rousing the ire of Chodo Contague and his daughter Belinda. Chodo and Belinda do not allow themselves to be constrained by traditional legal customs or the normal rules of evidence. They hurt people. And they kill people. They're supposed to be my friends and they scare the whiskers off me.

At the time it did not occur to me that Bic Gonlit might have wanted to collect a bounty on me.

"What do you want to do?" Playmate asked.

"Besides find Bic Gonlit and whip fifty pounds of lard off his broad butt? Go home and get cleaned up." TunFaire's alleyways aren't paved. Neither are they kept clean. Where they exist at all they're little more than broad, shallow trenches where refuse can accumulate in anticipation of eventual rains heavy enough to carry some of the waste down into one of the storm channels that drain into the river.

It takes a conscientious sort, willing to make an extra effort, to take advantage of the travel opportunities offered by TunFaire's alleys. The King's good and lazy subjects employ them when they're too shy to dispose of something in the street out front. So by the grace of Bic Gonlit I made the intimate acquaintance of some of my neighbors' greatest embarrassments—most of which, of course, would seem trivial to a disinterested witness.

Often the secret vice that concerns you most is of no interest whatsoever to anyone whose opinion you dread. The main problem exists inside your own head.

That's one of those things most of us learn too late. A life-skills version of the destroyer comeback that pops up

wearing a big, goofy grin three hours after some boor quali-
fies for a sound verbal caning.

"Thanks," I told Playmate. "Your timing was perfect."

"We aim to please."

"Where's the other one?"

"Who?"

"The guy we came out here to watch. The weird elf."

Playmate shrugged. "If he was still here he had a knack
for the invisible. Maybe the Dead Man was able to keep
track."

Probably wouldn't admit it if he did. "Let's say I'm cynical about his ability." There was no sign of the Goddamn
Parrot, either. Nor any of pixies. Did some small-size skulls
get cracked, too? Might be worth the headache if somebody
capped that dodo. "Did you notice what happened to Mr.
Big? My bird?"

Playmate shook his head.

"Never mind." I wouldn't bet two dead flies on tripping
over the amount of good luck necessary to get me shut of
that magpie cleanly. "Let's get out of here."

Playmate grunted. He was uncomfortable there. He was
a preacher, not an adventurer. And unwanted adventures
seemed to bubble up around me. Maybe it's my diet.
Though if complained at I'd point out that he'd brought
this one on himself.

We abandoned the alley, brokenhearted over our failure.

Folks on Wizard's Reach raised eyebrows, pinched their
noses, and turned away. But nothing helped me. It didn't
matter which way I turned my head or how tightly I
pinched my nose, I could still smell me. And I was way
past ripe.

Maybe a sudden thunderstorm would come up and wash
me down to the river.

Maybe they ought to put all the unemployed ex-soldiers
to work cleaning the city.

Never happen. Makes too much sense. And it would cost
public monies that can be put to better use lining somebody's pockets.

The neighbors lost interest in me when somebody hollered,
"There goes one!" and everything came to a halt while the

entire population stared at the sky. I was a couple beats late. I saw nothing. "What the hell is that all about?"

Playmate looked at me like he'd just flipped a boulder and discovered a new species of fool. "*Where* have you been? There've been strange lights in the sky and weird things hurtling around overhead for weeks. Longer than that, if you believe some people. I thought everybody in TunFaire knew about them and was watching for them."

"Well, not me. Tell me."

Playmate shook his head. "You have to get out of the house more, Garrett. Even when you're not working. You need to know what's going on around you."

I couldn't argue with that.

6

"What the hell?" My front door stood wide open.

"Maybe Kip ran away." From the vantage of his superior altitude Playmate surveyed Macunado Street, uphill and down. "Which would be stupid. He can't find his own way home."

I gave him a raised eyebrow look. "Where do you find them?" He's worse than Dean is. Dean being the antediluvian artifact who serves as my live-in cook and housekeeper. Who has several huge personality flaws. Those include acting like my mom and my dad and having a soft heart bigger than my often somnolent sidekick. But Dean does confine his overweening charity to kittens and strange young women. Playmate will take in anything, including birds with broken wings and nearly grown boys who need a guide to get around their own hometown.

Playmate was too concerned to talk. He charged up my front steps and into the house. I followed at a more dignified pace. I wasn't used to all that exercise.

"Hey, Garrett! He's right where we left him."

Absolutely. Kip was nailed to the client's chair, wearing an expression like he'd just enjoyed a divine visitation. The Dead Man was holding him there. But that couldn't account for the goofy expression.

"Then who left the door open?"

Your lady friend became distressed when she could find no one willing to make her breakfast. When the boy just stared at her and drooled she stormed out. That sparkling sense of amusement hung in the air once more, rich and mellow, with well-defined edges.

"But you had plenty of brainpower left over to hold and manage this nimrod."

Being dead had corrupted somebody's sense of relative values. The streets are swamped with goofballs. But Katie is unique. Katie is like a religious epiphany. "And what happened to the talking buzzard?" He would know. The Goddamn Parrot was almost a third arm and extra mouth for him anymore. He's going to weep great tears when that vulture bites the dust. Though Morley is fond of reminding me that parrots can live about a million years. If something doesn't wring their scrawny necks.

I'll weep myself when he's gone. Tears of joy.

Mr. Big is tracking the creature you failed to capture because you were unable keep your attention on the matter at hand.

"You mean Bic Gonlit, the guy who made his escape on a galloping donkey? Because nobody bothered to warn me that it was him hanging around in the alley, leaving me unprepared?"

Apparently an oversight on my part. I detected no second presence out there. Which is no longer of any consequence, now, anyway. But I would be remiss if I failed to point out that you should have been better prepared, knowing there could be difficulty.

"No consequence? Difficulty? You aren't the one the little pork-ball whapped upside the head."

Spare us your unconvincing histrionics, Garrett.

Unconvincing? I was convinced. I took a deep breath. I'd never gotten in the last word yet but like an old-timer married fifty years I'm an eternal optimist. It could happen. There might come a day. It might be today.

Actually, it'll probably come when I'm on my deathbed and the Reaper snatches me before Old Bones can come back at me. Except that Chuckles might decide to come after me. He's already got a head start.

Death. Now there's a guy who knows how to have the last word.

Mr. Big is following the creature I sensed in the alley,

Garrett. Not any sad little manhunter named Gonlit. I had thought you would understand that. A most unusual creature this is, too. Nothing like it has entered my ken before. Most notably, it seems capable of rendering itself invisible by fogging the minds of those around it. It is amazing.

"And you keep telling me there's nothing new under the sun."

Playmate's scrawny young buddy finally collected himself enough to notice us. "What happened to you guys? You smell awful."

My good and true friend Playmate announced, "What you smell is Garrett. I myself am redolent of roses, lilacs, and other sweet herbal delights."

I glared at Playmate. "We ran into Bic Gonlit." I turned my glower on the boy. He did not leap at the opportunity to have a chuckle at my expense. Maybe he wasn't a total social disaster at all times. Maybe he retained some rudimentary, skewed sense of self-preservation.

That's Mama Garrett's big boy. He can find a silver lining inside the ugliest sow's ear.

Maybe he didn't have any sense of humor at all.

Kip looked to Playmate for confirmation. Playmate told him, "It was Gonlit." Then he told me, "Do something about your sweet self. I have a strong feeling we're about to get out amongst the people. I wouldn't want you to embarrass yourself."

Yet again the stardust of amusement twinkled in the air.

I would propose that Mr. Playmate has offered excellent advice, Garrett.

I smelled doom. I smelled it like I'd smelled leaf mold in the jungle every time it'd rained while I was in the islands. It was in the air, sneezing thick. I did not have to sniff to catch a whiff.

I was about to be cursed. Squirm as I might I was about to have to go to work. All because I had been dim enough to open my door and let trouble walk in.

I whined, "Where on the gods' green earth is the beautiful girl?" It'd never failed before. I'd always gotten some wonderful eye-candy out of . . . "Yike!"

Old Dean, who pretends to be the chief cook and house-

keeper around here, but who is really the wicked step-
mother, had stuck his bitter, persimmon-sucking face into
the office. "Mr. Garrett? Why is it that I return home to
find the front door standing wide open?"

"It was an experiment. I was trying to learn if crabby
old people will kick a door shut *before* they start complain-
ing about it having been left open. Of particular interest
are crabby old men who live in a household where their
status more closely approximates that of a guest than something more eternal. So you tell me. Do you have any idea?
Where's the girl?"

Dean doesn't have much of a sense of humor. He offered
me the full benefit of his hard, gray-eyed stare. As always,
he was rock-confident he could demonstrate to the world
that my second greatest flaw is my frivolous, incautious
nature.

He believes my greatest failing to be my persistent bache-
lorhood. That from a character who never got within rock-
flinging range of matrimony himself. I put up with him because he *is* a wonderful cook and housekeeper. When the
mood takes him. And because he's cranky enough to hold
his own with the Dead Man—though when he has his
druthers he has nothing to do with Old Bones at all.

"Let's not fuss," I told him. "I have a client here."

Bad word choice. That brightened Dean right up. Little
pleases him more than knowing that I'm working.

I ground my teeth a bit, then continued, "So let's get
this sorted out quickly. I've got to catch up with Katie."
Before she developed an attitude toward me that I was
sure to regret.

Dean scowled as he headed toward the kitchen. Katie
isn't one of his favorites. He doesn't approve of Katie. He
hasn't been able to charm her the way he did my few other,
occasional female friends.

I fear Miss Shaver will have to wait, Garrett.

"No. Not hardly. Right now there's nothing more important than Miss Shaver."

Playmate and Kip appeared startled. Old Bones hadn't
included them in his message. Though Kip did look baffled

and kept rubbing his head and looking around like he knew something was going on.

I have exceeded myself somewhat, ethically, in reviewing the boy's memories. There being so many questions accompanied by so few answers it seemed possible that the best course was to see if he might not know something without being aware that he knew it.

Plausible, if prolix. I had used that argument on him a time or three, trying to prod him into becoming a little more aggressive in mining the thoughts of visitors and suspects. "And what did you discover?" You have to give him his line or he won't communicate.

Very little, to tell the truth. This boy has no more than two toes anchored inside our reality. His head is occupied by a totally eclectic jumble of fantasic nonsense and it is amidst that that he lives most of the time. He is always the hero in his own tale.

Well, aren't we all?

Some of his fantasies recall well-known epics and sagas. Some have their genesis in common storytellers' tales. Some are mutant versions of historical events. And even a few things might possibly have some basis in truth—behind the fantasy stuff he has built on top of genuine events. Inside his head it is impossible to discern the real from the imagined.

"If most of it concerns girls it sounds like the inside of a normal boy's head."

You would think that way. And you would be incorrect. While it does concern girls, some of it, it does so principally in the clever and daring methods by which he rescues the enchanted princess or other damsel in distress. While there are several of them I have yet to discover any of his fantasy women less than chastely clad or treated.

I gave Kip a quick glance consisting of about eighty percent worry and twenty percent accolade. Though I suspected that respect for women was not a real part of the equation. Naïveté would be the real culprit

The Dead Man continued, *He* is *acquainted with creatures he knows as Lastyr and Noodiss. They are not human but the boy has not cared enough about the answer to find out what they really are. The images in his mind are not familiar to me.*

The image that appeared in my mind, then, was unfamiliar to me as well. "Inbreeding? Or interbreeding?" You need only stroll around TunFaire a few hours to see the incredible range of Nature's artistry and her bottomless capacity for the cruel practical joke.

Perhaps. And, perhaps, they are something never before seen. In this world.

"Let's not turn alarmist!" I growled. Alarmed. Once upon a time not long ago I got into a head-butting contest with something never before seen at that time: very nasty, never-brush-their-teeth and talk-back-to-their-mamas foul, elder gods who thought that the god racket would be a lot softer if they could bust out of the dark place where they were confined and could come set up shop in our world.

There was nothing supernatural about the watcher in the alley, Garrett. Quite the opposite, I think. There was no magic in it at all. It seemed as though it stood entirely outside the realms of the magical, the metaphysical, and the supernatural.

I gobbled a couple pints of air while I tried to make sense of that, trying to sort through the countless implications. A world without magic! A place of order and predictability, with all evil fled!

Darker possibilities occurred to me as well.

Playmate began to poke and prod me with a singletree forefinger. "Garrett, I know it's a big, empty wasteland without many landmarks but how about you don't get lost inside your own head right now?"

I shook the gourd in question. The waste space was anything but empty right now. Most of that speculation seemed to be leaking over from the Dead Man's secondary minds. Suggesting that the puzzle had him sufficiently intrigued that he had become incautious where his thoughts strayed.

"Sorry. Chuckles got me going for a minute."

" 'Twould seem that he's gotten Kip going, too."

The boy was as rigid as a fence post. All the color had drained from behind his freckles. His eyelids were closed.

When I lifted one I found his eyeball rolled up so that he seemed to have no pupil.

"What did you do here, Smiley?"

The Dead Man launched a long-winded paean of self-exoneration. I sensed its complete lack of substance right away and focused on Playmate. "So cut the bull and tell me what you want from me."

"I suppose what I really want is for you to look out for him. Kip's a royal pain sometimes, Garrett, but that's mostly because nobody ever taught him how to get along with people. He befriended a couple of strays. Lost souls in the physical sense. He took care of them. They were grateful. That made him feel important. Same as I feel when I take care of him and the horses. He shouldn't get hurt for that."

Playmate was right. The world needed more helpful and considerate people. But I was looking at something else. Some very complex things seemed to be going on inside Playmate right now. He was taking this more personally than he should.

"You wouldn't be the missing father here, would you?"

That stunned Playmate. He chomped air a couple of times, in a way that left me wondering if I hadn't somehow struck nearer the mark than I'd thought possible. One glance and even the most cynical student of human folly would understand that Cypres Prose was no kin to Playmate.

"Don't try to provoke me, Garrett."

"Huh?" Provocation isn't my style. Not with my friends. Not very often, anyway. Not the ones that're three feet taller than me and strong enough to hold a horse under one arm while using the off hand to change the monster's shoes.

"I'm sorry. I apologize. This mess is keeping me on edge."

"Why is that?" By now I had resigned myself to not being able to make peace with Katie anytime soon. "Why don't you just lay this whole thing out so we don't have to pick you guys apart just so we can assemble enough information for me to start?"

I've found that clients never want to tell the whole story.

Never. Another given is that they're going to lie to you about half of what they tell you. They want results without having to reveal anything embarrassing. They lie about almost everything. The worst offenders are those who have fallen victim to their own greed or stupidity. They expect results, too.

Playmate was not a bad client. His fib quotient was pretty low, probably, as much because he knew about my partner as because he's naturally a good guy. He talked a good deal but failed to tell me much more than I had gotten already. Kip had become friendly with a pair of oddballs named Lastyr and Noodiss, no other names given. He had helped them learn their way around. After a while other oddballs turned up looking for the first two. Inasmuch as they never explained their interest, that was not taken to be benign. Especially considering recent events at the stable and Kip's home. Not all of the oddballs were necessarily the same kind of oddball.

Lastyr and Noodiss had been around for most of a year. Those hunting them had shown up only recently. All the elves seemed very determined.

Kip nodded a lot and didn't add anything. I trusted the Dead Man would collect anything that reached the surface of the boy's thoughts.

Playmate told me, "It may be coincidence. Kip's always made up fantastic stories. But it was right after those first two characters showed up that he started inventing things. I mean, things that worked or looked like maybe you could make them work."

The boy's head is bursting with the images of the most amazing mechanisms, Garrett.

He seemed completely thrilled.

I asked, "What would you suggest I do?"

"Just stick with us for a while," Playmate said.

Investigate.

"Investigate what?"

Let your experience be your guide. And, *Whatever else you do, do try to catch one of those creatures and bring it here to see me.*

"I'm the miracle worker of TunFaire, aren't I?"

Aren't I?

7

There was no sign of Katie when we stepped out the front door, me freshly bathed and cleanly dressed in hand-me-down apparel that approached the respectable. My sweetie had an hour head start now. And would be boiling like an overheated teapot.

Katie was going to require some cautious cooling down. I definitely didn't want her getting too cold.

I did spot Dean. Headed home. Where the hell had he been? He wasn't carrying anything.

He dropped a coin—a coin that belonged to me because he'd never give away a chipped copper of his own—onto the tattered blanket of a streetside fortune-teller. That caught her completely by surprise. Nevertheless, she gave him a toothless blessing.

There was an idea. I ought to hang out a shingle proclaiming myself a great psychic. Old Bones could rummage around inside their heads and feed me the items I would use to impress them enough to make them turn loose of their money.

An open mouth precludes open ears.

"What the hell does that mean?" I hadn't said anything. "I hate it when you talk that ancient wisdom stuff. The butterfly is silent when the eagle walks upon the sand."

I patted myself down. I was equipped with an arsenal of—mostly—nonlethal tools of mayhem. "Lead on, Play."

Playmate descended the steps and turned left. I followed, keeping Kip between us.

Dean met us at the foot of the steps. "Where you been?" I asked.

"Running a couple of errands."

"Ah." I said no more. No point letting him know he gave himself away whenever he was sneaking around doing something on the Dead Man's orders. "Let us continue, friend Playmate." I studied the street as we resumed moving. I saw nothing out of place.

Macunado Street is a busy thoroughfare, day or night. A ferocious downpour or bitter winter weather are about all that will clear it. The street was particularly busy today. But it was conventionally busy. Not one known villain, nor a potential riot, was anywhere in sight.

"Who was that?" Playmate asked after I waved to a neighbor.

"Mrs. Cardonlos. The police spy. Sometimes tormenting her is the only fun to be had."

"There're occasions when I despair of you, Garrett. There're times when you appear to be your own worst enemy. Why on earth would you want to taunt someone who has the power to tell lies about you to people who'd just as soon feed you to the rats?"

"Because Relway's bunch would be more suspicious if I didn't." Deal Relway is the master of TunFaire's unacknowledged secret police force. I know him because I was there when that particular terrorbird hatched. Its existence has become an open secret, anyway.

I do get nervous sometimes, knowing what I do know about some key individuals. Relway wouldn't hesitate to bend or break the law in his determination to maintain law and order. He might not hesitate to bend or break me.

Playmate's livery establishment was less than an hour away. We reached it without running into trouble. Once we did I borrowed his kitchen to brew myself a fresh mug of headache medicine.

8

Kip's little workshop didn't tell me much. It was evident the kid knew his tools, though. He had a hell of a collection, half of which I didn't know what they were. He had a hundred unidentifiable projects going. As soon as we walked in he grabbed a file and went to work on notches in a round metal plate about eight inches in diameter. It took him only a few seconds to become totally focused.

"What the hell?" I asked.

Playmate shrugged. "I don't know. Part of one of his machines. I can show you the picture he had me draw."

"I meant, how come he suddenly goes from being something you have to keep on a leash to being somebody who's blind to the whole damned world?"

Another expressive shrug. Playmate showed me into his forge area, which had expanded considerably since my last visit and which was an amazing clutter of junk and what looked like things half-built. I wondered how he got any shoeing done.

From some niche Playmate produced a leather folder filled with dozens of sheets of good linen paper. He shuffled through unsuspectedly good bits of artwork until he located the piece he wanted. I glimpsed my own likeness in passing. "Now that was a good-looking young man."

Playmate grunted. I think that was meant to be neutral but failed to sound like it when he observed, "The operative word being 'was.' "

There were more portrait sketches. They were all good. I recognized several people.

How many hidden talents did Playmate have? He surprised me every few months.

The portfolio contained more sketches of devices than of people. Some were really complicated, highly unlikely mechanisms. And a few didn't seem complicated at all. One of those was a little two-wheeler cart with a pair of long shafts sticking out in front. A man had been sketched in as pulling it, conveying another seated in the cart.

Something like that, without the shafts, sat about ten feet from where I stood. "You're trying to build some of these things?"

"Unh? Oh. Yeah. All of them, eventually. But there're problems. With that thing I'm having trouble finding long enough poles that're still light. But we did test it. It'll work."

"Why?"

"Because we have an extremely lazy complement of wealthy people in this town. And a lot of unemployed young men who need something to keep them out of trouble. My notion is to build a fleet of those things and rent them out at nominal fees so some of those young men have a way to make a living. Which will keep them out of trouble at the same time."

Having a way to make a living didn't keep me out of trouble.

That was Playmate, though. Finding a way to get rich doing good deeds. Except that then he would end up giving away any wealth he acquired.

Next to the cart stood a second mechanism. I could not figure it out. It had three wheels. Two were about a foot in diameter and were mounted at the ends of a wooden axle. The other was about two and a half feet in diameter, turning on a hardwood pin which passed through the ends of a two-tined wooden fork. That rose through the upper end of an arc of hardwood that curved down to the two-wheel axle. A curved crossbar above the hardwood arc allowed the larger wheel to be turned right and left.

I did not see a sketch of that in Playmate's folio. "What is that?"

"We just call it a three-wheel. Let me finish showing you

this. Then I'll let you see how it works. Here. Check this. It's a two-wheel. It's a more complicated cousin of that." He extracted a drawing.

This mechanism had two wheels of equal size, fore and aft, with a rider perched amidships, as though astride a horse. "I'm not sure I get this."

"Oh, I don't, either. Kip explains these things when he has me draw them but I seldom understand. However, everything he finishes putting together does what he says it will do. And sometimes it seems so obvious afterward that I wonder why nobody ever thought of it before. So I take him on faith. This engine—and that one there—gets around on power provided by the rider's legs. If you want to know much more than that you'll have to ask Kip. He'll turn human after a while. Come here." He led me to the three-wheel.

"Climb up here and sit down."

The wooden arc part of the mechanism boasted a sort of saddle barely big enough for a mouse. When I sat on it my butt ached immediately. "So what is it? Some kind of walker with wheels?" If so, my legs were too long. "I've seen lots better wheelchairs." Chodo Contague has one that is so luxurious it comes with a crew of four footmen and has its own heating system.

"Put your feet up on these things." He used the toe of a boot to indicate an L-shaped bar that protruded from the hub of the big wheel up front. "The one on the other side, too. Good. Now push. With your right foot. Your other right foot."

The three-wheel moved. I zipped around in a tight circle. "Hey! This's neat." My foot slipped off. The end of the iron L clipped my anklebone. I iterated several words that would have turned Mom red. I reiterated them with considerable gusto.

"We're working on that. That can't be much fun. We're going to drill a hole down the center of a flat piece of hardwood . . ."

I got the hang of the three-wheel quickly. But there wasn't enough room to enjoy it properly in there. "How about I take it out in the street?"

"I'd really rather you didn't. I'm sure that's why we've had the trouble we've had. Kip took it out there, racing around, and before he got back he had several people try to take it away from him. And right afterward the strange people started coming around."

I scooted around the stable for a few minutes more, then gave up because I couldn't enjoy the machine's full potential under such constrained circumstances. "Are you planning to make three-wheels, too? Because if you are, I want one. If I can afford it."

Playmate's eyes lighted up as he saw the possibility of paying my fees without having to part with any actual money. "I might. But honesty compels me to admit that we're having problems with it. Especially with getting the wheels and the steering bar to move freely. Lard doesn't seem to be the ideal lubricant."

"And it draws flies." Plenty of those were around. But the place was a stable, after all.

"That, too. And the kinds of hardwoods we need to make the parts aren't common. Not to mention that we'd have to come up with whole teams of woodworking craftsmen if we were to build even a fraction of the number of them we think we'd need to satisfy the demand there'd be once people started seeing them in the streets."

"Hire some of those out-of-work veterans to make them."

"How many of them, you figure, are likely to be skilled joiners and cabinetmakers?"

"Uhn. Not to mention wheelwrights." I walked around the three-wheel. "That geekoid kid over there actually thought this up?"

"This thing and a whole lot more, Garrett. It'll be a mechanical revolution if we ever figure out how to build all of the things he can imagine."

I slid down off the three-wheeler. "What do you call this?"

"Like I told you. Just three-wheel."

There had to be something that sounded more dramatic. "Here's a notion. You could train your veterans just to do what it takes to manufacture three-wheels. That wouldn't be like them having to learn all about making cabinets and furniture."

"And then I'd have guild trouble."

I stared at the three-wheel, sighed, told Playmate, "I guarantee you, somebody's going to get rich off this thing." My knack for prophecy is limited but that was a prediction I made with complete conviction. I had no trouble picturing the streets of the better neighborhoods overrun with three-wheels.

"Someone with fewer ethical disadvantages than I have, you mean?"

"That wasn't what I was getting at, but it's a fact. As soon as you get some of those things out there you're going to have people trying to build knockoffs." I had a thought. Lest it get lonely I sent it out into the world. "You said Kip took this one out and somebody tried to take it away from him?"

Playmate nodded.

"Could it be that Kip's having problems because somebody wants to steal his ideas?" I'm sure that I'm not the only royal subject bright enough to see the potential of Kip's inventions.

Playmate nodded. "That could be going on, too. But there's definitely something to the trouble with the weird elves. And right now I'm more worried about them. Stay here and keep an eye on Kip while I make us all a pot of tea."

Ever civilized, my friend Playmate. In the midst of chaos he'll take time for amenities, all with the appropriate service.

9

Kip tired of filing his metal wheel. He put it aside and started fiddling with something wooden. I watched from the corner of one eye while I thumbed through Playmate's drawings and sketches. The man really was good. More so than with portraits, he had a talent for translating Kip's ideas into visual images. There was a lot of written information on some of the sheets, inscribed in a hand that was not Playmate's.

"How do you come up with this stuff?" I asked Kip. I didn't expect an answer. If he heard it at all the question was sure to irritate him. Creative people get it all the time. They get tired of questions that imply that the artist couldn't possibly produce something out of the whole cloth of the mind. It was a question I wouldn't have asked a painter or poet.

Kip surprised me by responding, "I don't know, Mr. Garrett. They just come to me. Sometimes in my dreams. I've always had ideas and a head full of stories. But lately those have been getting better than they ever were before." He did not look up from the piece of wood he was shaping.

He had become a different person now that he was settled in the sanctuary of his workshop. He was calm and he was confident.

I wondered how much puberty had to do with his problems and creativity.

Tucked into the back of Playmate's folio, folded so I nearly overlooked them, were four smaller sketches of strange "elves."

"Would these be some of the people who're giving you a hard time?"

The boy looked up from his work. "Those two are Noodiss and Lastyr. Left and right. They're the good ones. I don't know the other two. They may be some of the ones Play ran off."

Playmate arrived with the tea. "They are."

"I told you your talent would be a wonderful tool in the war against evil. See? We have two villains identified already."

"Do we, then?"

No, we doedn't, doed we? We had sketches of a couple of likely baddies about whom we knew nothing whatsoever. I wasn't even sure they were the same kind of elves as the other two. They didn't look like the same breed in the sketches.

I changed the subject. "I have an idea, too."

Man and boy looked at me skeptically.

"It can happen!" I insisted. "Look. You see how much work it was making the steering handles for your three-wheel? You could use ox horns instead. You could get them from the slaughterhouses." Though the two of them began to look aghast I warmed to greater possibilities. "You could get them to save you the whole skull with the horns still attached. You could produce a special death's-head model three-wheel for customers from the Hill."

Playmate shook his head. "Drink your tea, Garrett. And plan to go to bed early tonight. You need the rest."

I offered him a hard glower.

Guess I need to practice up. He wasn't impressed. He just smiled and told me, "You're starting to hallucinate."

"And I should leave that to the experts. All right. Why don't I do some work? What can you tell me about these maybe elves that you haven't told me already?"

"They eat a lot of ugly soup," Playmate told me. "My drawings don't do them justice."

None of them appeared particularly repulsive to me. And I said so. Those homely boys didn't know it but I was looking out for them.

"Call it an inner glow kind of thing. You'll see what I

mean when you meet one." He sounded confident that I'd do so.

"Kip? Anything you can say to help out here? It's really your ass that's on the line."

Playmate advised, "Despite earlier events Kip still isn't quite convinced that he's in any trouble himself."

Most people are that way. They just can't believe that all this crap is raining down on them. Not even when somebody is using a hammer to beat them over the head. And they particularly can't believe that it's *because* of them.

We talked while we enjoyed our tea. I asked more questions. Lots of questions, most of them not too pointed. I didn't get many useful answers. Kip never said so, of course, but now that he was where he felt safe himself his main concern was his friends with the absurd names. He had decided that not telling me anything was the best way to shield them.

"It's not me you need to protect them from," I grumbled. "It's not me that's looking for them." He might not know exactly where they were hiding but I was willing to bet he had a good idea where to start looking.

Playmate offered nothing but a shrug when I sent him a mute look of appeal. So he was going to be no help.

Playmate is a firm believer in letting our young people learn from their mistakes. He had enlisted me in this thing because he wanted to keep Kip's educational process from turning lethal. Now he was going to step back and let events unfold instructionally.

"You do know that I'm not real fond of bodyguard work?" I told Playmate.

"I do know you're not fond of any kind of work that doesn't include the consumption of beer as the main responsibility of the job."

"Possibly. But asking me to bodyguard is like asking an opera diva to sing on the corner with a hurdy-gurdy man. I have more talent than that. If you just want the kid kept safe you should round up Saucerhead Tharpe." Tharpe is so big you can't hurt him by whacking him with a wagon tongue and so dumb he won't back off from a job as long as he's still awake and breathing.

"It was your remarkable talents that brought me to your door," Playmate responded, his pinky wagging in the wind as he plied his teacup. "Saucerhead Tharpe resembles a force of nature. Powerful but unthinking. Rather like a falling boulder. Unlikely to change course if the moment requires a flexible response. Unlikely to become proactive when innovation could be the best course."

I think that was supposed to be complimentary. "You're blowing smoke, aren't you? You can't afford Saucerhead." I'd begun roaming through the junk and unfinished inventions, growing ever more amazed. "He'd want to get paid up front. Just in case your faith in him was misplaced."

"Well, there is that, too."

The rat. He'd counted on the Dead Man's curiosity to keep me involved with this nonsense, whether or not I got paid.

Don't you hate it when friends take advantage of you?

I picked up the most unusual crossbow I'd ever seen. "I used to be pretty good with one of these things. What's this one for? Shooting through castle walls?" Instead of the usual lever this crossbow was quipped with a pair of hand cranks and a whole array of gears. Cranking like mad barely drew the string back. Which was a misnomer. That was a cable that looked tough enough for towing canal boats.

"We're trying to develop a range of nonlethal weaponry, too," Playmate told me. "That's meant for knocking down a man in heavy armor without doing any permanent injury."

I didn't ask why you'd want to do that. Didn't mention that, sooner or later, the guy was going to get back up and get after you with renewed enthusiasm. I just hefted the crossbow. "Supposed to be a man-portable ballista, eh?" It had some heft to it.

"The bolts are there in that thing that looks like a pipe rack."

"Huh?" I wouldn't have recognized them otherwise. They looked more like miniature, deformed juggler's clubs. Two had padded ends. Again I refrained from telling Playmate what I thought.

I believe I understood what Morley feels each time I shy off what I consider gratuitous throat-cutting. Playmate's boundary of acceptable violence was as much gentler than mine as mine was gentler than friend Morley's.

I loaded one of the quarrels, looked around for a target, shrugged when Playmate grumbled, "Not inside, Garrett," exactly as he no doubt had at Kip a few hundred times.

"All right," I said. "Kip. You never did tell me why these elves want to catch your friends with the strange names."

"I don't know." He didn't look at me. He was a lousy liar. It was obvious that he had some idea.

I looked at Playmate. He gave me a little shrug and a little headshake. He wasn't ready to push it.

I asked, "So where do we go from here?"

Playmate shrugged again. "I was looking at doing the trapdoor spider thing."

"That'll work."

The trapdoor spider hunkers down in a hole, under a door she makes, and waits for somebody edible to come prancing by. Then she jumps out and has lunch. Playmate's reference, though, was to an ambush tactic used by both sides in the recent war in the Cantard, employing the same principle. He meant he was going to sit down and wait for something to happen.

10

Without going headlong I kept after Kip about his strange friends. He frustrated me with his determined loyalty. He could not fully grasp the notion that I was there to help.

I needed more time with the Dead Man. I needed to figure out what Old Bones knew as well as how to insert myself into the fantasy worlds where Cypres Prose lived. Apparently his fantasy life was so rich that it influenced his whole attitude toward real life.

After a half hour of mostly polite tea conversation during which my main discovery was that Cypres Prose could avoid a subject almost as slickly as my partner, I was getting frustrated. I was prowling like a cat, poking at half-finished engines and mysterious mechanisms again.

"Garrett!" Playmate exploded. He pointed. His eyes had grown huge.

A small hole had appeared in the stable wall. It glowed scarlet. A harsh beam of red light pushed through. It swung left and right, slicing through the heavy wooden planks. Hardwood smoke flooded the stable, overcoming the sweet rotted-grass odor of fresh horse manure. It made me think both of smokehouses and of campfires in the wild.

Campfires do not have a place in any happy memories of mine. Campfires in my past all had a very nasty war going on somewhere nearby. They always attracted horrible, bloodsucking bugs and starving vertebrates with teeth as long as my fingers. Hardwood smoke gets my battle juices going lots more often than it makes my mouth water.

I picked up the overweight crossbow and inserted the quarrel that had no padding.

The wall cutout collapsed inward. Sunlight blazed through. An oddly shaped being stood silhouetted against the bright.

I shot my bolt.

I used to be pretty good with a crossbow. Somebody found out that I still was. I got him right in the breadbasket. With plenty of *oomph!*, because the recoil was enough to throw me back a step and spin me halfway around.

The villain folded up around the blunt quarrel, out of action. Unfortunately, he was not alone. His friends did not give me time to crank the crossbow back up to full tension. A shortcoming of the instrument that I would have to mention to Playmate. Its cycle time was much too long.

I snatched up a smith's hammer. It seemed the most convincing tool I was likely to lay hands on. The things I had hidden about my person wouldn't have nearly as much impact.

Two shimmering forms came through the hole in the wall, unremarkable street people who flashed silver each few seconds. The one I had shot lay folded up like a hairpin outside, entirely silver now. Another silvery figure ministered to it, briefly flashing into the form of a bum every ten seconds. Only the fallen one didn't shimmer like I was seeing it through a lot of hot air. My bolt must have disrupted a serious compound illusion sorcery.

Playmate stepped up and tried to talk to them. In Playmate's universe reason should be able to solve anything.

I've got to admire his courage and convictions. My own response to those critters was the only behavior I could imagine.

One invader had something shiny in his right hand. He extended it toward Playmate. The big man folded into himself as though every muscle in his body had turned to flab.

I let the hammer fly.

Ever since I was a kid I've had a fascination with the hammer as a missile weapon. I used to enjoy playing at throwing hammers, when I could get my hands on one without anyone knowing that I was risking damage to something so valuable. I knew that in olden times the hammer had been a warrior's weapon and the little bit of Cypres Prose resident within me had woven mighty legends around Garrett the Hammer.

Garrett the Hammer was dead on with his throw. But his target saw it coming and shifted its weight slightly, just in time, so that the speeding hammer brushed its shimmer only obliquely, ricocheted off, and continued on in a rainbow arc that brought the metal end into contact with the back of the head of the silvery figure trying to resurrect the villain I'd knocked down earlier.

That blow should've busted a hole in the thing's skull. No such luck, though. The impact just caused it to fling forward and sprawl across the creature that was down already.

These were Playmate's elves, it was obvious, but equally obvious was the truth of his contention that his sketches did not capture their real nature.

The one who had downed Playmate closed in on me. The other one chased Kip. Kip demonstrated the sort of character I expected. He had great faith in the patron saint of every man for himself. He made a valiant effort to get the hell out of there.

Kip's pursuer extended something shiny in his direction. The kid followed Playmate's example. He demonstrated substantially less style in his collapse.

I avoided the same fate for seconds on end by staying light on my feet and putting great enthusiasm into an effort to saturate the air with flying tools. But, too soon, I began feeling like I had been drinking a whole lot of something more potent than beer. I slowed down.

The dizziness didn't last long.

11

I do not recall the darkness coming. My next clear memory is of Morley Dotes with his pretty little nose only inches from mine. He's reminding me that to stay alive one *must* remember to breathe. From the corner of my eye I see Saucerhead Tharpe trying to sell the same idea to Playmate while the ratgirl Pular Singe scuttles around nervously, sniffing and whining.

The disorientation faded faster than the effects of alcohol ever do. Without leaving much hangover. But none of those clowns were willing to believe that high-potency libations hadn't been involved in my destruction. When people go on a nag they aren't the least bit interested in evidence that might contradict their prejudices.

Pular Singe, ratgirl genius, was my principal advocate.

What can you do? "You two are a couple of frigid old ladies," I told Morley and Saucerhead. "Thank you for your faith, Singe. Oh, my head!" I didn't have a hangover from this but I did have one from last night. The latest headache powder wasn't helping.

"And you'd like us to believe that you don't have a hangover," Morley sneered. Weakly. One side of his face wasn't working so good.

Not a lot of time had passed since the advent of the silvery people. Smoke still wisped off the cut ends of some of the wall planks. I suppose it was a near miracle that no fire had gotten going. Perhaps, less miraculously, that was due to the sudden appearance of Dotes, Tharpe, and Pular.

"Singe!" I barked at the ratgirl. "Where did you guys

come from?" She was likely to give me a straight answer. "Why're you here?" Bellows that Morley and Saucerhead would accept indifferently could rattle Singe deeply. Ratfolk are timid by nature and Singe was trying to make her own way outside her native society. Ratfolk males don't yell and threaten and promise massive bloodshed unless they intend to deliver. They don't banter.

When Singe is around I usually tread on larks' eggs because I don't want to upset her. It's like working with your mom wearing a rat suit.

She didn't get a chance to answer. Morley cracked, "This one's all right. He woke up cranking."

"What're you guys doing here, Morley?"

"Thank you, Mr. Dotes, for scaring off the baddies."

"Thank you, Mr. Dotes, for scaring off the baddies."

"See? You can learn if you put your mind to it."

"I was doing pretty good there on my own." The side of his face that wasn't working well had a sizable young bruise developing. "That's gonna be a brute when it grows up. What happened?" Morley's stylish clothing was torn and filthy, too. Which would hurt him more than mere physical damage could.

"I had a special request from the Dead Man. Round up Singe and a squad of heavyweights, come over here and keep an eye on you. You're a major trouble magnet, my friend. We're not even in place yet and we find the excitement already happening. What were those things?"

With more help from Singe than from Morley I made it to a standing position. "Where's the kid?"

"There was a kid? Maybe that's who your silvery friends were hauling away. Who were they, Garrett?"

"I don't know. You didn't stop them?"

"Let me see. No. I was too busy being bounced off walls and rolled through horse excrement. You couldn't hurt those guys." He looked as sour as he could manage with only half a face cooperating. "I broke my swordcane on one of them."

I couldn't resist a snicker. Morley is a lethally handsome half-breed, partly human but mostly dark elf. He's the guy fathers of young women wake up screaming about in the

wee hours of the night. His vanity is substantial. His dress
is always impeccable and at the forefront of fashion. He
considers disarray a horror and dirt of any sort an
abomination.

Dirt seems to feel the same way about him. It avoids
him religiously.

I snickered again.

"It must be the concussion," Morley grumped. "I know
my good friend Garrett would never mock me in my
misfortune."

"Mockery." I couldn't resist another snicker. "Heh-heh.
Misfortune." I glanced around. "Damn! Where'd he go? I
only looked away for a second. Too bad. You're stuck with
his evil twin instead of a friend."

"I hate it when that happens."

Singe had seen us in action often enough to discount
most of what she heard but she still couldn't quite grasp
what was going on. She watched us now, long fingers en-
twined so she could keep her hands from flying around. Her
myopic eyes squinted. Her snout twitched. Her whiskers
waggled. She drew more information from the world
through her sense of smell than with any other.

She tended to be emotional and excitable but now remained collected. If she had learned anything from me it
was better self-control. I felt it to be a cruel miscarriage of
propriety that my companionship hadn't had a similar impact on the rest of my friends.

She took advantage of a lull to inquire, "What is this
situation, Garrett? I did not understand the message I received from the Dead Man."

And yet she had come out of hiding. Because she had a
chance to help me.

Morley smirked. I would hear about that as soon as Singe
wasn't around to get her feelings hurt. She had an adolescent crush on me. And Morley, known to have broken the
bones of persons having thrown ethnic slurs his way,
thought it was great fun to torment me about being mooned
over by a ratgirl.

He could commit every crime of prejudice he hated when
they were directed toward him, yet would never, ever, rec-

ognize any inconsistency. Because ratpeople were a created race, products of the malificent sorcerous investigations of some of our lords of the Hill during the heyday of the last century, most people don't even consider them people. Morley Dotes included.

I told her, "Anything you heard from His Nibs makes you better informed than I am, Singe." Her particular line of ratpeople place their personal names second. Just to confuse things, other lines do the opposite, in imitation of local humans. "He didn't tell me anything. Not that he was interested in what's happening here nor even that he was planning to make you a part of things."

"What *is* happening here?" Morley asked.

"Can you handle that one, Playmate?" Saucerhead had the big stablekeeper up on his hind legs now.

"I don' t'ink," Playmate mumbled.

I tried to tell everybody what I knew, not holding back anything, the way my partner would. Well, some little details, maybe, like about how good the Dead Man was at sneaking peeks into unprepared minds. Nobody needs to know that but me.

"You sure you ain't been jobbed?" Saucerhead wanted to know. "That sure ain't much. Play, you runnin' a game on my man Garrett?"

I waved him off. "It's not that." Chances were good the Dead Man would've clued me in if that were the case. My concern was more that Kip and Playmate were being manipulated. "But I do wonder if someone isn't running a game on Kip. Play, you ever met Lastyr or Noodiss?"

"Not formally. Not to talk to. I've seen them a few times. Not so much recently, though. They used to come around here a lot. When they thought Kip would be here alone."

I grunted, irritated. Atop all the aches and pains it looked like the only way I was going to learn anything of substance would be to catch me a silver elf and squeeze him.

Which was a conclusion my partner must have reached before I left the house. Else how to explain Singe's presence?

Besides being my only friend from TunFaire's lowest lower class, Pular Singe is the finest tracker amongst a species known for individuals able to follow a trail through the insane stew of foul odors that complement the soul of this mad city.

"Singe? You find a scent yet?" I knew she was sniffing. She couldn't help herself. And she was clever enough to understand why she had been invited to the party.

She tried to shrug, then to shake her head. Ratfolk find both human gestures difficult. Singe wants to be human so bad. Each time I see it I hurt for her. I get embarrassed. Because most of the time we aren't worthy of imitation.

Failing, she spoke: "No. Not the elves. Though there is a unique odor where the two fell. But that exists only there. It does not go anywhere. And it does not smell like any odor from a living thing."

"Wow." Her human speech had improved dramatically since last I had seen her. It was almost free of accent— except when she tried a contraction. Her improvement was miraculous considering the voice box she had to use. No other rat in my experience had come close to matching her. Yet she was said to suffer from a hearing deficiency. According to the rat thug Reliance, who first brought her to my attention. "You've even mastered the sibilants."

Determination can take you a long way.

Her sibilants still had a strong serpentine quality. But Singe needs a lot of encouragement to keep going. She gets almost none of that from her own people.

"So what do we do now?" Morley asked. He wasn't interested, really. Not much. He was trying to work out how he could get back to The Palms and get cleaned up and changed before anyone noticed his disreputable condition. I had a feeling that, any minute now, I would find my best pal missing.

Singe said, "I cannot follow the strange elves. But Garrett taught me to follow the horses when I cannot follow a target who becomes a passenger in a vehicle that horses are pulling."

What a talent, that Garrett guy. After a moment, I confessed, "The student lost even the teacher on that one, Singe."

She looked at me like she knew I was just saying that so

she'd feel good, getting to explain. "The elves took the boy. Him I can track. So I will follow him. Wherever he stops moving, there will we find your elves."

"The girl is a genius," I said. "Let's all go raid Playmate's pantry before we go on the road."

That idea was acclaimed enthusiastically by everyone not named Playmate. Or Morley. Playmate because his charity is limited when its wannabe beneficiaries are solvent. Morley because the weasel wasn't around to vote.

Ah, well. My elven friend would be out there somewhere, a desperate fugitive fleeing the wrath of the good-grooming gods.

12

Saucerhead's impatient pacing took him across the narrow street and back three times as he tried to establish a safe passage around a particularly irritable camel. No owner of the beast was in evidence. I was surprised to see it. Camels are rare this far south. Possibly no one would have this one. Possibly it had been abandoned. It was a beast as foul as the Goddamn Parrot. It voided its bowels, then nipped at Saucerhead. I muttered, "That's what I feel like right now."

"Which end?" Singe asked, testing her theory of humor. She giggled. So bold, this ratgirl who came out in the daytime, then dared to make jokes in front of human beings.

"Take your pick. You know what that thing really is? A horse without its disguise on."

Even Singe thought that was absurd. And she has less love for the four-legged terrors than I do. You could say a state of war, of low intensity, exists between her species and theirs. Horses dislike ratpeople more than most humans do.

Playmate said, "One day I fully expect to find you on the steps of the Chancery, between Barking Dog Amato and Woodie Granger, foaming at the mouth as you rant at the King and the whole royal family because they're pawns of the great equine conspiracy, Garrett."

The Chancery is a principal government building where, traditionally, anyone with a grievance can voice it publicly on the outside steps. Inevitably, the Chancery steps have acquired a bevy of professional complainers and outright lunatics. Most people consider them cheap entertainment.

I said, "You shouldn't talk about it! They're going to get you now." Singe started looking worried, frowning. "All right. Maybe I exaggerate a little. But they're still vicious, nasty critters. They'll turn on you in a second."

The resident nasty critter spit at Saucerhead. Saucerhead responded with a jab to the camel's nose. It was a calm, professional blow of the sort that earned him his living. But he put his weight and muscle behind it. The camel rocked back. Its eyes wobbled. Its front knees buckled.

Tharpe said, "Come on." Once we were past the camel, he added, "Sometimes polite ain't enough. You just gotta show'em who's boss."

We walked another hundred feet. And stopped. The street didn't go anywhere. It ended at a wall. Which was improbable.

"What the hell?" Saucerhead demanded. "When did we start blocking off streets?"

He had a point. TunFaire has thousands of dead-end alleys and breezeways but something that happened in antiquity made our rulers issue regulations against blocking thoroughfares. Possibly because they'd wanted to be able to make a run for it in either direction. And while what we were following wasn't much of a street, it was a street officially. Complete with symbols painted on walls at intersections to indicate that its name was something like Stonebone. Exactly what was impossible to tell. The paint hadn't been renewed in my lifetime.

The wall ahead was old gray limestone. Exactly like the wall to our left. Needing the attention of a mason just as badly. But something about it made all four of us nervous.

"It sure don't look like something somebody threw up over the weekend," I said. Believe it or not, some Karentine subjects are wicked enough to ignore established regulations and will construct something illegal while the city functionaries are off duty.

Nobody stepped up to the wall. Until Singe snorted the way only a woman can do when she's exasperated with men being men. She shuffled right up till her pointy big nose was half an inch from the limestone. "The track of the boy goes straight on, Garrett. And this wall smells almost the same as the odor I found where the two elves fell on one another."

Playmate took a few steps backward, found a bit of broken brick that hadn't yet been scrounged by the street children. (They sell brick chips and chunks back to the brickyards, where they're powdered and added to the clay of new bricks.) He started to wind up, but paused and said, "Garrett, have you bothered to look up?"

I hadn't. Why would I?

None of the others had, either.

We all looked now.

That wall wasn't part of anything. It might not even be stone. It just went up a ways, then turned fuzzy and wiggly and lizard's belly white. Then it turned misty. Then it turned into nothing.

"It's an illusion."

Playmate chucked his brickbat.

The missile proceeded to proceed despite the presence of a wall that appeared completely solid, if improbably cold and damp when I extended a cautious finger to test it. Saucerhead Tharpe isn't nearly as careful as Mama Garrett's only surviving son. He reached out to thump that wall. And his fist went right on through.

We all stepped back. We exchanged troubled looks. I said, "That's an illusion of the highest order."

Singe said, "I hear someone calling from the other side."

Playmate observed, "An illusion that persists, that can be used as camouflage, requires the efforts of a master wizard."

I grunted. In this town that meant somebody off the Hill. It meant one of six dozen or so people who are the real masters in Karenta.

Singe said, "There is somebody over there. Yelling at you, Garrett."

I asked Playmate, "What do you think?" I admit to being intimidated by Hill people. But I've never backed down just because they stuck a finger in somewhere. I wouldn't back down now. Kip's kidnapping had me irked and interested. Of everyone I asked, "Anybody want to walk away?"

Nobody volunteered to leave, though Saucerhead gulped a pail of air, Playmate seemed to go a little green and Singe started shaking like she was naked in a blizzard and didn't have a clue which way to the warm. She made some kind of chalk sign on a real wall, maybe to ward off evil.

"You're the Marine," Playmate said. "Show us your stuff."

Saucerhead pasted on a huge grin. He was ex-army, too. And he had heard my opinions concerning the relative merits of the services more often than had Playmate. He refused to see the light. It's a debate that seems doomed to persist forever because army types are too dim to recognize the truth when it kicks them in the teeth.

Saucerhead's whole face threatened to open up. I thought the top half of his head was going to tip over backward onto his shoulders. He gasped out, "Yeah, Garrett. Let's see some of that old Marine Corps 'Hey diddle diddle, straight up the middle.' "

Ominously, Singe said, "There is no yelling anymore."

"I'm thinking about giving *you* some of that good old, big boy." I took a deep breath and squared off with the illusory wall.

Saucerhead chuckled. He knows I'd never come straight at him if I did think I had to get after him. Business led us to butt heads briefly once upon a time, long ago. The results had been far from satisfactory from my point of view.

I whooped like I was going in, back in my island warfare days, straight up the middle indeed. Something that we did not actually do very often, as I recall. Us and the Venageti both very much preferred sneaking around, stabbing in the back, to any straightforward and personally risky charging.

That wall was more than just an illusion. It resisted me. Hitting it felt a little like belly flopping, though with more stretch and give to the surface. Which popped after a moment. And which felt as cold as a god's heart until it did.

My efforts evidently weakened the wall considerably because the big army types followed me through as though there wasn't any resistance at all. And the civilian followed them. But I wasn't really keeping track.

We'd overtaken our quarry where they'd holed up temporarily, either so they could interrogate Kip or so their
injured buddies could recuperate. There was another imagi-
nary wall beyond them. That one had a bricklike look even
though it was semitransparent. From my point of view.

My heart jumped. Our approach had to have been noticed.

In that instant I sensed movement. The corner of the eye
kind of movement you get when your imagination is running wild. Only what I wasn't imagining was happening
right in front of me and I couldn't get a solid look at it.
Then, for a moment, I saw silver elves and Kip with something clamped over his mouth and I realized that Singe's
sharp ears must've caught his cries for help back when
she'd kept talking and nobody had bothered to listen.

A shimmering silver elf extended a hand toward me.

I dodged.

I didn't move soon enough.

Once again I didn't feel the darkness arrive.

13

Morley Dotes was right there in my face again when I woke up. "Some kind of party you must throw, Garrett. Blitzed into extinction again. And the sun still hasn't gone down." He looked around as I tried to sit up. My head pounded worse than before. "But in an alley? Even if it is a pretty clean one for this burg?"

"Gods! My head! I don't know what they did to me but it's enough to make me consider giving up liquor."

"You give up your beer? Don't try to kid a kidder, kid."

"I said liquor, nimrod. Beer is a holy elixir. One shuns beer only at the risk of one's immortal soul. I see you're all freshly prettied up. How'd you find us?"

Two of Morley's henchmen had accompanied him. I didn't know them. They were clad in the outfits waiters at The Palms usually wear but they were much younger than Sarge and Puddle and Morley's other traditional associates. Maybe the old guys were getting too old.

"Your girlfriend left us a trail to follow. Standard rat chalk symbols. You didn't notice? A trained detective like you?"

Pride made me consider fibbing. "No. I didn't. Not really." Ten years ago I couldn't have admitted any failing. Which, at times, had left me looking just a whole lot stupider than a simple confession would've done.

People are strange. And sometimes I think I might be the strangest people I know.

Morley's boys didn't lift a finger to help anybody. Dotes himself didn't do anything but talk. Which told me he thought none of us had been hurt badly. "What happened to the illusion?"

"What illusion?"

I explained. Morley wanted to disbelieve but dared not in the face of Saucerhead's confirmation. Tharpe doesn't have the imagination to dress himself up with excuses as complex as this.

"So you scared them into running when they're not really up to it. They have two casualties and a prisoner to manage."

"We don't know that any of them were hurt."

"Yes, we do, Garrett. Use that brain the Dead Man thinks you have. If they don't have someone injured they don't have any reason not to just drag the kid straight off to wherever it is they want to take him. Let's get back on the trail. They can't have gone far."

Maybe he was right. Maybe the villains were just around the corner. But I didn't have any way to track them. Right now.

Singe was still out, stone cold.

"I wonder if they understand how we found them." I was afraid the elves might've given Singe an extra dose of darkness because of her nose.

"Me, I'm wondering why they didn't hurt you a lot more than they did," Morley countered. His cure for most ills is to exterminate everybody involved. "For some reason they've slapped you down twice without doing any permanent harm." He has difficulty comprehending that kind of thinking.

He emphasized "permanent" because my expression revealed the depth and breadth of the temporary harm I was suffering.

"You all right, Saucerhead?"

"Got a miserable headache." Tharpe's voice was gravelly. His temper would be extremely short. Best not to disturb him at all.

"How 'bout you, Play?"

"What he said. And don't yell. Makes it hurt even more."

He didn't need to yell back.

Maybe I was lucky. All the practice I've had dealing with hangovers. I turned to Singe. "Seems a shame to disturb her." She did look rather peaceful.

"Kiss her and let's get on with it," Morley grumped. Without having been blessed by the elves.

"What?"

He opened his mouth to crack wise about the sleeping beauty, thought better of it, beckoned me. I followed him for as far as he felt was far enough to keep his remarks from being overhead by sharp rat ears. "She isn't really out, Garrett. She's giving you a chance to show some special concern."

The fact that he didn't make mock let me know that he was serious, that he was concerned about bruising Singe's tender ego. Though the motives behind his concern were, probably, wholly selfish.

"Understood," I told him, though that wasn't entirely true.

I don't like the responsibility that piles onto me when Singe gives way to these juvenile urges to manipulate me. That smacks of emotional blackmail. In fact, it *is* emotional blackmail. She just doesn't understand that it is. And I'm not all that well equipped to deal with it. More than one lady of my acquaintance would suggest that I'm not far enough away from adolescence myself.

I went to the ratgirl, dropped to my knees beside her. "Singe?"

She didn't respond. I thought her breathing was too rapid for someone who was supposed to be unconscious, though.

How do you tell someone that their relationship fantasies can never become anything more than that? Everything I could possibly say to Singe would be true but would sound so stupidly cliché if said that I could do no good talking to her. She was important to me, personally and professionally. She had become one of the half dozen closest friends I had. I enjoyed teaching her how to cope in a world where she was less than welcome. But she could never be anything but a friend, a business associate, and a student. And I have no idea how to make her understand that without causing her pain.

When she first broke away from the dominance of her own people, where females have fewer rights than do horses amongst humans, I considered letting her move into my place. I thought of making her part of the team. I still think well of that idea. But the Dead Man did assure me that, in her desperation to be wanted and liked and loved, Pular Singe would give the offer far more weight than I intended.

I touched her throat. Her pulse was rapid. I glanced around. There was no immediate salvation apparent. Morley was grinning, exposing about a thousand bright white needle teeth in a silent taunt.

"You want I should carry her, Garrett?" Saucerhead asked. There went Tharpe, being thoughtful despite his pain. Like most human beings, he can be a mess of contradictions.

"That might be good. Any of you guys know anything about doctoring ratfolk? If we can't fix her up ourselves we'll have to take her back to Reliance."

That ought to be the perfect medicine. The very philosopher's stone.

Reliance is a sort of ratman godfather, a highly respected and greatly feared leader of that community who's involved in a lot of questionable and some outright illegal activities. Reliance believes that Pular Singe belongs to him. There's a chance he's right within the rules of rat society. There is some sort of indenture involved. But rat society isn't paramount in TunFaire. And that guy Garrett don't much care about anybody's customs or rules when he makes up his mind what's right and what's wrong.

"She wouldn't be real happy about the boss rat getting his paws on her again, Garrett," Tharpe assured me. With a wink, showing he'd gotten it. "He tried to hire me once to bring her back." He grinned a grin filled with bad teeth.

Well. Maybe I was going to get some help with this after all, from the least likely source.

Saucerhead really can be a sensitive kind of guy.

And Singe, wonder of wonders, was stirring suddenly.

"So why didn't you take the job?"

"Old Reliance, he's too damned cheap for one thing. He

just can't get it through his head that it ain't just a matter
of rounding up one dumb female and dropping her off
where he wants her delivered. He can't get it through his
skull that she can actually think for herself and that she
can have made friends who'd be willing to look out for her.
He just figures you're trying to hold him up on your fee
when you try to explain it to him."

"You'd think he'd have figured it all out from direct
experience. Whoops! Look here. It's alive. Hi, sleepyhead.
You're the last one awake."

Singe mumbled something.

"We're just waiting on you."

Singe smiled a weak rat smile. She probably thought she
heard relief in my voice. Possibly she did. I was relieved
that her problem wasn't real.

Pular Singe's recovery was dramatically swift once she
decided that she needed to get healthy. Reliance's name
made a great whip.

Morley told one of his waiters to make a bread and
cheese run while the rest of us sat around staking claims
on being in worse shape than the other guy. Food was a
great idea, I thought, but when the man came back with a
basket filled with chow I didn't feel much like eating.

A similar lack of appetite afflicted Saucerhead, Playmate,
and Singe. And none of those three liked it even a little,
either. They loved their food. Singe, in particular, always
ate like a starved alley cat or one of her feral cousins.
Everything in sight, steadily, gobbling so fast that the bugs
never got a share.

I grumbled, "I think we've got us an invention right here.
A new weight loss program for the lords and ladies." Nobody else in this burg ever gets fat.

Soon enough, heads still aching and stomachs still empty,
we proceeded as Singe picked up Kip's trail. Though it had
begun to get dark she had no trouble finding the way. Sight
was never her master sense. Though it did become more
important after nightfall. She could see in the dark better
than Morley. And Morley has eyes like an owl.

This time the chase didn't last twenty minutes.

This time the camouflage didn't catch us unaware, either,

though it existed as an addition to a building rather than as something thrown across a street. From the viewpoint of the silver elves the trouble was that the building they'd scabbed onto was one that Saucerhead and I knew. And had we not known it ourselves there were at least twenty local Tenderloin folk hanging around in the gloaming trying to figure out what was going on. That addition hadn't been there half an hour earlier.

Playmate observed, "These people aren't very good at what they're doing, are they?"

"I get the feeling that this isn't anything they've had to do before. What do you say we just charge in there and grab the kid back?" I wasn't eager to get myself another bout of sleep because of my habit of waking up afterward with a ferocious hangover. I didn't need another one of those. I was working on a couple already.

Still, they had the boy. Obnoxious though he was. Which didn't incline them to throw him back out, apparently. They wanted him pretty bad.

I suppose a throbbing headache can impair your judgement. And a friend like Morley Dotes can have a similar effect. Once he had winkled out the complete details of our last encounter he was ready to go. "They aren't going to kill anybody, Garrett. There are six of us." Singe bristled, knowing she hadn't been included in the count. "They can't get all of us."

14

They got all of us, most of the bystanders, quite a few passersby, and even a handful of people inside neighboring buildings who didn't know what was going on and never knew what hit them.

I came out of it faster than before, my head pounding worse than last time. The first thing I saw was my eager beaver buddy Morley Dotes. Yet again. Only this time he had his temples grasped tightly and looked like he was working real hard on trying not to scream. Or was, possibly, contemplating the delights of suicide.

I grumbled, "Now we know why they didn't ask you to be a general during the recent scuffle with Venageta." Though considering the performances of some of the generals we'd had, who'd earned their bells by picking the right venue as a place of birth, Morley might've fit right in.

Dotes whined something irrelevant about the whole thing having been my idea and registered a plea for a lot less vocal volume.

"Pussy. I wake up feeling like this three or four times a week. And I function. What the hell are those people roaring about?" Neighbors not struck down were rushing into the street. In normal times their voices would have been considered restrained. Not so now.

They all stared at the sky.

I looked up just in time to see something large and shiny and shaped like a discus disappear behind nearby rooftops, heading north. "What the hell was that?" I glanced at Morley.

"Never mind. Don't tell me. Your cousins just got away in one of those flying lights that people keep seeing."

"Cousins? Those things weren't elves, Garrett. Not elves of any kind. Their mouths and eyes were all wrong. They didn't have elven teeth. Maybe they're some kind of foreign, deformed humans. You might look into that. But they're definitely not elves."

Playmate came around. Between groans he asked, "Did we get him back?"

"Kip? We didn't even get a wink this time. Let's see what we did get. Maybe that whore Fate has a heart of gold after all."

We managed to collect a few scraps of silvery cloth and nearly a dozen other items of wildly varying shape and no obvious utility. Those included several small, torn bags made of a silvery, somewhat paperlike material. The rest resembled smooth gray rocks with a very unrocklike feel that came in varying regular shapes. Most had markings in green and red and yellow that looked like writing but which were in no familiar alphabet.

One of Morley's men came up with a bag that hadn't been opened. Its contents turned out to be two thick biscuits the texture of oatmeal cakes. They had a sorghum molasses odor.

"Food," Playmate said. "We broke up a meal."

"I could use something to eat," Saucerhead said by way of announcing his recovery. "We still got that cheese basket?" He rubbed his forehead as he looked around. He has an amazingly high threshhold of pain but now he had begun to respond to it. "What happened?" He reached out and helped himself to the elven oatmeal cakes. He wolfed them down before anybody could remind him of the legends about fairy food.

Nobody answered his question. Because nobody had an answer.

"Lookit there!" somebody shrieked. In a second half the crowd were pointing skyward again.

The silver disk was back. And it was in a big hurry. It left a thunderclap behind as it streaked off southward.

"Hey! There's another one!"

One turned into three in a matter of seconds. Only these weren't disks. They looked like giant glowing gas balls. On a smaller scale I'd seen something similar in the will-o'-the-wisps of the swamps on the islands I'd visited during the war. The glowing globes chased the silvery disk.

Morley murmured, "I've been hearing about these things for weeks but I'd about made up my mind that they were pure popular hysteria."

I looked around for an easily accessible high place. I wanted a clear line of sight to the west, toward the heart of town. Toward the Hill. To discover if those lights ended up there. Because this looked like the sort of thing those people would pull. Squabbling amongst themselves using experimental sorceries while the folk of the city got run over.

Morley asked, "You think your friends the unemployed gods might be back, Garrett?"

That hadn't occurred to me. "I doubt it. They were more reserved. They didn't show themselves unless they wanted to be seen. Mainly because they couldn't be seen by nonbelievers unless they made a huge effort."

"I don't think that these people would attract attention if they were given an option. Something intense is going on with them, sufficient to make being noticed the lesser concern."

"Probably." I did think he was right. Logically, if you were a foreigner running around in an alien town you wouldn't let yourself be noticed unless it was unavoidable. "You think Saucerhead is going to croak on us?"

Tharpe had turned several indescribable colors, near as I could tell by torchlight. Torches and lanterns were turning up now that the curious felt safe enough to come out of their homes. Just as well that they hadn't before, too. We'd have awakened to find ourselves plucked of everything but our toenails.

"I think he might want to die," Morley said. "I think we ought to discover ourselves in another location sometime soon. This much activity is bound to attract lawmen."

And he wouldn't want the notice, however much he protests his innocence of the illegal of late.

Maybe old habits die hard.

These days, with the postwar economic depression becoming entrenched, the new secret police are very interested in any center of excitement. A minor bit no more scary than a street party can turn into a riot at the bump of a belly between an unemployed human and almost any nonhuman he might suspect of having moved into a human's job while human soldiers were away risking their lives on behalf of the kingdom.

These are social problems that aren't going to go away anytime soon.

I said, "We do have everything we need for a blowup."

Morley nodded. He understood. He shared my concern.

He has become very sensitive in these changing times. He doesn't like the way things are headed. Though it isn't the conflict that bothers him. That can be exploited to produce big profits. What he abhors is the growing power of the Crown and its determined interference in our everyday lives.

An elven trait, to believe that that government governs best which doesn't govern at all. Chaos is more fun. Anarchy is the ideal. And only the strong survive.

Morley would admit that a sustained harsh dose of genuine anarchy most likely would result in the extinction or expulsion of every species of elf currently calling Tun-Faire home.

I told Morley, "That was an absolutely marvelous suggestion, old friend. Can I assume that it'll be you carrying Pular Singe . . . ? What?"

Singe was still unconscious. But I wasn't concerned about her. "Morley. I just saw Bic Gonlit. He was watching us from across the street."

"So let's get Singe put back together and see if she can get on his trail. He just might know where to look for Playmate's kid."

"You don't think she can track Kip from here?"

"Not if he got carried away inside a giant flying wheel, I don't."

An excellent point. Not one I'd wanted to look at close up yet, though. You hope you can catch an occasional break.

Singe was getting her feet under her now, with a little help from Playmate.

"Let's see about traveling on, then," I told Morley. "I just spotted another familiar face. This one I recollect seeing in the vicinity of Colonel Block and Deal Relway in a none too distant past." I made a big effort to remember such faces so I can exercise some sort of exit strategy when I see one again. "I'll help with Singe."

15

The secret police evidently didn't have an interest strong enough to pursue us. At the moment. But I was willing to bet that I'd hear from Westman Block if anyone in the Tenderloin had recognized me.

Colonel Westman Block, erstwhile acquaintance of that handsome Marine named Garrett, oversaw all police forces and functions in TunFaire. That included the secret police. Theoretically. On paper.

We gathered in a dark place, half a mile from the excitement, and considered, "What now?"

Singe said, "I cannot possibly follow a man who flew away through the air, inside a flying boat made out of metal." She then wondered aloud, "Why are you looking at me like that?"

"Because Morley said almost exactly the same thing just before you woke up. We decided to chase Bic Gonlit instead." She knew the name from discussions of what was happening, back when we were tracking Kip. "As soon as we were sure we'd shaken the police."

"You must tell me more about this Bic Gonlit."

Playmate and I both tried to explain Bic Gonlit and his place in what was happening. A challenging task, of course, since we had almost no idea ourselves. I added, "Only, I'm not sure if he's actually part of what happened this afternoon."

"You people like to think you are so much smarter than us but sometimes you are really dumb, Garrett. You start talking before you think. How do you expect me to follow someone who is just another face in a crowd?"

"She's got you there," Morley said, content to leave all the blame with me. "I could use a little more information myself. Bic Gonlit is only a name to me."

"He's this little round fat guy who wears funny boots—"

"There was a little round fat man with hugely thick-soled boots I saw several times on the way down here. I thought he might be doing something for you because your parrot was right there near him."

"I didn't see him," Playmate said. "Not the bird, either."

"Nor did I," I confessed. My parrot. Following me around. And I never noticed.

It might be time to consider alternative careers.

"I noticed the bird," Singe said. "I saw the fat man, too. But I did not know Mr. Big was following him. I thought he was following you, Garrett. He is still around. I saw him just a minute ago. Yes. Over there. Where we came from. Up on that cornice thing where the pigeons are sleeping."

"I've made up my mind. I'm going to see Weider and tell him I'm taking the security job at the brewery." I felt completely blind and useless. It was so dark I couldn't find the end of my arm.

"There is a short little fat man over there watching us, too," Singe told me. "He is hiding behind those steps right under the parrot."

Like anybody could see all that if they just looked. Grrr! The only thing I could see was a glow in the distance, about where we'd lost track of Kip.

I really was inclined to tell Max Weider I was ready to come on board. Truly. At that moment. But, before I hung it up, I had to try another stunt or two. "I have a thought. We're all tired. Why don't we head for my place? If Gonlit really is following us, we can lead him to the Dead Man."

I was past ready to go home. I was desperate for something to take the edge off my headache. And I was hungry. And I was tired. Getting knocked unconscious regularly takes the vinegar out of you fast, even if you're not going out by getting bopped on the head.

My plan, as proposed, didn't stir a word of protest. Much to my amazement. Morley is naturally contentious. He'll get involved in arguments just to entertain himself. But all he said was, "I'm worn-out, too. And The Palms is headed into its busiest time. And I left Puddle in charge."

"I got a thing going myself," Saucerhead said. "I need to get back, too, unless something starts happening."

Even Playmate was willing to shut it down for the night. And to desert me when he did. "Nobody's been at the stable all day. I need to get back there before the animals get so upset they . . ." He stopped. I think he was about to let slip something terrible about the conspiracy amongst horses but realized that me finding out might turn out to be bad luck for him. He changed the subject. "And somebody's going to have to tell Kip's family what's happened."

A while later, after a period of silence, Playmate asked, "You wouldn't consider taking care of that for me, would you, Garrett?"

"Not likely, old buddy. Not likely. After today's adventures you're not real high on my 'please, God, let me do him a favor' list."

The tiniest flicker of a smirk crossed Playmate's features before he settled on an expression of stolid resignation. I had the feeling that I'd just gotten jobbed but couldn't figure out how.

16

I never saw the Goddamn Parrot before he dropped onto my shoulder in Wizard's Reach, two blocks from home. Or one block through the alley to my back fence. By then the only companions I had were the bird and Pular Singe. None of us were inclined to lose any sleep looking for Cypres Prose anymore.

Maybe I was just telling myself what I wanted to hear when I reasoned that Kip was in no physical danger because the silver elves had shown no inclination to do anyone any permanent harm.

So far.

Kip's personality might trigger the extra effort.

The bird said nothing. His presence was the message. The Dead Man knew we were coming. And he knew that Bic Gonlit was on our trail.

Now we would see how well the little fat man had done his homework.

If he knew much about the Dead Man he wouldn't get too close to the house. Not as close as he'd gotten in the alley. Though how close is really too close is something even I don't know.

The Goddamn Parrot whispered, "He has stopped, Garrett. He has positioned himself behind the Bailnoc stoop. From there he can see the front of our house while he stays far enough removed that I cannot read much more than his moods."

He didn't seem to mind Singe finding out that he could chat with me through the ugly rooster. I didn't think he

was dumb enough to believe that she was too dim to catch
on. So he trusted her completely.

Handy to know just how trustworthy your associates are.

I looked back. I couldn't see a thing. I wondered how
Gonlit could be watching me. I wondered about his connections. He'd have to have some potent ones helping right
now. Otherwise, he wouldn't be able to follow me around
unnoticed.

That takes some advanced magic.

I think I'm pretty good at this stuff I do. I don't normally
get tailed without noticing unless the tail comes armed with
some pretty potent sorcerous tools.

As Singe and I climbed the stoop a sleepy-angry tittering
broke out somewhere up under the eaves. Something as
fast as a hummingbird dropped down and circled us several
times too swiftly to be seen clearly.

My front door opened. Dean must've been alerted by
the Dead Man. He stood there in his nightshirt, scowling,
holding a lamp above his head, disapproving of birth, death,
and most everything in between.

"Early night?" I asked. The nightshirt was for commen-
tary only. It wasn't yet time for him to retire. He doesn't
change until he's ready to slide into bed. Unless he wants
to make some point that will remain obscure to everyone
but him.

He grunted and rewarded me with an even blacker scowl.

"What's with the gang of pixies up there?" I expected
their presence would keep us arguing like pixies for weeks.

"Ask the thing. He's the one who decided to adopt
them."

Ah. Live and learn. And discover the real root of Dean's
bad temper. The Dead Man had done something to offend
his sense of rectitude.

Dean was aggrieved further because I'd been all set to
blame him. Because that's the kind of thing he's likely to
do. Every time I turn around he's trying to take in another stray.

This might require some untangling.

"I'll talk to him," I promised. I wasn't really happy,
either.

Living near pixies is like setting up housekeeping inside a colony of sparrows. The squabbling never stops. And this bunch was making themselves at home right above my bedroom window.

None of that would bother Old Bones. He's dead. He doesn't have to listen to the racket.

Darkly, I added, "Failing him seeing reason, I know where I can come up with a nest of bumblebees." Bumblebees and the smallest of the little people were feuding before the appearance of the first men. If you credit the legends of the wee folk.

Dean growled something about, "Then how do we get rid of the bumblebees?"

He grows ever more pessimistic as he ages.

"One step at a time, brother. One step at a time. Right now we've got trouble on a grander scale. I lost the boy who came here looking for help today. In circumstances surpassing strange. Make some tea, slap together some sandwiches, bring everything in with His Nibs, and I'll fill you in."

The old man headed for the kitchen. I'd triggered his concern for the lost and the hopeless. Earlier he'd been ready to stuff Kip into a gunnysack with a couple boulders so the boy could have a close-up look at the lost treasures on the bottom of the river somewhere off the Landing.

Singe watched while I took the Goddamn Parrot to his perch in the small front room. The Dead Man had withdrawn his control and inhibiting influence. The feathered weasel was returning to normal. He muttered like a stevedore but his big interest at the moment was food, not obnoxious chatter meant to get his owner crucified. He let Singe stroke his feathers as long as she didn't interfere with his dining.

Singe was pleased. Normally that jungle buzzard is less kind to her than he is to me. She looked up at me and tried to smile.

"Wish you wouldn't do that."

"Am I doing it wrong?"

"No. But you're not people. Be content to be the brightest and best ratwoman who ever lived. Be true to yourself."

I felt like somebody's dad, spouting clichés. Then, of course, I felt really awful because I was old enough to understand what the clichés were all about. Embarrassment followed that as I remembered the cocksure boys we'd been when we were getting showered with the stupid stuff that turned out to be Joe Everyman's way of trying to pass along his accumulated wisdom.

She is young, Garrett. And she has only just escaped a state closely approximating slavery. She will need time and numerous opportunities to shore up her belief in herself.

Old Bones has a soft spot for Singe, too. Though he'd never admit that if it were suggested aloud. He'd never confess to any form of emotional vulnerability or sentimental weakness.

I kept thinking about old men and clichés. And I kept trying to avoid considering how often the Dean Man threw those things my way. Because I resented his advice almost as much as I'd resented advice from men of my father's generation when I was fifteen. I guess neither the old men nor the young men ever learn, but they keep on trying.

Dean nearly beat us to the Dead Man's room with the refreshments. I got a lamp going. Singe dragged in a special chair I'd had made that let her sit without having to worry about her troublesome tail. In moments she and I were hard at work. On the tea and sandwiches.

"Damn!" I woofed around a glob of bread and ham. "I didn't realize how hungry I was. The effects of that knockout spell must be all the way worn off now."

Singe grunted. She didn't have time for anything else. Once she gulped down everything Dean didn't nibble and I didn't devour, she looked around like she hoped there was still a whole roast pig she'd overlooked. I knew a reinforced battalion of young women who'd gladly kill, and who'd certainly hate Singe, for her ability to eat and eat and never gain an inappropriate ounce.

There are no fat ratpeople.

The Dead Man had me tell my story first.

I have a knack for accurate recollection. I provided the details I believed were necessary for an understanding of events while the Dead Man observed those events as mem-

ories drifting across the surface of my mind. He asked only
a handful of questions, waiting until I was finished talking
to go to the first. He seemed particularly interested in even
the most minute details of the silver elves' sorceries.

*At first blush I would have to agree with Mr. Dotes' as-
sessment that those people are not elves, Garrett. Perhaps
they belong to a single family of unusual breeding. A mixture of human and kef sidhe sounds plausible, considering
their descriptions. Though their apparel seems most unusual.
Let us examine the materials you managed to recover at
your last contact site. All three of you, please. So that I may
have the benefit of three divergent viewpoints and minds and
sets of eyes.*

Once scattered atop the little table that is one of the few
pieces of furniture in the Dead Man's room my plunder
did not appear especially exciting. Because he was able to
see the inside of my head, anyway, I admitted, "It seems
to be mostly trash."

Having contemplated the take through our several viewpoints, Old Bones responded, *You are correct, Garrett. The
silver people did abandon what they considered to be waste.*

How did he know?

*Through exactly the same process you used to come to
that identical conclusion, supplemented by experience and
unlimited intellect. It is a pity, however, that neither of you
can recall the exact circumstances of the kidnappers' final
escape.*

"A huge pity," I grumped. My headache remained on
duty, totally devoted. Singe, though smitten harder at the
time, had recovered completely already.

The Dead Man must've been more interested in events
than he let on. When I started feeling sorry for myself and
lusting after a beer he interfered with nature. He reached
inside my head and did something that made the pain fade
away. Some. Enough. Though a reminder remained in the
background, eager to come back.

What can we tell from the kidnappers' trash? the Dead
Man asked.

I couldn't tell a thing other than that they were no more
fastidious than any other Karentine subject.

Singe sniffed each item yet again before carefully showing us her best imitation human shrug. From its look she'd
practiced a lot. Ratpeople don't move like that normally.

She said, "This all smells very cold. Very sterile. There
is no soul in it. There is no magic."

That was an interesting observation, considering what
we'd seen and suffered. But I kept my thoughts to myself.
Singe needed her confidence. And for all I really knew, she
was right on the mark.

She might be indeed, Garrett.

I scowled his way. He was not supposed to eavesdrop on
the inside of my head when I wasn't reporting.

*I am not prying into your mind. I just know how you
think. I believe that it is now time to interview Mr. Bic Gonlit. His place in all this appears to be anomalous. Though I
do have several hypotheses about what could be transpiring.
His testimony should tell me which of those I can reasonably discard.*

"Why do I get the feeling that I'm going to do all the
work, inviting him in?"

*Perhaps because you are irrationally pessimistic. Your
part will require very little work, Garrett. I will be the one
forced to stretch himself to his limits after you have invested
just a few minutes in rounding him up and bringing him
here. Be sure you take your convincing stick.*

"Never leave home without one." That's my partner.
Like some kind of priest or professor, his vegetating is hard
and honorable work. All my sweat and agony is barely
worth a mention because what I do involves occasionally
engaging a muscle.

17

Bic Gonlit had no intention of cooperating. Bic Gonlit could pick his dogs up and put them down when he was scared. Who'd have thought a little round guy with chubby, stubby legs could lead me on such a long chase?

Not me. Not before I lived it.

After several blocks I was glad the Dead Man had insisted on sending the Goddamn Parrot out to scout for me. By then it was obvious that Bic Gonlit could see in the dark. And I could not, which wasn't a major news flash. And the people of my neighborhood aren't rich enough to maintain adequate streetlamps.

The multicolored chicken did his part. He kept up a running lot of howling and cursing, some evidently adapted from the cant of old-time formal hunts. Highbrow and embarrassing. And, likely, everybody he woke up would assume that it was all my fault.

There'd be complaints. There'd be angry presentations. There'd be intemperate talk about chasing me out of the neighborhood. That would be followed by calmer heads appealing for reason. The older residents all know I share my place with a cranky dead Loghyr. An *irritated* cranky dead Loghyr can make life a lot more unpleasant for a lot of people for a long time. Why go looking for trouble?

I needed to stop playing around. I needed to put on a burst of speed that would nail the fat man.

I should've planned for this phase before I let everybody go home.

Just off the Arsenal High Street, a little my way from

the brewery district, is a small remnant of old-time imperial TunFaire that wasn't consumed in the Great Fire. It's known as Prune Tastity for reasons nobody recalls anymore. Prune Tastity is a sort of museum of ancient times, all cramped-together buildings and covered alleyways barely wide enough to let the air circulate. Following the fire wider alleys and streets were mandated by law.

There is less disease in areas where the buildings are farther apart, too.

The wonder buzzard's shrieks told me my quarry was going to try to lose us both by ducking into Prune Tastity's tangle of covered alleyways.

I've been in there a few times. The place is a maze, at times rising five stories high. What Gonlit apparently didn't realize was that I was familiar enough with Prune Tastity to know that there're only a handful of entrances to the maze. He'd gone in the far side hoping I'd follow and get lost. If he meant to leave without running into me again he'd have to come out not far from where I stood listening to the Goddamn Parrot's progress report.

I got myself into position with minutes to spare. I used every second to get more wind back into my lungs. I needed my breathing under control if Gonlit wasn't going to hear me puffing for a block before he arrived.

I needn't have worried. Bic was puffing so hard himself that he couldn't have heard the ringing of the bell that's supposed to announce the end of the world. His head was down, his arms and legs were pumping, and he wasn't even making a fast walk anymore. But he was still moving. He sounded like he was going to expire if he didn't take a break and concentrate on his breathing.

I timed my move, caught his collar as he shuffled past. He made one feeble attempt to get away, then gave up. And I mean gave up completely. He just folded up on the street and refused to do anything but gasp for air.

Ten minutes later he was still curled up like a pillbug, daring me to make him do anything he didn't want to do. He seemed confident he knew enough about me to be sure I wouldn't kill him for being uncooperative.

Morley is right. I need to become less predictable. And I need to develop a more savage reputation.

Because of the Dead Man's reminder I had not left the house without my convincing stick, eighteen inches of oak with a pound of lead in its active end. It proved useful on this unfriendly night.

I tapped my new friend just below the kneecap on each leg, not hard enough to break anything. Just hard enough to turn his legs to water temporarily. I didn't want him able to put up much of a fight when I took his precious boots.

He understood before I got the first boot off. He started yelping. He called for help. He begged for mercy. The Goddamn Parrot came down and chimed in, carrying on loudly in several obviously nonhuman voices. Not that any witnesses were likely to drop their street sense in order to jump in and rescue any of us. That was not the way of the city.

"You sonofabitch, you want to keep your pretty boots, you'd better get real cooperative real sudden." I thumped Mr. Gonlit once atop each shoulder, briskly, not far from the sides of his neck.

Instantly, Bic began to have trouble lifting his arms.

The little man was tough in his way. He never stopped struggling—until I dragged the second boot off him. Then he went limp again. Without volunteering to make my life any easier.

"Bic, I'm gonna take your shoes home with me. Maybe give me a good shine." It had been my intention to drag him along with me, too, but I'd just heard a troubling sound, one I'd honestly never expected to hear. But rumors had been circulating for weeks so I recognized it in plenty of time.

The sound was a whistle. Rather like the shrill of a boatswain's pipe. Somebody from the guard's foot patrol wasn't far away and he'd heard that there was trouble. He was summoning assistance.

Changing times. Relway and Block just have way too many ideas for advancing the case of law and order. Not that I mind too much when they interfere in someone else's business. But my business is mine.

I said, "My friend and I have to run. I'll take good care
of your boots. You know where to find them. When the
mood hits you, drop by the house. You can pick them up."

I was drawing to an inside straight, betting his boots were
that important to him. I would've talked more but now whistles from several sources were sounding closer and closer.

I headed for home. I was halfway there before I realized
that the Goddamn Parrot wasn't with me. When I got home
I went straight to the Dead Man to find out why.

*The manner in which you dealt with the exigencies of your
situation seems well chosen. However, it did leave considerable leeway in the hands of Mr. Gonlit. It seemed prudent
to keep watching eyes and a nagging voice somewhere near
him. Lest he surrender to a fit of common sense and just
abandon his boots.*

*You do have those still? Excellent. Would you summon
Miss Pular? She is in the kitchen helping herself to a snack.
Dean has retired for the night.*

*We will try to discover why the boots mean so much to
our rotund nemesis.*

*Did you, by the by, discover how it was that he was able
to see in the dark?*

" 'Fraid not. The question went right out of my head
when I heard those whistles."

Old Bones was wide-awake and in rare form, nothing
escaping the notice of his several minds. I wasn't going to
be allowed anything less than wide-awake myself until he
sucked up all the outside information he wanted.

18

Singe sniffed Gonlit's boots. That wasn't a task I envied
her. Their fragrance had been less than appealing while I
was toting them, even carried at the ends of their strings.
But ratpeople don't seem to be repelled by odors the same
way we humans are. Nor are they offended by the same
scents.

Hard to credit in some cases but I've been around Singe
long enough to know that it's true.

The famous Gonlit boots had soles layered more than
two inches thick. They had fake glass emeralds and rubies
and little brass rivet heads all over them. I thought they
looked pretty shabby these days. Maybe old Bic was farther
down on his luck than rumor suggested. He wasn't so big-
time that popular interest tracked his every step.

At one time the boots had been white. At one time, so
the story went, Bic Gonlit had dressed all in white, even
unto the extremity of an all-white, wide-brimmed version
of the Unorthodox missionary's hat.

That would have been years ago, though, when Bic
would have been more prosperous because he was less well
known. That would have been during the days before he
learned that having a signature look was no advantage in
the bounty-hunting business. Your quarry would see you
coming.

The boots themselves, by reputation, were enchanted.
How so remained an open question. They hadn't added
anything to his getaway speed. But, on the other hand, he'd
been able to see in the dark.

Maybe we'd winkle out all the facts when Bic came to reclaim his treasures.

The Dead Man and Singe communed about those boots.

I jumped suddenly. My eyes had fallen shut. I don't know for how long. Long enough for the lamp to have gone out. Now just a single candle burned on the top shelf of the Dead Man's memorabilia case. He and Singe weren't troubled by the shortage of light.

Garrett.

I heard a racket up front.

One of the two nuisances had awakened me.

The Dead Man wasn't going anywhere. I got up and stalked to the front door. The racket there persisted. I began thinking that maybe Mr. Gonlit needed a whipping, just to remind him of his manners.

I used the peephole for its dedicated purpose.

Surprise. That wasn't Bic Gonlit trying to make my neighbors dislike me even more. That was three or four guys who had no manners to be reminded of. The loudest was none other than our beloved chief of the city Guards, Colonel Westman Block himself.

It'd been a while since we two had crossed paths. He seemed to have grown in that time, both in stature and in confidence.

I turned away on the theory that he could use a little deflation.

Allow the colonel to enter, Garrett. That will serve us better in the long run.

"Took you long—" Block snarled as I swung the door inward. "Damn! Garrett!" he barked when I swung it right back shut, bruising his nose.

Garrett!

"Just a little courtesy lesson." I opened the door again.

Colonel Block appeared more flustered than angry. And his goons—three gorillas damned near as big as Saucerhead Tharpe—wore dazed looks, as though they were asleep on their feet, with their eyes open.

"Good evening, Colonel. How can I help you?"

Evidently the shock had been enough to startle Block

into a case of the courtesies. That or some light touch from the Dead Man. "Yes. We've had reports of some unusual events, Garrett."

"This's TunFaire. We have wizards and priests enough here to supply the world with weird."

I led Block into the Dead Man's room while we talked. His goons remained outside, still as memorial pillars. He replied, "But in this instance there's reason to believe that you might be involved."

"What? Me? How come I get blamed for everything?"

"Because someone fitting your description, accompanied by persons fitting the descriptions of known associates of yours, including a cursing parrot, was seen near the sites of several unusual incidents. I'm disinclined to accept the explanation that your evil twin was out there trying to scuttle your reputation. You don't have one."

Go ahead and tell him the truth, Garrett.

I've cooperated with the authorities on most occasions. It rankles but, to be honest, it's never been that huge an inconvenience.

So I told him the whole story. Sort of. Almost. In the young peoples' abridged form.

Then he told me a story. His was a lot shorter.

"Coming up here we ran into a crowd of ratpeople. Twenty or thirty of them, trying to work up their nerve for some villainy. When they recognized us they scattered like roaches. A couple of my guys mentioned seeing a little fat man running with them. Either one of you want to say something about that?"

"I would if I could, boss. But I don't have any idea."

The Dead Man had no comment at all.

Block asked, "Any ideas about these lights in the sky, these flying helmets and whatnot? People keep seeing them and getting upset about them so other people keep telling me that I have to do something about them. Nobody has any suggestions about what the hell that might be and I don't have any brilliant ideas of my own."

"You've started to regress. You had your language so cleaned up you could've fit in at court."

"That's what's causing it. Polite society. Those folks have

more demands, and can make bigger pains in the ass of themselves, than any three normal human beings."

"Who's telling you to do something about those things? Do they really think you'd interfere in wizards' experiments?"

"Get real. It's wizards doing the demanding, Garrett. They can't figure out what's going on. So they expect Colonel Westman Block of His Majesty's Royal TunFairen Civil Guards to unravel the mystery for them. Meantime, Wes Block can't keep his own feet untangled. But they don't need to know that. How much does the Prose kid know?"

I'd been afraid we'd get to that as soon as he'd mentioned the failed investigations of our lords of the Hill. "I don't know. Not much more than squat, but he'd like everybody to think he's in on the secrets of the universe. He's a loon. Eighty percent of what he says is complete 'I-want-you-to-think-I'm-special' hooey."

"Does he know where to find those stray elves he picked up?"

"My guess is, he can get in touch somehow if it's critical. But we don't know where he is."

"Yes. That's right, isn't it? That other bunch snatched the boy up. So you say." He gave me a look filled with suspicion. He was succumbing to Relway's Disease. Trusting no civilian.

Sometimes I think Deal Relway divides the population into three categories. The smaller two consist of known criminals and of policemen, with a very fuzzy boundary in between. The other, largest category includes all the rest of us. And we're all just crooks who haven't been found out yet. And we should be treated accordingly.

Block eyed the Dead Man. "Is he asleep again?" Old Chuckles had shown no sign of sentience since the colonel's arrival.

"An excellent question. Lately I'm getting random moments of nonsense but nothing consistent. I'm worried. He may be on that last level ground before he hits the slippery slope down."

Block scowled, still suspicious. He had heard this one before.

I said, "Indulge my curiosity. How come you're out prowling the streets yourself? I thought you guys had a division of labor where the colonel stays back at the Al-Khar snoozing and harassing prisoners while the rest of the guys do all the real work."

Block didn't respond right away. He glanced at the Dead Man again, definitely wondering if he could get away with telling me less than the whole truth. "When your name came up I knew it was bound to get exciting. It made sense to get close to the center of the action right at the beginning."

I didn't need the Dead Man to tell me that Block was dealing me a steaming hot load. The Hill might not be behind the flying lights and pots but somebody up there wanted to be involved. And when the Hill wants something even its biggest detractors put on a show of flashing heels and flying elbows. Not many people relish the notion of spending the rest of their lives dead and being tortured.

Which is no contradiction where the top-ranked sorcerers are involved.

You might, by a stretch, be able to say that Colonel Block and I are friends. Not thick and thin, hell and high water, blood brother friends but guys who like and respect one another, who are willing to lend a helping hand to one another, where it's possible to do so.

It was conceivable that Block was doing so at the moment, so that I wouldn't walk into something entirely blind. And so that, in return, he could tap me for a little information that would keep him in good odor with the people prodding him from behind.

I can do that for him. It's worked out for us in the past. The tricky part is keeping outsiders from forming the idea that we can get along.

Block observed, "You really are a big old barrel of nothing, aren't you . . . ? What the hell is that?"

The pixies out front had declared war. Possibly on themselves, they were so raucous.

They'd been silent since my return. So much so that I'd begun to suspect an evil influence at work.

"Pixies," I told Block. "I seem to have adopted a mob.

Against my will. I'd better see what's got them excited."
Inasmuch as the Dead Man didn't seem inclined to inform me.

I heaved out of my chair and headed up front. In the small front room the Goddamn Parrot was asleep already, muttering in his diabolical dreams. No doubt he had protested his recent utilization by making a mess Dean would nag me about for weeks.

Block followed me. Through the peephole I watched one of his escorts fling something upward. I said, "Your boys are tormenting my pixies."

"I'd better get them out of here before it gets out of hand, then. Don't hesitate to let me know if you learn anything useful."

"You wouldn't accidentally let slip which sorcerer types are interested in my problem, would you?"

"Not hardly. Not even if I knew. But I think you can safely assume that just about anybody up there would be interested in gaining the secrets of flight." He opened the door, went out growling. "What the devil do you men think you're doing?"

"They started it. They were throwing . . ."

Chunk! The door cut it off.

19

I returned to the Dead Man's room. "So how come we needed to chase Block and his pals away? And how the hell did the Goddamn Parrot get back in the house?"

Mr. Bic Gonlit is out there awaiting an opportunity to reclaim his magical boots. Colonel Block was unable to add anything more to our meager knowledge.

Miss Pular opened the door for Mister Big while you were napping.

"*Did* Block add anything to our meager knowledge?" I didn't like that business about Singe opening the door with nobody to back her up. Old Bones isn't always attentive to detail.

Only internal confirmation of most of what he told you. The people on the Hill have become exceptionally interested in unusual celestial events of late. In Block's mind they're convinced the flying objects represent a threat from foreign sorcerers. Although a minority believe that a rogue cabal of Karentine wizards are behind what has been happening, hoping to elbow the rest out of the inner circles of power. Whatever the truth, the root concern is those people's fear for their positions.

"Oh, they wouldn't like to lose their power, would they? Do I need to go out and catch Bic Gonlit?" Because I was bone-tired. I was ready to hit the sack, skipping the evening's last five or six mugs of beer.

Judging by your stunning success in that direction before, perhaps your ideal course would be to wait for him to come

*to you. He does seem to be extremely superstitious about his
boots. They are a controlling factor in his life.*

Singe came in from the kitchen carrying a tray. She'd
hidden out there while Block was in the house. And she
hadn't wasted her time. She'd made more sandwiches. And
had drawn me a mug off the keg in the cold well.

I gave her a look at my raised eyebrow trick as I went
to work on a sandwich. Her whiskers twitched and pulled
back in the ratkind equivalent of turning pink.

"It's all right, Singe. You're welcome. Old Bones. I'm
not going to be able to keep my eyes open much longer.
If I get him in here can you handle the interview?"

His exasperation with mortal weakness became palpable.
*Get him in here. That is the key first step. Then you two
can run off to bed whilst I labor. . . .*

Singe squeaked. Her whiskers went back so far it looked
like they were about to pop out.

"He doesn't mean *that*, Singe. He just means sleep. You
take the guest room on the third floor." She was familiar
with it. She'd used it before. "I'll see if Block's gone."

*He is. Though an observer remained behind and is seated
on Mrs. Cardonlos' stoop, pretending to be drunk. He is
about to fall asleep at his post.*

I went to the front door certain that any sleepiness being
experienced by Colonel Block's man had an artificial origin.
Unlike my own.

Singe followed me. She carried a lamp. Its light silhouetted me when I opened the door.

Bic Gonlit arrived five minutes later. He was about as
hangdog as it's possible for a man to look.

"Bic, old buddy," I said, "why'd you want to go and
bring a bunch of ratpeople around to my place?"

"You still got my boots?"

"They're in a place of honor. But I'm going to burn them
and scatter their ashes on the river if I don't hear some
explanations."

"You don't have a reputation for being that hard,
Garrett."

"You've got a rep as a bring them in alive kind of bounty

hunter, Bic. So besides the answer to my ratpeople question—which I want to hear real soon now—I'd sure like to
know why you're hanging around me. But where are my
manners? Come on in. We don't want to do business out
here. The Guard keeps a watch on me."

Gonlit jumped. He looked back nervously. He sure was
a worried little man. And barefoot, too.

He slipped past me, taking one final troubled look back
as he did so.

"Tell me about the rats, Bic."

He stared at Pular Singe. "Because there's a huge reward
out for her. Reliance wants her bad. I thought I'd get my
boots back during the confusion when Reliance's gang were
grabbing her."

"Plus you'd've made a few marks," I said. "I appreciate
your honesty. So I'm not going to hold a very big grudge.
All you need to do is explain why you were hanging around
in the alley out back and just had to slug me. We're going
in here." I held the door to the Dead Man's room. Bic's
boots were in there, sitting on the table next to Singe's
sandwiches. But I had a feeling it would be a while before
they enjoyed a loving reunion with Bic's feet. "Take a
seat, brother."

"I just want my boots, Garrett."

"We all have dreams, Bic. Sometimes we have to give a
little something to attain them. What about the alley?"

"What alley?"

"Now we're going to play tough?" Exasperated, I
snapped, "The goddamn alley behind my house. Where you
bushwhacked me and pounded me over the head with a
sap."

Gonlit looked at me like I'd just sprouted antlers.

Garrett.

I jumped. So did Bic and Singe.

"Yeah?"

*Bizarre as it may seem, the man really does have no idea
what you are talking about. I now find myself examining the
hypothesis that the Bic Gonlit you encountered in the alley
was not the man who is here with us now. Either this man*

*has a twin or what you ran into was the creature I sensed
and set you to collect, somehow projecting an illusion based
upon the expectations of Cypres Prose.*

*I now agree that it is time you went to bed. Have the man
sit down.* Bic hadn't yet accepted my invitation. *Then go. I
will see that he dozes off, too.*

Pular Singe made an offer that was difficult to refuse
because she was so fragile emotionally. "Not tonight, Singe.
I'm so tired I'd fall asleep in the middle of things. And
you'd get your feelings hurt. While you kept telling me that
it was all your fault." She was getting used to hearing me
yell at her about embracing blame for what other people
did.

That wasn't as honest as I should've been. But it did buy
me time to think about an answer that would leave Singe
with her tender dignity intact, feeling good about herself.

The more I considered it the more I suspected that I'd
need the Dead Man's help to work this one out. Singe was
at an age and stage where she wasn't going to hear much
from me that she didn't want to hear.

Though I must say my "not tonight, another time" response certainly seemed to ease her anxieties for the
moment.

Maybe she wouldn't find the nerve to bring it up again.

20

Those damned pixies woke me up twice during the night. And both times I got a touch from the Dead Man indicating that we had a prowler outside. He didn't trouble himself enough to report what kind of prowler. And I was too groggy to care.

The pixies made good watchdogs. Yet if that was what I wanted I'd just as soon get something big but quiet that would eat the prowlers without waking me up or disturbing my neighbors.

It was near the crack of noon when I stumbled downstairs and found a sullen Dean sharing his kitchen with Pular Singe. Singe was at the table eating. She had dragged her custom chair in from the Dead Man's room.

Dean was doing dishes and wrestling with his prejudices. Not many folks have much use for ratpeople. I've always belonged to the majority myself. But I do try my best to contain my dislike. That's been a lot easier since Singe came along.

I mumbled, "You're going to get fatter than the Dead Man, Singe." I flopped into my own chair. "My head still hurts." Though a lot less than it had.

Dean said, "I've warned you and warned you to ease up on the beer, Garrett."

"It wasn't beer this time."

Dean rattled some dishes and snorted, not believing me.

"It's not. Singe can tell you. I got knocked out by some kind of wizardry a few times yesterday. And every time I woke up I had a worse headache than before."

"Then explain why I had to send out for a new keg this morning. It hasn't been ten days since you finished the last one."

"New keg? But the old one shouldn't be . . ."

Singe had developed a fierce interest in a fly doing acrobatics from the ceiling.

"And you don't have a bit of a hangover from all that, either. Do you, girl?"

She shook her head, tried one of her want-to-be human smiles.

"Gah! This's the cruelest of all cruel worlds." I would've teased her about selling her back to Reliance or something but she'd probably have taken me seriously.

Dean took his hands out of the water long enough to pour a mug of tea and set a breakfast platter in front of me. That was mostly seasonal fruit, accompanied by small chunks of cold ham.

A typical meal, really. Which left me wondering how Dean managed to produce so many dirty dishes, pots, and pans.

I downed a long slug of tea. There was something in that cup besides plain tea. It left a bitter taste underneath the honey. So Dean had counted on me showing up with a headache. Since he doesn't coddle my hangovers he must've been forewarned. So his fuss was all for form.

So the Dead Man was good for something after all.

Though he wouldn't have coddled a hangover, either.

Singe tried to fuss over me. Dean looked disgusted. I showed him my evil eye. Of all the females to pass through my kitchen the one he'd pick to dislike actively would be the only one who was willing to treat me special.

He was plenty willing to climb all over me when it came to me not treating every girl as if she was uniquely special.

I tossed back some more tea while thinking my house was turning into a nest of cranky old bachelors.

The pixies started acting up out front. Dean ignored them. He had his cutting board out and was getting ready to mutilate vegetables.

"You going to check that out?" I asked.

"No. Happens every fifteen minutes. If it means anything the thing in the other room will let us know."

If he wasn't asleep. The Dead Man has a habit of falling asleep, sometimes for months, usually at the most inconvenient times, businesswise.

I finished feeding. The medication in the tea had begun its work. The world seemed a less dark and cruel place already. "Singe, let's go see old Chuckles." Got to keep that premature optimism under control. And he was just the boy to rein it in.

"Hey, Old Bones. What's on the table today? Bic Gonlit. How you doing this morning, man? Dean get you something to eat?"

Whatever Dean put into the tea, maybe he used a little too much.

I got no response from the Dead Man. Gonlit did respond with a big scowl. "I want my boots, Garrett."

"I'm sure you do. They say you've got your whole personality tied up in those things. So why do you want to get them all filthy, romping around in the alley behind my house?"

Bic rolled his eyes. "Not again!"

I have exhausted that line of inquiry, Garrett. Mr. Gonlit sincerely believes that he has never been in that alley. There is no shaking his conviction on that count. Therefore, I am inclined to believe him. However, he cannot account for his whereabouts at the time of the alley event. He is more troubled about that than we are.

I wasn't troubled at all. "Maybe it was him being used by one of the silver guys the way you use the Goddamn Parrot."

That possibility occurred to me. There is no residue in Mr. Gonlit's mind of the sort I would expect to find if he had been manipulated. What is there consists of hints that he may have been asleep. Inasmuch as he does not recall sleeping, we might reasonably suspect that the sleep was induced. Perhaps by the same means as were used on you yesterday.

"All right. And?"

The boy, Cyprus Prose, brought Mr. Gonlit's name into play first.

I'd just been thinking that. Had Kip set us up somehow? Could the Dead Man have missed that while the kid was here?

No.

"Bic, did anybody hire you to hunt down a couple elves name of—"

"Lastyr and Noodiss. I'm tired of that one, too. Give me my damned boots."

He believes he never heard those names before he came in here last night.

I growled. The excitement and optimism were beginning to fade. "Then how come he was following me and you were following him with the Goddamn Parrot?"

Are you genuinely certain you want Mr. Gonlit to hear more about my abilities than you have given away already?

"All right. I wasn't thinking."

Not a first, I might note.

"You might. You might also answer me."

He was following Miss Pular, Garrett. Mr. Big was following you. Insofar as I have been able to determine, their appearance of being together was caused by the proximities of yourself and Miss Pular.

"There've been too damned many coincidences already, Old Bones. You know I believe in them but I don't like them. Next thing you're going to tell me is that good buddy Bic just happened to stumble over Singe as she and Saucerhead were coming to help me out. And being the ingenious fellow that he is, Bic just latched right on. Seizing the day, as it were."

That is quite close to the truth. As Mr. Gonlit knows it. Except for the fact that he was hunting Miss Pular long before we became involved in events. He had traced her to the area where we had her hidden. My call for assistance, unfortunately, brought her out just in time to be spotted.

I generated harrumphing old man noises. I didn't like the way things were going.

You never do. But you have a knack for blundering around, knocking things over, until everything works out.

I harrumphed some more. Practicing. I have plans for an extremely extended old age.

I was profoundly embarrassed by the fact that it took me so long to discover Mr. Gonlit's presence on your backtrail.

"Oh-oh." The Dead Man seldom admits lacks, flaws, or shortcomings. He is, after all, the most perfect of that perfect race, the Loghyr. Just ask him.

When he messes up it's always someone else's fault.

Behold! *Then I began to understand. The description I had was entirely inadequate.*

"So you didn't figure it was unusual for a guy to be turning up everywhere Singe and I did?" It really is pointless to indicate the holes in his excuse-making. At best he just ignores you.

I should like to engage in a much deeper look into your encounter with the false Bic Gonlit of the alleyway. It is entirely possible that you may have noticed something we passed over as trivial when we were confident that we knew who your conqueror was.

The real Bic Gonlit had grown very restless. "Let me give the man his soles back so he can go on his way." Charged up with uncertain ideas about his place in the grander scheme, his head a nest of confused, false memories.

Turn the bird loose once Mr. Gonlit is a block down the street.

"Of course. There's always hope he'll run into a parrot-eating eagle. Bic, here're your boots. Get going. Stay away from me and stay away from Pular Singe. I guarantee you, Reliance's reward isn't worth it. Belinda Contague used to be my girlfriend."

Bic went pale. He'd heard that rumor. I was still alive. So maybe I could conjure the helpmate of death.

Foolish, Garrett.

He was right. That was a stupid threat. If word got back to Belinda I could end up on crutches. If she happened to be in a generous mood.

I waved bye-bye from the stoop. Then I flung our lowlife, low-profile spy into the air. Then I rejoined Singe and the Dead Man.

21

Returning to life after having the Dead Man dig around in the muck in the cellars of my mind was less painful than getting whomped unconscious by a silver elf's spell but it did leave me feeling just as lousy emotionally. It left me wanting nothing more than to go back to bed, where I could curl up in a ball and suck my thumb.

That kind of invasion doesn't happen often. And never happens without my permission. But each time it does I swear I'll never let it happen again, no matter how desperate the crisis. But when the time comes I always go ahead, trusting him and knowing I'll get through it. And maybe it's even good for me in the long run. That dark, unhappy memories always seem to settle a little deeper and a little more comfortably, like a bucket full of gravel when you shake and beat it.

I took some cleansing breaths. Some of that martial arts stuff of Morley's really does work if you let yourself believe in it. I found a place removed from my center by just a few miles. "Did we learn anything that makes it worth all my misery?"

I believe we did. Though it is indeed a small thing at first glimpse.

He didn't go on. He wanted me to ask him to show off his brilliance. I wasn't feeling patient enough to get involved in the usual games. "And that was?"

The Bic Gonlit in our alleyway was not wearing the signature boots. You had mentioned missing seeing them earlier but at that time I overlooked the chance that you had not seen them because they were not there. At that time there was no reason to look beyond the obvious. Also, the Gonlit you met out back was several inches taller than this specimen, even without the leather lifts.

"So where does that leave us?"

Essentially still lost but now forearmed with the knowledge that the opposition might appear to us in the guise of someone we know. But not in the form of a perfect replica.

Grumble. "Don't tell me it's shapeshifters again."

I promise. There are no shapeshifters here. There does seem to be some remarkable illusory sorcery, however.

"You said there wasn't any sorcery in the alley."

I did. I do not believe there was. It is a conundrum, is it not?

"Great. So good old Bic is innocent of everything more sinister than trying to score the bounty on Singe. Stipulating that, I want to know how come Kip knew the name and thought Gonlit was after his strange friends. And I'd like to know how that elf got to know Bic well enough to masquerade as him without Bic knowing there was anything going on."

All excellent questions, Garrett. You are learning to think. Unfortunately, Mr. Gonlit does not have any of the answers. We will have to flush those out somewhere else. Inasmuch as we have no hope of uncovering a direct trail to the boy I suspect a visit to the mother has some chance of being productive.

"You think she might know . . . ? I see. Anything she can give us could be a thread to pull or a pointer to a path that might lead to somebody who does have an idea where to look for the boy."

Indeed. Which is why I suggest the mother. She may even have an idea where to find the mysterious Noodiss and his associate.

A possibility that, no doubt, must've occurred to the people already in that hunt.

"I get the feeling these others are real amateurs." How much less gentle would have been the hunt had the Outfit been seeking the missing elves?

True. Miss Pular should remain here. It is a certainty that Reliance has people watching the house.

"Relway, too, probably."

Just so.

"Then maybe I shouldn't go out there, either." A career in the home-based beer-tasting industry sounded good at the moment.

You are too concerned about your reputation. I will ensure that any spies remain ignorant of your departure.

Once again, a hint that he had greater abilities than those to which he admitted. Though this was a trick he had used before, several times. I've never been sure how it works. It might blind everyone in the neighborhood to my movements.

Which would be handy if I had to raise some cash real fast.

I had been considering a career change. Why not become an invisible pickpocket?

The air seemed to crackle. Like the sharp whispering of river ice just starting to break up. My partner didn't approve of my thoughts. Not even with those being entirely in jest.

When this day was done I was going to get away from all these people. Maybe I'd get me off to one of the taverns where old Marines gather to slough off the dust of lesser mortals. Or possibly somewhere where I might glimpse a shapely ankle.

Garrett, there will be no diversions, neither of the heart nor of the mind nor of the flesh, if you do not get out and try to find some threads that I can unravel while you are reviving your reputation as a rogue, a rake, and a wastrel.

He did have a point.

22

I went to Playmate's stable first. He'd have to show me where to find Kip's family.

"I don't know if that'll do any good," Playmate said when I explained what I wanted. "I guarantee you his mother doesn't know anything useful. If she did she'd already have been out there wherever yanking those elves' ears till they talked."

"Thought they didn't have ears."

"Maybe they ran into Kayne Prose already."

"Hardcase, eh?"

"A very determined mom. You don't mess with her kids. Otherwise, she's just a hardworking widow looking for enough work to get by."

There're a lot of those in TunFaire, though in the final few, most desperate years of the war the Crown tried taking younger conscripts so there wouldn't be as many widows created.

"Uh . . ." I said. "I must be confused. You didn't say anything about her being a widow yesterday."

Playmate looked at me like he wondered if I was really that dumb. Widow is a euphemism as old as mothers without husbands. "She wouldn't brag about having three out-of-wedlock children by three different fathers, one of them maybe off the Hill. Though two of the fathers really are dead. And the maybe wizard probably is. He hasn't been seen since the supply boat he was aboard left the TunFaire waterfront. When Kip was still a bun in the oven. The *Leitmark* never made it to Full Harbor."

"Pirates?"

Playmate shrugged. "At this date it doesn't matter. Kayne has bad luck with men. They die on her. Or they go away. But she's an unswerving optimist. She keeps on trying. After Kip came along I finally managed to convince her she should invest in avoiding any more pregnancies. She owed that to the kids she already had."

"You sound like you might have a little emotion invested in the Prose family yourself."

"I like the kids. They turned out pretty good, considering. And Kayne is a good woman who doesn't really deserve everything she's suffered. But she does bring it on herself."

"Self-destructive, eh?" I might know a little about that myself.

"Definitely. But mainly in the area of men. She keeps rejecting everybody who might be good for her and welcoming the villains who're sure to treat her badly."

There might've been a slight hint of disappointment there. If so, it was so faint that I didn't think it was worth pursuing.

Time would tell me about Playmate and Kayne Prose. I was about to see how they acted around each other.

23

Leaving Playmate's stable, we walked about a mile toward the river, skirting Prune Tastity, to reach the southwestern-most fringe of the garment district. Which actually takes up less land area than Prune Tastity. It was on the fringe that we found Kip's mom.

Kayne Prose was doing seamstress work in a small co-op operated round the clock by teams of women whose situations were all much the same. They were all dirt-poor, with children, without husbands, without other salable skills, and most with too many miles on them to compete as prostitutes or taxi dancers. I found the atmosphere inside that place oppressive. The walls had become impregnated with despair.

But every woman there had an air of grim determination. They were survivors, those women, doing what they had to do. Same as me, back when it was crocodiles on the one hand, Venageti rangers on the other, and poisonous bugs, snakes, spiders, and bats everywhere else. Neither we, then, nor these women, now, would let the despair work its seduction. These ladies would battle on until doom sounded its final bell.

Give them the supreme compliment. They would've made good Marines.

There were eight women sewing when we arrived. I picked Kayne Prose out immediately. There was a lot of her in Kip. Only . . .

"Damn, Play. She's a looker. You sure . . . ? That woman's got three kids, one of them nineteen years old?" No doubt the weak light did her a favor but she didn't look much older than me. If that old. She *could* have competed in the flesh markets. And would've done pretty well, I'd guess.

Maybe it was the long blond hair that shone like that of a girl half her age. Maybe it was her skin, which seemed far too smooth for a woman of mature years. Maybe it was her face, which the hardships of poverty hadn't etched nearly as deeply as I would've expected. Maybe it was some sort of inner fire. There are those one-in-a-thousand people who just never seem to get old.

I guess I stood there stunned, maybe dribbling from the corner of my mouth, for a while, because I heard this whisper: "That's exactly how everyone reacts when they meet her for the first time."

Everyone male, I figured.

Kayne Prose's sparkling baby blues met mine. The twinkle there told me she could read my mind as surely as the Dead Man could. A tiny smile told me she didn't mind my sort of thinking, either.

Oh, the gods had been generous when they'd shaped Kayne Prose. And some real artists had gone in on the architecture. Nor had childbearing been unkind. There would be plenty of women ten, even fifteen years younger who'd just plain hate Kayne Prose for existing.

Seven of that sort were planted right there in that room.

"Hello, Play," she said. And, oh my, her voice was as deep and husky and sensual as Katie's. It turned my spine to water. And I was there on business. Feeling guilty because I'd let her son get spirited away. And she was fully aware of the effect she was having. It was an effect she'd been having on men for twenty-five years, probably.

I was willing to bet there was elven blood in her, no further than a grandparent away

She said, "I can't get up. I fell behind yesterday. Who's your friend?" She looked me over like she was checking out vegetables at the market, yet from her it was flattering rather than offensive.

And the same from me right back.

She definitely liked being looked at. Which was probably a symptom of her problem.

Playmate's expression soured. Proof that there was substance to my earlier suspicion. I tried to rein in my boyish charm.

Playmate said, "Kayne, this's Garrett. The man who was going to help Kip. Now he's going to help us find Kip."

For a moment Kayne Prose turned entirely into a worried mother. She turned up a look I remembered from childhood. Which left me nose to nose with the scary speculation that my mother might have been capable of that other, nonmotherly behavior, too.

No. Never. She was Mom.

"Whatever I can do to contribute, I will, Mr. Garrett," she said. All business now, I'm afraid. Well, almost all business. Kayne Prose was incapable of stifling her sensual side.

Man.

I said, "I'm here because I don't know where else to start. Can you talk while you work?" The place wasn't a sweatshop, it was a co-op, but none of the women were pleased to have Playmate and me upsetting their routine. Though a couple of them eyed Playmate like they were measuring him for a wedding suit.

It being a co-op there wouldn't be killer piecework quotas but, still, for the women to make much income they'd have to put in fourteen-hour days. They'd have some formula for a fair division of the co-op's income.

"Talk away. But there ain't much I can tell you. If I knew anything I probably wouldn't've lost my kid. Those two goofballs don't mean anything to me."

"Noodiss and Lastyr?"

"We know any other goofballs in this mess?"

"The four who weren't those two, that took your son. And the three who tried and failed earlier." I didn't think the two crews were the same. But I hadn't seen Playmate's female elves. Then, inspired, I said, "Tell me about Bic Gonlit." If Kip knew the guy, then so might she.

Pay dirt.

Her needle slowed for a moment, possibly snagging

somehow. She studied her last stitch for half a second. Then she glanced up at Playmate. Her stitching fell back into rhythm. "What do you want to know?"

"Everything." There was something here. Maybe nothing I'd find useful but definitely a connection.

Again she glanced at Playmate. So I did the same, only to have him shrug in response, then ask, "Will you be more comfortable if I go outside, Kayne?"

Kayne Prose winced.

I doubted that the woman was long on sensitivity. Life wouldn't have afforded her the luxury. But she had something on her mind. She thought Playmate would be disappointed or hurt. She cherished his good opinion. Or maybe needed it as an emotional foundation stone. Whatever, she could see some value in a man who was too good to become an active accomplice in her game of self-destruction.

Playmate is one of those guys who is just too damned nice for his own good. And everyone in the place recognized that Playmate felt that his good could be the woman who looked like she had made a pact with the agents of darkness. Except for Kayne Prose herself, of course.

Kayne Prose told Playmate, "You don't need to go, Play. If I'm embarrassed by something I tell Mr. Garrett, then I deserve the full impact. Mr. Garrett, I enjoyed—for want of a more appropriate description—a brief relationship with Bic Gonlit not long ago." Her fingers flew, sewing a sleeve onto something for a child maybe six years old. Something for a little girl who would never suffer the miseries and indignities so intimately known to the woman who had assembled her dress. "I don't believe he saw it in the same light as I did, though." With an intonation implying that they never do.

"Interesting." The Dead Man hadn't mentioned this tantalizing tidbit. Did he want me to find out for myself? Or wasn't there anything interesting there? Or maybe Bic hadn't remembered because it wasn't important to him. "Was this anytime recently?"

Kayne nodded. "I ended it three days ago. When I realized he was using me." Damn! The woman made the act of breathing a sensual promise. No wonder old Bic took her wrong.

The rest of the women adjusted their positions as Kayne finished, each commenting without saying a word. Possibly unfairly. I didn't get the feeling that Kayne Prose made herself a public utility, only that she really enjoyed men but always conspired with her own inner devils to make sure she picked the ones who would be bad for her.

"I see. This was a good idea, Play. I've learned more in the last three minutes than I did up till then. Kayne, did it get physical? Did he ever take his boots off?" Rumor suggested that Bic might not.

Kayne Prose turned bright red, something her co-op pals probably found amazing. I wondered if that would have happened had Playmate not been with me.

"He . . . He had a problem. He said . . . What do you mean about boots?"

"Bic Gonlit's big legend revolves around his custom-made, hugely ugly, possibly magical boots. They're boots a ratman wouldn't steal. They're white with fake gems all over them. They have thick elevator soles. You're probably a good four inches taller than Bic in his bare feet."

"He's as tall as me. And I never noticed any special boots. Or shoes. Or anything else."

I exchanged glances with Playmate.

"What?" Kayne demanded.

I told her, "That wasn't the real Bic Gonlit, then. That was one of the elves who're looking for Kip's friends. He uses some kind of sorcery to make people think they're seeing Bic Gonlit. But the illusion doesn't include the boots. Or enough of the short."

"You know, you're right. I never thought about it before. When we were kids Bic always had a thing about his shoes."

"You've known him a long time?"

"Not well. But since I was Kip's age. We grew up on the same street. I saw him around sometimes. We said 'Hi.' I never paid him much attention. And he never paid me any. I thought that was because he might be a little . . . fey. Like maybe he didn't know what he wanted to be. And he

was always kind of a jerk. But a month ago he started
coming around and acting like he was really interested.
He'd gotten a case of the manners and he could talk a
pretty good game. But he never did nothing else. Sooner
or later, and mostly sooner, the conversation got around to
Kip and his friends. He was always asking questions. A
man who never does nothing but talk about your kids don't
stay real interesting and ain't much fun."

You hear that, Play? I thought. This one has a "me"
streak. And it's what keeps causing her problems. Clever
men would play to it. And would think less of her because
they were able to.

"I stand cautioned. But I do have to bring the brats up
some in order to get my job done."

One of the women groaned dramatically.

Playmate blessed the lot with a righteous glower. He
drew himself up stiffly erect, like he was about to go on a
rant about hellfire and sin and chucking first rocks.

I asked, "Kip did know this Bic, too?"

"Better than I did. He figured out right away that Bic
just wanted to get next to the two spooky critters."

"Lastyr and Noodiss."

"Still the ones, buddy." The furnace wasn't burning
nearly as hot as it had.

I'd managed to work myself down off the A list.

"You have any idea how I could find this Bic Gonlit?
Could you get ahold of him somehow if you wanted?"

She thought about her answer for a while. I'd begun to
suspect that her lights didn't burn too bright and that the
woman was something of a flake besides. More factors con-
tributing to her string of failed relationships.

The substance behind the beauty and the intense sensuality
was thin. Which I wouldn't find all that big a handicap most
of the time. But, businesswise, it makes for endless problems.

From the corners of my eyes I noted the other women
watching to see how long it would take me to catch on—
and if it would matter. Maybe with a touch more malice
toward me than toward Kayne Prose. In some ways they
might live vicariously through Kayne. Kayne wasn't afraid
to indulge herself.

She let me look and think for a while, probably so I could reflect on what I was talking myself out of, before she said, "Yeah. Play, take Mr. Garrett over to my place. Rhafi can show you guys where Bic used to hole up. And if the creep is still there, break a couple limbs for me. All of them if he don't give Kip back."

I was about to explain that it wasn't likely the false Bic Gonlit had the boy. Playmate nudged me. That was irrelevant. It was time to go.

Good idea, too. Because, atop everything else, Kayne Prose had a kind of narcotic quality to her. I could see myself sliding into addiction. Just like my dusky pal.

I kept thinking that, if she hadn't had so many incompatible personality quirks, she could've set herself up for life by getting into the mistress racket. In a prime position.

That she was where she was, looking as good as she did, never having done better, was one more warning flag about the woman inside that marvellously attractive shell.

A long time ago, almost a whole day now, Playmate had told me that Cypres Prose's mom was different and had pointed to his temple. Based on information gleaned, I'd say the man was right. But that didn't stop me from wanting to turn right around and go back and try to score some points for the future.

24

Playmate asked, "What did you think of Kayne?"

"Honest answer, Play? I never saw her before in my life. But I wanted to trip her and beat her to the floor. And ten seconds after that I just wanted to beat her. And ten seconds after that I was completely confused about what I wanted. And right now the animal side of my soul is screaming at me not to walk away from this wonderful chance. There's a perverse, self-destructive urge in there somewhere that she just shrieks out to."

He wasn't offended. "That's how a lot of men react. You a little faster than most, but that's just you being you. And after years of studying Kayne Prose I think it's all because of what's going on inside her. She doesn't just hurt herself in these doomed relationships. And the harder it is on the guys, the harder they try to make it work."

We were strolling. Playmate needed to air out some thoughts. It was clear that he was a Kayne Prose addict and willing to risk destruction. And maybe Kayne Prose thought too much of Playmate to give him a hit of poison.

People are the strangest creatures.

"What's it all mean?" I asked, just to keep open the windows of his mental house.

"I think it means that Kayne has a low-grade form of what the Dead Man has. The mind thing." Which could mean *another* wizard in the woodpile, a generation further back. "Just enough to read you faintly and to touch you just as weakly. Without knowing it on a conscious level. But using it all the time when men are around. In such a way that whatever is going on inside her will be reflected right back at her from outside. And maybe it'll feed on itself if it starts running into something dark."

I considered. "You could be right." I started trying to compare, in my head, Kayne Prose's impact with the jolt my friend Katie could deliver. Katie can reduce this man to jelly with just a look. When Katie gets interested there are no distractions. Katie is the closest I've ever come to having had a religious epiphany.

I'd just considered that to be a matter of focus. But maybe it was something more. Maybe there was a weak, crude mental connection involved.

Playmate said, "It's just a hypothesis." With a tone so defensive that an apology was implied.

"A damned good hypothesis, I'd say. You ought to get completely alone with her sometime, no distractions whatsoever, and test it out."

He sputtered.

"Play? You're embarrassed?"

"I'm not that kind of guy, Garrett."

"Maybe you ought to be. Tell me about Kayne's other kids. Are they problem folks like their mother and brother?"

"Not like their mother and brother. But problems enough. You'll like Cassie."

He didn't tell me much more. But he was right about Cassie. Cassie was a very likeable child indeed.

25

Cassie Doap was nineteen. Physically, Cassie was her mother a decade and a half younger, with the overpowering sensuality less controlled. Cassie Doap would break hearts just by going out where men could see her and understand that they would live out their years never having gotten any closer than they were at the moment when first they spotted her. Cassie Doap filled up a room with her presence but didn't spark the confusion that came with being around her mother.

Cassie Doap was smarter than Kayne, too. She understood the impact she had on men but had no intention of letting that define who and what she was. If Kayne Prose had done one useful thing for her daughter it was to set an example of how not to live her life.

All that I understood before Cassie Doap and I exchanged a word. Because Cassie Doap was an easy read. She wanted it that way.

I wondered what hidden, horrible flaw had a poor woman as gorgeous as this still living with her mother at her age. A hyperactive sense of self-worth?

Playmate performed the introductions. I managed to shake hands while avoiding stepping on my tongue, distracting myself by concentrating on business. I'm able to do that occasionally, though there're some who would have the world believe otherwise. It's just that the Kaynes and Cassies of the world make it so hard.

With Cassie there I almost overlooked her brother Rhafi. He wasn't the sort to attract much attention.

I told Cassie, "We're trying to find Kip. We think . . ."

"If Play hadn't guaranteed it was the real thing I would've bet the little twerp staged the whole damned thing."

"Why would you think that?" I noted that, unlike her mother, Cassie did nothing to make sure I understood just how much woman she was.

"Because that's the way his evil little pea brain works." Brother Rhafi nodded his head vigorously. "He lives inside his own imagination. Everything in there is high drama. Perilous chases, deadly duels, narrow escapes, beautiful princesses, and monstrous villains."

Playmate chuckled. "Sounds like your life, Garrett," he quipped.

"Except for a severe shortage of princesses, beautiful or otherwise. You wouldn't be a long-lost princess, left in a basket on your mother's doorstep, would you, Cassie?"

"Long-lost, anyway. If that was intended to be a compliment you get points for being a little more subtle than the usual, 'Gods, you're beautiful. Lie down because I think I love you.' "

"Must've been army type guys. Marines are all smooth and crafty." Had we just gotten a hint of why Cassie Doap hadn't wriggled her way into the sweet life? Everybody knows that's a girl's easiest way out of the poor side of town. Or was she in a constant rage because Fate had decreed she should be so beautiful that everybody wanted her? I don't recall ever having run into a woman who resented her own appeal, only women who hated their sisters for having more of it than they did. But I could understand the notion, in principle. In someone who could, genuinely, separate self from body.

Possibly Kayne's past behavior had loaded Cassie up with outside expectations as well. Perhaps the whole neighborhood figured like mother, like daughter. That's the sort of ignorant thinking you can expect from human type beings. And the sort that would park a big old chip on somebody's shoulder.

Playmate said, "Kayne told us you could show us where Bic Gonlit stayed when he was coming around here." His tone was strained, neutral. And Cassie heard that. And she understood.

"I can't. I stayed away from that creep. He was always trying to get me to go somewhere with him when Kayne wasn't around."

But Kayne had told us that Bic hadn't shown any physical interest in her. If he hadn't gone for the mom why would he take a run at the daughter?

Make the assumption he wasn't a good, red-blooded Karentine boy and you might think he could want something else. Maybe he'd had a notion that snatching Cassie would give him a lever he could use to get Kip to tell him what he wanted to know.

Hard to imagine just wanting Cassie as a hostage. She was the kind of girl you have to keep away from the old men. Or you'll have them dropping like flies from strokes and heart attacks. Hell, I was having palpitations myself and I was just there looking for her nimrod brother.

I had trouble seeing anything else. Especially not brother Rhafi, who vanished in Cassie's glare. That poor kid didn't even have Kip's unpleasant character traits. He was just there, a gangly six-footer with unkempt dark hair, brown eyes, a ghost of a mustache, the beginnings of a set of bad teeth, and no meat on his bones. I got the impression that he'd rather be somewhere else. That, like his brother, he had a preference for the habitués of worlds of his own devising.

Physically, it was obvious that Rhafi did not share a father with Kip. Cassie . . . She might pass as Kip's full sister if anybody wanted to pretend. But she did have that different last name.

No matter. As pleasant a task as it was staring at Cassie and drooling, I was in the business of rescuing obnoxious teenagers. "Rhafi, I'm Garrett." Like maybe he'd forgotten. But I'd decided to deal with him the way I dealt with Singe. Carefully. He seemed of an age to be volatile. "I specialize in finding things that get lost." Or about anything else that needs doing, that clients don't want to do for themselves, and that I don't think is wrong.

"Like Bic Gonlit."

"Well, sure. Though the reason I want to find him is because he may know where to find your brother."

Petulantly, "I mean, Bic Gonlit finds things that're missing. He said so."

"The real Bic Gonlit specializes in finding people for
other people. People who're willing to pay well to have
them found."

Playmate told me, "Let's don't complicate things, Garrett. Rhafi, please show us where Bic Gonlit stayed."

"He tried to get me up there, too, you know. Like he
did Cassie."

"And you found out where he stayed. Good job." Playmate's approach was the same as mine but the boy responded better. Probably because he knew and trusted
Playmate.

Playmate does exude trustworthiness. I've seen total
strangers entrust him with everything but their souls.

Playmate kept talking. And Rhafi responded.

The boy did not enjoy Kip's one redeeming quality. He
wasn't bright. And he was spoiled. As much as a near-
destitute child can be spoiled.

I stepped back and let the master work.

"Shall we?" I asked Cassie, offering her my arm and a
glimpse of my raised eyebrow. The trick that kills them
dead.

"I think I'll just stay here."

Whimpering, every bone crushed, I dragged my battered
carcass out of the Prose flat, following Playmate and Rhafi.

26

Playmate said, "I told you you'd like Cassie."

"Hell, I love her. But I'm not so hot for the thing that's inside of her, wearing her like a suit."

Rhafi started laughing. I mean, he got one of those cases of the giggles where you just can't shut it off, no matter how hard you try.

"I didn't think it was that funny," I said.

Playmate agreed. "It wasn't funny at all."

Rhafi gasped, "But you don't know Cassie. You don't have to live with her. You don't have to suffer through it when she tries on different personalities like some rich bitch trying on different clothes." He hacked and gasped all the way through that. "I know it isn't that funny. But it was just so perfect for the bitch that she's trying to be this week."

"She's always been an actress," Playmate said, demonstratively not using the word in its pejorative form, which means whore. "That's her way of coping."

"Ever get the idea that the dysfunctional folks outnumber those who aren't? Every damned day I'm more of the opinion that everybody's knot is tied too loose or too tight. And some just cover it up better than others. It's only a matter of time. Except for me and thee, of course."

"And sometimes we wonder about thee, Garrett. I'm sorry you feel that way. You might consider surrounding yourself with different people. Excluding myself, naturally. Or you might find a different line of work. One less likely to turn you cynical."

"Me? Cynical? That's impossible. I am one with the universe. I have the perfect life. Except for the fact that I do have to work once in a while."

"You should've picked a mother who lived on the Hill."

"That was a little shortsighted of me, wasn't it?"

Rhafi, in a moment when the giggles were under control, observed, "You guys must be getting older than you look." Outside of the Prose flat, out of the shadow of his intimidating sister, he developed some substance.

"Yeah? How come do you say that?" That was a bitter draught, even from a kid as strange as he.

"You both think too much."

The little philosopher. "Damn!" I said. "There's an accusation that hasn't been flung in my face for a long time."

"Possibly never," Playmate opined. "I recall the opposite fault getting mentioned with some frequency, however . . . Hello. What do we have here?"

Clumps of people occupied the street ahead, staring down a cross lane and pointing at the sky.

"I have an uncomfortable feeling. Rhafi, how far to Bic Gonlit's place?"

"Next block. I bet they're looking at one of those . . . Oh, yeah!"

The crowd all made awed noises. Everyone pointed, reminding me of crowd scenes in paintings of the imperial circus, the people saluting as the emperor arrived.

A silvery discus, that I guessed to be pretty high up in the air, had appeared from behind a tile rooftop. It drifted our way for a few seconds, then moved back out of sight again. Some of the watchers complained bitterly because it hadn't come closer. I supposed similar groups of gawkers could be found all over town.

I overheard several people claiming to have had contact with creatures who lived inside the silver disk. One insisted that he had been a captive of creatures who lived inside the balls of light I had seen last night. That turned into a contest: who could concoct the tallest tale about the outrages done them by the silver elves.

The human imagination is very fertile. And exceedingly grotesque.

"Did I say something about them outnumbering us?" asked. "Play, you heard of those silver things coming out in the daytime before?" Sightings had been going on for a least a month but I hadn't paid much attention. There's always something weird going on in TunFaire. Like most of His Majesty's subjects, if the something weird ain't happening to me I don't worry about it.

"Oh, sure. Just as often as at night. As I recollect, all of the earliest sightings, over a year ago now, came during the daytime."

"I do remember. It was one of those one-day wonders. Nothing happened so I forgot about it. These people are getting a little thick here," I grumbled. I eased into Playmate's wake. He had little trouble pushing through the crowd. Many of them probably recognized him. He was always out here doing the charitable side of the ministry thing.

Always something weird happening. These flying things. The silver elves. People catching on fire and burning up, up on the north side. The other day news that another juvenile male mammoth had wandered in through an unwatched gate and was creating havoc, also on the north side. If one of Block's people was supposed to have been on duty there he'd better be prepared to eat the mammoth. Dereliction of duty was close to a capital crime in the eyes of Colonel Westman Block and Deal Relway.

It might behoove me to keep better track since so much of the weird stuff pulls me in eventually.

"Is something the matter, Mr. Garrett?" Rhafi asked from behind me. "You jumped."

I'd thought about voluntarily creating work for myself, that was what was the matter. No need to share that with the kid, though. "Aren't we there yet?"

"The yellow brick dump."

And dump it was. The tenement in question, easily more than a hundred years old, was a hideous four-story memorial to the disdain lavished on housing for the poor during the last century. When they actually still built tenements with the idea that poor people needed housing. I knew the inside perfectly before we ever passed through the doorless entry, stepping over and around squatters, trying not to inhale too deeply. The nearest public baths would be miles away.

Cooking smells, heavy on rancid grease, did help suppress the body odors somewhat.

Every room in the structure would be overcrowded. Entire extended families would occupy a space at most ten feet by eight, some members possibly sleeping standing up, leaning on a rope. Certainly sleeping in shifts, the majority always on the street trying to score an honest or dishonest copper. When you're that poor that distinction is too fine to notice.

It's the way of much of the world. And once you've looked into a place like that tenement you tend to appreciate your own better fortune a good deal more.

That tenement made Kayne Prose's situation appear considerably less awful.

I asked Rhafi, "You know where he stayed here?"

The boy shrugged. "Upstairs. I think he said the top floor."

"Oh, my aching knees."

"Not exactly the digs you'd expect of the Bic Gonlit who enjoys gourmet dining and fine wines," Playmate observed.

"Definitely not. You think Bic maybe used this place as a safe house?" I stepped over and past several big-eyed ragamuffins, the eldest possibly four, all huddling on the bottom steps of the stairs.

I knew the answer to my question. The Bic Gonlit who had come to see me in search of magical boots knew nothing about the other Bic. The Dead Man would have winkled that out right away.

The opposite, of course, could not be true.

Possibly the real Bic had a relationship of some sort with the artificial Bic and didn't know it. Puffing, I asked Playmate, "Bic have any brothers or cousins?"

"Only child of an only child, far as I know. Top floor. How come you're having so much trouble breathing? Which room, Rhafi?"

Rhafi didn't know. Rhafi wasn't bright but Rhafi was cunning enough not to let himself be lured into something by

someone weird. Unless that someone happened to be flashing coin.

There were eight doorways on that fourth floor. The one
farthest back on the right had an actual door in its frame.
Several others had rag curtains hung up. A couple had
nothing. And the doorway on the right, next forward from
the one with a real door, had been boarded up. So well
that no entrepreneur had been able to pry the boards off
and return them to the local economy.

I said, "Has to be the one with the door, Play."

Curious faces poked out of neighboring doorways, most
of them low to the floor and dirty. Only a couple of older
people had the nerve to be nosy.

In TunFaire nosiness can be a deadly disease.

Playmate said, "Look at that. A key lock." He knocked.
There was no response. "Looks like the one you have over
at your place."

"That's because it was made by the same crooked lock-
smith." After having suffered Dean to spend a young fortune to buy and install a lock I'd learned that the machine
could be picked easily. I knew how myself, having had to
develop the skill because, once he got the lock installed,
Dean used it. Without regard to my location in relation to
my front door, or whether I'd remembered to take my key
when I went out.

I knocked, too. There was no response to my magic
knuckles, either.

I felt the door. Like maybe that would clue me in to
what was going on behind it. It wasn't hot or cold or wet
so the weather was fine. The door did rattle in its frame,
which was no surprise in that dump. It was a replacement
door, likely to vanish as soon as some entrepreneur could
get on the other side and reach its hinges.

I tried the knob.

It turned. "What the hell?"

The door wasn't locked. It wasn't barred or chained on
the inside. It creaked inward at the slightest shove.

With our backs to the wall either side of the doorway,
Playmate and I exchanged looks of surprise. There were

whispers down the hall, tenants kicking themselves for not having noticed and seized the day.

If you want to live alone in a place this low you'd better have a pet thunder lizard or be able to leave some really nasty booby traps behind when you go out.

Nothing with lots of teeth and bad breath came to see who was calling.

I produced my oaken headknocker. I used it to push the door open a little wider.

The room behind it appeared clean and neat, almost sterile. Its plaster was in perfect repair and had been painted gray. The wooden floor had been sanded and polished. Overall, the place appeared to be in better shape than it had been the day it first accepted a tenant.

There were rugs on the floor. The furniture included a small table and two wooden chairs. One of those sat in front of a fine cherrywood writing desk cluttered with paper and both quill and metal-tipped pens. There was an overstuffed chair that faced the one small window. That window had real, clear glass in it. A little table beside the chair supported a top-quality brass-and-glass oil lamp.

I whispered, "Looks like our man does a lot of reading." There were shelves beside the cherrywood desk. Those held at least thirty books, a veritable fortune. The bindings on the bound volumes suggested old and expensive and rare, which almost certainly meant stolen.

Playmate grunted. "This fellow isn't poor."

"Makes you wonder, don't it?"

"Be careful going in there."

"What's this, army telling Marines how to play the game? Here's an idea. Why don't I just toss Rhafi in? We can wander on in after the smoke clears away." I was beginning to suspect sorcery. I couldn't think of any other reason for anybody to have so many books.

"Do that and you'll ruin your chances forever with Kayne and Cassie both."

"Right now I'm not sure that'd bother me a whole lot, Play. I must be getting old. I'm taking Morley seriously. I'm losing my taste for women who're crazier than me." I dropped down, reached inside with my stick, felt around. Slowly and carefully. The setters of traps like to put their triplines down where you're less likely to notice them. I didn't find the threads I expected. Which is what I'd have used if I was rigging a setup like this. "I can't find anything here, Play. But it still don't smell right."

This time army didn't have any advice. This time army awaited Marine Corps' professional assessment.

The Marine chose to use his magic wand some more. There was a very small throw rug lying right inside the doorway. I started to push it away, to see what was underneath it.

I heard the sound of water falling into a vat of boiling grease. Then came a blinding flash of light accompanied by a baby thunderclap. I flung myself sideways, dragged me upward until I was sitting with my back against the wall.

When my vision cleared and my hearing returned I saw Rhafi swatting at a smoking patch of wall across the narrow hallway. A couple of tenants were yelling for water. The precursors of a human stampede were taking shape.

I smelled the stench of burnt hair.

Playmate told me, "My man, you're going to have to wear a hat for a while."

I felt the top of my head. I spoke a few syllables that my mom wouldn't have approved even on this occasion. "I'll just have Dean give me a haircut. I'm sure he thinks I'm overdue, anyway." I got back down on my belly and poked that little rug again.

Crackle. Flash. Clap. But all much less energetic than before.

I slithered into Bic's place, disturbing that little rug as I went. The booby trap barely popped. And that was the end of that.

27

"This guy had a whole lot of time on his hands," I said. We'd been over the place three times. We hadn't found anything to help us trace Kip. But we knew this Bic Gonlit liked to read books about TunFaire and Karenta, modern and past, and we knew he must enjoy rehabilitating run-down property because he'd completely redone this room and the sealed-up place next door, which he reached through a doorway he'd cut through the separating wall.

"Not to mention having enough spare change to afford several expensive hobbies." Those had to include paying someone to steal all those innocuous texts."

"We need to interview the neighbors."

"They aren't going to say anything. None of their business."

"You just have to know how to ask, Play. They'll sing like a herd of canaries if you happen to have some change in your hand while you're talking."

"Don't look at me."

"All right. Tell me something, then. Who's the client in this case? I didn't come to you and Kip. Am I getting my head shaved by some kind of lightning just for the exercise? I don't like exercise. Am I short the most focused and talented girlfriend I've had in a while because I'd rather be out rolling around in the slums with the lowest of the low-lifes, spending my own money so that they'll maybe give me a clue how to find a kid who probably should've been sewn into a sack with some bricks and thrown in the river ten years ago?"

"Don't go getting cranky on me, Garrett. I need some time. I honestly didn't think it was going to get this complicated."

"You didn't think. You're an idealist, Play. And like every damned idealist I've ever met you really think that things should happen, and will happen, because they're the right things to happen. Never mind the fact that people are involved and people are the most perverse and blackheartedly uncooperative creatures the gods ever invented."

"Garrett! That's enough logs on the fire."

"I'm just getting going."

"Never mind. You've made your point."

"So we'll start talking to people out in the hall. You will." I didn't want anyone else getting into our quarry's rooms. There'd be too much temptation to make off with inexplicable trinkets.

There were unknown items everywhere that resembled the little oblongs and soap bar–size boxes that had been left behind when Kip was snatched. They had foreign writing on them. Which in itself is a big so what in TunFaire, where almost everyone speaks several languages and maybe one in ten people can even read one or more. They had little colored arrows and dots. I assumed they were some sort of sorcerer's tools and left them alone.

There wasn't much else to see in the first room. The second was used as a bedroom and was set up pretty much like my own, with the wall where the hallway door used to be concealed behind a curtain, which made a closet. That contained clothing in a broader range of styles than you'd find anywhere else, and a rack of sixteen wigs. The diversity amongst those told me our boy enjoyed going out in disguise. But nothing I uncovered ever moved us one step closer to finding Cypres Prose.

I gave Playmate what coins I had. After a careful count. "Don't be generous. These people won't expect it."

"What should I tell them when they ask me why we want to know?"

"Don't tell them anything. We're collecting information, not passing it out. Just let them see the money. If somebody tells you something interesting, give him a little extra. If he sounds like he's making it up to impress you, kick his ass and talk to somebody else. I'll listen in from back here."

Rhafi wanted to know, "How come you want Play to do all the asking?"

"On account of he looks more like a guy they can trust." It was that preacher man look he cultivates. "I look like a guy who'd send for the Guard if I heard anything interesting. If I'm not underground Guard myself."

The simple existence of Deal Relway's secret police gang was making life more difficult already. People were paranoid about those in authority. No doubt with good reason in most cases.

I continued to potter around the place while Playmate and Rhafi held court in the hallway. I invested a fair amount of time examining the door lock.

It exhibited no scratches to indicate that it had been picked. There was no damage to show that the door had been jimmied. There was nothing else to make me think anything but that our man had gone out without locking his door.

I found that hard to credit. This is TunFaire. Despite having heard a thousand times from country folk how they never had to lock their doors at home, I couldn't believe that anyone would do it here. But there was no evidence whatsoever to indicate otherwise. Unless the man who lived here *wanted* somebody to walk in. And maybe get blasted.

I called Rhafi in from the hallway. "Is there any way you know of that Bic Gonlit could've been warned that we were coming?"

"Huh? How could anybody know that?"

How indeed?

28

I'd caught a whiff of a red herring. And in less time than it takes to yell, "I'm a dope!" I sold myself a duffel bag full of wrong ideas.

Lucky for me somebody came along before I invested a whole lot of time and anger in trying to figure out how Kayne or Cassie or somebody had gotten word over in time for a trap to be set.

First hint came when the fourth floor hallway suffered a case of illuminated roaches effect. In less than a minute, without explanation to anyone whatsoever, the entire population of the ugly yellow tenement took cover in their home rooms.

I beckoned Rhafi and Playmate into Bic's room. "Go hide out in the bedroom. And stay quiet." I pushed the door shut behind them, locked it, then recalled that it hadn't been locked and undid that. Then I nudged the little throw rug into place just behind the door.

We waited.

I wasn't yet sure what for. When a whole crowd of people suddenly do something all together, like a flock of birds turning, and you don't get it, you'd better lie low and keep your eyes open.

That was my master plan for the moment.

The door handle jiggled as a key probed the lock. I tensed. The tenant was home? Was that why everybody had scattered? Playmate's interviews hadn't achieved much but to reveal that the denizens of the tenement were scared of him. Though nobody had produced a concrete reason.

How would he respond to finding his door unlocked?

Probably with extreme caution. Unless he'd left it unlocked.

I continued to nurse a paranoid streak on that matter.

The door opened. Nobody came in right away. I held my breath. I was thinking that only a blind man could've overlooked the scorching on the wall across the hallway. Only a man with no sense of smell would miss the stink of burnt hair.

But then somebody did a little hop forward, over the throw rug.

I shoved the door shut. "Play."

Playmate popped out of the other room before the man finished turning toward me. He considered his options and elected to do nothing immediately. He was trapped in a confined space, between two men much bigger than he.

He was just a little scrub, maybe five-foot-seven, and skinny. He was much too well dressed for the neighborhood.

I asked Playmate, "You know this guy?"

Playmate shook his head.

"Rhafi? How about you?"

"I seen him around. I don't know him."

"Sit, friend," I directed. "Hands on top of the table." Playmate moved the chair for the elf, then positioned himself behind it. Mindful of what we'd found in the other room, I said, "Pull his hair."

His hair came off. And when it did bits of flesh began to peel back along the former boundary between hair and naked skin. The part of the head that had been covered by the wig was hairless and pale gray.

I tugged at the peeling edges of the face. It came off. What lay beneath was a ringer for one of Playmate's elf sketches. The gray face betrayed no more emotion than had the motionless human mask when that had been in place.

"Holy shit!" Rhafi burst out. "It really is one of them things Kip was always talking about. I never believed him, even when he got Mom to say she'd seen them, too. He was always making up stories."

"I've seen them, too," Playmate said. "So has Mr. Garrett. But never quite this close."

"Which one is this?" I knew it wasn't any of the ones I'd seen before. It had more meat on it.

"I don't know. Not one of Kip's friends, though. It might be the first one who came looking for them."

I considered the elf. So-called because we didn't know what he really was. The Dead Man's suggestion of kef sidhe half-breeding didn't seem more likely than true elven origins. Maybe it hailed from the far north or from the heart of the Cantard. Some strange beings have been coming out of that desert since the end of the war with Venageta.

The elf seemed calm. Even relaxed. Without a concern.

I said a little something to Playmate in the pidgin dwarfish I could manage. Playmate nodded. He thought the elf was too confident, too.

I told the critter, "I owe you one for bopping me in that alley, guy. But I'm going to try not to remember that while we're talking."

My words had no effect. In fact, I got the distinct impression that the elf felt that he was in control of the situation, that he was playing along just to see how much he could find out.

I said, "Rhafi, go into the other room and see if you can find something we can use for a bag. A pillowcase, for instance. Anything will do."

Rhafi was back in seconds with an actual bag. It was made of that silvery stuff we had found right after Kip was taken.

I said, "Just start throwing in all the little odds and ends and knicknacks. Keep your back to us when you do. And stay between whatever you're bagging and our friend." I wasn't quite sure why I was giving him those instructions but it sure seemed like the right thing to do. And Rhafi was a good boy who did exactly what he was told.

I told Playmate, "Kayne maybe did her best job with this one."

"Don't be fooled," he whispered. "You're on him at a good time. He can be more trouble than the other two put together."

I jerked my head toward our captive. "Does this guy talk?"

"I expect so. He's been getting by by pretending to be human. Can't manage that without saying something sometime."

A touch of tension seemed to have developed in the elf. He wasn't pleased with Rhafi's activities.

"Good job, Rhafi," I said. "When that bag is full I want you to take it downstairs and leave it in the street." It shouldn't take more than a few minutes for the contents to disappear forever, whether or not anyone could figure out any use for the trinkets.

I watched the elf closely. So did Playmate. This would be the time when he would try something. If he was going to do so.

The gray elf's strange Y-shaped nostril opened wide. Air whistled inside. The nostril closed. The elf's skinny little mouth began to work, though no sounds came forth.

The elf exhaled, then drew a second deep breath. I got the notion he'd tried something he hadn't expected to work and had been disappointed by the results.

The elf spoke. "Mr. Garrett. Mr. Wheeler."

Who the hell was Mr. Wheeler?

Oh. I'd never known Playmate by any other name, except once upon a time when I'd told everybody his name was Sweetheart, just to confuse things if they decided to go looking for him.

Playmate shook his head and pointed at Rhafi. Three different fathers. Well. I hadn't thought about the kid's patronymic. Or even that Kayne might have used it if she wasn't married to the man. But she had been, hadn't she? As I recalled Playmate explaining it.

Meantime, my new pseudoelven buddy was going on, "I believe that we may be able to help one another." His Karentine was flawless, upper-class, but more like a loud, metallic whisper than a normal voice. It took me a moment to realize that that was because he wasn't really using a voice.

More legs on the millipedal mystery. Every intelligent creature I've ever met had a voice. Even the Dead Man did, back when he was still alive.

"Who are you?" I asked. "What are you?"

"Policeman? One who tracks and captures evildoers and delivers them to the justiciars? Do you have that concept?"

"Sure. Only in these parts it's track and catch lawbreakers, not evildoers. Big difference, here in TunFaire. Where are you from?"

He ignored my question, more or less. "The distinction, perhaps, is not always observed in my country, either, though there are those of us who refuse to bend in the wind."

Damn! I got me a gray-skinned Relway?

He continued, "Be that as it may, I have come to your country in search of two criminals. They have proven extremely elusive. And lately my search has been complicated by the arrival of other hunters, newly alerted to approximately where these two now can be found."

Damn. Wouldn't it be great to have the Dead Man listening in here? The guy's story was good, so far, though hard to follow because it was delivered in six- or eight-word puffs separated by long inhalations.

I was inclined to suspect that the creature normally communicated mind to mind, like the Dead Man.

I asked, "How can we help each other?"

"You wish to recover the boy, Cypres Prose, who has been taken captive by the recently arrived Masker elements. I wish to capture the two villains I was sent to apprehend. My superiors are growing impatient. I believe I may be able to locate the boy by locating the criminals holding him. I do not have the power to wrest him from the hands of his captors alone, however. Join me in doing that. Then get the boy to tell us where my criminals are hidden. Once I have them in hand I'll go away. Life here can return to normal."

"That's just about good enough to gobble up. Even if life here is never any normaler than it is right now. What do you think, Play? Are Lastyr and Noodiss desperate criminals?"

"I don't think they're any danger to Chodo Contague, based on the little I saw, but they never really acted like innocent men. Sounds like a workable swap. What are those two wanted for?"

"They are Brotherhood of Light. Their exact crimes are unknown to me. I do not need to know those to do my job."

I said, "If we're going to be partners we're going to have to call you something besides, 'Hey, You!' You got a name of your own?"

He had to think about it. "As If, Unum Ydnik, Waterborn. Which I cannot explain so that you would understand. Call me Casey. I heard that name recently. I like the sound. And it will be easier for you."

In words my friend Winger might have used had she been around, this old boy was slicker than greased owl shit. He always had a good answer ready to go. Though I got no sense of insincerity from him. I was almost certainly less sincere than he was.

All the time we were talking Rhafi kept maneuvering back and forth, trying to reach the door with his sack of plunder. While trying to keep facing away from Casey and keeping me or Playmate in between.

I told him, "You can forget what I said, Rhafi. I think we're all going to work the same side."

The boy stayed behind Playmate while he said, "Kip won't give those guys up."

"Then maybe we'll just toss him back to the bad guys." I hadn't fallen in love with Cypres Prose during my brief exposure to the kid. I kept wondering what I was doing, not just dropping the whole thing. Doing a favor for a friend? I did owe for all those times when Playmate had done really big favors for me.

"Just leave the bag on the table, please," Casey told Rhafi. "I will return everything to its proper place. Mr. Garrett, when would you like to pursue this matter?"

"I'm going to take it as stipulated that you're the expert on the people holding Kip. How dangerous is that situation?" There was a time when I did a lot of work related to kidnappings and hostage holdings. Unless the villains belong to one of just a handful of professional gangs the victim's chances are slim. And they deteriorate with time.

"By the standards of your city those scoundrels are a waste of flesh. You people are more casually cruel to your own families and friends, without thought, than Maskers can be under full force of malice. The dangers enveloping Cypres Prose are almost entirely emotional and spiritual, perils of the soul your people almost entirely discount as irrelevant at best."

I could buy that. I didn't know what the hell he was talking about. Which was, probably, his point. "They aren't breaking his teeth or shoving hot needles under his nails?"

Casey managed to project an aura of horror so strong that it got me thinking about some of the other feelings I'd experienced since he'd shown up. "No. Nothing like that."

"Then, if he's in no immediate physical danger, I'm going home and getting something to eat. And maybe I'll take a nap." And then maybe I could dash over to Katie's and see what I could do to patch things up. Hoping her father wasn't home. Katie's father doesn't realize that she isn't twelve years old anymore. "And I'm sure Playmate is worried sick about his stable." Down deep Playmate has to know what monsters he's harboring.

Casey shuddered. He projected quietly controlled terror. He knew the truth.

I might like this guy after all. Even if I didn't trust him farther than I could throw the proverbial bull mammoth.

I suggested, "Why don't we all wrap up all our other business, then meet at my place in the morning. We can go find Kip from there."

"Your morning or real morning?" Playmate asked. "We need to get that established." He couldn't conceal his sneer.

In addition to his completely self-delusory regard for the equine race Playmate is a devoted adherent of that perverse doctrine which suggests that it's a *good* thing to be up and working ere ever the sun peeps over the horizon. Which goes to show just how broad-minded a guy I am. I still consider him a friend.

"Solar morning. But no before the crack of dawn stuff. Moderation in all things, that's my motto."

"Even in telling us what your motto is, evidently," Playmate cracked. "Because I've never been there to hear you state it. Before now."

"After sunrise," I grumped. "Rhafi, we're leaving now.

You go out first. Playmate, you follow. Casey, I know you're a stranger here. But you've been here a while and those books tell me you've been trying to learn your way around. Here's a tip. Don't ever leave your door unlocked again. I guarantee you, next time you do these people here, your neighbors, will steal everything but your middle name before you get down the stairs to the street."

I backed out of the room myself. I retreated cautiously until I reached the head of the stairs. Needlessly. Casey never stuck his head out of his room.

29

"That was clever, Garrett," Playmate said after we hit the street.

"I thought so myself. But, knowing my luck, the Dead Man will be sound asleep when Casey shows up tomorrow."

Playmate chuckled.

I stopped the parade half a block from the yellow tenement. "Rhafi. What did you take?"

"Take? What do you mean? I didn't take . . ."

I had been fishing because it seemed in character. His response betrayed him. "I saw you. I want it. Right now. And no holding back."

"Aw . . ."

Playmate explained, "Look, if you make Casey mad he might not help us get Kip back."

There followed an exchange during which Playmate almost lost his temper because he couldn't make the kid understand how Casey could guess that *he* had taken anything that turned up missing.

Rhafi hadn't gotten the brains or the looks.

Rhafi began to look like he wanted to cry. But he held it in. He produced three small gray objects, two dark and one light, in varying shapes and sizes, though none had a major dimension exceeding four inches. Except for colored markings on their surfaces all three items looked like they had been cast from some material that resembled ivory or bone when it hardened. All three items had slightly roughened surfaces.

We stood in a triangle, facing inward, examining Rhafi's loot. I handled everything with extreme care. There was almost certainly some kind of sorcery involved with those things and I had no desire to wake it up. I concealed them about my person carefully. "Good. Now I have a job assignment for you, Rhafi. I want you to stay right here and watch that yellow brick tenement. See if anybody who might be our friend Casey ever leaves. Keeping in mind that he'll be wearing some kind of disguise. You saw the clothes and stuff he had."

"You want me to see where he goes?" As I'd hoped, he was all excited.

"No. No. Don't do that. I don't want you to end up like Kip. You just stay here till a man named Saucerhead Tharpe shows up. You'll know him by how big he is and because he has bad teeth. If Casey does leave, make sure you can give Saucerhead a good description of his disguise. Whatever, once Saucerhead shows up, you go home. I want you to tell your mom that we don't think Kip is in any physical danger, that we're on the trail, and that it looks like we might get them back as early as tomorrow. Got all that?"

"Sure, Mr. Garrett."

"Excellent. You make a good operative."

As soon as we were out of earshot, Playmate asked, "Do you believe that? That Kip's not in any real danger?"

"I think our new pal Casey believes that. I'm not sure how come but I could tell what he was feeling. Maybe it's because of all the time I spend around the Dead Man. Then I get close to somebody who probably communicates the same way and I just kind of cue in. I'll ask His Nibs."

"Uhm. Darn. I've got to find somebody to watch the stable. I can't keep walking away like this. The horses need attention. Somebody has to be there to deal with customers."

"Not to mention thieves."

"That's not a problem in my neighborhood." He stated that with complete conviction. I hoped his optimism wasn't misplaced.

"You ought to get yourself a wife."

"I'm reminded of an old saw about talking pots and black kettles."

He would be. "I'm doing something with *my* bachelor-hood. I'm laying in memories for those long, cool years down the road. Look, I've got to send Saucerhead down to relieve Rhafi. Saucerhead will know where to find Winger. I can have him tell her to come over and cover for you."

Playmate made growlie noises. He grumbled. He whined. Winger has a million faults but her country origins qualified her to baby-sit a stable. And she'd probably do a decent job as long as she was getting paid. Assuming Playmate had sense enough not to leave any valuables lying around. Winger has a real hard time resisting temptation.

It was the getting paid part that had been giving my large friend problems throughout this mess. He'd made commit-ments without first considering the fact that somebody would have to part with some money to see them met.

Winger would expect to be paid. Saucerhead would ex-pect to be paid. Garrett the professional snoop might be gouged for a favor or two but you couldn't expect him to pay his own expenses. And he was out of pocket already for help from several people, including Mr. Tharpe, Pular Singe the tracker, and the generous assistance of the Mor-ley Dotes glee club and bone-breaking society.

Hell, even my partner, who didn't have much else to do and didn't require much upkeep, might insist on some sort of compensation, just so the forms of commerce were observed.

He can be a stickler for form and propriety.

Sometimes I suspect he isn't aging all that well.

Playmate said, "There isn't any money in this, Garrett! You saw Kayne and her kids."

"We could always auction off a few horses. They're beg-ging for them down at Kansas and Love's, way I hear."

Playmate was so aghast he couldn't even sputter. From his point of view my simple mention of a slaughterhouse was so far beyond the pale that he found it impossible to believe that such words could have issued from a human mouth.

And I just couldn't resist needling him. "Which is hard to understand, what with all the surplus horses there ought to be these days."

"Garrett!" he gasped. "Don't. Enough. Not funny, man."

"All right. All right. You'll wake up someday. And I'll sing a thirty-seven-verse serenade of 'I Told You So,' outside your window."

He just shook his head.

"I'll get Winger headed your way. Maybe we can work out a deal where we'll all take a percentage of the profits from Kip's inventions."

That actually began to sound like a good idea once it got away. I might talk to the Dead Man. And to Max Weider at the Weider brewery, where I'm on retainer, next time I ran a surprise check on floor losses for him. Max Weider has a good eye for what people might want to buy and plenty of practical knowledge about how to get them together with your product so they have an opportunity to realize just how much they can't live without it.

Moments after Playmate and I parted my head was awash in grand schemes that would make me one of TunFaire's great commercial magnates.

30

The Dead Man was still awake. And still intrigued. Which left me vaguely uncomfortable. Usually a major part of the work I do consists of getting him to wake up, then getting him interested enough to participate, then keeping him awake until we finish. Any prolonged period of self-stimulated interest and cooperation generally constitutes a harbinger of an equally prolonged period where neither cataclysm nor calamity will stir him.

I described my day and refused to rise to the bait when he chided me for having knocked off work so early.

It might be interesting to interview the mother and sister. Arrange to bring them around. . . . You are incorrigible, sir.

"So don't incorrige me."

A weakness for punning is one of the onset signatures of senility, Garrett. I would suggest that a hands-off approach might be the safest policy with these women, if indeed your characterization captures the reality.

"I probably can't argue with you there. But, oh, are they scrumdidlyicious to look at."

A status you appear to accord almost any female you encounter if she is able to stand up on her hind legs.

"Unless she's related to Dean. It's a marvel how many homely women that family can pull together in one place."

The Casey creature. You did indeed feel that he was honest?

"Yeah. Well, he thought he was. We need to talk more about how I was sensing him. If that was for real, and I think it was, I want to be able to use it. As long as I have a good feel for what he's thinking I can keep him from putting one over on us primitives."

Primitives? He knew what I was getting at but wanted me to articulate it better so I'd be clearer about it in my own mind.

"Possibly 'primitive' is the wrong word. He had an aura of superiority about him. It had a strong moral edge to it. A self-righteousness. Like Dean, only much more carefully concealed."

Dean doesn't hide much. He isn't concerned about getting along with anybody. He knows he's right. When you're right other people have to worry about getting along with you.

We reviewed my day again, me underscoring events that had attracted my attention. "You see how I came to that conclusion? Even the criminals are too civilized to hurt somebody. If they're actually criminals."

Intriguing. It might be interesting to explore a system of thought that is, indeed, that alien.

"I set it up so we'll all get together here in the morning."

He will not come.

I didn't think he would, either. But I could hope.

"Where's the Goddamn Parrot?"

In transit here as we converse. The watch on the genuine Bic Gonlit has not been particularly productive. However, Mr. Gonlit did meet with Reliance's people. He has not given up on collecting the bounty on Miss Pular. He did have a prolonged argument with the ratmen concerning his fee. He took the not unreasonable position that he ought to be paid because what he had been hired to do was to find her. Which he did. But now they insist that he has to get her out of this house, away from you, and deliver her to them. Mr. Gonlit then argued that they were destroying their own credibility by changing the terms of a contract while that contract was in force and that that could not help but come back to haunt them. They would not listen. They seem to have an exaggerated and irrational fear of your prowess as a street fighter. I suppose it is possible that they have confused you with someone else.

"That must be it. I sure never worried anybody before. Now what's going on?" The pixies out front were acting up.

Mr. Big has arrived. But take your time letting him in. There are watchers. They do not need to know that we are aware of the bird when it is out of our sight.

"Watchers? Reliance's people or Relway's?"

Both of those and possibly more.

"More? Who?"

I believe Colonel Block mentioned a strong interest on the Hill.

He had, hadn't he?

Singe suddenly bustled in with a tray of food and drinks suitable for a party of ten. She offered me one of her forced smiles. "Dean is teaching me how to prepare meals."

"Tell him he has to let up on the spices a little when he's working with you. You have a delicate and precious nose."

"And hello to you, too, Mr. Garrett. How was your day?"

"Evidently sarcasm is on the training schedule, too. My day was pretty much like every working day. I walked a couple thousand miles. I interviewed a lot of people who were either crazy or born-again liars. Tomorrow I'll round up some of them and go check out something that might sort out the liars from the loons."

"I will go with you."

I barely got my mouth open.

She will go with you.

"Well, that's nice of you. I hope Reliance isn't in too black a mood when he catches us."

"I do not fear Reliance. Reliance fears me." Singe spoke around a mouthful of roll. The already-depleted state of the tray she'd brought warned me that I'd better grab fast if I wanted my share.

What she said was at least half-true. Getting Pular Singe back must, by now, be as much a fear of consequences matter as it was a bruised ego thing for Reliance. Strongmen, and even strongrats, have to keep on demonstrating their strength. The moment they show a hint of weakness some younger, hungrier strongarm is going to reach up and pull them down.

I glanced at Singe—she waved a fried chicken wing and nodded to let me know it was some good eating—then at the Dead Man. Old Bones wasn't sending it out but I could sense that he was entertained. He knew I was eager to run off and find Katie. I'd been rehearsing my most abject excuses and humble apologies all day long. I wanted to get cleaned up and get going, to take my personal life back.

I wondered how much Singe knew. I wondered if Dean's sudden interest in Singe might not be anything but another triumph of the old man's basic decency. He didn't approve of Katie, though you'd never guess it from overhearing one of their conversations. Katie was too much like me. And I've mentioned his attitude toward my approach to life.

Ain't none of us going to get out of it alive so we might as well get all the enjoyment out of it we can while we've got it.

I said, "I need to get cleaned up."

First you need to let Mr. Big into the house. He is becoming impatient. I believe he is hungry. In any event, he is about to denounce your taste for—

"I'm on my way." That damned wonder buzzard was invincible.

Somebody, once upon a time, said you surround yourself with the friends that you deserve. I need to take some time to lean back and think about that.

31

Katie's dad wouldn't let me in. Katie was home but he refused to tell her I wanted to see her. He didn't like anyone male, liked anyone interested in his daughter even less, and me least of all. I've never been real good on any musical instrument so I couldn't get her attention with a serenade. Grumping, I stood around in the street wondering, "What now?" I could wander over to the Tate compound and see if Tinnie was talking to me this week. I could try a couple of other young and incredibly attractive women of my acquaintance, though it was getting late of a workday evening to be turning up on anybody's doorstep. Or I could go somewhere and hang out with other guys like me—dateless and not wanting to stay home—and pay five times retail price per mug of Weider beer not bought at home by the keg.

Laziness and a long lack of the companionship of men who remembered drew me toward Grubb Gruber's Leatherneck Heaven. Which is as fat a misnomer as the one that used to hang on Morley's place back when he called it The Joy House. Grubb's joint isn't exactly a pit of despair where lost souls go to drink in solitude, perhaps in search of oblivion, certainly nurturing a sad pretense that camaraderie might break out at any moment. But you don't hear a whole lot of laughter in there. As the evening progresses the reminiscing turns inward, private, and maudlin, to memories that as individuals we cannot easily share. And I'm always surprised when there isn't any of the whimpering and screaming that had so often come around in the darkest hours of the night, down in the killing zone.

When those memories come, and somebody in Gruber's place starts wrestling with them, somebody else will hoist a mug and summon a ghost. "Banner-sergeant Hamond Barbidon, the meanest mortarforker what ever . . ."

And the cups will rise up. And ten thousand ghosts will rise with them.

"Corporal Savlind Knaab."

"Lance Fanta Pantaza."

"Andro Pat."

"Jellybelly Ibles."

"Mags Cooper."

And each name will remind somebody of another. "Cooper Away, the best damned platoon sergeant in the Corps."

Plenty of men would be prepared to dispute that because everybody remembered a particular sergeant who brought him along. The sergeants are the backbone of the Corps. And if you lived very long out there you grew up to become one.

Chances are you never heard of any of the toastees because they'd fallen in different places and different times. But they were Corps, so you honored them. You remembered them and you wanted to weep because those people out there in the street didn't know, didn't have any idea, and already, just months after the long war's end, were beginning not to care.

Sometimes it isn't that difficult to understand why the really ugly, militant, racist veterans' organizations have so much appeal for men who survived the Cantard.

Nobody who wasn't down there will ever really understand. Not even those who shook our hands when we left. Not even those who welcomed us back with mighty hugs and no conception whatsoever what it was like to sit there watching the life bleed out of a man whose throat you'd cut so you could go on, undetected, to murder some other poor boy whose bad luck had placed him in your path at the wrongest time possible in the entire history of the human species. So that someday, somewhere far away, some woman would cry because she no longer had a son.

I decided that what I wanted was to spend an evening at Grubb Gruber's place. But, apparently, I never arrived.

32

Eventually a moment came when I was rational enough to realize where it was that I was regaining consciousness. Guess who was looking down at me with an unhappy glint in his eye? I croaked, "We godda sta dis romance, Morley. Wha da my doin' here?"

"I've been hoping you could explain that to me, friend. The evening is just getting started. I've got some swanks from the high ground down here slumming, carpeting the floors with silver. Then you burst in, obviously not part of the entertainment. You're all torn up. You have blood all over you. You have a snarling ratman hanging on your back. You crash through three tables before you collapse. Five minutes later I'm standing here watching you leak all over a Molnar rug because all my customers have abandoned me and I don't have anything else to do."

I tried to get up. My body wouldn't respond. I'd used up my reserves talking, evidently.

Morley looked up as his man Puddle entered my field of vision. Puddle was about eighty pounds overweight and appeared to be about as out of shape as a man could be and still stay upright. He had a lot of miles on him, too. But looks are deceiving. He was strong. He was hard and he was tough and he had a lot more stamina than was credible for a man his size. He was dressed as a cook. He needed a shave.

"Need to shave, Puddle," I crooned.

I thought about going back to sleep. But I thought I probably ought to hear what Puddle had to say first.

Morley asked, "What did you find?"

"A long trail, a broken ratman and puddles a blood, boss. Da skink was a reglur one-man army."

"Corps," I said, not loud enough to be heard.

"And the ones who were after him when he staggered in here?"

"Split. Hauled ass out'n here da second we come out a da door."

"Reliance's gang, you think?"

"Not sure, boss. But dis's his part a rat city." TunFaire can be considered as many cities which occupy the same site. In some cases this fact is acknowledged publicly but in most the pretense is strongly in the other direction.

"No matter. We'll get the real story when Sleeping Beauty over there wakes up."

I managed to roll my head a short way. A ratman in worse shape than I found myself was sort of strewn around the floor ten feet closer to the front door, being stepped over and around by people cleaning up the mess.

Morley said, "Sarge, come give Puddle a hand. Get Garrett sitting up in a chair. Then we'll find out what happened."

Good. Good. Because I really wanted to know.

A second very large man, who could've passed as Puddle's tattooed big brother, appeared beside Puddle. Straining for breath, both men bent toward me. Each grabbed a hand. Up I floated. I tried to say something. What crawled out of my mouth didn't make sense even to me.

They dropped me into a comfortable chair. At least, it was comfortable under the circumstances. I wasn't yet quite certain what the circumstances were.

I had the uncomfortable feeling that I'd been on the losing side in a major brawl.

Morley said, "Somebody bring the medical box." The existence of which I noted. A fact that would weigh in on the other side the next time my good friend insisted he was completely out of his former underworld life. Which he might want me to believe because he thought I was thick with Colonel Block and Deal Relway. "Sarge, start checking him out."

Sarge is Sarge for the obvious and traditional reason. And, some think, for his tattoos, which let the whole world know that here's a man who made something of himself in the army. Here's a man who was tough enough and ferocious enough to have survived years of leading men in the witch's cauldron that was in the Cantard.

What that name and tattoos don't tell is what kind of soldier Sarge was.

Not many know, Sarge never brags. He doesn't look the type. But if he wanted he could stay drunk the rest of his life on drinks bought for him by other guys who'd been to and come back from the land beyond the far walls of Hell.

Sarge was a field medic down there. Which means he spent more time with his neck under the blade than did most of us. *And* during most of that time he couldn't have enjoyed the luxury of fighting back against the Venageti trying to kill him because he was too damned busy trying to do something to salvage something from amongst an overabundance of freshly mutilated bodies.

I tried to tell Sarge he was all right for a groundpounder. Almost an honorary Marine. Maybe he understood some of what I was trying to say because a sudden, horrible pain shot from my neck down my spine, through my hips and into my legs, all the way to my toenails. I believe I squealed in protest.

"He's been worked over real good," Sarge said. "But not by nobody who was able ta do whatever he wanted. What he's got is da kin' a wounds and bruises ya see when a whole bunch a clumsy guys gang up on somebody what's fightin' back."

So I put up a fight. Good for me.

If I'd been worked over like a plowed field, then how come I didn't ache in places I didn't even know I had?

"Anything broken?" Morley asked.

"Nah. He'll heal."

"Damn!" Puddle observed. "An' here I was tinking we could finally grab us a break, assuming we could a caught dis ole boy. . . . Oh, my stars! Da man his own self is awake."

Puddle is full of it. I consider him a friend even though

he's always saying things like that. Because he doesn't just say them about me. You could get the idea that he wants to drown Morley and Sarge. In fact, he's always rooting for everybody to get out of his life and leave it a whole lot less complicated.

Morley leaned closer. "So what was it, Garrett? To what do I owe the pleasure of your presence this time?"

I croaked, "I don' know. Can' remember. Goin' to Katie's."

Morley gave me a dark, unforgiving look. He'll never forgive me for having found Katie first. Her impact on him is just as ferocious as it is on me. Which is hard to believe, considering how I start drooling and stammering whenever she comes around me and how much more practiced and slick Morley is when dealing with the obstinate sex.

"Maybe you got there."

Puddle got it and laughed his goofy laugh. Sarge asked, "Den how come dem ratmen was all over him when—" Puddle nudged him with an elbow, hard enough to loosen a lever or two somewhere inside his bean-size brain. "Oh. He caught da wildcat. Dat's pretty funny, boss."

"And maybe he didn't. That cat would've scared those mice away. So what's your game with the ratpeople, Garrett?"

I couldn't remember. But if ratmen did this to me there could be only one answer. "Singe. I guess."

"Reliance. The old boy does seem to be getting a little fixated on that particular subject. Don't you think?"

"I do t'ink." I had a strong feeling that Singe was becoming a major issue inside the world of ratfolk organized crime. Reliance was ancient for one of his kind. The up-and-coming youngsters must be getting impatient.

I tried explaining that to Morley. I faded in and out a few times before he got it.

"Bet you're right, Garrett. It isn't about Singe at all. Not really. And I think I know how to settle the whole mess. And turn Reliance into your best buddy while we're at it. Sarge, the rat's breathing just picked up. He'll be ready to sing in a few minutes."

"What're you gonna do?" With stalwart assistance from

Puddle I was having considerable success at staying in my chair. My speech was clearing up some, too.

"I'll just remind Belinda that a broken-down ex-Marine named Garrett, with help from his ratgirl honey and a certain suave and incredibly handsome restaurateur, saved her sweet slim behind not all that long ago. I'll include some suggested topics for discussion with Reliance and his troops. Like the troops should leave the general alone. And the general should remember that he's indebted to you now, not the other way around."

"I don' like it."

"Of course you don't. You're Garrett. You have to do everything the hard way. Marshall. Curry. Help Mr. Garrett to a seat at the table in the back corner. And whichever one of you heathens has a little brandy squirreled away, I'd like to see a dram turn up in front of my friend."

Guys started looking for the apocryphal friend. The usual uncomplimentary remarks passed between Puddle and Sarge. I didn't think I liked the guy they were talking about very much myself. We needed to track him down and spank him.

Marshall and Curry turned out to be the young thugs Morley had brought along for the Cypres Prose chase.

Somehow, while Morley was away consulting his two weightiest henchmen, a beer stein brimming with spirits appeared before me. The smirk on the mug of the cook who delivered it told me it had been donated involuntarily from someone else's stash. Probably that of *faux* cooks Sarge and Puddle.

I am amused by the fact that none of Morley's guys share his tastes for vegetarianism and teetotaling. They respected him enough not to bring their slabs of dead cow to work with them, but a few can't, or don't want to, get by without a little nip of firewater now and again.

A few sips got my brain clanking along. Just well enough to make me wonder why I wasn't hurting as much as I ought to be. Those ratmen must've tried to get some kind of drug into me. And they must've had some success.

I didn't feel well but I didn't feel nearly as badly as I knew I would when whatever it was wore off.

Morley dropped into the chair opposite me, showing a lot of pointy teeth. His place was ready for business again. And, naturally, customers began to drift in.

Dotes said, "Bring me up to date on your adventures."

I could talk in fits and starts now, almost clearly, so I did. But I still couldn't tell him anything about what'd happened in the last few hours.

I noted that my cohort in delivering disaster, the ratman, had indeed been swept up and taken away. Some of Morley's less skilled waitstaff and kitchen help were not in evidence, either.

I'd say it wasn't a good evening to be a ratman foot soldier.

Of course, so far, it wasn't that great an evening to be me, either.

33

I wasn't seeing double from drugs or concussion anymore. I was doing that from the bite of a pretty good brandy. Suddenly, I spotted a couple of Katie Shavers coming in the front door, dressed to stop the hearts of celibate clerics and to start those of guys who'd taken up layabout duty in the morgue.

I gawked. And muttered, "One for each of us."

Morley said, "Excuse me?"

"What's she doing here?"

"Well . . . I believe she received a message explaining that you'd been badly mugged on your way over to her place. So make like you've got one foot over the line and she's the only thing holding you back."

"Not to worry. She ain't the only thing but as long as she's here on this side, I'm staying, too. Hello, darling."

Katie just kind of smiled and ate me alive with her eyes. Which is part of what Katie does so well. She doesn't say much, most of the time, but she's great to be with when she does. She has red hair, an all-time crop of freckles, and eyes that are a sort of gray-blue slate instead of the green you might expect. Nor is the red hair that brilliant shade that always comes with a difficult nature.

Conversations stopped while Katie walked the length of The Palms. Women punched or gouged their men. Yet for all that, Katie is not a great beauty—though not even a madman would try to make the claim that she's the least little bit unattractive.

What she has most is tremendous presence and animal

intensity. Every minute with Katie is like a minute spent in a cage with a restless panther.

"You are in bad shape," she told me, like she was surprised to encounter the truth. Her voice husked, of course, yet managed to sound like she was going to bust out laughing any second.

I tried to tell her she ought to see the other guys. My mouth wouldn't form the words. The effects of the drug kept coming back.

Katie scooted a chair around beside me, sat down next to me, took my hand, and leaned against me. "Cure for most anything," I croaked in Morley's direction. And all was right with the world.

Morley nodded and drifted away.

After a long time purring I managed to get out words to the effect, "I tried to see you to apologize for getting tied up with my work but your dad wouldn't even tell you I was there."

"That's all right. I tried to see you, too. But Dean said you were out and he wouldn't let me in to wait."

And never mentioned the fact that she'd come around, either. "What time was that?"

"Midmorning."

Ah. I *was* out. But she wouldn't believe that if I told her because she knows my habits. If I defended Dean at all she'd decide that I must've been with somebody else. Sometimes her mind works in nonsequential directions, disdaining cause and effect. "We need to get those two together."

"Who?"

"Dean and your father."

"That's probably not a good idea. The only thing they'd agree about is that they should keep us away from each other."

"You're right."

"I'm always right, darling. You need to remember that."

"You're right." They all are. All the time. Which means that there're really tens of thousands of realities all around us, happening all at the same time. Has to be, on the face of the evidence.

Which brings to mind a joke first told me by Winger, of all people, and by just about everyone else I know since. If a man speaks in the heart of a forest and no woman is there to hear him, is he still wrong?

Katie asked, "Have you been drinking?"

"Yes I have. A little bit. Medicinal brandy. But the reason I'm goofy is because the ratmen tried to drug me."

Morley returned now, accompanied by Marshall and Curry. The whole gang dragged me upstairs and put me away in a guest room, where Katie did her best to keep me awake while I was suffering a threat of concussion.

34

The Palms by daylight is a different world. As a soft light will flatter some women, so night and candlelight do wonders for Morley's nightclub. By day the cheap wall coverings and decorations that had upgraded the place from its former status as The Joy House revealed their shabbiness.

The Joy House hadn't been what it sounds like. It used to be the same thing it was now, just patronized by a different clientele. Lowlifes. Grifters and pickpockets and low-level professional criminals. Ticks on the underbelly of society. The Palms, on the other hand, caters to parasites able to afford new clothes. But the upscale appurtenances have begun to show wear.

I sat at that same back corner table sucking down herbal tea and trying to figure out if my head hurt because of the ratmen's drug, the brandy I'd consumed, or because various blunt instruments had thumped my skull in passing. It was a valuable exercise, in theory. If I could figure it out I could shun the causes in future. All I'd have to do is give up drinking or get a real job.

Morley bent down to look me in the eye. He couldn't restrain a smirk.

I grumped, "This place is starting to look tacky, buddy. Maybe you ought to start setting yourself up for another format change. Try selling granite wine to dwarves and trolls for a while, maybe."

"Those kinds of people are much too hard on the furniture. The overhead would be too high. You started to remember anything about what happened?"

He knew blows to the head sometimes work that way. Chunks of memory from right before the trauma disappear.

"Some. I was headed for Grubb Gruber's place. Katie's dad had just told me to get lost. I hadn't seen the guys down there since before that business with The Call. It seemed like a good time to drop in."

Morley offered me a thinly veiled look of despair. He asked, "Why would you want to hang around with that tribe of has-beens?"

Because what they has been is what I has been, I didn't say. Morley would never understand. Guys down at Gruber's know what everybody else went through. Not many others do. And less than anyone those who stayed home to comfort the lonely soldiers' wives. Some of us don't need to go in there as often as others. "Because I learn more from them about what's going on around town than I can anywhere else. None of those guys feels like he's got anything to hide or anything to hold back."

"Ouch! How the bee doth sting."

I asked, "Did you perchance send word out about what happened? I was supposed to meet some people this morning."

"I informed your partner. At his request I passed the word along to Playmate, too." Morley grinned. "He had a huge row with Winger. About whether or not she ought to get paid. Until he decided he had to relay the news to someone else."

Morley seemed more curious than I found comfortable. Naturally suspicious, I examined that from a couple of angles while also wondering if it wasn't natural to want to know what was going on when you were involved. Hell, I wanted to know what was going on myself.

Some of Morley's guys were sweeping, mopping, otherwise halfheartedly getting ready for the coming evening's business. Of a sudden, with no perceptible change in attitude or speed, they all headed for the kitchen. In moments the place was empty except for myself and the owner. And the owner no longer looked happy.

I muttered, "Maybe I should head for the kitchen, too."

Because I had a feeling I wasn't going to like what was about to happen.

Imminence became actuality.

The approaching coach, the rattle of which had cued the troops to vanish, wasn't approaching anymore. It had arrived.

Morley said, "I do wish she'd take a little less of a personal interest in her business. It's your fault, you know. Nobody ever sees her till your name comes up."

Two thugs pushed into The Palms. Once they stepped out of the bright sunlight they looked like miniature trolls, ugly and hard as jasper. I don't know where they find them. Maybe there's a mine where they dig them up. One held the door for Belinda Contague.

Despite being who and what she is, Belinda persists in dressing herself as the Slut of Doom, the Vampire Whore in Black. She wore black today but with the light behind her not much of her shape remained a mystery.

That ended when the door closed. Her dress was black and unusual but not particularly revealing without the backlighting.

She said something to her henchmen. Both nodded. One went back outside. The other assumed a relaxed stance watching Morley and me.

Belinda approached, perfectly aware of the impact she had because she worked hard at creating it. She was tall, with a shape well-favored by nature. She had a particularly attractive face, which, unfortunately, she insisted on covering with makeup as pale as paper. Her lips were painted bright red and slightly exaggerated by the color.

We have been lovers. We might be again if she really insists.

Very few things frighten me. Belinda Contague is one of them.

Belinda isn't sane. But she has her madness under control and uses it as a weapon. She is deadlier and scarier than her father ever was because she's so much more unpredictable.

She bent and kissed me on the cheek, lingering in case

I cared to turn for something with a little more bite. I had to fight it.

Belinda has her positive attributes.

She sensed my temptation and was satisfied. She dropped into the seat beside me. The one Katie had occupied just last night. Luckily, Katie had gone home.

Sometimes it's a curse being a red-blooded Karentine boy. Especially when the red-blooded Karentine girls won't leave you alone.

I asked, "How'd you get here so fast?" I did know that Morley had sent her a message about the Reliance situation.

"I was in town already. There was a matter I had to see to personally. I'm making arrangements for my father's birthday. This one is the big six-zero. I want to give him a party. I'll want you guys to be there. I wouldn't be around if it wasn't for you."

Morley and I exchanged the looks of men suddenly and unexpectedly condemned.

Belinda said, "Tell me about your problem with Reliance."

I did so.

"Why's this Pular Singe so important to you?"

"She's my friend."

"Do you make her squeal?"

"She's *just* a friend, Belinda."

"I'm *just* a friend but you've made me squeal a few times."

"It isn't like that, Belinda. I've also helped you out a few times because you're a friend."

She showed me some teeth and a flash of tongue. She was pleased with herself. "I owe you for Crask and Sadler. So I'll send out word, the way you suggested. That'll set you up. And it'll close out my debt to him for his part in saving me from those two."

"You all over that now? You all right?" She'd been tortured and brutalized during the incident she'd mentioned.

"Back to my old self. Able to best a Marine two falls out of three. Know where I could find a Marine who wants to wrestle?"

"You're turning into a forward little sweetmeat."

Morley made a face but kept his groan to himself.

"Sometimes you've got to be direct. When all anyone does is worry about whether you're planning to cut their throat. I'm no black widow, Garrett."

So she said. I had no trouble picturing her with a scarlet hourglass on the front of that dress, accentuating her already-enticing shape. She had no reputation for that sort of thing but there was ample precedent in her own father's treatment of her mother.

"I don't think you are. What I wish you weren't is somebody who twists my head into knots every time I see you because that really gets in the way when I try to do business with you."

She leaned against me. "Poor baby."

Morley sat there in absolute silence, showing no inclination to draw attention to himself. He had no personal relationship with Belinda to help shield him from her unpredictable wrath. He preferred by far to do business at a grand remove.

Belinda told me, "Tell me a little more about this case you're working." So I did. I could see no way that it would hurt. And there was always a chance she'd get a wild hair and do something that would help.

"How does that tie in with your rat girlfriend?"

"It doesn't, far as I can see."

"I'll look around."

In TunFaire it's far harder to hide from the Outfit than it is to hide from me or Colonel Block. The Outfit commands far vaster resources.

"This have anything to do with all those flying lights everybody's been seeing?" she asked.

"It might," I conceded, grudgingly, not really having considered the possibility before. There was no evidence to suggest it.

Belinda popped up, in a bright good mood suddenly. Her mercurial mood swings are another thing that makes her a scary thing. She's much more changeable than most women.

She planted another kiss, this time at the corner of my mouth. "Give my best to Tinnie."

"We're on the outs. This week."

"Alyx, then."

"Nothing going on there, either."

"There's hope for me yet. I'll definitely want you to come to Daddy's party." Out the door she went, bouncing like she'd shed a decade of life and a century of conscience.

Morley exhaled like he'd been holding his breath the whole time. "You know what that means?"

"Belinda having a party for the kingpin?"

"Yes. He's not going to be sixty. Not yet. And I think his birthday really isn't for a couple of months yet, either."

"It means she's confident enough of her hold on the Outfit to roll Chodo out and let everybody see what his condition really is."

The purported overlord of organized crime in TunFaire is a stroke victim, alive still but a complete vegetable. Belinda has been hiding that fact and ruling in his name for some time now. Questions have arisen but the combination of Chodo's past propensity for bizarre behavior, a little truth, and Belinda's utterly ferocious, ruthless suppression of challengers have kept the kingpin position safely a Contague prerogative.

Morley said, "There're some old underbosses who'll revolt. They won't take orders from a woman, no matter who she is."

I sighed, too.

Chances were good Belinda knew that better than we did. Chances were good that Belinda was ready to retire those old boys, and might do it at this marvellous party.

I could figure that but they couldn't because they didn't know what I knew about Chodo.

"How many times have you saved her life?" Morley asked. "Several, right?"

"Uhm." He'd been there a few times.

"I think she's gotten superstitious about you. I think she's decided you're her guardian angel. That no matter how bad it gets, if she's in trouble good old Garrett will bail her out."

"That's not true."

"But she believes it. Which means you don't really have anything to fear from her."

"Except for her expectations."

A sly look flicked across Morley's features. "You think she bought your story about Singe?"

It took me a moment to get it. "You butthead."

35

I said, "I was afraid of something like this."

Another woman had just stamped into The Palms. She headed toward me and Morley, elbowing Morley's men aside.

Winger definitely survives more by luck than by any good sense.

"Winger." Morley's greeting was less than enthusiastic. I suspect he'd had a bad personal experience there, once upon a time. Which would teach him to pay attention to his own rule about not getting involved with women who're crazier than he is.

"The very one," she retorted.

Winger is a big old gal, more than six feet tall, and solidly built, though she's actually quite attractive when she bothers to clean herself up. If she was a foot shorter and knew how to simper she'd be breaking hearts wholesale just by looking the wrong way.

"Hey, Garrett," she roared. "What the hell are you doing sitting on your ass in this nancy dump? You was supposed to—"

"You don't listen too well, do you? Word went out that I got the snot beat out of me last night. To you, too. The man who told you is standing right over there. Meantime, I've got bruises on my bruises. I'm stiff all over."

"Yeah? How 'bout where it counts? Didn't think so. You're another one that's just all talk." She glared at Morley. "Get up and walk it off."

Winger is something like a thunderstorm and something like

a female Saucerhead. Except with better teeth. And she's a lot more stubborn than Tharpe. It may take Saucerhead a while to work something out but he'll change his mind. Winger has never been wrong in her life. Unless it was that time she thought she was wrong but it turned out that she wasn't.

Big, blond, meaty, goofy, completely dangerous where your valuables are concerned, she's likely to be part of or taken in by the most outrageous scams imaginable. And yet she's one of my friends. One of the inner circle. One of those who'd take steps if something happened to me. And I've never figured out why we like each other.

"Come on, Garrett. Get up off that fat ass. Don't you figure you done left Saucerhead twisting in the wind about long enough?"

I did think that. But Saucerhead was getting paid. And he, too, had been told of my misfortune.

I asked, "Where's Playmate? You're supposed to be covering for Playmate."

"Oh, he went off somewhere this morning, before your messenger came. When I got bored I decided . . ."

I sighed. Morley shook his head.

"What?"

I said, "I'm sure you've heard the word 'responsibility' a few times. You have any idea what it means?"

Chances were she did but just didn't care.

"What?" Winger demanded again.

"If you came over here because you're bored, who's minding Playmate's stable so the other crooks don't walk off with everything in sight?" It was really stupid of us to have left all of Kip's inventions unguarded. But the gods of fools had been with us. Word had come that Playmate hadn't suffered any losses. He had wonderful neighbors. "Who's getting paid to make sure that doesn't happen?"

"Other crooks? What do you mean, other crooks? Wiseass. Look, I'm actually here because I'm kind of worried about Play. I thought he was going off to meet you. I figured he'd come back when he heard you wimped out on account of you got a couple of bruises and a scrape."

I said, "Well, I've had all the fun here that I can take. I'm going home."

It took me nearly a minute to get out of my chair. Then I couldn't stand up straight. "Guess I'll have to look on the bright side." I looked left. I looked right. "So where the hell is it?

"Winger, for heaven's sake, go take care of that damned stable." I had visions of footpads absconding with my own personal three-wheel. "And don't give me any of that crap about I'm picking on you because you're a woman. I'm picking on you because somebody hired you to do a job and you're just letting it slide. Again."

"Gods. Somebody get this man a drink. He's gone totally cranky."

36

Singe and Dean both awaited me on the stoop. The old man came down the steps to help me make the climb.

Winger had been right. A little exercise had loosened me up. But hardly enough. I still moved like somebody twice my age, suffering from rheumatism. I'd begun to worry that the ratmen might have done me some internal damage.

Once I'd eaten and downed a quart of Dean's medicinal tea, though, I no longer felt like we needed to send for a witch doctor.

With Singe's help Dean moved a padded chair from the small front room into the Dead Man's room. I occupied it, prepared to discuss business. Instead, I went to sleep. I stayed that way a long time. When I awakened Dean was there with more food and fresh tea. Singe fluttered about nervously.

We find ourselves facing a disquieting development. Mr. Playmate has disappeared.

"No. I didn't want to hear that." I don't like losing a client. That means I have to work three times as hard. Usually for no pay.

Miss Winger sent word to the effect that he has not yet surfaced. I took the liberty of sending Dean to Mr. Dotes with an appeal that he send a few men to support Miss Winger. This would seem an opportune time for raiders to try scooping up Cypres Prose's inventions.

"It would, wouldn't it? And it's Mrs. Winger. She's got a husband and a couple of kids she abandoned, somewhere out in the country."

*The good news is, an hour ago a messenger delivered a
letter from Reliance. It was a bit formal, stiff, and strained,
but he renounced all further interest in Miss Pular.*

"Hear that, Singe? You can go outside without worrying
about the bad guys. . . ."

*Reliance cannot, and does not, guarantee the good behav-
ior of all ratmen, Garrett. Call it a weasel clause if you like,
but he did advise us that he is not able to control the actions
of some of the younger ratmen. He denounced a certain
John Stretch in particular.*

"To be expected, I guess. We're still better off than we
were. I can't imagine too many of those youngsters being
crazy enough to want to get the Outfit after their tails."

*The young often cannot connect cause and effect, Garrett.
You see stupid behavior on the street every day. It will take
only one fool who believes he can outwit Reliance and the
Outfit to ruin Miss Pular's prospects.*

"I'm pretty sure Miss Pular is bright enough to outwit
any of her kind who might be stupid enough to come
after her."

Indeed.

Singe preened.

*But she will have to remain alert and ready for trouble
for some time to come. Until the rat tribes acclimate themselves to the new situation. Reliance's letter is there before
you. I asked Dean to leave it when he finished reading it
to me.*

His mention of the letter was a hint that I should read
it. I did so, wondering who had written it. I'd never heard
of a ratman who could read or write.

"I'd say this is less than a total victory for Singe."

That is correct.

Singe asked, "What is wrong?"

"The way Reliance states this, he isn't just giving up his
claims on you, he's telling us you don't have any more
claims on the community of the ratpeople. He won't let
you."

Singe thought for a while. Then, "Please explain more.
In case I do not understand correctly."

"He's exiled you from your people. You know exile?"

She nodded. "He's basically saying that since you won't play by his rules he isn't going to let you have anything to do with your own people. I guess you'll have to decide if that's a price you're willing to pay."

"I have decided already."

"Are you . . . ?"

"Reliance does not have much longer. And while he does last he cannot be everywhere, keeping me from making contacts I might want. He is too old and too slow. And an enforced exile will compel me to learn my way around the rest of the city more quickly."

"Wow!" I said.

Yes. Perhaps you should marry her after all. In five years you might be a king.

Old Bones let Singe in on the part where he showed that he was impressed. The rest he sent only to me. One of his poor excuses for a joke.

Garrett. Miss Pular. You will have to pick up Mr. Play-mate's trail at his stable. Track him to wherever his hidden demons have taken him. You might search the boy's work-shop. It is conceivable that Mr. Playmate found something there that led him to believe he could find the boy on his own.

Actually a notion that had occurred to me when first I'd heard that he was still missing.

I said, "Excellent thinking, Old Bones. I see only one problem with the scheme. I'm so beat-up I can hardly move. At my best speed today I can grow a foot-long beard faster than I can make it to the river."

A difficulty anticipated and overcome. In my communica-tions with Mr. Dotes I arranged for you to be transported wherever Miss Pular's nose leads her.

"Who's going to pay for all of this? We've got Saucer-head out there somewhere getting gray. We've got Singe and Winger working. We've got who knows how many of Morley's gang backing up Winger. Where's the money com-ing from? Kayne Prose don't have a pot to pee in. Her kids don't seem to be producing. Playmate isn't much better off than Kayne. Anytime he gets two extra coppers to rub to-gether he gives one of them away."

*You are going to pay for it. As an advance cut out of
your share of that lake of gold you see yourself tapping in
the future.*

"What? Are you digging around in my head again?"
There was entirely too much of that stuff going on around
here lately.

The outbreak of warfare amongst the pixies prevented
me from going off on a rant.

The Goddamn Parrot wanted a part of this action. He
started hooting and hollering and cursing the pixies.

I believe your help has arrived.

37

Somebody knocked on the door with a battering ram. Plaster dust fell all over the house. The pounding didn't stop. Dean came roaring out of the kitchen armed with a cleaver, ready to offer somebody some advanced training in etiquette. He beat me to the door. He was in such an evil temper that he opened the door without first using the peephole.

"Gah!"

Who would've thought a man that old could jump that far? And backward at that, while inscribing sagas on the air with the edge of his lightning cleaver.

I caught him "Hey! Maybe you want to settle down. Before you damage the woodwork. It can't be all that bad."

"I'm all right," Dean insisted right away. "They just caught me by surprise."

An odor wafted in through the open doorway, like the southern extremity of a northbound skunk or, more likely, the last thing you smell when you meet up with one of the big flesh-eating thunder lizards out in the woods. It was bad breath on an epic scale. I hadn't encountered it in a long time but I knew it of old. Its provenance was just coming back to me when I got up to the door and leaned out just in time to get the full benefit of the exhalations of a pair of humongous creatures who'd bent down to peer into my house.

These boys both fell out of the ugly tree at a young age, hitting every damned branch on the way down. Then their mommas whupped them with an ugly stick and fed them

ugly soup every day of their lives. They were *Uh-glee*, with
a couple of capital double-ugs.

"Doris. Marsha. How're you fellas doing?"

Doris and Marsha Rose were two of three brothers who
insisted they were triplets born of different mothers. Doris
and Marsha have a greenish cast and stand twenty feet tall.
They have teeth that stick out all which way. One is cross-
eyed and one is walleyed but I can't keep that straight.
Sometimes they trade off. They're grolls, a seldom-seen result of what can happen when giants and trolls fall in love.
Doris and Marsha aren't very bright. But they don't have
to be. They're so big hardly anything else matters.

"We're all doing marvellously, actually," a small voice
piped. Of course. The grolls seldom went anywhere without
the third triplet, Dojango, who, being a half-wit, was the
brains of the family.

Dojango Rose isn't much over five feet tall. Well, taller
than Bic Gonlit, so maybe he's five and a half. He's indistinguishable from a thousand other weasel-eyed, furtive little grifters on the streets of TunFaire. He'd have no trouble
passing for human if he wanted, though he can't be more
than one-eighth human in reality. In some fashion he's dis-
tantly related to Morley Dotes. Morley tosses snippets of
work his way when finesse and a low profile aren't critical
components in the grand scheme.

I descended the front steps amidst booming greetings
from the larger brethren and the worst carrying-on by the
pixies since their own arrival. I barely noticed. Already
their hell-raising was becoming a commonplace, part of the
background noise of the city. Seldom is TunFaire completely quiet.

Dojango Rose had himself in harness between the shafts
of Kip Prose's two-wheeler man-hauling cart. He grinned.
"Bet this's something you never thought you'd see,
actually."

"Actually. You really think you can haul that thing
around town with somebody in it?" Dojango seemed to
have gone a few rounds with consumption since last I'd
seen him. He looked lucky to be able to shift himself.

Based on prior experience chances were good he had his brothers carrying him most of the time.

"I am kind of counting on my brothers to help, actually," Rose admitted. "But there's more to me than you think, actually."

"Actually." Dojango Rose had some annoying verbal tics. "There just about has to be. Hey! Knock it off! Let her go."

Doris unpinched thumb and forefinger. A pixie buzzed away in dazed, staggering flight.

Amazing. Some people will respond automatically to any loud, commanding voice.

"Ah, Garrett, I was just—"

"I know what you was just." I climbed into the cart, every muscle arguing back. "Save it for the villains. We're liable to run into some. Godsdammit!"

There I was in the street about a thousand steps downhill from my front door and I hadn't brought anything out with me. . . . Dean and Singe materialized, each with arms filled. They clattered down the steps. Singe dumped her load into my lap. That consisted of enough instruments of mayhem for me to start up my own small army.

Singe and Dean stayed busy around the back of the cart for a while, with trips into the house and outside again. Then the old man headed back up the steps. Eventually, Singe came up beside me. "We are ready to travel." She tossed Dean a cheerful wave. Dean returned the gesture.

She had outstubborned him and overcome his prejudice by force of personality. Singe was, indeed, a wonder girl.

"What were you doing back there?"

"Storing provisions. You do not plan your travels properly. Especially in the area of food. So Dean and I fixed us something to take along."

While I was digesting that Dojango suddenly called out, "Where to, boss?"

38

There were subtle signs that some parts of Playmate's place had been searched. I asked Winger, "Has anybody been in here since you took over? Since Playmate wandered off?"

"No."

"You're sure?"

"Absolutely." She was irked. I was daring to question her faithfulness to her commission.

"I didn't think so. So *you* have to quit going through Playmate's stuff." While she sputtered I took a lamp into Kip's workshop. At first glance the only change there was the absence of the cart I'd ridden over here. Behind one or another of the grolls, mostly. As I'd anticipated.

Three blocks from my house Dojango was already trying to mooch a ride.

With Doris or Marsha pulling the cart, though, there were problems. Problems which sprang from their size. Neither could fit between the cart's long shafts. So whichever one was on the job dragged the cart along one-handed. The ride became a series of wild jerks as the groll swung his arms.

Then there was the problem of height. The grolls' hands were eight feet off the ground when they stood up straight. When they pulled the cart I ended up lying on my back.

But we had arrived at Playmate's stable. Marsha had volunteered to carry me around in his arms when he saw how much trouble I had levering my stiff old bones out of the cart. "I'd take you up on it, too," I told him. "Except for the fact that you're too tall to go anywhere inside here."

That was one big problem with being those two guys. Hardly any structure in Tun-Faire was tall enough to accommodate them.

So I limped a lot and leaned on things. I was crabby. I snarled at people for no good reason. And I didn't find a single clue as to where Playmate had gone. But I did have Singe. She'd located Playmate's newest track and was ready to move out on it long before I finished my rounds of Playmate's digs. I swore there had to be something incriminating somewhere. Something to tie him into the evil equine empire.

I kept returning to Kip's workshop, convinced that there was something I was overlooking. There was nothing missing and nothing wrong there but something deep inside me kept telling me to watch out for something.

I never did figure out what it was. But I trusted my hunch. I told Morley's associates to keep a close eye on Kip's junk. "Something here has something to do with what's going on. I don't know what it is yet. So I don't want you to let anybody in. Don't let anybody touch anything. And in particular, don't let Winger touch anything. But otherwise, consider her to be in charge."

I gave Winger a big grin and a glimpse of the old raised eyebrow trick.

Winger gave me the finger.

"Promises, promises."

That earned me a matched set of flying fingers.

39

Singe was having trouble concentrating. Dojango kept distracting her. He wouldn't shut up. Which was a habit of his that I'd forgotten. Kind of the way you forget how much a broken bone hurts until the next time you bust one.

I explained, on three separate occasions, how difficult it was for Singe to follow a trace as old as Playmate's, to explain that she had to concentrate all her attention on the task at hand.

"Oh, yeah. Oh, yeah. I understand, Garrett, actually." And thirty seconds later it would be, "This's just like the time me and Doris and Marsha was running the bag for Eddie the Gimp, actually. If we wasn't right on top of what we was doing every second . . ."

I sent a look of appeal up toward Doris, whose turn it was to walk beside the cart. But it was too dark out for him to notice. So I asked, "Doris. How the hell do I get your little brother to shut up?"

"Huh?"

I got ready to groan.

"I don't know. I just shut him out. Is he running off at the mouth again?"

"Still. I can't get him to stay quiet for twenty seconds straight. He's driving me crazy and he's making it impossible for Singe to keep her mind on her work." I suffered a moment of inspiration. "If we don't pull this thing off, if we don't find this guy, we blow the job. Which means that none of us will get paid."

"Dojango, shut the fuck up. You even cough, I'm gonna

slug you." Doris waved a fist about the size of a bull's head in his brother's face. "Where we gonna put him when I do, Garrett? 'Cause I'm guaranteed gonna gotta do it on account of he can't even keep his mouth shut when he's asleep."

"He managed to shut up when he had to that time we all went to the Cantard."

"Yeah. But like they say, long ago and far away. And times change."

They do indeed. I'd just gotten more words out of one of the grolls than I'd heard before in all the years I'd known them.

Dojango couldn't help observing, "Actually, it ain't really polite to be talking about somebody like they ain't even there when you—"

Bop!

Doris's blow was almost casual. Dojango rocked and wilted. His brother scooped him up and carried him like a baby.

I asked, "Wasn't that a little harsh?"

"He ought to be getting used to it, Garrett. Actually." Doris grinned broadly. Moonlight glistened off his snaggle teeth. "This ain't the first time his mouth has caused us some trouble."

"Amen, brother," Marsha said from up front. "We gotta love the guy on account of he's family, but sometimes . . . If it wasn't for his connection with Cousin Morley . . ."

"Guys, we all have relatives like that. I've got a great-uncle Medford that somebody should've poisoned a hundred years ago."

Singe stopped. "You are quite right about Medford Shale, Garrett." Great-uncle Medford had figured prominently in the case where I'd first made Singe's acquaintance. "Just as you were right about me needing no distractions if I am to follow this trail. Perhaps I can have Doris knock you out, then have Marsha knock Doris out, then pray that a building collapses on Marsha."

"Or we could all take a hint and save the chatter till later."

"You could do that. But I am willing to bet that none of you are able."

Was it Mama Garrett's boy who'd said that this ratgirl desperately needed some self-confidence? She sure didn't lack for it in this crowd.

Ten minutes later, I called, "Singe, I know where we're going." We were headed for the Prose homestead. Maybe Playmate's luck had changed. Or, from his point of view, maybe he had given in to temptation. "We're headed for the boy's mother's flat."

"All right. If you think so. If you want to go there and wait for me, go ahead. I would prefer to stick to the trail. That will reveal if there were other stops he made along the way."

A gentle admonition from the expert. I decided to heed it. The girl had a point. Suppose Playmate was headed for Kayne Prose's place but never made it there?

40

He did make it. But he'd gone away again. Singe explained that to me before I ever went upstairs and found a very frightened Cassie Doap holed up behind a barricaded door, refusing to open up for anybody.

· "Cassie, come on. This's Garrett. The man Playmate hired to find your brother Kip. Now Playmate's disappeared and I'm trying to track him down, too." I hoped he turned up soon. My body was doing a lot of aching. "He came here about . . ." I looked at Singe, whispered, "How long ago?"

"This morning."

"He came here this morning. Why was that? Where did he go from here?"

Cassie kept telling us to go away. She was terrified. But Singe could detect no odors that would justify such a strong response. And none of the neighbors showed any curiosity, which suggested that great dramas by Cassie Doap were not at all uncommon.

I recalled Rhafi telling me that Cassie was an actress. She put on characters like clothing. Maybe she was overacting now.

I wished I had one of my human lady friends along. Particularly Tinnie Tate of the shoemaking Tates. That professional redhead would know how to manage a mere blonde. Tinnie was an accomplished actress herself. At least where the manipulation of guys named Garrett was concerned.

Singe did make a few calming remarks, loudly enough to be heard through the door, while I tried to talk Cassie out of her hysteria. Singe's comments were kind of childish but they had their effect. At some point Cassie decided to open the door a crack to see who was out there in the hallway with me.

I don't know why my having a ratgirl along should've been reassuring, but it was enough so that Cassie decided she'd talk to us. She asked, "What do you want to know, Mr. Garrett?"

My heart broke. That delectable young woman had called me "mister." I was nothing but a "mister." I wasn't on her list of prospects.

It's a cruel world indeed.

Probably just as well, though. Cassie was the kind of woman Mom warned me against. One goofier than me.

"Where's Playmate, Cassie?"

"I don't know. He went to find my mom."

All right. That made sense. Maybe. To her.

She was definitely afraid, for real. She had referred to her mother as Mom. She'd always called her Kayne before. "And why did he do that, Cassie? Was she in trouble?"

"I don't know. She went to find Rhafi when he didn't come home. Then she didn't come home. So I went and got Playmate. And he decided to go looking for both of them. . . ."

Without bothering to inform me. Or even Winger. Who hadn't mentioned Cassie. Which probably meant that Winger wasn't paying attention to what she was supposed to be doing.

"Just as an aside, did you see a tall blond woman at Playmate's stable?"

"No. Is that important?"

"Probably not. All right. Let's go back. Rhafi disappeared? What's the story on that?"

"That man you had watching Bic Gonlit. Rhafi was hanging around with him. Covering for him when he had to go off. Like that. Then Rhafi just disappeared. While that man was away getting them something to eat. He told us when Kayne and me went to find Rhafi on account of Rhafi was supposed to start a new job today. It's getting really hard to find somebody who'll give him a chance anymore. Kayne really didn't want him to screw it up this time."

Now that she'd decided to trust me Cassie gushed, getting rid of the fear and the tension through a flood of words. She didn't really have much to say except that Rhafi had disappeared, then Kayne had gone looking for him while sending her to tell Playmate. Then Playmate had gone after Kayne. And *he* hadn't been seen since. And now Cassie was firmly convinced that the forces of darkness would come for her soon.

"You get back inside and barricade your door again. I'll take care of it." I hoped. I'd done somewhat less than take care of things on several occasions lately.

41

"You still have a trail?" I asked Singe.

"Yes. Getting better than it was."

I grunted. I didn't try to shortcut this time, though I expected the track to lead us straight to Saucerhead.

Which it did. More or less. Though Tharpe wasn't at his post.

I didn't even ask. I just left Singe to work her wonders.

"It is not entirely clear but it seems that Mr. Tharpe accompanied Mr. Playmate. Or he followed him within a very short time."

"And they went over to that ugly yellow building, right?"

"They were headed in that direction when they left here."

That was Singe. Making no assumptions.

"Can you detect any other odors here? That you might've noticed in that place we just visited?"

"That blond woman was here earlier today. And maybe others who left traces in that building. The odors are very faint."

"But there's nothing to contradict the story Cassie told us?"

"You do not trust her?"

"I've found that it's best to trust no one completely when I'm working a case. Nobody is ever completely honest with me."

"Truly?"

"Truly. Nobody wants to admit that they're desperate. But they are. Or they wouldn't come to me in the first place. They almost never do until things are out of hand. But that's human nature. You don't want people to know you can't manage your life. You're afraid to look weak."

We walked while Singe and I talked. I was moving more freely now but I still hurt. Doris and Marsha were doing a wonderful job of keeping their mouths shut. Dojango was still napping. He was in the cart.

I had everybody wait in front of the ugly yellow structure while I gave it a careful once-over from outside. The grolls attracted attention wherever they went, of course, but they knew how to discourage gawkers. A growl and a wave of the club each carried, more as decoration than as armament, were enough to discourage most people. For a while.

I wondered if they would use their clubs if pressed. They'd employed them during our visit to the Cantard but they hadn't really wanted to. They were actually gentle people, the Rose triplets. Though the two big ones did get a kick out of panicking people once in a while.

It seemed to me that it might be useful to know what was happening inside Casey's place before I went storming upstairs. "Doris. I need you to hoist me up so I can peek through a window."

Only there wasn't any window.

I stared at the blank brick, tried to visualize the inside of the tenement to see if I'd gotten turned around. I hadn't. So how had I misplaced a window made of glass?

I had Doris put me down. Then I worked my way around the ugly structure. It did have a few unglazed windows, but very few, indicating that it had been erected during the last attempt at establishing a window tax, with the minimum legal number of openings. None of the existing windows were on the fourth floor.

What the hell?

Which was what the place had to be in summer.

"How high can you count?" I asked Doris.

"Garrett, I don't think questions like that are polite."

"You're probably right. But I suspect that I don't much care. Here's what I want. Six minutes after I go in the front door you take your club and knock a hole through the bricks right up there where I was feeling the wall. Don't be shy about it. Haul off and pound a hole right through."

"And then what? When they come to arrest me. Go down fighting? I don't think so."

"Hey. . . !"

"You're a big-time bullshitter, Garrett, but you ain't big-time enough to bullshit me out of knocking somebody's building down."

"All right. All right." The recent outbreak of law and order was getting to be a real pain. "So don't bust a hole through the wall. Just thump on it hard enough to distract whoever's on the other side. Better give me eight minutes to get up there, though. That's a lot of stairs."

Doris grunted, shuffled over to his brother. They muttered at one another, not pleased because whatever happened here would do so in front of witnesses.

The grolls were beginning to attract gawkers who wouldn't run from a growl and a brandished club. Mostly they were youngsters who should've been asleep, but adults would gather, too, if it became obvious that the grolls would have some entertainment value.

"Singe, you come with me." I headed for the entrance to the tenement. That was filled with spectators who wanted to know what was going on. "We're hunting for Kagyars," I told them, which dumbfounded everyone.

The people of TunFaire and Karenta aren't much interested in their own history.

My remark would've melted their spines half a millennium earlier. The Empire was still in place then but was suffering a swift decline because it was being choked to death by fanatic members of the Orthodox Rite. The Kagyars had been members of a gentle, nonviolent heretical cult whose beliefs must've terrified the hierarchy of the established religion. They invested all their energies and all the treasure of the state in a hundred-year campaign to exterminate the Kagyar heresy.

All that horror and cruelty and evil and today not one Karentine in a thousand can tell you what a Kagyar was. Possibly not even one in ten thousand.

42

"What will you do?" Singe asked.

"Knock on the door and see if anybody answers. Whack them over the head if they do." I brandished my headknocker. There was no peephole in Casey's door so he would have to open up in order to respond.

I knocked. Singe looked around nervously. And sniffed. She said, "It's hard to tell but I think they may have gone back downstairs again."

I knocked some more. "Playmate, Rhafi and I did come up and go down before."

Still no answer to my knock.

The building shuddered. Doris was on the job.

Something fell behind the door.

I did a fast picklock job between club strokes. "Get back against the wall," I told Singe. "Squeeze your eyes tight shut." I pushed the door inward, knelt, tripped the rug booby trap. I got the same crackle, pop, and flash. I avoided problems with my hair this time but did get the fuzz crisped off the outside of my forearm. Casey must've adjusted the aim of his sorcerous implement.

A glance across the hallway assured me that was true. The wall was smoking at a site two feet removed from the previous. And the crisped area was significantly larger.

I began to suspect that Casey might not plan to honor our new alliance. And I began to reflect on the fact that this particular silver elf wasn't as reluctant as the others to resort to violence.

"Don't expose yourself yet," I told Singe. "This thing's going to pop a couple more times."

Second try wasn't a charm. As before, the fury of the sorcery was considerably lessened. But its aim had shifted since the first flash. I lost most of my stick and got a mild case of roasted knuckles. The lead from the end of my stick was still liquid when I peeked.

We were collecting witnesses now, the older ones probably thinking about launching a raid as soon as the dangerous people got out of the way.

Doris kept whapping the outside wall. That was sure to attract attention out there. Police attention, eventually.

I told Singe, "We probably won't have much more time." But haste could be painful. Or even lethal.

I got down on the floor and slid my arm in to trip the third flash. It was more feeble than the last time I'd done this, though plenty bright enough to have me seeing spots.

Then I recalled Casey having just hopped over the trigger carpet.

Better safe than sorry.

I hopped.

There were no changes in the room behind the door. Casey had returned his possessions to their appointed places. Every item in the place looked precisely positioned.

I had a suspicion that Deal Relway's place would be very much like this.

I looked at the window that wasn't there on the outside of the building. The view it presented was impossible. What it should have shown was the wall of the building next door. Instead, I found myself looking down into the street out front.

Interesting.

Something thumped behind the closed curtain of Casey's bedroom.

"Come in and close the door," I told Singe. "Keep an eye on this window. Look for anybody who might belong to the Guard. Or who just gives you the feeling that they might be trouble." I yanked the curtain aside. And said, "Well, hello."

I'd found some of my missing people. Rhafi and his mother. Kayne was unconscious. So was Rhafi, but he was restless. Neither had a stitch on. Rhafi's clothing lay on the floor,

as though discarded by someone undressing in a hurry. Nowhere could I find anything that looked like it might have
come off Kayne.

I tried not to get distracted by the still life.

"Hey, Singe. You think you could track somebody's
clothes if somebody else was wearing them?"

She stepped over where she could see what I saw. "My."
She kept looking back and forth between the window and
the naked people. "Well." And, "Can you wake them up?"

I was trying to do that already. I wasn't having any luck.
I tried to avoid any expression as Singe took her opportunity to inform herself of the nature of human bodies.

"Would you consider the female attractive?" she asked.

With any other woman I know I'd have to consider that
a trick or loaded question. Singe, I guessed, actually wanted
to know. "Yes, she is. Especially considering her age and
the fact that she's borne three children."

Singe becomes horrified whenever she contemplates the
size of human babies. Her people have babies in litters of
up to eight, the aggregate weight usually being less than
that of one human newborn.

"And the male? Is he attractive?"

"Not to me. But that's partly because I know him. He
could be attractive to some women." Nature appeared to
have blessed Rhafi in one respect. I returned to my question. "Could you track the woman's clothing? I think our
villain might've used it to disguise himself."

Singe eyed Rhafi dubiously, looked at me in mild alarm,
then shifted her attention to the window. She thought. I
kept trying to waken Kayne and her son.

It became obvious that they were under some kind of
enchantment that I couldn't penetrate.

After several minutes of silence, Singe told me, "I can
follow the horses again."

"Meaning?"

"Following the clothing would be extremely difficult. But
I will have no trouble following Mr. Playmate and Mr.
Tharpe. Who would have been with or who would have
been following what they believed to be this woman." She
eyed Rhafi again, growing more uneasy with what she saw.

I opened my mouth to ask a question, then realized that I'd been outreasoned by a ratgirl. A ratgirl who had other things on her mind.

Rhafi was getting more of her eye time than that window was.

Casey had spun the tables on me.

He needed help to get to Kip. He'd told me so. But he didn't want to be anybody's partner. So he became Kayne Prose and lured Playmate and Saucerhead into going where he wanted, where they would, doubtless, fight like lions to defend the lovely Kayne from the villainous silver elves.

"Garrett! Something's happening!"

Dopey me, I glanced at Rhafi first, figuring maybe he was having a happy dream. But nothing to startle Singe was happening there.

"What?"

"The window. It keeps showing different things."

I stepped over.

She was right. It kept alternating between four different live scenes. "Did you touch it? Did you do anything?"

"No! I was over here, looking at . . . I never thought they were so big. . . . I *was* picking at the colored spots on this strange gray stone." She shoved a paw at me. Her whiskers were way back. But she just had to take another look at Rhafi.

I took the "stone." A number of not dissimilar items were scattered around the room. But not nearly so many as there had been during my previous visit. Which suggested that Casey might have taken some with him.

Those elves we'd chased, who'd knocked me out over and over, had used some small fetish or amulet or whatnot to do so. Maybe all those things were different magical devices.

Which got me thinking. We had a small collection back at the house, from that last place where Kip's kidnappers knocked us down, plus those I'd taken away from Rhafi. Should they stay there, dangerously near my partner, when we didn't know their capabilities? Might it not be more useful to surrender them to Colonel Block? That might earn me some obligation points. And might even be a service to the Crown. If these silver elves actually were a sorcerous threat from foreign lands.

Singe made a squealing sound that might have been surprise, fright, dismay, or all three together. I glanced into the other room.

I asked Singe the same question. "Did you touch it? Did you do anything?"

Singe backed out of the room but couldn't stop staring until I closed the curtain. I chuckled but didn't pursue the subject. I did suspect that in future she'd be less inclined toward romantic experimentation.

I thought it might be a good idea to gather up everything of potential interest to the people Block represented because minutes after Singe and I left it, Casey's place was going to get picked clean.

"Garrett?"

"Uhm?"

"You said tell you if I saw anything interesting?"

"You found Rhafi interesting, did you?"

"Not that." Her tone put me in my place for my having my mind in the gutter. "In the window."

I saw what she meant when the view of the street out front came up.

Three silver elves had taken station across the way. They weren't out in traffic but, even so, you'd think people dressed that weird would attract some notice. That they attracted none whatsoever told me that some sort of enchantment concealed them from passersby but couldn't fool the window's eye.

A hint of a flicker of afterimage indicated that they were pretending to be women. Women who didn't know their ways around. One stared at something in her hand as she swung her partially extended arm right and left.

"We did something to attract Casey's enemies," I said. "And they got here fast. But they still don't quite know where to find him. We'd better get out of here while we can." I squinted at the window when the street view came back up. Did those elves really have waists and breasts? That was a fine crop of nubbins, to be sure, but damned if it didn't look like *something* was there, putting a little appeal into those elegant silver lines.

43

The silver elves weren't visible anywhere when Singe and I reached the street. I felt them vaguely, though, in the back of my mind.

"Can you smell anything?"

"Something cold. . . . Like what I smelled when we were tracking that boy. But not quite the same."

"I think that's because this's a different bunch of elves. We have some kind of pyramid here. There's one guy, Casey, who's hunting two guys, Lastyr and Noodiss, because they're wanted for unspecified crimes. Then we have these three elves, evidently all female. In times past they raided Playmate's stable and the Prose flat, trying to lay hands on Kip. Then we have the four who actually did capture Kip. Unless Casey was lying—and his lips weren't moving at the time, on account of he doesn't have any— these people are all involved in criminal enterprises of some sort."

We were moving away from the ugly yellow structure, Singe picking the way, me limping along in her wake lugging a sack filled with trinkets rescued from Casey's digs. I nodded to Doris and Marsha as I passed. I felt the invisible elves start moving behind me.

Singe observed, "Reliance is involved in criminal enterprises. But a lot of his activities don't appear to be morally questionable."

Though she hadn't stated it perfectly I was proud that Singe could reason to that level. "True. The law isn't always about what's right. Or wrong. A lot of times it's about somebody being guaranteed an advantage over somebody else. And that's human nature. That's the nature of any sentient species, I think. Damn! Those invisible people really are moving back there. I get the feeling that they're crossing to Casey's place."

I hoped that was what they were doing, rather than falling in behind us.

They were sure to walk in on some excitement if they went upstairs. I hoped they'd find Casey's place crawling with scavengers and voyeurs.

I said, "I think it might be a good idea if we checked back to see how Rhafi and Kayne are doing, later." Those two could end up in deep trouble if that sleep spell didn't wear off.

"Shush. I need to concentrate."

So now it was me who was the distraction. The triplets weren't because they were keeping their distance, pretending they weren't with me. Good on whichever one of them thought of that. But I needed to toss my swag bag into the cart with Dojango. I wasn't about to carry it forever.

My aches and pains had receded somewhat but they continued to hamper me. I limped and gimped and had no sense of humor at all. I couldn't even work myself into a state of amusement over Singe's recent discombobulation. And that was pretty damned funny. It could become a classic after a few retellings polished it up.

When our path took us around a corner, thus taking us out of sight of any eyes tagging along behind, I halted. I didn't move until Doris and Marsha appeared.

I tossed my swag bag into Dojango's lap. The results were satisfactory. Rose's enthusiastic barking demonstrated that he had been faking unconsciousness.

I left him to his brothers. Singe and I traveled on into the night, me limping and groaning and demonstrating grand vigor in protesting my determination to find a new way to make a living.

"Where in hell are we going?" I muttered. We'd been walking for hours. It was the middle of the night. I felt every step in every muscle and every joint. We were way up north, passing through neighborhoods where real elves roamed. Singe and I drew stares from folks curious about whether we were a couple. I could've told them that we were a couple of idiots.

This was dangerous country. But if we stuck to the main thoroughfare, the Grand Avenue, we should be all right, partly because it was customarily safe ground, partly because Doris and Marsha were ambling along with us, their clubs dragging the cobblestones and their knuckles threatening to get down there soon.

"I am following the trail, Garrett. I am not creating it." Singe was getting cranky, too. Probably needed to get some food in her.

"This is why I hate working. Once you get started you can't just knock off when you feel like it and have a couple of beers. You've got to keep going until you drop. Why don't you eat one of your sandwiches?"

Singe immediately went to the back of the cart and dug out several. "If it makes you feel better knowing, we are much closer than we were. Their scent is almost fresh. They are less than three hours ahead."

Every silver lining has a cloud.

"That's the godsdamned gate up there!" I grumbled, glaring at an island of light in the far distance. "Please don't tell me they left town."

"All right." Singe sounded troubled. And she should. For ratpeople TunFaire's outer wall constitutes the edge of the world. Go past it and you fall off into the misty void.

The situation wasn't much better for me. I don't like notcity. I don't go outside often. When I do I prefer to visit some rich man's estate, where I can be comfortable while I take care of business. I get back to town as fast as I can.

If we kept going this general direction for a few hours we could drop in on the Contague estate.

Although I know better intellectually, emotionally I feel like the deadly wilderness is clamoring at the city gate, all carnivorous or poisonous plants and animals, most of them bigger and faster than me, while the air is so full of maneating bugs that you don't dare breathe deep. In reality, most of the countryside near TunFaire is well tamed. If it wasn't it wouldn't be able to feed the city. The exceptions are some bits unsuited for exploitation or which the wealthy and powerful have set aside as hunting reserves or whatnot. The rare incursions of thunder lizards, mammoths, or even bears or giant ground sloths, are just that: rare. But they sure do get talked about plenty.

Marsha said, "We maybe need to take a sleep break first if we're really going to go out there, Garrett."

He had a point. A good point. Or, at least, a damned good excuse for us not to go wandering around the wilderness in the dark. Even if we were only a few hours behind our friends.

44

Wilderness is relative. Before sunrise we were in wild country compared to where I live. But we were in a carefully tamed and only mildly unkempt park compared to the places where I fought my share of the war.

Of course, this was the worst nightmare wilderness Singe had ever seen. She couldn't take ten steps without stopping to sniff the morning air for the warning stench of approaching monsters. I kept after her to move faster. "The quicker we get there the quicker we get it over with and the quicker we get back to town. You don't want to spend the night out here, do you?" But instinct is hard to overcome. I prove that every time I get too close to Belinda Contague. "Besides, the grolls can handle anything we're likely to meet."

Dojango had been yakking all morning, inconsequentialities. Typical of him, actually. So much so that nobody paid him the least attention. Though Doris did drag him out of the cart and have him pull it as one way of slowing his jaw down.

"Wait a minute," I said. "What was that?"

Because Dojango's mouth runs with no real connection to his brain he just chomped air for a minute. What might he have said that could interest me? He hadn't been listening. Then he went into mild shock because somebody *was* interested in something that he'd said. "Uh, I don't remember, actually."

"About the thing you saw in the sky."

"Oh. That happened while you were all asleep, actually."

When the time had come we'd all just planted ourselves at streetside, grolls on the flanks, and started snoring. We hadn't been bothered.

Size *does* matter.

Dojango continued, "I decided I'd stand watch on account of all of the rest of you were out like the dead."

He was fibbing. He hadn't been able to sleep because he'd spent all that time snoozing in the cart. It's easy to tell when Dojango is revising history. He forgets to use his favorite word.

"And?"

"And a ball of light came in out of the east, from beyond the river. It went somewhere south of us. It stopped for a while. I could see the glow. Then it came north, slowly, drifting back and forth over Grand Avenue. I had a feeling it was looking for something, actually."

"And it came to a stop up above us?"

"Yeah. After a while it shined a really bright light down on us. And that's all I remember." He shuddered, though. So there was something more.

"What else?"

He didn't want to talk about it but Dojango Rose is incapable of resisting an invitation to speak. "Just a really bad dream where the light lifted me up and took me inside the glow, into a weird, lead-gray place. They did really awful things to me, these weird, shiny little women. This one wouldn't leave my thing alone."

"I see." He'd healed wondrous fast if he'd been tortured. "Something to keep in mind." I did some thinking. Some consideration of the circumstances. I came up with some ideas.

The first time we approached a sizable woodlot which boasted enough tangled undergrowth to suggest that it wasn't used much I had Doris and Marsha carry the cart and its cargo deep inside and camouflage it with branches.

Dojango cried like a baby.

"I guarantee you I don't have a whole lot of sympathy, buddy. Why don't you use your sore feet to make the rest of you mad enough to smack some of those elves around when we catch up with them?"

That bought me a respite. Dojango Rose is a lover, not a fighter. He probably heard his mother calling but couldn't run away as long as his brothers stuck it out.

We passed gated estates. The grolls attracted considerable attention. Most of the guards were friendlier than they might have been had I tried to engage them in conversation on my own. Doris and Marsha make a convincing argument just standing around, leaning on their clubs.

Some of those guards had seen Saucerhead and Playmate go by. But not a one had seen Kayne Prose. Or any other willowy blonde. Tharpe and Playmate had been bickering, according to several witnesses. They were, also, not making very good time. We were still only a few hours behind them despite our pause to enjoy a stone mattress.

"We keep on with this and we're going to find ourselves out in the real country pretty soon," I observed. We were past the truck gardens and wheatfields and starting up the slope into wine country. Ahead the hills started growing up. Fast.

We popped over a ridgeline, me cursing the day Kayne met Kip's pop and, even more bloodily, the day I let myself get into debt to Playmate. "Whoa! There it is. That's perfect."

"There what is?" Dojango asked. I'd stopped. He'd sat down. He had one boot off already.

"That bowl of land down there. Filled with trees. It has a pond in there. You can see the water. Runs down off all these hills. Looks like a great hiding place. Bet you that's where—"

Some sort of flash happened under the trees. A dark brown smoke ring rolled up through the foliage. There was a rumble like a very large troll clearing his throat.

"That was different," Dojango said. He levered his other boot off.

"My guess is, our friends just found the elven sorcerers."

Nobody rushed off to help. Dojango massaged his blisters and distinctly looked like he'd rather head some other direction. Any other direction.

Singe had the sensibilities of a soldier. "If we can see

what is happening down there, then whoever is down there can see what is happening up here."

"Absolutely." I responded by dropping into the shade of a split rail fence. The Rose boys didn't need the whole speech, either. The big ones made themselves as scarce as possible on an open road that ran downhill through a vineyard where the plants were seldom more than hip high. To me. Dojango rolled into a ditch.

A look around showed me a countryside not made for sneaking. The wooded bowl was entirely surrounded by vineyards. I could cover some ground on hands and knees amongst the vines but there wasn't a whole lot of cover for guys twenty feet tall.

And there were people out working the vineyards. Some not that far from us, eyeing us askance because of our odd behavior. Before long most of the workers began to amble downhill to see what was going on.

"There's our cue, people. Look like you've got grape skins between your toes."

Dojango began to whine in earnest. Once out of his boots his feet had swollen. He couldn't get them back on.

It was real. We'd have to leave him behind. Which was just as well, actually. Dojango has a talent for screwing things up by getting underfoot when times begin to get exciting.

I told him, "We'll pick you up on the way back."

He didn't act like his feelings were hurt.

45

Most of the vineyard workers reached the wood well before we did. Which was fine by me. Because something unpleasant was going on in amongst the trees. Something flashy, noisy, then smoky. Another doughnut of brown smoke rolled up out of the trees.

The vineyard people decided they wanted no part of that. They went scooting right back up the hills. Not a one was interested in wasting valuable running time gawking at my odd company.

At a guess I'd say people in the area had had bad experiences down there before.

Once you penetrated the dozen yards of dense brush and brambles on the outer perimeter of the wood you found yourself in a perfectly groomed, parklike grove. Without undergrowth. With grass almost like a lawn. With a pond an acre in size, somewhat off center to the west. And with a big silver discus thing smack in the middle, standing eight feet above the grass on spindly metal legs. A flimsy ladder rose from the grass to an opening in the disk's belly. A silver elf lay at the foot of that, unconscious or dead. Likewise, one Saucerhead Tharpe, right hand gripping the elf's ankle, whose scattered attitude suggested that he'd been dragged back out of the discus.

I saw nothing to explain the brown smoke rings, nor all the racket we'd heard while we were coming down the hill.

The wood was perfectly still now. Not a bird had a word to say. Not a bug sang one bar to his ladylove. A few leaves did stir in the breeze but they kept their voices down. The only sounds to be heard were the distant, excited voices of vineyard workers who had decided they were far enough away to slow down and gossip.

When I stopped and counted them up in my head I doubted that there'd been more than a dozen workers, total.

We four froze with the moment, some listening, some sniffing. I turned slowly, trying to get a direction for the sense of presence I'd begun to feel.

I whispered to Singe, "The Casey creature is here in the grove somewhere. Can you scent him?"

"The odors here are very strange, Garrett. I am confused. I do scent something that might be Casey but I cannot locate him."

A breeze stirred the leaves and branches. My eye kept going to an oddity of shadow that didn't stir with everything else. I examined it from the corners of my eyes. I squinted, right and left and direct. I moved several times so I could try everything from a variety of angles. Several times the dance of bright sunlight and deep leaf shadow made me think that I had glimpsed something that might have been Kayne Prose crumpled up beside a stump, trapped inside something like a heat shimmer. When I concentrated I discovered a shadow being cast onto the ground by something not apparent to the naked eye.

I looked left and right. Nothing told me why the vineyard hands had run for it. Nothing told me where Playmate might be now. Nothing indicated the current whereabouts of the three silver elves not sprawled underneath their silvery discus. Nothing told me much of anything.

I drifted toward the shadow that shouldn't have been, beckoning Marsha to follow, laying a finger to my lips. I got a few more glimpses of Kayne Prose. She didn't appear to be awake. The invisibility spell keeping her unseen was sputtering and maybe needed a little punching up from somebody who'd had enough schooling to know what they were doing.

The spell did a whole lot of nothing to fool my sense of touch.

I got Marsha down on his knees, guided his hands.

"That's his head. You hang on in case he wakes up. If he does, let him know who's in control. Without killing him, if possible."

"Gotcha."

I began the task of frisking and disrobing a body I couldn't see. The stripping part didn't go well at all.

A totally bedraggled imitation Kayne Prose materialized suddenly. In the same moment Singe said, "Gleep! Where did Garrett go?"

Inasmuch as I had not gone anywhere I gazed with suspicion at the small gray fetish I'd just taken off Casey. "Singe. Come over here." When she arrived I put the device into her paw. She vanished. I assume I reappeared. "Now you're invisible. Hang on to that. It might come in handy."

"Nobody can see me? Whoo! Ha-ha! What I could do with this!"

"What couldn't we all do? Why don't you sneak over there and see if Saucerhead is still breathing?" I had a recollection of having turned up horizontal myself a few times after running into these elves. Only they hadn't knocked themselves out, too, those times.

I couldn't see Singe but she did still cast some shadow when she stepped into the light. She said, "Mr. Playmate must have climbed up the ladder."

"Singe! Don't go in there!"

My last two words even I couldn't hear over the *Crump!* as a sudden ring of brown smoke blew down off the bottom of the discus. The smoke hit the ground, ricocheted back upward, into the sky. It seemed much less substantial than had the earlier clouds.

"Singe? You all right?"

A ratlike squeak resolved itself into, "Garrett? Can you hear me? I cannot hear right now. But otherwise I am all right. I am going to finish climbing the ladder now."

"You damned fool! That's what just—"

"I found Mr. Playmate. He is right inside here. Out cold. Lying on a metal floor with two more elves. One has a broken arm. At least it is bent the wrong way."

Meanwhile, on the ground, I was continuing to make sure that Casey and the other unconscious elf wouldn't be able to go anywhere when they woke up. "Let's see if we can't get this costume off this one." I'd given up trying to strip Casey. And to Singe, "That's a good job, Singe. Don't go wandering around in there. Singe?"

She didn't respond.

The girl was getting a little *too* sure of herself. "Would one of you guys reach up in there and drag Playmate out?"

Doris had taken over trying to get Casey's silver suit off him so Marsha crawled under the discus. It was a tight fit. He ended up twisting himself around so he was seated on the grass, his head and shoulders inside the opening. "Gosh, Garrett, it's weird in here." A moment later he dropped an elf.

"Hey! You damned near hit me with that." I was having no luck stripping the elf who had fallen with Saucerhead. The new arrival didn't look like he'd be any easier.

"Here comes the one with the broken arm. You might want to take him so he don't get hurt any worse."

I jumped up just in time to grab the body Marsha handed down.

The elf weighed hardly anything at all.

"Hey, Garrett! Look at this."

I turned. Doris was standing up, his top half up in the foliage. He seemed to be looking back up the hill that we had descended to get to this adventure. I shed my burden, skipped a dozen yards to a point where I could see the hillside myself.

I thought the vineyard workers would be up to something. But they were just making tracks.

Instead, Dojango was in deep sludge. But he hadn't noticed yet.

46

It was kind of funny, actually, because he didn't see it coming until after Doris and I began watching. He was, probably, just sitting there throwing pebbles at grasshoppers and congratulating himself on having gotten out of all the work when he spotted the glowing balls. By that time they'd bracketed him and were descending.

Doris said, "Maybe he didn't make up all that shit about them pulling him inside and doing something to him. They sure didn't have no trouble finding him again, did they? Even after we ditched that cart and all that magical stuff."

"An excellent observation, brother." I watched Dojango jump up, try to run in several directions, all of which turned out to be blocked as soon as he chose them. He never stopped trying though, like a squirrel in a box trap. While prancing on stones because his tender feet were bare.

I noted that the vineyard workers were trying to make themselves seem scarce while they watched, too.

Once the balls of light were on the ground they faded to become three eggs of lead-gray metal with little in the way of exterior features.

I said, "We can probably expect their company in a few minutes. We'd better roll up our sleeves and get ready." Playmate came flopping down out of the discus. Marsha started dragging him away. I said, "Hide all these people in the woods. Under the brush, maybe. Then get yourselves out of sight. Where is that girl?" I hopped over the foot of the ladder. "Singe!"

Singe didn't respond.

I said, "On second thought, leave Saucerhead and Play-mate lying out in the open. This guy, too." I used a toe to nudge the silver elf lying nearest the ladder. "That'll give them something to focus on. So they'll maybe overlook the rest of us. You guys hide. Take whatever steps seem appropriate."

Gritting my teeth, I reached out and touched the metal ladder. Quick and cautious, using just the tip of one finger.

Nothing happened.

Not even a hint of brown smoke.

47

The ladder took me up into a small metal room that was maybe ten feet across. Its ceiling was five feet high. I had to move in a stoop that started my back aching in moments. At its extremities the room's floor conformed to the external curve of the discus. The room itself seemed suitable only for storage.

"Singe?"

My voice sounded strange in that place.

Singe didn't answer me.

"Don't be playing games just because you're invisible."

Still no answer.

The back side of the ladder went on up to another level. I swung around there, looked up.

There did seem to be an opening—which was closed. Mostly closed. A bit of fabric had gotten caught in a gap where the closure abutted the head of the ladder. The lighting was poor but the fabric resembled that of Singe's shirt.

I pushed. Nothing gave but the muscles in my back. I tried again, twisting. The closure slid sideways an inch. I thought I had it now. I pushed and twisted some more. The crack widened a few more inches, then wouldn't respond to any effort I made.

I tried to look through the crack. I couldn't see anything but nothing. I followed up by snaking a cautious hand in to feel around. Nobody stomped on my fingers. It's a wonderful life when the highlight of your working day is that nobody stomped on your fingers.

I felt around some more. It seemed that the main reason the entry wouldn't open any farther was that Singe was lying on it. Getting her off proved to be a challenge. But I was up to it. I was a trained, veteran Royal Marine.

Eventually I slithered through the gap. Singe was lying in plain sight, mostly on another metal floor like the one below. This room was perfectly round, with another ceiling that had to be uncomfortably low even for the elves who used it. One of those was slumped in one of four chairs gracing the room. The chairs were all fixed to the floor.

The wonders of that round room were too numerous to recount. I think I was too numb to recognize a lot of them as anything special. There seemed to be thousands of little glowing lights, for example. Some were green or red, or yellow or purple or even white. Some kept flashing on and off. Most seemed content just to be there, showing themselves.

I've seen some wild sorcery in my day, including the kind that melts mountains. Yet I was more impressed with this vision than I'd been with anything I'd seen before. The numbers were what did it.

Then there were windows something like the one at Casey's, most of them more nearly horizontal than vertical. But the really eye-popping thing, the overwhelming thing, was the outer wall, all the way around the room.

It was like that was missing, not there at all until you touched it. The woods were visible there pretty much as I would've seen them had I been standing on a fifteen-foot-high platform. I was seeing the world from the altitude that Doris and Marsha saw it.

I couldn't hear anything, though.

I checked Singe's pulse. She'd be all right. I checked the elf. Somebody had slugged this one from behind. I'd bet on any invisible ratgirl. I couldn't find a pulse in any of the usual places but he was twitching already. I got him plucked of his possessions and tied up with odds and ends. Just in time.

And just in time for the arrival of the three glowing balls. Those touched down carefully after a wary approach.

When he saw that happening, my captive elf began to kick and struggle. He wasn't pleased. I felt an inarticulate mental pressure but he never said an actual word.

I shut the door in the floor and parked both Singe and the elf atop it. When he tried to move I admonished him gently with a toe. He learned faster than a pup.

I looked outward again.

The three glowing objects gradually stopped doing that. They turned out to be dull gray lopsided metal eggs not more than ten feet tall, the fat half of each egg downward. Each stood on three metal legs as skinny as broom handles.

Nothing happened for a while. Then, as an opening began to appear in the side of one of the gray eggs, Doris came bounding out of the woods and dealt that very egg a mighty overhand smack with his club. The blow left a sizable dent.

Then there was a flash. And Doris staggered away, not knocked down but not real sure where he was anymore. A vaguely feminine silver elf dropped a ladder from the assaulted egg and scrambled down to the ground. She seemed to be seeing the fact but didn't want to believe that Doris hadn't been destroyed by the flash.

I got all that from feelings within me and from elven body language that probably meant nothing of the sort because the creature wasn't human.

It hit the ground running toward Doris, in a truly foul mood. The groll himself had gotten lost in the woods. He was blundering around in confusion.

The other two silver elves left their eggs. They showed hints of femininity, too. From the remove at which I watched I couldn't be completely sure, however. Though there did seem to be minor physical differences from the other elves, nothing was absolutely convincing. Maybe if you were a silver elf you could tell. Kind of the way slugs can tell the boys from the girls.

Plainly, they didn't label themselves the way humans do, sexually or by pinpointing weirdness, physical disparity, or attractiveness.

Never mind. I don't need to get my ulcers burning about human nature. I'm all growed up now, Maw. I know we ain't gonna get nowhere wishin' an' hopin'. People are too damned stubborn.

Speaking of stubborn. Here came Marsha, half the size of a house, crawling on his belly, sneaking up on the lead egg only abandoned a moment earlier by a silver elf with cute little crabapple breasts. Marsha had learned something while watching his brother precipitate attack.

When he was close enough Marsha reached out and, with a sideways swipe of his club, swatted one of the egg's legs out from under it.

Which didn't turn out to be quite as clever as I'd thought before he did it.

When the egg fell it tipped straight toward him. He had to scramble to get out of the way. And even then he wasn't safe.

The elves decided to chase him.

The violence of the egg's fall shook the discus. For a second I was afraid I was going down, too.

The fallen egg began to glow in a patch on its bottom. Then it started sliding around drunkenly, darting and stopping like a water bug, spinning, tearing up trees. It knocked over the only uninjured egg, struck the discus a ferocious glancing blow, and panicked the new arrivals. They didn't know which way to run. Finally, the egg blistered off in a straight line, ripped through the pond and the woods beyond, then plowed a deep furrow through a vineyard almost all the way to the top of the slope before it came to rest. At that point it seemed both to melt and to sink slowly into the earth.

Marsha had to be amazed by what he'd accomplished.

The silver elves were amazed, too. And distraught in the extreme.

I was now reasonably confident that they did communicate the way the Dead Man does. I couldn't pick out any words but the atmosphere was pregnant with emotion. There was a lot of blaming and finger-pointing going on, driven by a terror of being marooned. That fear became a notch more intense when the three examined their surviving egg and discovered that Doris's ill-advised attack had crippled it somehow.

"Uh-oh."

The three all stared at the disk like it might be their salvation. After a brief commune they all produced a variety of gray fetishes and began poking at them with long, skinny, nailless fingers. One of the little girls came forward, toward me, passing out of view beneath my feet. Two minutes later there was a whining noise from the area where Singe and the captive elf lay sprawled.

I scooted over there. The door in the floor was trying to move. The weight piled on it kept it from doing so. I sensed a considerable frustration down below. That was one—maybe—lady who didn't think things ought to be going this way. A—maybe—woman whose day had been on the brink of triumph, but which had turned to shit in her hands in a matter of minutes.

"Been there, sweetheart," I muttered. I began to look around, seeking something identifiable as a nonlethal weapon. I didn't want to hurt anybody if I really was dealing with women. Possibly the most bizarre aspect of this business so far was the fact that no one had gotten killed. We had one elf with a broken arm and we had me with a bumper crop of aches and bruises—acquired from rat-people not directly involved in the case—but otherwise the whole thing was almost civilized. And no silver elf had yet done anyone a direct physical injury.

I didn't find anything that could be used as a weapon. Maybe I could rip an arm off the elf I did have and use it to harvest the new crop. I did retain plenty of pieces of steel in a variety of shapes and sizes, all with very sharp edges, should the situation grow hair, though.

Even so, these weird people didn't seem to be impressed by weapons. Which left me wondering just how bright they could be.

The elf downstairs tried to get the floor door open again. I sat down nearby, ready to crack her knuckles with the butt of a knife if she stuck a hand through the way I had. I'm not always a perfect gentleman.

Some of the little flashy lights expired suddenly. Outside, the most voluptuous elf began to jump up and down. Evidently she'd solved some puzzle and was totally excited. She didn't jiggle much, though.

The other elf looked over her shoulder. Clearly, she disapproved of her sidekick's demonstration but was pleased with their results. Her daddy longlegs fingers began to prance across another of those gray fetish things.

More lights went out. There was a declining whine, fading fast, never noticed until it went.

"I don't think that's a good sign," I told myself.

Still more lights went out.

"Definitely not a good sign."

Up on the see-through wall—which I just now noticed had a curved shape in the vertical dimension that allowed it to show a lot more than a flat window would—I saw a large piece of deadwood come arcing out of the woods, spinning end for end horizontally. It was a log I would've had trouble lifting.

It got both silver elves.

I felt their rush of pain inside my head.

48

The elf downstairs made a run for it. She dropped out the bottom of the disk and headed up the path already blazed by the self-immolating egg. Marsha didn't have any luck catching her. I didn't let it worry me. She was completely weird and doubtless had no clue how to get by in the country, without help from her strange, sorcerous toys. She should not be hard to track. Just follow the commotion she caused.

Maybe Colonel Block could get me a big fat medal for having saved Karenta from the foreign sorcerers and sorceresses. Maybe the flying pigs would start evicting the pigeons from their traditional roosts. Which sure would leave a mess around all those dead and incompetent generals posing outside the Chancery.

The common wisdom among former grunts is that *competent* generals wouldn't have screwed up so bad they got themselves killed and therefore there wouldn't have been any need for a memorial.

Soldiers are a cynical bunch.

In the process of exploring the interior of the discus I discovered Cypres Prose installed in a padded box behind a door that locked from the outside. The little horizontal closet was soundproof. It was on a floor above the one with the marvelous lights and the wonderful view.

The upper level seemed to constitute of crew quarters and such, if you went over it just guessing.

My years in the Corps, with its ancient and traditional naval associations, clicked in at last. This thing had to be some kind of aerial ship or boat. With a crew. With decks and bulkheads and hatches instead of floors and walls and doors. With heads instead of toilets and galleys instead of kitchens—and all that special navy talk us Marines always resented.

The silver elves must have been trying to teach Kip something, stashing him in a padded box. But they hadn't been harsh enough. Their rewards and punishments must have been too subtle. The boy began to complain the second the door opened, never once going for a "Good to see you again," or, "Thanks for coming to find me, Garrett." That being the case I shut him back in while I went on to explore the rest of the aerial ship.

After a while I reopened the hatch confining Kip. "Where can I find Lastyr and Noodiss?"

Bitch, bitch, piss, and moan.

"All right. Your call." I shut the hatch.

I went back outside "Hey, Marsha, did you happen to look for Dojango? I'm pretty sure they dragged him into one of those lead eggs."

In the excitement we'd forgotten the little brother.

Marsha went over to the fallen egg and yelled in the doorway. He didn't get a response. For a moment he and I both stared up the hill along the path taken by the berserk egg. Then Marsha went and yelled into the dented egg. That didn't do any good either.

"I'd better look," I said. "Chances are they wouldn't have left him in any condition where he could do some mischief." These silver elves were highly weird but I doubted that they were highly stupid.

I was right. I found Dojango in the dented ship, as unconscious as Singe and Playmate and Saucerhead Tharpe. "This is not good," I kept muttering to myself. Until my superior intellect finally seized the day.

I went up into the vineyards and asked around until I found a somberly clad, gloomily serious young man willing to abandon his post for a fee. I gave him messages to deliver to the Dead Man, to Morley Dotes, and to Colonel Block. In that order. I gave him half of his handsome messenger's stipend before he departed, giving him to understand that receipt of the balance was contingent upon his getting the job done right. He nodded a lot. All his mates seemed to think his going to the city was a huge joke.

Then I just felt like I could lie back and take it easy until reinforcements arrived. Taking a few minutes every hour to go see if Kip had started to catch on yet.

That boy was slow. After a while he mentioned hunger. "That right there's you one more motive for turning cooperative, I'd say. Whew! It's really starting to get ripe in there, too. Guess those good old silver boys let you out when you had to go." He refused to understand that right away, too.

Back outside, I asked, "How is Doris looking, Marsha?" I'd been rooting for a swift recovery. Making small talk with the healthy brother had worn thin in a hurry. Once we'd used up business and gossip all Marsha could talk about was the shortage of suitable females within his size range.

"An' you can stuff them ideas right there, Garrett. On account of I've already heard all the jokes about mastodons and blue oxen."

"Then I shan't belabor the obvious. Actually, I was going to suggest that you jog up and get our cart back. Singe packed us a load of sandwiches." She'd also eaten a load of sandwiches along the way but I hoped a few might have survived. And if not, I'd at least get a respite from the mighty lover's whining.

Marsha thought that was about the best idea he'd heard all week. He took off right away, tossing back, "Keep an eye on Doris, will you?"

"I will indeed." On account of I didn't want to be in the wrong place when the big goof tripped over his own feet and came tumbling down.

I made my rounds of prisoners and patients. They were all being incredibly stubborn about recovering, though I now saw some signs that they were coming back. Singe had begun babbling in her sleep, thankfully mostly in ratfolk cant. My grasp of the dialect is feeble. I was embarrassed only about half the time.

Doris was coming along fine. He made sense about seventy percent of the time. He stayed fine as long as he didn't get up and try to walk around. His sense of balance was out of whack. When he did try to walk he drifted sideways. Then he fell over.

Twenty minutes after Marsha left we had a visitor. Some sort of vineyard manager or overseer or supervisor, name of Boroba Thring. Boroba was a fat little brown guy on a skinny little brown donkey. He believed devoutly in his right to claim everyone and everything in sight in the name of his employer, evicting me in the meantime. Evidently he seldom dealt with anyone who told him "No." He'd come visiting alone and didn't see that as a disadvantage. He was one of those particularly irritating characters who couldn't conceive of anyone thwarting him, let alone ignoring him. Which is what I did for a while when first he spouted his nonsense. Once I became sufficiently sick of his voice, I said, "Hey, Doris. You can have this one to play with."

Thring didn't last long. I had Doris dump him in with the other prisoners. After that I passed the time amusing myself by figuring out how to strip silver elves.

The material they wore was tough but I discovered that it wouldn't stand up to a really sharp piece of steel.

Marsha arrived with the cart. "You're probably gonna want to keep those people in the shade, Garrett. I've seen albinos with more color to them."

"They definitely don't get out much." My, oh, my, the cargo area on the back of the cart still contained sandwiches that Singe hadn't eaten. And some beer in stoneware bottles. That was a nice surprise. I shared the sandwiches with the grolls. I shared the beer with me. I reserved the last sandwich and went to see Kip.

49

"This is the way it goes, kid." I waved the sandwich, took a small bite. "You can talk to me, the nice guy who's here to help you. Or you can talk to the Guard when they get here and take over. I know. You're a tough guy. You've been getting yourself ready for this in your daydreams for the last fifteen years. And so far it hasn't hurt much more than an ordinary dream. But when the Guards get here they'll have someone from the Hill with them. And you know those people won't think any more of stepping on you than they would of stomping a roach."

I looked into Kip's eyes and tried to imagine what he was seeing as he looked at me. Definitely not what I thought I was. Probably just a minor villain, laughing and rubbing his hands together while cackling about having ways to make him talk.

Time was getting to be a problem.

What I had to get around was Kip's absolute vision of himself as the hero of his own story. Which at this point meant crushing him in a major way because I couldn't come up with a means by which he could see an honorable escape route he could use without believing his escape was some sort of wicked betrayal.

I did some estimating of how much time I might yet have before those I'd summoned arrived. Seemed like it should be quite a while yet if things ran their usual course in officialdom.

I did some soul-searching, too. Because I wanted to know

why some part of me was so convinced that it was important for me to get to Lastyr and Noodiss.

When I start thinking, and wondering about my own motives, life really starts to slow down. I can see why Morley gets impatient with me.

Marsha built us a fire. Doris had recovered enough to help without falling in. I gathered some of my favorite people in the circle of warmth. Singe. Playmate. Saucerhead. Casey and a member each from the other crews. They didn't look like much naked. The males were like shriveled up old prunes. Like mummies. One of the two females wasn't much more promising. The other got barely passing marks from me because I possess a prejudiced eye.

I hoped somebody would thaw out and tell me something interesting.

Neither Doris nor Marsha had any trouble leaving brother Dojango a subject in the realm of silence. Dojango never said anything interesting. Dojango just said.

Saucerhead recovered first. He was in a predictably foul temper. He insisted he was starving.

"Save yourself some agony," I told him. "I've been where you're at now, three times. If you try to eat anything it'll come right back up."

"Let me learn the hard way." His stomach growled agreement.

"Your choice. But the only edibles in the area are those grapes up yonder. And if those were ripe they would've been picked already."

Saucerhead wasn't interested in common sense or rationality but he could handle them when they happened. "Then I'm going back to sleep." Presumably a trick he'd learned in the army. Doze as much as you can until flying misfortune makes you get up and go to work.

"Don't get into it too deep. I sent for the Guard. I can't see you wanting to be lying around here napping when they show."

"Which won't be for a while. And I can count on my good friend Garrett to kick me in the slats and wake me up as soon as he sees them coming over yonder ridge. Go on and get away from me. My head is pounding and I ain't in no mood."

I did get a smile out of Playmate before he turned nasty on me. Somehow, while he was unconscious, all his pain and misery had become my fault. Ignoring the incredibly stupid thing he'd done, chasing after a Kayne Prose who wasn't even the real deal, a dozen miles into the countryside.

Singe tried harder to be nice when she came around, but she did find it difficult to be understanding about the food shortage.

Seems I spend my whole life listening to people complain.

Maybe I should get into the priest racket. But I'm either too cynical or not cynical enough.

I told Singe, "If hunger becomes a bad enough problem we'll eat our pal Casey over there."

Casey didn't respond even though he was awake.

None of the elves seemed able to communicate without their clothes on.

50

I took a nap myself. It lasted through most of the night. I awakened to find my accomplices feeling better physically but no less testy. They all complained of hunger. The prisoners were all awake now, too, but were unable, or unwilling, to communicate. When I gave Casey his suit back, in hopes that that would help, but he just stared at the ruins and shook his head. Evidently my knifework had deprived him of his sorcery permanently.

I said, "I've had a thought."

Saucerhead grumbled, "Don't go spraining your brain."

"This one just popped right up, no work at all."

"Like a toadstool, probably. Growing on a cow pie.'

"Somebody from town should be showing up pretty soon. But they don't need to find the rest of you here. They don't know about you so there's no need for you to deal with their crap."

Playmate said, "They'll just hunt us down later."

"Not if I don't tell them. None of these elves can talk."

"There's that grapestomper."

"He's only seen the big guys. I can make him a deal that'll guarantee his silence."

Playmate gave up arguing. He enjoyed official scrutiny as little as the next man. "What about Kip? We haven't found Kip. Kip is what this mess is all about. It's all a waste of time, money, and pain if we don't get the kid back."

"I'll keep looking. He's got to be here somewhere."

"I have to take him back, Garrett."

"I know." Overly moral me, I'd decided that I couldn't

let a kid fall into Colonel Block's hands. Not even that kid. Block is a decent enough guy—for a royal functionary— but there are a lot of people, way nastier than me, that he's obliged to keep happy. And Kip meant nothing to him personally. There were ten thousand Kips in town.

Maybe I get him together with Kayne Prose. Make Kip mean something long enough for the Hill folk to lose interest.

I strolled over to the discus. I climbed inside. The bulk of a sandwich awaited me beside the hatch to Kip's compartment. I was tempted to enjoy it myself. But I was concerned, too. That sandwich had drawn no flies. When I reflected on the matter I realized that I had yet to see any insect inside the aerial ship.

Now there was a sorcery worth stealing.

"Hello, Kip. This could be your lucky day. I have something for you to eat *and* a chance for you to get out of here before Baron Dreadlore and the Civil Guards arrive." Dreadlore was a fabrication but somebody with a name very much like that would turn up soon. Maybe several of them, considering how much damage a sorcerer could imagine himself doing if he owned the secret magery of flight.

"Water."

"Dang me, Kip." I hadn't even thought about water. I should have. I must be getting senile. "There's a whole big pond of the stuff right outside. And a nice cold spring. You still want to be stubborn?"

Yes, he did.

I told him, "They got hold of your mother and Rhafi, you know."

He croaked, "That was Casey."

"How would you know? How would you know that name?"

"The Drople and the Graple both told me. They have ways of observing things that are happening in the city." He didn't explain who the Drople and the Graple were. Two of his captors, presumably.

"They talked to you?"

"They hoped to convert me to their cause. They didn't get the job done." It was nice to see the kid too weak to be a smart-ass. "I couldn't understand what they were talking about. Lastyr and Noodiss are the only ones of them that I ever actually do get. They just want to go home."

"How'd they get here in the first place?"

"In a sky vessel. Like this one. But they didn't know how to work it well enough. They crashed it."

"I don't recall the incident."

"They crashed in the river. Whatever's left of their ship is underwater."

At last I was starting to dig something out. Not that it made a lick of sense.

"That being the case, why not let Casey take them home?"

"Because Casey isn't here to take them home. Casey is here to take them to prison."

"They're escaped convicts?"

Kip was losing patience with me and my questions. "No. They have the wrong politics. Although politics isn't exactly what it is. Not like what we mean when we say politics here. It's all politics and philosophy and science and law and research with all three groups. And even though I've talked and talked about it with Lastyr and Noodiss I still don't understand much better than you do without ever having heard them explain anything. It seems like there's a war going on between people who've got different ideas about how knowledge should be handled. The party Lastyr and Noodiss belong to, the Brotherhood of Light, believe that knowledge is the birthright of all intelligent life-forms. That it should be freely shared with anybody able to understand it. That's why they came here. So they could teach us."

I believe I've mentioned my tendency toward the cynical reaction. I sneered at the charity of Kip's friends.

I said, "The way you're hacking and croaking, I'll bet you're ready for a long, cool drink of springwater."

Kip grunted.

"So point the way for me."

In complete exasperation, the boy told me, "I don't know where they are!"

"You know how to contact them. Let's go, Kip. It isn't

a game anymore. It isn't an adventure. People are coming for you who'll pull pieces off you like you're a bug. The stakes are probably a lot bigger than either of us can imagine."

He gave me a look that belittled my imagination. I kept plugging. "We need to do whatever we can to get ourselves out of their way."

The kid looked at the stale sandwich but didn't fold. I had to admire him even if, from my point of view, he was being stubborn for all the wrong reasons.

"You win, kid. Eat hearty." Time to change over to Plan Q.

51

"I found him," I told Playmate. "They had him stashed in some kind of locker. Marsha! Get everybody ready to hit the road. We're gonna move as soon as we can get the kid cleaned up. Playmate, take him to the pond."

My instructions inspired a hundred questions. I ignored them all, located my local buddy Mr. Thring. He had value under the new plan. He glared daggers once I removed his blindfold but he'd begun to understand that bluster and attitude weren't his best tools here. "Mr. Thring. Good morning. I've been talking with my associates about what we should do with you. Most of them think we should take you over to the pond and hold you under until you can't remember names or faces anymore."

Surprise and fear lit up the dusky round face of the estate manager.

"But it seems to me that you might be more use to us healthy. If you'll help us with a little something and can leave us comfortably assured that you wouldn't discuss your adventures with anyone later on."

Thring was eager to provide assurances. He couldn't by virtue of having been bound and gagged.

"What I'm looking for is a little-known path or road we can use to slip away from here." Inside I was kicking myself for not having pulled this together last night, when we'd had a lot bigger lead on the folks who'd be headed our way now.

That messenger was going to end up having to whistle for the second half of his stipend.

"You do know this country well enough to help us with that, don't you? Probably grew up around here? Came right back after you did your five? Right?"

The man nodded his head.

"Good. I'm going to take your gag off now. And we'll get started on making you one of the crew."

I scanned the group. This wasn't a promising crowd for making a running retreat. Kip was in no shape to travel. Neither was Mr. Thring. Dojango would whine a lot but he could walk. Limping. He'd soaked his feet. Playmate and Saucerhead would manage what they had to manage. Doris and Marsha would end up doing more than their reasonable share, as usual, probably by having to carry somebody. And I would want to take an elf or two along.

The females seemed the most promising hostages. They were lighter and from what little I could sense of what was going on inside them, they seemed more cooperative, more likely to talk about things none of the several crews wanted known.

Playmate, Saucerhead, and I could take turns pulling our prisoner cart.

Saucerhead approached. "What's up, Garrett?"

"I've decided not to wait for Colonel Block. Mr. Thring here has been generous enough to offer to guide us out of here by back ways so we can get out and go home without having to deal with those special people who're likely to show up here with the Guard."

"I gotcha. Good idea. You suppose he could guide us somewhere where we could get something to eat?"

"I'll talk to him about that."

A little hunger probably wouldn't hurt us nearly as much as leaving a clear backtrail. Once we put some miles between ourselves and the wrecked skyships, though . . .

I was ready for a snack myself.

52

I was so agitated. All my paranoia went to waste.

When I reached home, after an epic death march that brought the survivors and me into town through the west gate, I learned that the Dead Man hadn't received my message at all. Neither had Morley, because Morley would've contacted His Nibs if he had.

What that meant was, there was still a gang of elves out there, tied up and maybe dying of thirst and exposure.

I headed for the al-Khar immediately. There wasn't much of me left when I got there. I need to work on my strength and endurance.

I had no trouble getting in to see Colonel Block. He really was interested in what I was doing.

I related a comprehensive version of my story. It ran light on the sorcery side and came up short on names but was solid enough to let the colonel know that here was a matter genuinely in need of his attention.

Block asked, "Did you happen to catch the name of this weirdly dressed fellow who was supposed to bring me your message?"

"Yeah. Earp. Eritytie Earp."

"Was he Michorite? That sounds Michorite."

"Possibly. Maybe one of those cults, now that you mention it. He dressed the part."

"And I'll bet all the other hands yucked it up when he volunteered to take the job. Am I right?"

"There was some amusement. But nobody else volunteered."

"You know what? Your boy is going to wake up in the Tenderloin stone-cold broke, without even his farmboy brogans, undoubtedly so wrecked that he can't remember his own name, let alone those of people he was supposed to give messages. Those ascetic cultists don't deal with temptation well when they come up against it without all their sour fart buddies watching over their shoulders, holding them back."

"Hell, that could be me. But at least I've been there enough times that I know what I'm missing."

Block gave me a concerned look. "You may end up with some legal problems if any of those elves die. Can you produce trustworthy witnesses to back you up when you say they kidnapped this kid?"

"Hell, Wes, you had a guy there when it happened."

"Not exactly. Oh, I do believe you. More or less."

"So why don't I just stipulate that you've got me over a barrel? Get somebody out there. Those creatures can't do you any good dead. If you *really* need me, you know where I live."

"I thought you'd go along. Be right there handy when questions start popping up."

"You thought wrong. I'm going home. I'm going to eat and sleep and not do anything else for about nine days. I'm allergic to the country. It takes me a long time to get over it. I'm just trying to do my civic duty here, anyway."

"You always were a bullshitter, Garrett. I'll let you know how it comes out."

I'd heard that before. He'd forget about me the second I left. The only reason he'd mentioned taking me along was to make me more eager to get out of there. He wanted to grab the benefits of this for Westman Block.

Damn, that was smart of me, being stupid enough to hire a messenger who'd get lost in the red-light district before he thought of doing anything else.

From the little I've heard about the Michonites and related cults, that's a rite of passage. They—the men—get one chance to sneak away and wallow in sin and depravity. Then they spend the rest of their lives keeping an eye on each other, every miserable man making sure nobody else has any fun ever again.

"In your hands," I said. "I hope you get more out of it than I did."

"Go on. Before I change my mind."

He might, just to show me that he could, so I got.

The house was crowded, what with Singe, Kip, and the captive silver elves staying over. Singe offered to ease the crowding by moving into my room with me.

I begged off again. Kip and the elves ended up sleeping on the floor in the Dead Man's room, where he'd have the least trouble keeping them under control.

I'd really hoped that Singe's encounter with Rhafi unclothed would scare her off. It seemed to have whetted her curiosity instead.

The situation amused His Nibs immensely. He wasn't going to help me get out of it, either. I fell asleep in a household drenched in the miasma of his amusement.

53

Dean never gave the bitching a minute's rest but he did cook up breakfast enough for the whole wretched crowd.

The elf women joined in timidly. Dean tried them on everything in his arsenal. Tea they found acceptable. Honey seemed to be all right, in tea or straight from the pot. One nibbled a biscuit, also with honey aboard. Bacon revolted the two of them. The more obviously feminine member of the pair—the one who looked like she'd actually made it a few weeks into puberty—attacked the mustard once she discovered it. Dean scowled and muttered to himself. A lot of work goes into grinding seed and preparing the condiment. There's always a pot on the table, mainly because I don't much like mustard.

The other elf woman, the elder and senior woman—judging by wrinkles—seemed terrified, though no one even spoke to her. I got the feeling she'd never seen the inner workings of a Karentine household.

Fear or no, she did appear to me immensely curious about everything.

Kip was a shuddering zombie, controlled by an increasingly exasperated Dead Man. Kip never stopped fighting him. Something was missing in that boy's makeup. I couldn't understand how he'd managed to stay alive this long.

Singe and I removed to the Dead Man's room as soon as I'd had enough to eat. She brought a platter along with her, loaded with seconds or thirds. Having no better idea what to do with herself, the slimmer elf woman tagged along. She wouldn't sit when I offered her my chair because that would leave me standing between her and the door. The other one stayed with Dean, exploring the wonders of the kitchen.

"So where do we stand, Old Bones? Have we learned anything?"

Perhaps. At the first instance, probably that we should not have allowed emotion to sweep us away and get us involved in this. As I see it now, we have stormed into the middle of something that was none of our business. We have done nothing but trail chaos and dismay wherever we have gone.

"What do you mean, 'we,' Big Daddy Homely? You can't really talk about someone else in the royal plural, can you?"

Do not become tedious. I am struggling to translate what little recognizable material I find in the thin creature's mind. This is truly an alien intelligence, Garrett. I have encountered nothing like it in all my years. Nor have I ever heard of such creatures . . . Unless . . . There may have been similar folk here when I was a child. Visitors, they were called then. They were all murdered for their secrets. Inasmuch as they did not reveal anything they were soon forgotten.

I am having difficulty communicating not just because of what you would call a language barrier but also because of her fear. She is awash in fear, not just of us, here, whom she finds terrifying enough, but of being cut off from her own people. She is completely unmanned by the possibility that she may never be able to return home. And least of all, but still there in the mix, is a fear of the consequences of the failure of her mission.

"And that would be?"

I do not know. That is in a sealed part of her mind.

"What about the other one?"

She is frightened, too. And her mind is more closed. But behind her fear there is a hint of her seeing this personal disaster as a potential opportunity for . . . I do not know what. Something compulsive. Possibly obsessive. Possibly something wicked. Worms of temptation have begun to awaken way down in the black, mucky deeps. . . .

I hate it when he meanders off on a free association,

poetic ramble. I guess because I can't ever figure out what the hell he's babbling about. "What about Kip? Did you get anything new out of him?"

Yes. Once I became aware that there was something that should be there. But it is not much. And I do not know if we can justify hunting down Lastyr and Noodiss.

"Of course we can." But I couldn't think of any reasonable argument in favor of that. "Is there any chance some of those elves might've put a compulsion into my head somewhere along the way? Like one of those times when I was knocked out?"

At the moment I am unable to investigate. All of my mental capacity is occupied by the boy and these foreign women.

"They definitely are both women, then."

By birth. You unclothed them. You saw.

"I didn't see much." But what I had seen had been curiously interesting. "The one in the kitchen at least raised a crop of lemons."

Many human women are not as voluptuous as those in the range you usually find interesting. This one's primary sexual characteristics are somewhat atrophied. I would expect that to be true of the others, as well.

"I did notice that." In the women it all added up to a sort of virginal innocence that was attractive in its own fashion.

Singe hissed at me. I think it was supposed to be laughter.

I suspect that this is not an individual aberration. I suspect that we would find the males even more atrophied.

"Weird." I shuddered. "The ones I stripped down out there definitely weren't built to boogie. Maybe I ought to introduce this old gal to Morley."

The pixies out front launched one of their racket shows, which wakened the Goddamned Parrot.

She may be beyond seduction, Garrett. They may have tried to breed the sexual impulse out of themselves. The same madness has been tried by countless cults in our part of the world in a shortsighted effort to shove all those distractions aside.

"How the hell do they get little elves, then?"

Exactly. No such cult lasts more than a generation. Per-

haps the silver elves have found a way around that limitation. Possibly they have a separate breeder caste. I do not know. I do know that no living creature I have ever encountered, save the rare mutant, has lacked desire, however distorted the core impulse might have become because of stresses upon the individual. I would suspect them to be present in these elves. But buried deep.

"So have you gotten anything out of the kid concerning his two weird pals?"

Truly, he does not know how or where to find them. He does not have a reliable means of attracting their attention. His method worked only two times in five tries. The rest of the time they just turned up at their own discretion, almost always when he was alone. It has not occurred to Kip to wonder but they almost certainly knew that he was alone before they visited.

Dean stuck his head in. "That racket out front is because the wee folk have spotted Bic Gonlit."

Dean was talking to the pixies now? Times change. I gave him the fish-eye, on general principles. He wouldn't be feeding them, too, would he?

"Now why would Bic . . . ?"

I have him. Go bring him in, Garrett. He flashed me a pixie's-eye view of the spot from which Bic was watching the house. I noted that it was farther away than the Dead Man had shown he could reach before when trying to manipulate a human being. *After that, take Kip home to his mother. He is nothing but a distraction here.*

"This is the real Bic Gonlit?"

The genuine article. Evidently determined to be foolish. Help me find out why. He will not run this time. He will not see you leave the house.

54

Though he was mad as hell Bic couldn't get his body to move. He couldn't do anything but flinch when my hand settled on his shoulder. "Bic, my man, here you are again. Lurking. Let's go for a walk."

Gonlit stood up and zombie-walked over to the house with me. I talked to him all the way, mainly in an admonitory tone. There was no need to get any other watchers overly excited.

I did blow Mrs. Cardonlos a kiss. She was out on her porch, keeping her eyes open. She needed her reward.

Mr. Gonlit is after Miss Pular again. Now on behalf of a ratman who calls himself John Stretch.

"You get the joke, Singe? John Stretch?"

"No. Why would the name John Stretch be a joke?" The notion seemed to irritate her.

"John Stretch is what they used to call the hangman, before we got civilized and started lopping off heads instead."

"Is that true? I wonder who he could be." Singe had almost no accent left, despite her vastly different throat and voice box. Scary how talented the girl was. But her tone was so controlled even I knew she was dancing around something. I was surprised the Dead Man didn't get after her. Although, sometimes, he just doesn't pay attention to anything but himself.

Mr. Gonlit does not know who John Stretch is. He does not care. One of the hard-nosed youngsters with ambitions toward Reliance's throne, if you care to call it that. A some-

what naive youngster willing to pay part of Mr. Gonlit's fee up front.

Mr. Gonlit enjoyed a wonderful gourmet dinner last night. He followed it with a bottle of TunFaire Gold and a deep pipe filled with the finest imported broadleaf tobacco. Probably a Postersaldt. Now Mr. Gonlit finds himself in a position where he has to deliver something that will please John Stretch.

"Hey, Bic. You know we warned you to back away from us."

Gonlit shrugged. "People warn *you* off, pal. I don't recollect you ever running away."

That stuff is pretty obnoxious when somebody else is throwing it into *your* face.

"Must be the boots talking, Bic. Making you braver than you ought to be."

"What're you gonna do, pal? Send me to the Cantard?"

Bic tried hard not to betray his interest in the silver elf woman. Her interest in Bic, however, was both frank, blatant, and troubled. The manly posturing thing seemed both to excite and repel her. She was eager to see what happened next.

"There's an original question, Bic. Well, I have work to do. Errands to run. I hope you took that John Stretch for a potful of gold. By the time I get back home you'll probably be unemployed. Kip! Where the hell are you? Get your sorry ass ready. I'm taking you home." With a side trip to The Palms along the way, of course.

I needed to see my old buddy, my pal, Morley the celery stalker and carrot killer.

55

I passed the word to Morley. "The number one boy out to scrub Reliance is a rat who calls himself John Stretch."

"That's cute. What've you been up to?"

"I thought Reliance might be interested. What do you think? How do you mean, up to? Why do you want to know?"

"We've had some unusual people turn up here the last couple of nights. They're the sort who dress up in black and manage to suck all the joy out of a room just by entering it."

"Why would they come here?"

"I thought you might be able to tell me."

"Not a clue here." And I really didn't have one.

"That the kid you were looking for?"

"The very one. Am I good, or what?"

"So you got him back."

"Damn me with faint praise if you want. I'm taking him home to his mother now."

"You think he's smart enough to make it there, then?" Kip had just done something to test Sarge's patience.

"I have hopes. I'm counting on his ego. And once I'm shut of him I'll be the happiest boy in town. I'd go on a toot if I didn't have work to do."

"Ooh! You have another job lined up already?"

"Nope. Just studying the excesses of the rest of you. I'm considering entrepreneur stuff. Because I'm going into business for myself."

Morley looked at me for a while. "All right. This ought to be entertaining."

"What? You don't think I can be a serious business-man?"

"No. Because a serious businessman has to stay sober most of the time. A serious businessman has to make his decisions untouched by emotion. And, most of all, a serious businessman has to *work*. All day, every day, enduring longer hours than the most dedicated character on his payroll."

I took a deep, cleansing breath, sighed. "O ye of little faith."

"Exactly. Tell me everything you've left out about your adventures, Garrett."

When I got to the part about the Michonite messenger Morley began to laugh. He said, "I guess that explains the kid who turned up here a few hours ago."

"What?"

"He was a dark-haired boy of draft age, as handsome as they come, some mother's son, wearing nothing but a loin-cloth. But he stank like an alley in the drought season."

"How long did you fiddle with the words to put that together?"

"Then till now. Sounded good, didn't it? He couldn't remember why he was supposed to see me. The boys in the kitchen gave him some leftovers and sent him on his way."

I grunted sourly. "Hey, Sarge, no need to hold back on my account. The kid asks for it, smack him. Probably won't do any good. But he's got to learn somehow, someday."

Though I was just about convinced that Kip never would.

Only seconds later, *Smack!*

Kip bounced off Sarge's fist, slammed into a wall, folded up into a very surprised pile of dirty laundry.

Morley said, "Sarge wasn't just a medic. He did one tour training recruits."

I asked, "How'd you teach that kind when you were in the army, Sarge?"

"Ain't dat hard, Garrett. But foist ya do got ta get dere attenshun."

Excellent, in theory. But we were dealing with Cyprus Prose who, I feared, could not be reached by mortal man.

The kid got up, still looking surprised as he shook his head. He started to say something.

Sarge popped him again. Harder.

And, moments later, again, harder still.

And that was all it took. Kip looked right at Sarge, as though really seeing him for the first time.

"Dere. Dat's better. Let's you an' me talk, boy."

Then a miracle occurred.

Kip paid attention.

Morley opined, "I believe it has to do with Sarge having no emotional investment. Everyone else who ever tried to teach the boy manners didn't want to hurt him. Down deep he always knew they'd pull their punches. And they'd give up after they'd failed a few times. So he learned to outlast them. Sarge doesn't have an investment. He doesn't care if the kid lives or dies. He'll just keep on hitting, harder and harder, until he gets results. People sense that. They give him their direction. The way the boy has. *Ouch!*"

Sarge had smacked Kip again, this time turning him ass over appetite.

"A smart mouth always calls for a little reminder. Let the master work a while. You'll be glad you did."

So I did. I kept one ear turned Sarge's direction while Morley and I tried to figure out what the hell I'd gotten myself into this time. Sarge talked to Kip softly, gently, probing his core knowledge of courtesy and the social graces. Kip knew the forms. What he lacked was any understanding. Sarge managed to pound a few insights into his thick, young-adult skull.

I told Morley, "That sonofabitch just went up about ten notches on my approval board. He had me fooled. You think he could do anything with a blasphemous parrot?"

"Where is the lovable Mr. Big?"

"I'm sure he's out there somewhere, spying on me."

Morley chuckled, but said only, "There's more to almost anyone once you get to know them, Garrett. But you knew that already. It's the kind of thing you're always throwing at me when I've decided it's time to break some totally deserving jerk's arm."

Most of the time he goes for the neck, actually. "That's different."

"Oh, absolutely. Garrett, at the risk of causing you a seizure because of my departure from the norm, you're full of shit."

Morley gets a kick out of arguing morals and ethics with anybody who'll sit still for it.

I said, "I need to get going. I only wanted to get the word to Reliance."

"You're beginning to pile up a real debt."

"I don't think so. You do still recollect who it was who didn't bother to tell his buddy that he was lugging a coffin full of vampire to a certain meeting with the gentleman who was the kingpin before our current, lovable Chodo Contague? What was that villain's name?"

Dotes rolled his eyes, looked to heaven and to hell. "I'm never going to hear the end of that, am I? I'm *never* going to hear the end of that."

"Nope. At least not while I have a parrot on staff. Hey, Kip. It's time to take you home."

56

Naturally, Kip had to find out if it was possible to resurrect the old order. I told him, "I learned something today, too. Bottom line, what it adds up to is, I don't put up with any more attitude from you. You give me any crap, I pop you. You don't behave like a human being, I hit you even harder than Sarge did. Sarge is a good man but he never was a Marine."

I led Kip to Kayne Prose's co-op. Kayne was pleased. Kayne squealed in delight, like a girl younger than her daughter. She hugged and kissed her baby. She hugged and kissed her baby's rescuer. She refused to turn the latter loose until he promised her an opportunity to demonstrate her gratitude more fully.

But when the smoke cleared away and the emotions settled out, Kayne still had sewing to do. She asked me to take Kip home. Where I found his sister Cassie trying on a new personality. This one was much more appealing. This one was very friendly indeed. I account it a miracle that I was able to escape still wearing my trousers, trailing a "Maybe later" that started me drooling every time I thought even a little bit about Cassie Doap.

What a life.

Rhafi did get the job.

57

One of the good things to happen in my life has been the unshakable friendship I've formed with Max Weider, the brewery magnate. I've done several jobs for Max. They didn't all work out the way we hoped but we did become friends of the sort who trust one another absolutely.

Where money and women are not concerned.

Max has a very lovely daughter named Alyx. Alyx is a bit of an adventuress, in her own mind. Alyx could complicate things without even trying.

A new man answered the door at the Weider mansion. Max doesn't go out much anymore. Like the old *majordomo,* this character's pointy nose spent most of its time higher in the air than did that of any member of the Weider family. That nose wrinkled when he saw me. I told him, "Go tell Gilbey that Garrett is here. It's business."

I cooled my heels outside until I began to suspect that the *majordomo* hadn't bothered to deliver my message. Manvil Gilbey, Max Weider's lifelong sidekick, wasn't as keen on me as everyone would be in a perfect world, but he was certain to let new help know. . . . How do you get a job like that? If you're the employer, how do you find somebody to do it?

The door opened. This time Manvil Gilbey himself stood on the other side. Behind him lurked a disappointed doorman. "I'm sorry, Garrett. Rogers only started yesterday. In all the confusion I forgot to let him know that you're one of the people we always want to see. Is there something going on at the brewery?"

"Could be. But this don't have anything to do with it."
I told the doorman, "Thanks for nothing, Bubba. Hey, Gilbey, how do you go about finding and hiring a guy who
can be snooty about opening doors?"

"Max is in the study. Napping when last I checked. Let's
go up. Maybe if you needle *him* a little he'll show some
interest in life. Are you involved in anything? I believe it
would be useful if we had you work your magic at a few
of the smaller breweries we've acquired the past couple of
years. Two or three of them keep showing some screwed-
up numbers."

"You kept the original workforces, right?"

"Top to bottom." Max always did, till individuals proved
themselves not worth keeping. Weider wasn't sentimental
about deadwood or crooks. "We only put in a handful of
our takeover guys. To study their processes. We try not to
change the final product. Unless it's really awful. But we
do look for ways to increase profitability. You'd be amazed
how many inefficiencies persist in this industry simply because things have always been done a certain way."

From the day they launched their first brewing operation
Weider and Gilbey had produced a quality product the
most efficient way possible. Today they control seventy percent of the human-directed brewing in the city. And they
have shares in many of the nonhuman breweries. Even
ogres understand enhanced profit margins and good beer.

Gilbey pushed through the second floor door to Max's
study, held it for me. I passed through into the heat.

Max always has a bonfire going in the fireplace there,
these days.

I missed a step. Max had aged a decade in the weeks
since last I'd seen him. He used to be a little round-faced,
red-cheeked, bald on top, smiling, twinkling-eye sort of guy.
Not now. He looked terrible. He had suffered a severe
decline in a very short time. Which wasn't that huge a surprise. Life had been exceedingly cruel to Max of late. He'd
had two children murdered and his wife pass away, all on
one horrible day.

Max wasn't napping after all. "Garrett. I see that you're

not here to brighten my day. And that your wardrobe has begun to decline already."

"I guess I'm just a natural-born slob."

"Do we have trouble on the floor again?"

"Not that I'm aware of. Manvil did ask me to check out a couple of the new satellite breweries. And I'll get to that right away. Before the end of the week. But what I came for this time is to beg the borrow of some business expertise."

Weider steepled his spidery, blue-veined fingers in front of his nose. The rheum went out of his eyes. His now nearly gaunt face showed a bit of light. I'd managed to pique his interest.

Gilbey, who had moved to a post beside his employer's chair, shot me a look that told me to get on with it while there was a chance of getting Max interested and engaged.

I could do this. I know how to keep a corpse awake and interested. Sometimes.

Manvil Gilbey isn't just Max Weider's number one lieutenant, he's his oldest and closest friend. They go back to their war years together. Which makes for a hell of a bond.

"What it is," I said, "is that I've stumbled across this kid who invents things. All kinds of things. Some are completely weird. Some are completely useless. And some are really neat. What I want is for somebody with a lot more commercial sense than I've got to eyeball the inventions and tell me if I'm fooling myself when I think somebody could get rich making some of them."

"Ah," Max said. "Another business opportunity. First time this week we've been offered the chance to get in on the ground floor, isn't it, Manvil?"

I pretended to miss his sarcasm. "I'm not looking for anybody to go in on it with me. I have that part worked out. If I could just have Manvil give me his honest opinion of the stuff in the kid's workshop, and if it matches mine, I'll see if the Tates want to manufacture them. Now that the war's over there isn't much demand for the army boots and leather whatnots they've been making for the last sixty years."

Max asked, "What's your take, Manvil?" He was well aware of my precarious relationship with one of the Tate girls. And he thought I was a raving romantic instead of a tough, lone, honest man battling to scourge evil from the mean streets, which is what I know that I really am. As long as I don't have to get up before noon to work the flails.

"I think friend Garrett might be even less devious than we've always thought. You weren't going to cut us in, Garrett?"

"Huh? Why should I? You guys already got more money than God and more work than—"

Max stilled me with a wave. "See what he's got, Manvil. Garrett, Willard Tate is a good choice. He's an excellent manager. And he does have that gorgeous redheaded niece besides." He knows about Tinnie because Tinnie and his daughter Alyx are friends. "I like your thinking there." Maybe because a Garrett involved with a Tinnie Tate again meant a Garrett not involved with any Weider daughters.

We may be friends but he's also a father.

Max leaned his head back and closed his eyes. End of consultation. For now.

Manvil actually smiled. I'd managed to get his buddy interested in something, at least for a little while.

58

"Sounds like a riot," I said. Gilbey and I, in the Weider coach, were nearing Playmate's stable.

Possibly it was a neighborhood war. A lot of sturdy subject types, armed with knives and cudgels, were trying to adjust the larcenous attitudes of the biggest daytime mob of ratmen I'd ever seen. There were dozens of them. And things weren't going their way. The street was littered with ratmen already down. The survivors were trying to retreat, burdened with booty. And just as Manvil and I arrived the Domains of Chaos spewed another ingredient into the cauldron.

At least twenty more ratmen appeared. They attacked the smash-and-grab guys with a ferocity I hadn't seen since the islands. They were determined to leave bodies behind. And they got as good as they gave.

I leaned out the coach door and told our driver, "Just stay real still and try to think invisible thoughts till this blows over."

"What's happening?" Gilbey asked. There was no color left in his face. He didn't get out on the town much.

"We seem to have strayed into the middle of a factional skirmish amongst members of the ratman underworld. What it was before it turned into that I won't know until I get a chance to look around." But I had a feeling it boded no good for me and my industrial schemes.

"Your life is never dull, is it?"

"A little dull wouldn't hurt, some days. I've thought about calling my autobiography *Trouble Follows Me*. The problem with that is, the troubles in my life are usually waiting when I get there."

The battle outside turned tricornered. Playmate's sturdy subject type neighbors couldn't tell one ratman from another. And most of them just plain welcomed a chance to whack on a thieving ratman anyway.

Whistles sounded in the distance. The Guards were gathering. I expected that, like the Watch before them, they would move in only after they were confident that they had nobody to deal with but people who couldn't crawl away.

I slipped down out of the coach. "Better stay in here for now, Manvil."

"No problem. I used up my adventurous side a long time ago."

One thing that's never in short supply around Playmate's stable is the rough hemp twine his hay-and-straw man uses to bundle his products before he brings them into town. Playmate saves the twine and gives it back.

I gathered a load and started tying rats. Neighbors thought that was a marvelous idea and joined right in.

"Not that one," I told one of the sturdy subjects. "The ones wearing the green armbands are the good guys. Sort of. We can fail to see them getting away if they're able to go."

That earned me some dark looks but no real arguments. Emotions were surprisingly cool, considering.

I tied fourteen ratmen personally before the Guard arrived. There were more still unbound. Almost all of the neighbors had started to carry Playmate's possessions back into the stable. They ignored instructions not to disturb the evidence. Most of that, I noted, was stuff that had been looted from Kip's workshop.

I returned to the Weider coach. "Come on. Let's see if they left anything I can show you."

To my delight, the three-wheel, *my* three-wheel, hadn't been disturbed. "This's the main thing I want to make. The biggest thing. Right here. Watch this." I climbed aboard, zoomed around as best I could in the confined space. "I can see every rich family in town wanting one of these for a toy. Come on. Try it."

As Gilbey was trying to get the hang of making the big front wheel turn in the correct direction I caught a sound from behind me and whirled, expecting an attack from some desperado ratman who'd been knocked down earlier or who'd gone into hiding when the tide had turned. What I found was a weak, cross-eyed Playmate trying to get up from where he'd been laid low by a blow to the head.

I gave him a hand up, which wasn't the best thing to do for him in his condition. I supported him till he could get his backside planted on a bale of hay and his spine pressed against a post. "How bad does it look, Garrett?" I was checking the top of his head.

"You're going to need a real surgeon. You've got a piece of scalp peeled back. The wound needs cleaning. You need a bunch of stitches. You're going to be enjoying headaches for days. What did they want?"

"They never told me but they meant to haul off everything Kip ever made."

"Didn't I warn you?'

"Yes. You did. How's Winger?"

"I don't know. I haven't seen her. She supposed to be here? I'll look around. Manvil, would you keep an eye on my friend, here? You remember how to deal with a head injury? Don't let him go to sleep."

I found no sign of Winger anywhere. I went back to Playmate. "You sure Winger was still here?"

"I still have fresh blisters on my ears from the language she used when this started, Garrett. She was busting up ratmen like she was killing snakes or something. They won't be good to her if they took her away."

"You Garrett?"

I jumped. I hadn't heard this guy come in. He was way shorter than me but plenty wide and all muscle. He had big, brushy eyebrows that met in the middle over mean-looking little blue eyes that, surely, concealed a bright mind. He was clad in businesslike apparel that managed to look shoddy even though it was relatively new. I knew what he was before I asked, "Who wants to know?"

"I do. Lucius Browling. Extraordinary Guard Services. Reporting straight to the director." Lucius Browling didn't offer to shake. Neither was he rude or confrontational.

"The director? What director?"

"Director Relway. Of the Emergency Committee for Royal Security."

Good old Relway. Count on him to paint the outside of his house of righteous thugs with colorful, high-sounding monikers. Monikers that would change as fast as people figured out that each was a hollow mask for something more sinister, probably.

"In that case, Garrett just left. If you hurry you can catch him. He's a little weasely-faced guy with a skinny black mustache . . . You know, all of you guys would get along with the world a lot better if you could just figure out what it means to have a sense of humor."

"Quite possibly you have a point. The director occasionally mentions how much he values your opinion. Perhaps you can raise the matter personally once we get to the al-Khar." He raised a hand to forestall my next question. "Colonel Block and the director both want to consult you concerning recent events. I'm just a messenger. Just one of a dozen EGS men in the field, hoping to run into you at one of your known haunts."

Implications, implications. They knew I wasn't at home. . . .

There was no point fighting it. "I'll be with you in a minute, then. Let me wrap up here." I stepped over to Gilbey. Manvil had been smart enough to get off the three-wheel before any outsider could get a good idea of what he was doing. Right now he was just a civilian who happened to be hanging around. "Tell Max. Let me know what you guys think." I turned. "Playmate. I want you to go see Drak Shevesh about your head. I've used him. He's the best there is. And it won't bother him that you're human."

I told Lucius Browling I was ready. He didn't cheer. He didn't say much, either. Which was just as well. I was a little preoccupied trying to spot the Goddamn Parrot and being worried about Winger.

I did tell Browling, "If your people have any real interest in what happened here you should round up a bounty hunter named Bic Gonlit. He had something to do with it somehow."

I was getting piqued with Bic. He was as stubborn about sticking to his job as I could be.

59

Colonel Block was in a formal mood when Browling led me into the biggest chamber I'd yet seen inside the city prison. It appeared to be several cells converted into a meeting room. There was a large table of mediocre quality, some uncomfortable chairs, no windows, and not nearly enough light. You could hide werewolves and vampires in the shadowy corners. Today those only held Deal Relway, playing ghost. Lucius Browling vanished as soon as I'd been delivered.

Three other, silent men were present. Nobody introduced anybody.

I didn't push. Those three likely told Block what to do and when to do it, and whether or not to smile while he did it. They had that Hill look.

Block said, "We've gotten back our first reports from the country, Garrett."

"Wow. You guys move fast when you want to. I take it something didn't go the way you wanted."

"Our people found physical evidence and local witnesses to corroborate your report. But your silver elves were gone."

So. The girl who got away must've come back to rescue the others. Elven enemies possibly having more in common than silver elves and people do. Or maybe it had to do with wanting a ride home.

Block continued, "The disk-shaped flying engine was gone, as well. The pear-shaped flying engines had been destroyed. Melted down in a heat so fierce they'd sunk right down into the earth. A search of the area produced nothing but these." He showed me several of the gray fetish things, similar but not identical to one another.

Without invitation I suggested, "If they were that thorough about cleaning up after themselves you'd better consider the possibility that those things there were meant to be found."

A small stir. The observers exchanged uneasy glances.

"You been holding anything back on us, Garrett?" Relway asked from his shadow.

"Deal," Block cautioned. "Garrett? It's a pertinent question, despite Deal's tone."

I wondered if Relway ever got to be the nice guy. "And the answer is, probably. Without meaning to. Remember, I brought this stuff to you guys. I don't have any idea what you need to know, let alone anything at all about the much vaster category of 'want to know.' "

"We don't need to get into any pissing contests, Garrett. I have a job. All I want to do is to get it done."

"And I'm not up for any macho headbutting, either. Where we have trouble is, you don't want me to know *why* you want to know what you want to know. You even probably don't want me to know *what* you want to know. Which'll really make it impossible to answer your questions intelligently. But you'll still put the blame on me when you don't hear what you want to hear. Chances are good you'll even accuse me of lying or holding out."

One of the observers made a gesture. Block cocked his head slightly. Although I wasn't included in I understood that there was some communicating going on in much the same fashion as when I conversed with the Dead Man. A very small handful of the most powerful of our wizardly overlords have been able to develop that talent.

I *was* able to read the emotional overtones.

A man entered the room. His interruption earned him frowns from everyone but me. I didn't care. He whispered to Relway briefly. Relway studied me as though he'd just suffered a mild surprise.

That did nothing to make me more comfortable.

Colonel Block admitted, "Your argument has considerable merit, Garrett."

In private I would've accused him of being a poetaster or some other artsy critter equally heinous. In front of people, where I might embarrass him, I said only, "My thinking is that we're all on the same side despite maybe having different goals. . . ."

There was a sign from another of the observers. I shut up because I could sense that this particular guy had taken a negative shine to me and wasn't likely to invest a great deal of patience in me.

Block said, "These silver elves seem to control a lot of powerful sorcery, the flight thing being only the most obvious. We'd very much like to explore some of those secrets. And right now you're the closest thing to an expert on them as exists."

"And I've given you everything. . . . Wait a minute. There's Casey. Though you should know about Casey on your own."

"Casey?"

"The only silver elf I've actually talked to. His name is something really weird. He prefers Casey. He claims to be a cop. He says he was sent out to arrest two elves nobody's seen except maybe one crazy teenage boy. A boy who, after I grilled him mercilessly, turned out to have no clue how to find *any* elves. A boy who couldn't even find his own way home without help. Casey wasn't sure what crimes the fugitives had committed. And he didn't care. That was for his judges to worry about. He had an apartment . . ." I gave the directions and details and recommended extreme caution on the parts of any investigators. Questions arose. I answered as many as I could.

Relway had another visit from the whisperer. He took an opportunity to do some whispering of his own, to Colonel Block, before he left the room in a hurry. To put together a raid on Casey's place, I assumed.

Once he was gone, Block said, "There're people here looking for you, Garrett. Legal type people. Did Browling do something wrong? Did he manhandle you or insult you or in any way demonstrate a lack of courtesy?"

I paused, definitely puzzled, but then observed, "Either you're really naive or you just don't understand what you and Relway have created. There isn't any need for Lucius Browling to be anything but Lucius Browling for alarms to sound and people to get upset."

He didn't get it. We didn't lapse into a philosophical pissing contest in front of the wizards. For such they surely were, in mufti.

"You aren't a prisoner, Garrett. You aren't under arrest. You're an expert we called in to help us with a particular problem. And I wish you'd tell those people that. Evidently they're making life very difficult for the staff up front."

"They won't go away just because you trot me out. What kind of legal beagle is going to take the word of a man who's in the hands of—"

"Thank you, Mr. Garrett. I suspect that I've just learned a valuable lesson. And that I'll be happy that Relway wasn't here to pick it up as easily. Might I request your presence and assistance for as long as it takes Relway to investigate that elf's hideout. I'll provide a small honorarium."

"I'll go tell the folks in the waiting room. But if they're the kind of people I think they are, they won't leave until I do."

Block glowered.

And I was right about the lawyers.

60

The Casey raid was a disaster for the secret police. Almost everything had been removed from the place except for an extensive array of booby traps, most of them so cunning there was no way to detect them before they did their evil work.

"There were two corpses in the place when we got there," Relway told us. "According to people in the building both were tenants who sprang traps while they were looting the place. They'd been there a while. They were getting ripe. The same people told us the elf came back this morning, beat-up and dirty. He did whatever he did in his apartment, then went through the building reclaiming his stolen stuff, which he loaded into a waiting wagon. He did leave a few things behind because he didn't have time to recover everything. He was still there, at it, just ten minutes before we arrived. But, somehow, he knew we were coming. At ten minutes he dropped everything and took off."

I offered a suggestion. "Look for a livery stable in the neighborhood. A place that has donkeys stabled. Possibly for rent. And don't count on being able to recognize this guy if you run into him. He loves disguises. And he has sorceries that help him look like other people. And some of the other elves have demonstrated the ability to make themselves invisible."

"What was that about a donkey?"

I rehashed my first encounter with Casey, disguised as Bic Gonlit. And then explained that the real Bic Gonlit seemed to be making his living working for ratman crime bosses these days. And that I suspected that the raid on Playmate's stable had been incited by the false Bic.

Block wanted to explore the whole Bic Gonlit question more closely. There seemed to be one long coincidence right in the middle of things, that being that both Bic Gonlits would cross my path on unrelated matters.

"It probably wasn't total coincidence," I mused. "But I'm confident that there's no grand plot. In order to pretend to be Bic Gonlit, Casey would've had to get close to the real Bic to study him. So Bic's probably had an unexpected friend during recent months. You might see what he has to say about that."

Colonel Block gave me a hard look. I'd just set poor Bic up for some difficult times. But Block said, "Suppose there isn't a coincidence? Is it possible that this Casey wanted to pull you in? Maybe so he'd have somebody who really knows TunFaire looking for the two elves he wants to find?"

I considered the almost compulsive need I had, at times, for finding Lastyr and Noodiss. "It could be. I think it could be." So did that make it the grand plot that I was confident didn't exist?

I don't think so. I have a feeling there was a lot of opportunism and seizing the day going on around me, particularly by Casey and Bic Gonlit.

None by me, of course. I'm too damned dumb. And then some.

"It's been another long day, Colonel," I said. "And I don't see how I can possibly be any more help, no matter how much I might want to be. Other than to get those people up front out of your hair." I was curious about that. I didn't know anybody in the legal profession. Not well, anyway. Lawyerdom is a small community with very little official standing outside the realm of commercial relations. "And you do know where to find me if you need me."

Block seemed distracted as he said, "All right. You're right. You might as well go home."

As I rose, I said, "Here's an idea. Everything that used to belong to the elves. Whatever you've managed to gather up. Isolate it somewhere. Try not to talk out loud around it. And if you try to figure out how something's magic works, make sure you don't give away any of your own. I really believe they can spy on us through those little gray blocks, somehow."

Colonel Block got up and walked me out himself. Once we were well away from that meeting room and the heart of his little empire, he asked, "You do know who those people were, don't you?"

"Not specifically who. I know what."

"All right. Listen to this. You've crossed paths with two of those three before. As I understand it. One of them doesn't like you even a little bit. I don't know what you did to inconvenience him, when or where, but he's definitely not big on forgive and forget. If we convene one of these brainstorming sessions again, consider the remote possibility that you might do yourself the most good by not volunteering any information. Or suggestions. They don't trust anything they don't have to work to get. They're cynical at a level that makes your cynicism look like playacting."

I didn't argue. I didn't see any point. I wasn't quite sure I got the point he was trying to make, either. He was sort of doing that sidewise friend thing where he thought he didn't dare be direct. I guess he was telling me to watch my back where spooky people off the Hill were involved.

To me that didn't seem like a lesson that needed to be taught to anyone over the age of seven.

61

The legal talent had been laid on first by the Weider brewing consortium. Manvil Gilbey being quick on the draw. Later, a gentleman had arrived who, allegedly, was associated with a rather more sinister enterprise.

Harvester Temisk has been the legal point man for Chodo Contague for ages. He continues to handle some things in Chodo's name, even though Belinda is in charge now, secretly. Which likely is no secret to him.

I couldn't imagine how Harvester Temisk could've gotten involved with my problems. And he wasn't the least bit forthcoming when I asked. All he had to say was, "I want you to come see me as soon as your current calendar clears."

Inasmuch as his presence might've led to my elevation from detainee to paid consultant, I told him I'd look him up as soon as I could.

I was profuse in my gratitude to the Weider man, too, a skinny little critter with a balding head, a huge brush of a mustache, and the oddball name Congo Greeve.

Neither lawyer could've done a lot for me, legally speaking, because the Guard were pretty much making things up as they went. What the lawyers' appearance did was put the Guard on notice that influential people were concerned about my welfare. And influence, nepotism, cronyism, and bribery are how the system works, Deal Relway's mad notions of universal justice and meritocracy notwithstanding. And the actual producers and the gangsters have far more influence than our masters on the Hill see as reasonable.

                            *   *   *

I first spotted the Goddamn Parrot when I was only a
block from home. That animated feather duster was getting
too clever about going unnoticed.

And just after I spotted the bird I realized that I hadn't
been entirely forthright during my interview. I'd forgotten
to mention my elven house guests.

In fact, I'd forgotten them completely.

*Take care, Garrett. There are unfriendly ratmen in the
neighborhood.*

That seemed hard to credit after so many had gone down
at Playmate's stable. Still, Old Bones isn't in the habit of
being excitable.

It turned out there were only two unfriendly ratmen.
And one of those had a limp so profound he was no threat
to anyone but himself. The uncrippled individual approached me in a manner so bold that people on the street
turned to marvel. "Mr. Garrett?"

"Guilty." This close to the Dead Man I didn't feel any
special risk. "What do you need?"

"I bring a message from John Stretch. He has the
woman Winger."

This ratman was no Pular Singe. I could barely understand him.

*As a point of information, Garrett, this fellow is John
Stretch. He has only a handful of followers left, most of them
injured. He fears they will desert him if he demonstrates any
hesitance or lack of resolve.*

"Couldn't happen to a more deserving guy. I hope they
enjoy a long and prosperous marriage."

The ratman appeared nonplussed. "John Stretch says he
will trade the woman Winger for the female Pular Singe."

"Hell, so would I. You're kidding, right? One of my
friends put you up to pulling my leg. Right? Who was it?
You can help me get him back."

The ratman was confused. This wasn't going anything
like he planned. "John Stretch says he will harm the woman
Winger—"

"John Stretch isn't likely to live long enough to harm
anybody or to make deals with anybody. Rather than mak-

ing more enemies John Stretch ought to be trying to find himself some new friends."

Bic Gonlit.

Yes, indeed. "I *might* do business if Bic Gonlit was available for trade."

The ratman had been difficult to understand when he was delivering a rehearsed message. Now I had to rely on a relay from the Dead Man in order to grasp what he was trying to say.

"You do not want the woman Winger?"

"What would I do with her? Nope. She's all yours. And she's going to take some feeding, I'll tell you. But I am strongly interested in getting my hands on Bic Gonlit. Bic Gonlit has messed me around a couple of times lately. I'm ready to settle up."

"Perhaps that could be arranged." The ratman looked thoughtful.

"Actually, there're two Bic Gonlits. The real Bic is short for a human male. He wears white boots covered with fake gemstones. The second Bic is a pretender. He's a little taller and never wears boots. This false Bic Gonlit has created a lot of mischief. I believe he was responsible for the bad advice that led to the disaster at the stable today."

The ratman had questions, suddenly. He had big trouble asking them without revealing that he was, himself, John Stretch. He was no genius but he did understand that he wasn't going to come out on top if we got into a scuffle.

I told him, "The false Bic is really a wicked elf who has disguised himself so the real Bic will get blamed for the evil he does. I still haven't figured out why he wants to cause strife and unhappiness. I guess he just does. Maybe it's fun."

I didn't believe that but it sounded like the sort of behavior and motivation that would make sense to a John Stretch.

John Stretch was a record-setter of a ratman. He had berries the size of coconuts—but limited smarts to go with them. Though a lack of brains never has been a huge handicap in TunFaire's underworld. Guts and daring get you ahead faster.

"I want them both. But the false Bic more than the other."

The ratman twitched, mad as hell. But he maintained his self-control. "I will inform John Stretch. What should I tell him about the woman Winger?"

"I don't know. She's his problem. You could let him know she's involved with The Call. And that one of her lovers is Deal Relway. Of the Guard. He might find that information useful when he decides how to dispose of her."

The Call is a virulently racist veterans' organization, armed and organized as a private, political army. It shares a good many goals with Deal Relway. I wouldn't want to be a ratman who came to The Call's attention because I'd done harm to a human woman.

And Deal Relway is Deal Relway, increasingly the bogeyman to all those who practice wickedness in TunFaire.

I stopped to visit with some of the pixies. From brief encounters I knew two of the youngsters by sight, a daring boy who called himself Shakespear and a young lady named Melondie Kadare, who was so sweet and pretty I wished I could whack her with a transmogrification stick and grow her up to my size.

Melondie was the pixie who had followed me into the alley out back on the occasion of my first encounter with a silver elf in a Bic Gonlit disguise. Back then she'd been a precocious, curious adolescent. Now she was a serious, refined young woman. More or less. When the old folks were looking.

Pixie lives race away far faster than our own. I think that may be why we're uncomfortable around the little people. They're so much like us, in miniature. Their swiftly lived lives remind us, piquantly, that our own more numerous hours are still painfully and perfectly numbered.

62

Singe let me into the house moments after the Goddamn Parrot, evidently under the illusion that he was some kind of eagle, slammed down onto my right shoulder and tried to carry me off to his aerie.

He couldn't work up quite enough lift. So he gave up.

I feared Singe was going to climb all over me exactly the way I'd wished about a thousand young women of passing acquaintance would've done in days of yore. And she might've done so if the sexier silver elf hadn't come out of the Dead Man's room to see what was happening. She wore a tattered old shirt probably taken from Dean's ragbag. It might've served as a child's nightshirt before it acquired all those holes. It was barely sufficient to cover the subject. Most of the time.

That was distracting. Even on her. Because there was nothing but her underneath the tatters.

Maybe it was some sort of experiment by His Nibs.

Singe settled for clinging to my arm. "So what great adventures did you get to enjoy out there today, while the rest of us were locked up here, dying of boredom?"

I detached the Goddamn Parrot from my shoulder. "I traded you to John Stretch for two Bic Gonlits and a sugar-cured ham." I tossed the jungle chicken in the general direction of his perch, in the small front room.

"What?" Singe shrieked.

"John Stretch really wants you. You really turned his head."

Garrett, do not be a fool. Miss Pular is about to fly into a panic. What you are saying means more to her than it should.

"I'm sorry, Singe. I'm sorry. I didn't mean that like it sounded. I was teasing you. Yes, I did tell John Stretch that I'd trade you for two Bics. But his chances of . . ."

Garrett!

"All right! Singe, no matter what I told John Stretch, I'm not letting you go. Nobody is going to take you away. So relax. Take some time, again, to see if you can't figure out when you're being teased. And I'll try to rein it in. If I can. Humans seldom speak straightforwardly and direct. I find that frustrating myself, sometimes." Like almost every time I spend more than a few minutes in the company of most human women. "Anyway, even if I was that big a villain, how likely is it that John Stretch would keep his word?"

"Because he's nothing but a slimy little rat, you mean, and we all know that ratpeople are nothing but stupid, lazy, lying, thieving, smelly animals?"

While Singe shouted the Dead Man passed along one or two points of interest. *Well, well. The ratman who calls himself John Stretch was born Pound Humility, of the same female one litter before Miss Pular Singe. It may be that his interest in her is less political than personal. Miss Pular suspects an unwanted brother's concern for his sister's welfare. From the viewpoint of a ratman she would be making a huge mistake by getting involved with you.*

"Whoa! Whoa! Singe! I'm sorry! I apologize! That isn't what I meant at all." I felt a variant of Winger's question kicking in. If the woman who heard it wasn't human was the man still wrong? Apparently so. I'd tripped a triggerwire and I wasn't going to talk my way out of this one.

Good to see that you are not going to deny that she is involved with you, even if you do not feel that you are involved with her.

The Dead Man rescued me. This once. Because this wasn't a hole I'd dug for myself without help and because Singe was creeping up on the edge of true hysteria. And if there's anything the Dead Man dislikes more than females in general, or as a class, it's hysterical females.

There was one plus side to the whole emotional circus. Although ratgirls do get upset, they don't shed tears.

The silver elf woman just kept standing there, gaunt as Famine Himself in that old shirt, taking the scene in with those huge, strange eyes. She didn't seem frightened anymore. I wondered how much she was picking up from the Dead Man.

63

Dean brought food and drink to the Dead Man's room. He seemed to have adjusted to the extended presence of guests. He and Singe, in particular, seemed to have achieved a sound accommodation.

After relating my extensive adventures I asked the Dead Man, "Have you been able to learn anything from our elven guests?"

A great deal. Beginning with the obvious fact that they are not actually elves, nor are they members of any similar or familiar species. Nor are they a mixture of familiar species. Nothing that I have learned, by the way, was provided to me voluntarily. They suspect, but do not yet know, that they have revealed a great deal about themselves and their kind. This one knows herself as Evas, which is the diminutive for something even I cannot fathom. The other is Fasfir and was the captain of their party of three. They have much more complex interior lives than human beings, yet seem to envy your emotional freedoms. Fasfir, curiously, seems to have a rudimentary sense of humor.

"All right. Your talents are mighty and your cleverness surpasses anything the world has ever seen. What do we know now that we didn't know yesterday?"

We now know that Casey is what he claims to be, an officer of their law sent here a year ago to arrest Lastyr and Noodiss. Insofar as I can decipher the images in Evas' mind, which is much easier to penetrate than is Fasfir's, those two are religious missionaries originally sent out by an outlaw cult known as the Brotherhood of Light. Proselytization is a major crime under the laws of these people. Casey is supposed to arrest them, simply for their intent to proselytize.

They stole the skyship they used to come here. They were not skilled in its operation. They crashed it into the river. Their motives for teaching Kip to invent things have to do with wanting him to create things that have to exist before they can begin to make the tools that they will need to fix their ship.

Which takes them into another entire realm of crime entirely, apparently. That of revealing the secrets of state sorcery. Another department sent out Evas and her companions to seize Lastyr and Noodiss for betraying sorcerous secrets, the fact of those crimes having been included in Casey's reports, which somehow leaked over to the competing bureau.

"If they needed a ship why didn't they just go down to the waterfront and hire one?"

Evidently the journey is too long to make in a normal sailing ship, which supposedly cannot travel fast enough to make it to their country in even a Loghyr's lifetime.

"Wow." What else could I say? I've always known that the world is bigger than what I've experienced in my thirty years, but distances on that scale are beyond my comprehension. "And what about the elves from the flying disk? Who are they? Still more cops?"

They appear to be something resembling a sorcerer who, though he spends his whole lifetime studying magic and discovering new things about it, never does anything more practical with his discoveries than just write the information down. They are members of a fraternity where the search for knowledge is an end in itself. The excitement about Lastyr and Noodiss alerted them to the existence of Karenta and TunFaire, so they assembled an expedition to come study us. Apparently they wanted to grab Kip Prose because their ship is suffering its own problems and they thought that if they could open communications with Lastyr and Noodiss, working together they could produce one working vessel from the two cripples.

I do stumble into the weird stuff. And you can't get much weirder than this.

These last four may also have been doing commercial surveys of some sort, as a condition of gaining financial support for their research. At least one of them may be a ringer who really works for a law enforcement bureau that somehow oversees commerce. Fasfir holds all four in complete contempt. At the same time she is convinced that they are her crew's only chance of ever getting home. If their aerial ship can be made capable of completing one more long voyage, Fasfir sees two ways of accomplishing that. One calls for an improbable amount of good luck making repairs to the one aerial ship you saw up close in the wine country. The other requires that she and her friends find Lastyr and Noodiss so that their wrecked flying ship can be cannibalized to make repairs to the other. Fasfir is much more knowledgeable than is Evas, who seems to be the junior member of the mission.

The creature Casey will have a ship of his own hidden somewhere, of course. There is a general consensus that he will rescue no one but himself. He feels no responsibility for the others. But he will take Lastyr and Noodiss back as prisoners. And Fasfir is afraid that those two might be ready to surrender. They came here to save Karentine souls and teach Karentines forbidden magics that would make their lives easier but after a year of exposure to our savage ways, she fears, even those two have to have become convinced that we deserve our damnation.

"Not exactly original thinking there." A quick visit to the Chancery steps will expose you to all the outrage against the moral destitution of our times that you can possibly stand. Most of us are so poverty-stricken morally that we don't realize that we're missing something. According to the rant-and-ravers.

It was unoriginal when I was a stripling. It is a long slide indeed that never reaches bottom.

"You ever find any way to communicate with them directly?"

I have not yet given the matter much consideration. However, and despite any pretense to the contrary, this one understands spoken Karentine perfectly. They have a sorcery which allows them to learn very quickly.

Meaning she was tracking my part of the conversation.

Exactly.

"Ouch. But is there any solid reason for us to hide?"

Evas stood motionless, regarding me with those huge, unblinking eyes, possibly trying to see inside me, to the place where I was listening to the Dead Man. I wondered if she was having any success. I conjured a vivid erotic vision of the two of us rather energetically being boys and girls together. The Dead Man made his disgust known immediately. The silver elf did not, though by happenstance there was a huge crash in the kitchen.

I did get a somewhat puzzled look from Singe, which confirmed my suspicion that she might be slightly sensitive herself.

Very slightly. For which be grateful. Had she viewed that image we might be dealing with hysteria all over again.

"You know, I still ache all over anytime I sit still for very long. I don't want to be a detective anymore today. And when I get up tomorrow I just want to be an accountant trying to figure out how to make sure we get paid for all of this. Can they read and write?"

I do not know. And now I can no longer see inside Evas' head without hammering my way in. For some reason she has begun to suspect that someone here might be able to read her mind. You would not have any notion why she might suspect that, would you?

I shrugged. It didn't seem likely, did it?

I'm not usually much concerned about money—as long as I've got some. I was growing concerned because of this mess, though. We were spending and spending and spending to hire help and buy food and there seemed to be an ever smaller likelihood of us managing any return on investment. Kip was back home with his family. The silver elves seemed to have lost interest in him. After the country confrontation, they all knew that he couldn't finger Lastyr and Noodiss.

But Old Bones was having him one hell of a good time, I could tell. This thing was the most fun he'd had in years. It was something *new*. These two weird women, Evas and Fasfir, were, to him, as exciting and alluring as was my friend Katie to me.

I said, "This's the least violent, least traditional thing we've ever been into. I'm not comfortable with it at all. The stakes are trivial and these silver elves are too alien for me to find very interesting."

Perhaps you will feel differently in the morning. Try considering the stakes from a viewpoint not your own. I will be doing that myself now that I have the mind time free. One obvious avenue of exploration is the possible dangers the Lords of the Hill fear.

"Those old paranoids are only scared because they think the whole world is infested with people as cruel and wicked and mean-spirited as they are."

True. But that does not render them automatically wrong in every instance. They can be afraid in a huge way because it is possible for them to have huge enemies to make life terrible, not just for them but for us all. Just one of these silver elves needs to be wicked and willing to use their weird but powerful sorcery against us.

He was right about that. Those people controlled some very strange powers.

He was right about me feeling differently in the morning, too—for reasons entirely unrelated to any remotely within his consideration at the time.

64

I wakened suddenly, thinking those pixies had to go. But they were quiet. Instead, there was a weak light burning and I wasn't alone in my bed. When I turned to tell Singe, yet again, that this couldn't happen, a spidery gray finger fell upon my lips. Another spidery finger touched a large eye, then tapped my temple.

Oh, boy. What was this? The silver elf woman, Evas, knelt on the edge of my bed. She'd seen that naughty image after all. And she'd brought a sheaf of papers with her. I recognized them. They'd all been in my office, on my desk, before I'd come upstairs.

Evas could read and write Karentine. And she'd been a busy little scribbler.

She placed the papers in my hands. The top sheet said, simply, *Teach me*.

She removed that raggedy, short shirt. And again placed a finger on my lips when I started to tell her to go away.

That petite form definitely did have its appeal, suddenly. I couldn't resist wondering about its possibilities.

Later I would wonder if there was any chance my thoughts had been guided from outside.

Evas moved the top sheet of paper to the bottom of the stack.

Followed a story of an extremely ancient people who, ages ago, had decided to set aside the insidious and constant distortions of the intellect that are caused by the stormy demands of sexual reproduction.

I could relate to that. Some would claim that I'm intellectually distorted most of the time. I confess freely that I'd be much more respectable and much less emotionally vagrant if the gods hadn't seen fit to bless and curse the rest of us with women.

Evas declared herself a despicable throwback who suffered wicked urges and curiosities all the time. She'd fought those successfully until now only because she'd always been surrounded by people who wouldn't let her get into situations where she might embarrass herself.

Here, tonight, she had an opportunity to pursue the curiosities that were driving her mad. And her people would never be the wiser.

Chances were excellent that such an opportunity would never come to her again.

She knew the mechanics. She'd taken advantage of her ability to move around unseen to indulge her curiosity intellectually. They all had. She was the only one who hadn't been repelled.

Back to sheet one and *Teach me.*

Hers was a whole new, entirely intellectual approach to the art of seduction. Backed up by what my rude senses could gather of her mental state. Evas wasn't kidding. And in that weak light she looked far more exotic and desirable than weird.

I had fallen into every red-blooded boy's favorite daydream.

At some point Evas took time out to use a thin fingertip to trace letters on my skin to pass me the message, "I will not break." She wanted me to know that she wasn't nearly as fragile as she looked.

65

"Good morning, Sunshine," Dean told me, nudging me to let me know he'd brought my tea. I was half-asleep at the breakfast table, unable to stop grinning.

I grunted.

"Odd. You're smiling. And you got to bed at a reasonable hour for once. But you're as crabby as a mountain boozelt."

"Them damned pixies. They never shut up. All night long."

He didn't challenge me. That could only mean that he didn't know any better.

Singe appeared, obviously having been up since the crack of dawn. She was chipper, though possibly more conspiratorial than ever. She was pleasant to me. Nor was I getting any grief from the Dead Man.

When Evas turned up she was coolly indifferent to everything but some tea heavily sweetened with honey. She was exactly as she had been yesterday except, possibly, for projecting a somewhat more resigned attitude toward her captivity. Her sidekick Fasfir, though equally cool, presented a puzzle. She kept looking at me the way you might regard a twenty-foot python you found coiled atop the kitchen table: repelled, wary, awed, maybe a little intrigued and excited.

Still nothing from the Dead Man.

That must've been one hell of a dream I'd had. Especially since it'd reawakened all my aches and pains and had added a few that were new.

Evas might be willing to let me think it had been all a dream spawned by my wicked imagination but I noted, with some satisfaction, that she moved very carefully and did so mainly when she thought no one was paying attention. Fasfir noticed, though.

So. She knew.

My grin spread a little wider.

"What evil thought just burst into your mind?" Singe demanded. There was an actual teasing edge to her voice.

"Nothing special. Just a warm memory."

Once I finished eating, and began to feel a little more awake, I moved to my office. I was feeling positive and eager to get things done. But before I could start I had to go round up a pile of missing paperwork.

During the course of the morning, various people came by the house. Most wanted money. Playmate was effusive with gratitude but didn't bring one copper sceat to defray the costs of my efforts to salvage his madonna's useless infant. I responded to two written requests for clarification or additional information from the good people at the al-Khar. I received a note from Manvil Gilbey telling me that Max Weider wanted in financially. The same messenger brought a sealed note from Max's daughter Alyx, who complained that she was dying of loneliness and that that was all my fault and when was I going to do something about it?

There were other notes in time, including one from Kayne Prose, inscribed for her by a professional letter writer. That was meant to impress me. And it did, a little. Then there was a discreet letter from Uncle Willard Tate, who invited me to the Tate compound for dinner because he'd just enjoyed an intriguing visit from a certain Manvil Gilbey, associated with the Weider brewing empire. The paper on which the letter was written had a light lilac scent. The hand in which it had been inscribed was familiar and almost mocking.

It reminded me which redheaded, green-eyed beauty managed the Tate correspondence and accounts.

I'd have to gird my mental and emotional loins for that visit. Tinnie was sure to play me like a cheap kazoo if I was bold enough to venture onto her home ground.

The afternoon saw the arrival of a formal, engraved invitation to participate in the celebration of Chodo Contague's sixtieth birthday party, two weeks down the road. And a "Just wanted to say hi" note from solicitor Harvester Temisk, implying that he'd really like to visit before Chodo's birthday celebration.

Dean began to grouse about having to answer the door constantly—when he wasn't hard at work pursuing his custom of charming whatever woman happened to be staying in the house. It was he who took Evas far enough along to lure forth a spoken word of gratitude. She didn't pronounce the word right and she had difficulty saying it but she did demonstrate that at least one silver elf besides Casey came equipped with a capacity for speech. Yet one more talent unsuspected by us primitives until she betrayed herself. Possibly she was a throwback in more ways than the one.

Fasfir didn't seem pleased.

I had begun to develop an idea of the personalities of our reluctant guests. Evas was cool and brilliant and collected and always in control. In her own mind. But in real life she'd be her own worst enemy. A sort of foreign Kayne Prose with a mind. With her self-destructive urges skewed at a different angle. Fasfir would *be* cool and collected and always in control but, like the best officers and sergeants, would be skilled at failing to see those transgressions which did not threaten the world with an immediate descent into chaos and anarchy.

Singe invited herself into my office to preen and gossip. There wasn't a lot to gossip about, though, unless she wanted to discuss the recipes Dean had begun sharing with her.

I asked, "How close are you to your brother?" I didn't think family was important among ratpeople, but had only prejudice and hearsay to go by.

"I do not have a brother. What does this one say?" She had started leafing through my papers.

"Which side?"

With unerring accuracy she had chosen the side which said, *Teach me.*

I told her.

"What does that mean?"

"I don't know. This isn't a royal style business. I don't have a few million people I can gouge for taxes anytime the urge takes me so I have to make do with whatever bits and pieces of paper come my way. My stuff is on the other side."

I hoped Singe hadn't done any poking around in here. There were almost two dozen identical sheets of paper inside my desk drawer, with both faces still virgin to the pen.

I stuck to my subject. "What do you mean, you don't have a brother? What's John Stretch, then?"

"Oh. Well. We do not see some things the same way you do. Humility belongs to the litter before mine. He would have a different father." Ratpeople follow social and mating customs much closer to those of rodents than they do those of civilized beings such as myself. Chances were excellent that few of Singe's littermates shared the same father.

"Humility?"

Singe responded with one of her rehearsed shrugs.

"So his real name is Pular Humility?"

"No. It is Pound Humility." That's right. The Dead Man did tell me that. "His sire is believed to have been Hurlock Pound. Chances are good. My mother managed to retain some choice and self-control even during the peak of her season. I hope I will have the strength to do the same. Though I am less likely to go into season as long as I remain in exile."

The name Hurlock Pound meant nothing to me. "Never mind. I'm too groggy to keep up with all that. Let's stick with John Stretch. Why did you get upset yesterday when—"

"Because I have spent too much time around you people. I suppose. And because Humility was always good to me when I was little."

"But now he wants to use you as a counter in his effort to make himself king of the ratmen."

"Just do not go hunting him. All right? That way I cannot blame myself for whatever he gets himself into."

"I guess. Whatever." The child was strange. I was convinced that *she* didn't know what she wanted most of the time. Unlike her doomed brother, she didn't know where she wanted to go.

Then again, I'm sometimes wrong.

"I have been wondering, Garrett. Do you think it would be possible for me to learn to read and write?"

So that was where she'd been going when she'd chosen that sheet of paper. I gave it some thought because, honestly, "I've never thought about it. That's probably because of the prejudices all us humans are brought up with. Do you know any ratpeople who can read or write?"

"No. Reliance is the only one I know who needs to. So he has a couple of slaves to keep his books and write his letters. The same goes for the other ratman gangs."

I kept a straight face. "Have you ever heard of anyone who tried to learn?"

"I've met some who wanted to learn. Wanted to *try* to learn. But who would teach them?"

Who indeed? Nobody in TunFaire, of whatever race, wanted ratpeople getting notions, taking on airs, thinking above their station.

"All right. Karentine is the main language in TunFaire so it's what you'll know best." I recovered the sheet carrying the request, *Teach me.* Ironic. "Do you know any of these letters by name?"

She didn't then but half an hour later she knew them all and had a solid grasp on the concept of how characters and groups of characters represent the sounds that make up spoken words. That was because she'd paid attention most of her life. To everything going on around her.

I sorted out every paper I had that had anything on it in Evas' handwriting—which was, actually, laborious, tiny printing—and got that all put away. "We humans might ought to have you strangled right now, Singe. I swear, you're going to take over the world in a few more years."

For once she grasped the compliment. She was learning in every direction.

I hoped she was as good in her heart as she seemed. Otherwise, I'd be helping to create a monster.

66

I did hear the pixies get excited but missed the knock on the door. I'd fallen deep into contemplation of Eleanor, who seemed to be contemplating me right back. She didn't approve of the way I'd been running my life lately. When Eleanor disapproves I know it's time to do some serious reassessment. I thought I had a handle on it, too.

Dean stuck his head into the office. "There're some very nervous ratmen on the stoop."

John Stretch.

"John Stretch?"

"One gave me that name."

"I'm on my way."

Bring them to my room.

I swung the door open. "Get in here, guys. They're watching the place most of the time these days. Bic, bitty buddy. How're you doing? Not too good, I guess. And Casey," as a second Bic shuffled forward. "I know that must be you in that disguise. Screwed up, eh? Damn, John Stretch, you got them both. I didn't think you could do it." I made sure the door was solidly locked, just to retard any attempt at a hurried exit. "Go into the room behind the door on the right, please. Dean! These guys look like they're starved. Singe! Where are you? We've got company. Give Dean a hand."

In my heart I was wondering if, perhaps, Singe wasn't the only genius pup produced by her mother. And this other pup did want to be in charge.

John Stretch and his friends didn't know what to make of the Dead Man. It's hard to do, him sitting there like an idol that gives off just a hint of bad aroma. Chances were excellent that they'd never run into a Loghyr before. It could be, in fact, that they'd never heard of the Loghyr race.

They didn't know what to make of Fasfir when she invited herself in, either. She drew plenty of attention from Casey, though. Casey seemed amazed to find her alive and more amazed to find her clad in ragged native garb. But he kept his opinions to himself. The Dead Man assured me that Casey had closed his mind with a determination that was stunning. For the time being he was locked up tighter than Fasfir was.

He must suspect something.

Either that or he was a natural-born paranoid.

I took my seat. "Damn again, John Stretch. How in the world did you manage to round up these two?"

Interesting. He has a talent of his own. He can use his normal rat cousins to scout and spy for him, much as I employ Mr. Big. Though his reach is very much shorter than mine.

"It couldn't be any other way." I continued, "You put me in a nasty position, John Stretch. My reputation for keeping my word is my most important asset."

Last time we met, I thought John Stretch must be dim. He wasn't. Not even a little. He understood that I wanted to weasel out. "You agreed to a deal. *We* have fulfilled our undertaking." His Karentine remained hard to follow but was adequately understandable. His courage was beyond question. Ratmen don't talk back to humans, let alone imply threats.

"The problem is, long before I made the deal with you I swore a solemn oath to Singe that I wouldn't let any of you people drag her away from here."

"And he knows that if he does not keep his word to me he will soon wish he was enjoying the torments of one of his human hells instead of basking in my displeasure." Singe staggered under the weight of a tray of hastily assem-

bled sandwiches. She set that on the little table, began to
help herself. John Stretch and his ratmen waited only long
enough to get a nod from me before they assaulted the pile.

Singe brought her muzzle within inches of John Stretch's.
With her mouth full and crumbs in her whiskers, she demanded, "What the hell do you think you are doing, Pound
Humility? I am not a pawn in your game. I will not be a
pawn in your game. I will not be a quiet, obedient little
ratgirl who lets herself be passed around like a weed pipe."
John Stretch and his henchmen glared daggers at me. This
was all my fault, this ratgirl getting uppity. "If Garrett will
not whip up on you and throw you out of here I will kick
your mangy tail up between your hind legs myself. Then I
will go to work on your idiot friends."

John Stretch could not find words for a while. Finally,
he asked, "You are not a prisoner here?"

"What? A prisoner? You are an idiot. I live here. This
is where I want to live."

Gah! I had a feeling that the cunning ratgirl had just
jobbed me. A strong hint of Loghyr amusement supported
that hypothesis. That damned Singe could think on her feet.

*It is quite true that John Stretch believed Miss Pular was in
need of rescuing. In addition to being a clever and competent
criminal he appears to be an unabashed romantic and as
vulnerable as you might want to hope from that quarter—
as was, if you will believe it, Reliance, in his time.*

He was going to get bashed if he tried anything here.
"John Stretch, let's you and me step over to my private
office for a minute and talk, man to man. Go ahead, grab
another sandwich. Before Singe consumes the whole pile."

I started in while John Stretch was still reeling from his
first look at Eleanor. "What'll your guys do if they find out
everything they've been through was just to rescue a ratgirl
who refuses to be saved? There've been people killed. A
bunch have been dragged off to the al-Khar. You know
their prospects are going to be dim there."

"Those will not be much worse than out on the streets.
The war is over. There is no more work. Humans have no
more motive to treat us with respect. For those imprisoned

the misery just will not last as long. The stable disaster was bad luck. Bad timing added to the fact that we were not told just how much material we were expected to remove."

"Maybe you didn't know the temper of the neighborhood very well, either."

"Of course we did not. No ratpeople live there. But the promised payoff seemed worth the risk."

"It always does. Until the pain starts."

"Possession of Pular Singe is more than a personal matter. All ratkind is watching. Yes, I would have rescued her. Even having heard the words from her own mouth, in Karentine rather than cant, I find it hard to believe that she prefers to live among humans."

"I'll tell you why. You know the saying, 'Lower than a ratman's dog'?"

"I know it. I understand it."

"I'll tell you what's lower than a ratman's dog. A ratwoman. Think about it."

He got it. A point in his favor. Most ratmen wouldn't have if you'd drawn them a picture. "That may be another reason why Reliance considers her an important symbol. She is living proof that things can be done in ways other than the ways they have always been done."

"Reliance has been advised by a higher power. He's renounced his interest in Singe. In return the Syndicate will let him live. But he's just stupid enough to think he's clever enough to sneak around the Outfit, somehow. So I'm going to invest in some rough insurance as soon as we're done here."

"You mean that?"

"Singe is my friend, Pound Humility. She's one of the most remarkable people I've ever met, of any species. I want to see her become everything she can. I want to see what she can become if she's given the chance. Despite the customs and politics of ratpeople. Despite the prejudices of everybody else. You understand?"

"No. But I can accept. If Singe is safe from Reliance."

"Answer my question. What'll your friends do if they find out what you were doing?"

"If we do not have possession of Singe? They might be angry enough to kill me."

"Thought so. You ratfolk aren't subtle people. So maybe you'll want a running start. . . . No. Wait a minute. Wait just a minute. I might have an angle. Hang on here for a second."

I zipped across the hallway. "Singe, come out here. Yes, bring the sandwich." I shut the door behind her. "Singe, my sweet, whatever happened to that now-you-see-me, now-you-don't fetish we took off Casey out in the country?" I knew we hadn't turned it over to the Guard. Mainly because I'd forgotten all about it.

Singe's whiskers folded back. Way back.

The significance of which I intuited instantly. "Oh, no. You didn't. You wicked girl." Not only did she know about Evas, she'd been there to watch. "You figured out how to work the box." Now she was a sorceress, too. And she hadn't said a thing. "Old Bones. Are you listening?"

I am here.

"Then show Singe what I want her to do." There were too many untrustworthy ears in the place tonight

And now the Dead Man knew about Evas, too. He hadn't before, though three people in the house did know. Evas must have some considerable skill at sealing memory blocks, including those in minds not her own.

But I did know, Garrett. Because the pixies knew. However, it was none of my business. He had nothing to say about his failure to be a direct witness himself.

But the pixies, too. Who didn't know?

Dean. So far.

Even Fasfir?

Even Fasfir.

Grrr! He was right before. This was personal stuff. But when had that ever kept him from butting in with his opinion? And why hadn't the senior elf woman blown up like a bad batch of beer?

Now wasn't the time to worry. We needed to get on with business. "Keep Singe posted on what I'm saying." I returned to John Stretch. "Here's what we'll do. Singe will go with you, all docile and bashful, for your sake. Because we think it'll be good to have you for a friend. Let all ratkind marvel at your coup. But I want to warn you. Singe is going to vanish. Like a candle being snuffed. I want you to lie low for a few days after that. Things will be going on with Reliance and his like. Pay attention. Try not to repeat their mistakes after your luck turns."

John Stretch had no idea what I was talking about but he listened.

He'd know the whole story soon enough.

"Have another sandwich while Singe gets ready."

Stretch and his henchrats dug in, eating with an amazing devotion. I told Stretch how he could pick up a little extra pocket change by hunting elves.

I continued to have this strong desire to meet Lastyr and Noodiss.

I heard Singe's distinctive step descending the stair. I met her at its foot. I told her, "I want you to be careful. Don't let anybody get close enough to get a good hold on you. Disappear first time they're all looking at something else. Once you figure they can't blame it on John Stretch. Don't leave a trail they can sniff out."

"You care."

"Of course I care. You're my friend. I worry about you."

"Good. It is all right, you know. You and Evas. Or you and Kayne Prose. Or you and her daughter. That sort of thing does not trouble ratfolk like it does your people. I was curious. Evas suspected I was there after a while but by then she did not care."

If I'd had whiskers they would've been back far enough to tie behind my head. The more I saw of Singe the less well I seemed to know her. Maybe I needed to stop using her as a mirror.

"Please be careful."

"I will be careful, Garrett. Because I mean to have my turn. Someday."

Help!

67

"What have we got with these two?" I asked the Dead Man, after I'd seen the ratpeople into the street and after I'd turned the Goddamn Parrot loose to keep track of them.

Singe *needed* watching. Reliance couldn't be blamed if he attacked his enemies and, lo! Pular Singe happened to be tromping around with them. That wouldn't violate the letter of any agreement with higher powers.

"Other than a big-ass grudge, of course."

Very little that is new or interesting. Mr. Bic Gonlit did persist in trying to sell Miss Pular after you asked him to behave. For which effort his reward has been to end up here, traded for her.

Bic winced badly. He was getting the benefit of the Dead Man's wisdom.

The thoughts must have been particularly strong. Fasfir stirred back there in the darkness, where she sat cross-legged atop a stool. She would've been an elegant sight had there been enough light to reveal her. None of the silver elves seemed to be acquainted with the concept of under-wear. Or of modesty, either.

Officer Casey did hire those ratboys who just left. A great many of them, going well beyond John Stretch's gang. They were supposed to steal everything from Cypres Prose's work-shop, without exception, evidently because Casey's superiors had ordered him to see that it was all destroyed.

I didn't speak aloud, just articulated my questions softly

in the back of my throat. "He can do that? He has the sorcery to be able to talk to people in another country?"

Evidently.

No wonder the Hill crowd wanted to lay hands on these people. I had trouble imagining the full power of the weapon that would be instantaneous communication. There would be no defeating armies with that capacity.

Indeed. It is extremely difficult to dig information out of Casey. But it can be done, slowly, if one approaches the task with considerable patience. He does not appear to be as adept at concealing himself as Fasfir is, when worked over time.

"So maybe she can get him to cooperate. You have any idea where his ship is? It's the only working one left. If we knew where it was the rest of the silver elves would turn into our best friends."

Quite likely. And I do know where the ship is. Approximately.

"Approximately? And? Or is it a but?" It would be something.

Severe sorceries project it. And actually finding it might be difficult. Our visitors do not envision spatial relationships the way you do. They see different colors, hear different sounds, sense things you do not sense at all.

"Oh, well. Will Casey just do more mischief if we cut him loose?"

He will try. He is what he is. He shares many of your character traits. He will try to do the job he has agreed to do. He has, just recently, received those orders concerning the eradication of inappropriate knowledge. Whatever that may mean. I suspect that that means there is now an actual physical threat to Cypres Prose, simply because he has so many wonderful ideas. Ideas he received from his elusive friends.

"Then we'll just have to keep him around here." If he got too rambunctious, I could always send him off for a wondrous vacation in the al-Khar.

In a conversational sort of voice, I said, "Bic, we're going to give you one more chance to get out of our way with

your ass still strapped onto the rest of you. All it'll take is
for you to carry a letter from me to Colonel Block at the
al-Khar. Because I don't have time to handle it myself. Can
you manage that without getting distracted? Knowing that
the letter means enough to me that I'll hunt you down and
feed you your magic boots, one from each end, if my message doesn't get through within the hour?"

"Garrett, how come you're so damned determined to
make my life miserable?"

"Maybe you'd better look at the facts, Bic. Who did what
to who first? I think your beef is with Casey. This critter
right here, dressed up like you. He had you jumping
through hoops by pretending to be Kayne Prose in heat.
While he was working Kayne, pretending to be you." I'm
so clever. Sometimes I can spot a pothole only minutes
after I've stumbled into it. "And you and Kayne both
ended up screeching because you couldn't get all the way
lucky. Old Case couldn't pretend that part."

Bic growled. Bic didn't want to listen to any damned
theories.

"Look at him, man. He looks like you in a funhouse
mirror." A mirror that skinnied him down and talled him
up.

"Never mind. I'm not going to argue till you're
convinced."

"So just give me your damned letter and let me out of
here."

"And don't forget to remember me in your will. Because
I've treated you better than anybody else in town would've
done." I found myself lusting after a beer. Or something
with a better kick. I hadn't had a drop since our country
picnic. But I couldn't take time out now. I had business to
attend to, outside the home. "Bic, I'd kiss you good-bye
but then you'd just come back for more."

I shut the door behind the little man at last, leaned
against it. "I sincerely hope that that's the last time I ever
see Bic Gonlit." The man was like a mosquito. Not a major
problem but one persistent annoyance if you didn't kill him.

"Can he possibly have any other reason to buzz around my ear, now?"

Suppose the Guard arrest and question him.

"I didn't think of that." I hadn't, which seemed real dim of me the second the subject came up. "But he will. And he's clever enough not to let that happen. I wish the bird was here to send out to watch him."

You might send a pixie. They have not yet done much to earn their keep.

"That seems a little dangerous. For the pixies. Let's just trust Bic to do what he said he'd do. I'm going to clean up and change now. I'm heading up to the Tate compound. To see Willard Tate."

Old Chuckles failed to seize the opportunity, though I'm sure he noted my unnecessary explanation of why I had to put myself in close proximity to a certain ferocious redhead who couldn't quite seem to decide how big a part of my life she wanted to be.

68

"I think we're in business," I told the Dead Man when I returned in the wee hours, a little light-headed. Willard Tate enjoys his brandies and loves to share his pleasures with people he likes. He likes me right now.

The rest of the Tates are wine people, every one with a favorite vintage. I'm not much on the spoiled grape juice myself. I prefer that Weider barley soup with plenty of hops. But I couldn't be impolite when a taste was offered.

And it was hard to keep track of how much sipping I did when I was a little distracted, off and on, by Tinnie and her wicked cousin Rose.

I said, "I'll have a sitdown with all the principals as soon as I arrange for Morley to make space available."

I would take Morley on a nostalgic voyage into his past, returning The Palms to the days when it was The Joy House and neutral ground for meetings just like the one I planned. He was a good friend. He deserved to get the business.

Excellent. And though I do begrudge admitting it, I believe you have suffered one of your better ideas this time.

"Did Singe get back yet?"

More than an hour ago. All went well. She ate and drank like a lumberjack, then went to bed. That child has an amazing capacity for beer.

"If she's going to keep sucking it down here, she'd better start showing an amazing capacity for bringing in cash. What about the jungle chicken?"

Still out there. Watching the al-Khar now. To see how the Guard responds to your message.

"There's only one response possible. Don't tell me they haven't done anything."

Nothing dramatic. There have been comings and goings but, not being familiar with the routine around the jail, I do not know if they are unusual. And it would behoove us to recall that we live in a political world. What Colonel Block should do and what he is allowed to do might not be identical—if someone important upHill happens to be an investor in Reliance's undertakings.

"I know. I know. It's a blackhearted world. I'm going to go put away some beer myself. Then I'm going to sleep till noon."

A man's fondest dreams and dearest ideals often become storm-tossed wrack upon reefs of reality.

I wakened to find myself already deeply involved in some extremely heavy petting.

Evas had decided school was in again. Only . . . It took a few moments of exploration to determine that tonight's pupil wasn't Evas. Perhaps Fasfir had pulled rank.

Fasfir was a dedicated student, give her that. Her focus matched Evas'. It seemed she wanted to practice till she got it right. She didn't go away until people started stirring around the house.

Good thing I'd announced that I meant to sleep in.

69

Dean didn't get the word. Or didn't care. He wakened me. His stern look of disapproval was the one he reserved for my sloth, brought out on occasions when he felt he couldn't state his opinion aloud. He would've employed an entirely different and much uglier scowl had he known about Evas or Fasfir.

He told me, "You need to get up. There are messages awaiting your attention. And Miss Winger is in the street outside, apprising the world of all your shortcomings."

"I doubt that. She hasn't had a chance to catalog them. Unless you've signed on as her adviser."

He plowed ahead. "And the workmen have arrived." He said that last quickly and softly, as though it was a minor, mooshy afterthought of no consequence whatsoever.

I didn't think about it. Which was the point.

John Stretch had cut Winger loose. Good for him. Good for her. Maybe not as good for me if she was going to roam the streets accusing me of being in cahoots with those ugly fraternal twins, Mal and Mis Feasance. Although I certainly had trouble imagining why she might do that, considering she slept in their bed herself, most nights.

"None of that sounds all that pressing to me," I grumbled, knowing he was going to be disgruntled simply because I was in bed when it was light outside already.

Dean shrugged. His usual, aggressive morning attitude seemed to have abandoned him. He was intrigued by something on the floor. Something he might possibly have last seen hanging off Fasfir. He frowned deeply as he tried to get a mental grasp on the facts.

I saw the change when he decided he was imagining things.

I said, "I'll be down in a few minutes."

On instructions from the Dead Man, Dean let Winger into the house. She stormed from the front door directly into the kitchen, where I was working on breakfast while surrounded by my harem. "Have a cup of tea, Winger." Then I said, "If you insist on being abusive I'll just chuck you right back out in the street. Where you can keep on entertaining the secret police spies who watch this place every minute."

Winger was wound up. She blistered the air with her extemporaneous remarks. However, mention of Relway's gang got her stuttering fast. Unfortunately for her immortality, I wasn't paying enough attention to recall her exact words for posterity. Which was probably just as well. She hadn't been doing a whole lot of nun-style talking.

"You're running around loose, aren't you?" I wedged the question in while pouring tea for myself and Evas, who seemed astounded that something like Winger existed. "Imagine that. And you didn't get one single precious little hair on your pretty head harmed, either. Amazing." I wasn't responsible but she didn't need to know that.

Winger thought some. The implications made her stumble some more. She decided to sit down and enjoy an eating contest with Singe—at least until she'd worked herself up for a fresh round of accusations.

Once she had her mouth full, I asked, "How did those ratmen manage to capture you? I expected something to happen. Morley was supposed to send some men to back you up. Didn't they show?"

"Those pussies?" I think that's what she said. Her mouth was still full of dribbling crumbs. "Those assholes ran out on me."

I sighed. That wasn't that hard to translate. It meant she'd been such a bitch that Morley's guys had decided that the job wasn't worth it, that Winger deserved whatever she got. Morley would back them up. And would demand that they be paid for their suffering. And he'd have the moral right of it, probably.

Winger remains her own worst enemy.

Maybe she ought to try a little adult education with Sarge.

Some crashing and banging started up front. "What the hell? Sounds like somebody's beating on the side of the house with a sledgehammer." For a moment I envisioned Doris doing to my house what he'd refused to do to Casey's place.

Nobody told me anything. But Dean's attitude suddenly seemed evasive.

I recalled his having said something about workmen.

I drained my teacup and headed for the front door, noting that I wasn't hurting much of anywhere this morning. Which was wonderful. And surprising. I ought to have some cramps, or something, considering the rigors of my instructional duties.

The racket got the Goddamn Parrot going. "Help! Help! Oh, Mister, please don't. . . ." I leaned in to tell him, "Aw, shut yer ugly beak, ya little pervert," before I went on to the door. "Ain't nobody here who ain't heard it all before."

Wait.

"Huh?"

I believe we are about to have a caller.

"But somebody's trying to wreck the outside of the house."

Masons are removing a couple of bricks to permit the pixies access to the hollows in the middle course of the wall.

The outer walls of my place are three-course brick masonry, a very dark, blackish rough red brick. Typically, the center course of that sort of construction includes a lot of voids.

So some genius had gotten the notion that those voids could be turned into pixie apartments. Gah! Now I'd have them squabbling inside my walls, day and night.

I supposed chances were excellent the guilty genius spent most of his life making and unmaking messes in my kitchen.

As the Dead Man had predicted, someone knocked on

the front door. The knock had that peremptory character I associated with the secret police, that combination of confidence and impatience.

Nor was my guess in error, though my visitor was no one I recognized. And had been chosen, no doubt, because of that fact. If they had to deal with me directly, they would show me too many faces to remember. "Yes?"

"Courier. I have a message for you from Colonel Block." A written message at that. He slapped a small, scroll-style document into my hand, then turned and took off, stepping like he was marching to a drumbeat pitched too high for human ears. He headed straight up the street to Mrs. Cardonlos' rooming house, probably to collect the daily reports. Which meant they'd given up bothering to pretend.

Well?

Reading, I closed the door with shoulder and elbow. "A report on what they've been doing about Reliance and some other rat gangsters using human slaves to manage their bookkeeping."

Generous of the colonel.

"Yes, indeed. And I'll tell you this. I wouldn't want to be a known ratman criminal right now." What Block was willing to commit to paper would be just the tip of the iceberg. And what he'd been willing to set down was so vicious and wicked that I felt belated reservations about having unleashed the whirlwind.

"Here's an interesting 'Did you know?' Did you know that ratpeople, alone of all the intelligent peoples of TunFaire, have no legal standing whatsoever? Less, even, than an ox or a draft horse? That anyone can do just about any damned thing they want to them with complete legal impunity? Just the same as if they were regular rats?"

Easy to understand why, then, they would be bitter.

"Better believe." Not one in a hundred of my fellow royal subjects had a conscience sufficiently well developed to understand why I found that situation troubling, too.

Do not bruit that about. Few people know. Were that common knowledge, someone would soon be killing them for their fur or their teeth or their toenails, or something such.

And people capable of that were out there, strangers

to conscience, remorse, and pity, who were constitutionally
incapable of encompassing those concepts however often
they were explained.

"I've unchained a beast."

*This once may be for the best. Mr. Relway may know no
limits but those he imposes from within. Which may make
him appear infinitely ferocious even while those internal limits do exist. He will exterminate ratmen with wild enthusiasm
but everyone who perishes will have been a true villain.*

"Or if they weren't they wouldn't have gotten themselves
dead. Right? I know that game of old."

*Mr. Relway will dwindle away to that point someday, no
doubt. But it won't be today. Today he still recalls that he's
just a man. An overly idealistic sort of man.*

"Shall I tell Singe?"

She will learn of it anyway.

"Tell Singe what?" Singe demanded, having entered the
Dead Man's room soundly equipped to avoid starvation for
at least a generation.

"That the Guard have attacked Reliance and several
other leading ratmen. With the sort of acutely accurate intelligence you'd expect of Deal Relway. The Guard did it
because Reliance has been keeping human slaves." Though
the slaves' humanness shouldn't have mattered. Slavery at
its most blatant and obvious has been outlawed for generations, no matter the race of the slave.

Today we have indenture and apprenticeship and several
forms of involuntary servitude involving debtors and con-
victed criminals but nobody owns another intelligent being
outright. In law. Sometimes reality can be pretty ugly.

Acute and accurate intelligence? Then how come they
hadn't known about the slavery? Or had they?

My cynical side quickly had me wondering if the raids
weren't just image-building stunts launched at this point
only because somebody with a big mouth and an overly
moralistic attitude now knew what the ratmen were doing.

I told Singe, "The attacks have been remarkably vicious
and violent." Because the Guard wanted to make an unmis-
takable point. A major new power player had entered the
lists.

There would be truly big trouble if Relway ever got so overconfident that he went after the Outfit. Because there are a whole lot more of their bad guys than there are of his good guys. And those bad guys have far greater resources.

"And this would be the insurance you were taking on my behalf?"

There was no ducking the truth. "No Reliance, no threat from Reliance."

Singe did not get upset with me. What distress she did betray she directed at herself. She might not have willed disaster to devour Reliance but a disaster had occurred on her account. "You are right, Garrett. You are completely right. Life is a bitch."

"And then you die."

"Will Humility be all right?"

"I don't know. I tried to warn him. I hope he listened. I think he's someone I could get along with. And what I do, it's all connections."

"What *we* do, Garrett."

I started to speak.

Might I suggest a level of caution usually reserved for speech in the presence of Miss Tate?

He might. But that didn't mean I had a whole lot of use for it.

Singe continued, "I am part of this team, now. And I am not really asking for a salary, or anything."

"Nobody draws a salary here. But the more people there are around here, the more work has to be done to keep everybody in clothing and food. And the way you keep putting it away . . . You aren't pregnant, are you?" All I needed was a horde of rat pups underfoot, atop the rest of the zoo.

Not a smart suggestion, Garrett. Not a smart suggestion.

He was right. I'd managed to offend Singe at last. And her main complaint was a sound one: I'd tossed off a remark like that without ever having bothered to learn enough about ratpeople to know that she couldn't get pregnant unless she was in season. Unlike human women. And she hadn't yet gone into season, except once, her first time, under rigorously controlled conditions, with her mother and some older sisters there to make sure nothing untoward happened.

"After the first time any ratgirl with half a brain can manage her schedule. I go to the same apothecaries human women do. And the same hedge wizards." Singe rolled up her left sleeve, showed me a fancy yarn amulet not unlike those worn by every human female I knew who'd passed the age of nine. This is a cruel, wicked, unpredictable, and exciting world. Bad things happen to good girls. Good things happen to bad girls. Nobody with any sense risks having her life shattered by chance joy or evil.

Which isn't to say that there aren't scores of accidents happening out there every day. Common sense isn't.

"It is really easy. But a lot of males do not want females controlling their fertility. And very few ratgirls are as courageous as I am. It takes a lot of nerve to sneak away and get fitted for an amulet. Even though everyone knows where to get one."

"What happens if you get caught using one of those things?"

"Basically, they get really unhappy with you but, mostly, they just take it away. Then they crowd you till your season comes on you. They believe that once a female has enjoyed a vigorous season of mating she won't want to delay another one ever again."

"Is that male arrogance? Or is it true?"

"I cannot tell you of my own certain knowledge. I have seen females little older than myself swilling an herb tea they believe will bring them into season sooner. At the same time taking other concoctions supposed to prevent pregnancy or to terminate one if it starts."

Sounded to me like love amongst the ratfolk could be as mad as it is amongst human folk.

"It is a good thing to be a girl who thinks ahead," Singe said. "So my older sisters tell me. They say a girl can futter herself blind for weeks on end if she makes the proper preparations and takes the right precautions."

I was beginning to get uncomfortable.

Singe fluttered her eyelashes. "Weeks."

My luck was mixed. That didn't go anywhere because

Winger burst in. She started barking at the Dead Man and me. "You guys aren't gonna stiff me, Garrett."

"A straight line I cannot resist—"

"Don't give me no shit, Garrett."

"Winger, why do you have to be a pain in the ass every day of your life?" She wasn't, really. Most of the time she was good people. My directness startled her silent long enough for me to add, "I ought to hire the Rose brothers to follow you around with a couple of huge mirrors so every time you start in on somebody they can shove one in front of you so you can see what's happening."

Winger got a big, goofy look on her face. She isn't deep at all. She'll take that sort of remark literally, often as not. This time she cocked her head and thought about it for a few seconds before she decided it was just, somehow, some more of Garrett's candy-ass, goody two-shoes, crapola, pussy philosophy. A category which included anything I ever said that she didn't agree with or didn't understand. She gave her hair a violent toss. "You guys ain't gonna get outta giving me what I got coming."

"Oh, you're going to get what you've got coming. One of these days."

Her blind, fool, drunk good luck has got to run out someday.

Upon repeated advice from the Dead Man, in the face of my own deeply held principles, I sent Winger off with a little money in her pocket. She was happy to get it. She knew perfectly well that she didn't deserve it.

Now she'd go do some drinking, get into a fight with somebody who reminded her of her husband, maybe bed him if he survived the action. Then, while she was still drunk but already beginning to feel the bite of a hangover, she'd drag Saucerhead Tharpe out of bed and try to con him into helping her manage some criminal enterprise noteworthy for its complete boneheadedness. Like the time she got poor Grimmy Weeks drunk, bopped what little brains he had out, then talked him into helping her pilfer the Singing Sword of Holme Prudeald.

That damned sword has no value whatsoever. It's not fit

for fighting and its only magical property is its ability to sing. Badly.

The damned blade never shut up after they pinched it. Everywhere Grimmy and Winger went, it boomed out off-key operatic arias about henpecked top gods, brothers who plooked their sisters in order to create psychopathic, dwarf-murdering heroes who tended to forget that they were married to defrocked, doomed, and not very bright Choosers of the Slain. Which might not have been too bad if Winger hadn't gotten a wild hair and tried to sell herself as the nimrod Chooser.

They say it made great street entertainment.

Winger panicked when she figured the sword's owner would get word. She did a runner when Grimmy had his back turned, leaving the poor befuddled dope holding the scabbard, so to speak.

I'm probably the only guy in town who bought Grimmy's sad story about the big blonde who'd led him to his despair.

If Grimmy survives four years of forced labor in the silver mines he'll return to the street having learned a valuable lesson about getting to know your partners in crime *before* you begin to work together.

She hadn't even given him her real name.

"Hey, Chuckles," I said, popping into the Dead Man's room. "What're we going to do with Casey and the girls?" The male silver elf was too much trouble to keep under control. But if we turned him loose he would become dangerous. And he didn't deserve to be turned over to the Guard. And I didn't want to kill him.

I have been giving that matter some thought. It is not simple. I have been unable to find a satisfactory answer yet. I will continue to reflect. Possibly Casey himself will present us with an idea.

That didn't seem likely.

I was in my office. After our recent power spending our financial picture was no longer rosy. I scowled. That might mean having to take on more work.

Evas eased into the room, cold and aloof and remote. Today she wore an unflattering tattered dress that had been handed down by one of Dean's much heftier nieces. The dress wouldn't have been flattering when it was new and on the form it fit. The weavers had strung a lot of ugly thread into the woof.

Evas closed the door. Then she began to change into the very friendly Evas. "I . . . cannot . . . wait." I got the sense that she was mildly ashamed of herself because she couldn't control herself.

After a while I managed to get away. The first tentacles of a marvelous idea had begun to stir in the darkened rooms at the back of my mind.

Damned if it didn't seem like Eleanor winked at me.

Had to be a good idea.

If I could survive the next few days. . . .

"How well do you know my parrot?" I asked. "Come on. You should get to know him."

70

I made sure my crew were the first to arrive at The Palms. Even Dean came along, mainly to make sure Morley's barbarians did things right. If there was much surprise at the appearances of Singe and Evas, Morley's people hid it well. I'd left Fasfir behind. Fasfir seemed to have learned everything she'd wanted to know during her one protracted lesson.

Quite possibly nothing could surprise them.

One quick glance around and I asked Sarge, "What's going on? I paid you guys good money. You were supposed to set the place up for—"

"You jus' go on up da stairs dere, Garrett. Puddle's up top. He'll take care a you."

Puddle could make that climb and survive?

"Smart-ass," Sarge said, reading my mind. "Dey's gonna come a time when yer gonna have some slick pup mockin' you fer havin' stayed alive so long."

"Maybe so. I hope so." If my luck shaped up.

My manners were less than impeccable.

I scurried up to see what was what, leaving Singe and Evas under Dean's protection. Puddle pointed when I reached the top.

I've been in and out of Morley's place for as long as we've been friends. I'd been upstairs a hundred times. Morley has his office and living quarters up there. I hadn't thought much more about that floor. Now I discovered a narrow hallway beside his office that, on previous occasions, must have been covered with a panel that looked like part of the wall. The hallway opened into a banquet room, complete with dumbwaiter to the kitchen.

I suppose I should've suspected. The existence of the place seemed entirely reasonable once I saw it. There was a lot of room up there. It might be a major adjunct to Morley's business.

I wondered what went on there when he wasn't renting it out to me.

Morley materialized. In his most ingratiating, oily manner, he asked, "Is it satisfactory, sir?" He'd noted the fact that I was nonplussed. He loved it. "Is there anything else I can do?"

A double-width table array had been set up with seats for twenty people, eight along each side and two at each end. The settings were basic but correct as far as they went. Dean didn't register any objection when he arrived, which eventuality occurred while Morley and I were talking.

There was something else Morley could do but we'd get to that later. "No. This's fine. Except you've got extra places set."

"Don't give me that dark look. I'm not inviting anybody in. We've just found that setting extra places saves embarrassment when the invited guests decide to bring along someone you didn't plan to have attend. People do that. Even though it's terribly bad manners."

"I understand." All too well. Dean had brought in a covered birdcage containing one guest I hadn't wanted to invite. This one wouldn't be getting his own chair. And, if I could avoid it, the cover wouldn't be coming off his cage, either. He could be the Dead Man's proxy without participating in anything.

I remarked, "Your guys ran out on Winger at the stable the other day."

"And should've left an hour before they did. The woman is insufferable. And she keeps getting worse."

"She's got a problem with you that she was taking out on them?"

He didn't want to talk about it. So I asked, "You totally trust all your guys downstairs?"

"Of course."

I tilted my head toward Evas. "Colonel Block has some high-level friends who'd love to sink their talons into her. We took a coach over here so nobody would see her on the street."

"If you need to keep her secret, why risk having someone see her?"

"Her presence is an important ingredient for the success of my evening."

"She is a she, isn't she?"

"You'd better believe. Not extravagantly so, just to look at, but between us guys, don't let that fool you. Her public attitude, either. The ice does melt. In fact, it goes straight to steam. A touch of wine helps. So she has an excuse for making Katie seem repressed and distracted."

"You didn't. You know Tinnie will come with her uncle. She'll figure that out before she's all the way into the room."

The possibility had occurred to me. But the potential of the evening seemed worth risking Tinnie's wrath. I mean, that would come down on me sooner or later, anyway. It's like weather. Some days we're going to have some.

"She'll notice Kayne Prose and Cassie Doap long before she notices Evas."

"You didn't. You rogue."

"Rake's the word, I think. But don't go playing pot to my kettle, pal. It took a lot of arranging to get everybody here tonight. And I had to get away from the house for a while. At least none of them are married."

In general, Morley prefers women encumbered with husbands. Rich husbands are especially good. Their wives are much less likely to make demands he'd rather not meet. They have too much to lose. Besides, he's a married elf himself. So he claims. I've never met his wife. He hasn't seen her himself since he was a kid, supposedly. Or maybe she wasn't a wife, just a fiancée.

Arranged marriage. It's an elven thing. And an everybody else thing, sometimes. When substantial estates are involved.

I added, "The rules of our relationship, laid down explicitly by Tinnie herself, clearly state that neither of us has any right to demand anything of the other as long as the relationship remains informal. Which's the way she wants it kept."

"Garrett, you're thirty years old. Do you still believe in the tooth fairy, too?"

"I'd say there's a better chance of me running into the tooth fairy than there is of Tinnie actually living up to the letter of that."

"I hope you know what you're doing."

Morley left us in Puddle's care. He said he wanted to head downstairs so he could make sure my guests went the right direction when they arrived. Which probably meant he didn't want those lowlifes mixing with his class clientele.

I resisted the temptation to let the Goddamn Parrot get away.

Dean assumed his post, the seat to the left of what would be mine at the table head. He laid out paper, pens, and ink, and a couple of Kip's writing sticks. He'd try to record what got said accurately enough that there could be no arguments later. I was confident that others would do the same. I was just as confident that there'd be arguments over who said what and when later on. There's always somebody who insists the records are wrong.

Evas and Singe lurked behind the old man, both of them trying to read his notes as he made them. I wondered how much success they actually had.

It was scary how fast Singe was picking up the art. Writing was giving her trouble, though. Her body wasn't built to provide the necessary fine motor skills. I suspected she'd never manage anything but tedious block printing.

Even that would make her unique.

I separated Evas from Singe. "The man I was talking to was the one I told you about."

She showed an interest immediately. She'd reached the point where she was having trouble sustaining her public frost. She was obsessed. Which had been cute for a while but which had become disturbing once I found myself ambushed whenever I was alone.

I thanked the stars or fates that Fasfir had needed to try her wings just the one time. It had been sweet enough work keeping up with Evas.

I reminded her, "He'd be a better teacher than I am. Much better. Elves are known for their endurance." If you could believe a quarter of what this particular half-elf said about himself. "He's not bad looking, either. By our standards."

Near as I could read a silver elf's face, Evas seemed thoughtful.

I settled beside Dean. "All set?" He was studying one of Kip's writing sticks, looking dubious.

"I'm not sure I can do this anymore."

"If you can't get it word for word make sure you get the high points. Ah. Playmate's here."

As I moved that way, Singe sidled up. "What are you trying to do with Evas?"

"Nothing."

"Garrett."

"Just trying to help my best pal get a chance to experience an amazing phenomenon."

"I think you are up to something."

"Really? Look, I need to talk to Playmate." Playmate had Kip in tow but not Kip's mother or sister. Or Rhafi. Mustn't ever forget poor, invisible Rhafi.

Playmate looked exhausted. "It's getting to me, Garrett. Having the Guard watching the place all the time. Having them come around asking questions at all hours."

Even Kip seemed subdued. He hardly fidgeted. He made no effort to wander away from Playmate. He didn't insult anyone.

I asked, "Where are the rest of them?"

"I don't know if they're coming. Kayne said she was but I expected her to get here before we did."

"She has to come. We'll be on real thin legal ice if we put together a company where one of the partners isn't even old enough to draft. We need his mother here."

"I understand that. But you need to realize that Kayne's custodial status won't stand up if somebody big really challenges it. She's a woman. So she's pretty much handicapped when it comes to making contracts herself. If this turns into something involving really big money, you know the jackals are going to start gathering."

Playmate was right. Women who make a name and place for themselves have to do so against the ancient tide of the law. Kayne had the legal advantage of being a widow, had no living father, and neither son had reached his majority. Still, as Playmate said, add money to the mix and somebody would take legal action to become Kayne's legal guardian.

Playmate mused, "I'm worried that the father will turn up and stake a claim."

"I thought he was dead."

"No. He disappeared. He's presumed dead. Even if he is dead, somebody could claim to be him. It would be his word against Kayne's. A woman. Of questionable morals. The sorting out would give somebody plenty of time to do some mischief."

"People can't do much mischief if their legs are broken."

"It wouldn't be that simple."

"I hate people sometimes, Play. In times like these I have trouble convincing myself that Relway doesn't have the right idea about how to handle humanity's scum."

"Might not be your best simile, Garrett. The scum is what rises to the top. Well, somebody is here."

Somebody proved to be Max Weider and his beautiful daughter Alyx. Alyx was coifed and dressed to kill. Alyx loved every second of the attention she attracted. Manvil Gilbey and our first uninvited guest, Congo Greeve, straggled in behind, the bad and the ugly. Congo looked like he had broken out the special, formal occasions cranial wax. His eight-inch part glistened.

Wicked, wicked Alyx headed straight for me, blue eyes sparkling like a bucket of diamonds. She showed me a wicked, wicked smile and leaned forward to offer me a world-class glimpse of a wicked, wicked decolletage.

"Bad girl," I told her. "Daddy's going to spank."

"Promise?"

"You're hopeless."

"I've got plenty of hope. I know you can't resist forever. I see you took the trouble to dress up." She grabbed my right arm, did a little wriggle-and-spin move before I realized what she was doing.

Her daddy was not amused.

"I . . . What're you doing?"

"Tinnie was right behind us."

The devil herself stepped into the room. Red hair, green eyes, freckles, a shape to make men sit up nights cursing the sun and the moon and the stars because there was only one of her to go around. She wore green velvet. She eyed Alyx, checked the goofy look on my clock, shook her head and allowed Puddle to guide her to the side of the table where the Tates would be stationed. Like most everyone else I know who passes as more than a remote acquaintance, Puddle treats Tinnie like an empress.

Alyx said, "Damn. That didn't get a rise out of *her*. How 'bout you?"

"Well, you did get your dad all steamed up. You'll hear from him later." Max and I might be friends but there was no way he was going to let me get involved with his baby. Not that he's a snob. He just don't think my prospects are any better than those of highwaymen or pirates, professions notorious for their high rate of turnover.

Alyx went over and dropped inelegantly into a chair beside Tinnie. They fell into conversation instantly, probably beating up on me. They were close friends, despite Alyx's relentless campaign to slide her shoes under the end of my bed.

Morley reappeared. He had changed clothing. He wore a lady-killing costume now. I kept a straight face. He cast covert glances into the dark corner where Singe and Evas lurked, trying to avoid notice. Evas was busy playing peeka-boo with the Goddamn Parrot but didn't miss Morley's return.

Kip had discovered Evas, too. He was scared to death. I said, "Play, tell Kip it's all right. She's on our side."

Well, I was hoping she was. Things might change suddenly if she found out she had a ride home.

"Are you ready to begin serving?" Morley asked. "The kitchen is ready for you."

"Not yet. I'm waiting for the boy's family to show."

He stared at Evas and the jungle chicken, which Evas had just uncovered. "There's something about that creature . . ."

Something she was projecting herself. I'd felt it back at the house more than once. "Yes, there is. Would you like me to introduce you?"

"I'm talking about Mr. Big, Garrett," he lied.

"That's one of the better straight lines you've ever handed me but I'm going to let you off. You were distracted. Let me mingle with my guests. You want something to do, a wine course might be appropriate right now." A suggestion that Dean had offered on the way over, as a way of dealing with time that had to be filled.

There was an extra Tate as well as the Weider lawyer. His name was Lister. He was a cousin in his thirties. Outsiders occasionally confused him with Tinnie's deceased pop, Lester. Lister passed as the family legal expert. He was a square-jawed, dark-haired, immaculately clothed and groomed, painfully handsome character who had a hint of the weasel gleaming from the corners of his eyes. For some reason I think of him as the Lawyer of Times to Come.

I know of no one in the Tate clan who likes cousin Lister. He's tolerated because he's kin and because he's good at what he does.

Cousin Lister has no clue how his relatives really feel about him.

Like every human family in TunFaire, great or small, the Tates have menfolk buried in the Cantard. Full-length frog fur coats are more common than grown men who avoided military service in the war zone.

Lister Tate, without halfway trying, wangled himself an army assignment that kept him right here in TunFaire, as the armed forces' liaison with their biggest suppliers of boots and leather accoutrements. He didn't even move out of the family compound. Nevertheless, he promoted himself an out-of-barracks housing allowance that exceeded the pay rates of men like myself, at my highest rank, even including the combat bonus I got while I was in the islands.

I worked my way around to Tinnie. "My good fortune never ceases to amaze me. I was daydreaming about meeting a beautiful redhead. Look what walked through the door."

"I saw what you were daydreaming about. A slutty blonde young enough to be your baby sister."

Alyx snickered and bounced over a seat so I could settle between her and the redhead. She made some crude remark about the chair's warmth, that would've had her father looking for a switch had he heard it. I gave her a wink. "You could come be my baby-sitter."

Tinnie told me, "You ever call her bluff for real, big boy, you'd better have your running shoes on."

Alyx said, "If he does, he won't be able to do anything but crawl."

"You're going to put it all on me when she's talking like that?" I winked at Alyx again. She stuck her tongue out at Tinnie and started to hop into my lap. Then she noticed her father, Gilbey, and Congo Greeve all glaring at her. She needed to learn that some teasing wasn't acceptable in public.

"Yes. Because I expect you to know how to say no."

That seemed a tad unrealistic but I didn't insist. Instead, I said, "Uh-oh," with very little regard for Tinnie's opinion.

Kayne Prose had arrived. Making a grand entrance, just ahead of Cassie Doap, who seemed to have adopted a flamboyantly flirtatious personality for the evening. Tinnie stomped a foot. She wasn't used to this level of competition.

In fact, she was rather exceeded.

Mother and daughter wore newly made gowns. Their creation must've required the needles of all Kayne's cooperative sisters. Both gowns flattered outrageously what begged for very little flattery in the first place.

Slack-jaw disease raged among the menfolk in Morley's private dining room.

Even Dean's imagination seemed to come to life.

Rhafi came in behind his mother and sister, rendered almost invisible by their glory.

As happenstance had it, Lister Tate was the only married man in the room. The bachelors and widowers all looked ready to revel in their status.

When time and doom catch up with me and I have to slough off this mortal realm, I mean to thank the gods for having blessed me with the chances I've had to get to know so many comely women. I expect to start working on my speech about ten thousand years from now.

Manvil Gilbey caught my eye, projected the unspoken question: Was this something I'd laid on for Max? Max could not seem to stop staring at Cassie Doap.

I shook my head, mouthed, "But if it'll help . . ."

Puddle showed the newcomers to their seats, near Playmate and Kip. Even he was having trouble breathing. There were far too many beautiful women in that room, each of them trying to one-up the others.

Tinnie let me have an elbow, putting plenty of force behind it. "That's for what you're thinking."

"I apologize. I'll never think of you as an object again. From now on it's nothing but business. From now on you'll be Mr. Tate in my every act and thought."

That earned me a repeat stroke of the elbow. "I'd better not be." The fickle woman.

Alyx said, "Look at Dad! I think the old bull's in rut."

Tinnie muttered, "Alyx, sometimes you're *too* juvenile even to amuse me."

I moved up to my place beside Dean, which was my signal that the evening was about to become serious. Those who weren't in their official seats found them. Once everyone sat down there was very little room to spare. Morley had another place setting on each long side but it would've taken a shoehorn to get anybody in. I introduced everyone, including Morley as host, then Evas and Singe as they took their seats to the left of Dean and to the right of me, without explaining their presence. I thought they ought to stay mysterious. They drew stares but not even Lister Tate was gauche enough to demand information about them.

I let Morley know that we were ready to be served.

Kayne and Cassie both managed admirably during dinner. Tinnie was not amused by the regard they received. She was used to being the center of attention. But all the men at this banquet were related to her or had known her since she was a pup. Except for me and Dean and Kayne's drooling baby boys. And she already had Dean on a leash and me wrapped around her finger.

Alyx was amused. She liked seeing Tinnie have to take second chair. Just to rub it in she kept right on flirting with me. Her father wasn't worried about her anymore.

71

I tried not to cry when I thought about how much this evening was costing me. I tried to forget the fact that, if it didn't work out, I might end up spending several years working fourteen-hour days just to get back to the point where I could afford to save money buying beer by the keg.

As a business convocation the sequestered evening at Morley's place had to be some sort of precedent. The gang of us came out of there having created a company dedicated to the creation, production, and marketing of the fruits of the imagination of Cypres Prose, ingenious boy inventor. The Weider brewing empire would provide financing. The Tate family would handle the actual production. Kayne Prose and all her offspring would move into the Tate compound, where they would live much better than ever they had before, with no requirement that they do anything but be Kip's support and inspiration. I myself would be the genius who held it all together. Having been the genius who had gotten it all together.

I had a feeling Kayne Prose wouldn't have much attention to spare for industry. Not for a few months, at least.

When Kayne Prose met Manvil Gilbey it was lust at first sight both ways. All the rest of us had to be grateful that they didn't jump on one another right there in the banquet room.

Kayne's behavior wasn't exactly a surprise. I had a feeling she seldom met a man she didn't like. But Manvil Gilbey is as reserved as a wine butt normally.

The absolute absurdity of the universe is declared, in a bellow, once again, by the fact that Max Weider, age sixty, became infatuated with Cassie Doap, a completely ridiculous eventuation not unilateral in nature. Nor did either of those two seem conscious of the fact that Cassie was three years younger than Alyx Weider. And Alyx was the baby of Max's five children.

Max told me, "Of course it's stupid. But she's a dead ringer for Hannah when I first met her." And he was willing to play delusional games with himself in order to defy his pain.

More or less. Nobody cons Max Weider for long. Not even Max himself.

Cassie's positive response, wholly genuine, was a good deal more puzzling. We knew already that neither Cassie nor her mother were out for the easy ride, bought with their looks and bodies.

There're times when people do, honestly, connect on something besides the physical level.

That became one of the fine evenings of my life. One of those times when everything works out even better than you'd dared hope.

Sometime during the socializing, following the creation of the Articles of Agreement encompassing the founders of the new company, my good pal Morley Dotes and the silver elf Evas disappeared.

I suspect that couples who do that tell one another no one will notice but, secretly, don't give a rat's ass if anybody does because their minds are fogged by anticipation.

The capper came when Lister Tate proved he wasn't a complete waste of flesh by, belatedly, providing a device for getting around the legal age problem, as well as the potential problem of a fatherly return. "Willard Tate can adopt the boy. The device goes all the way back to imperial times, when the emperors wanted to handpick their successors. It's not much used anymore, except on the Hill, but the tool is there. Mrs. Prose can allow it. If nobody challenges right away only a Royal proclamation can reverse it. And we could argue against that that only an imperial edict is valid since the adoption went forward under a pre-Karantine law. I believe there are precedents."

I told Tinnie, "Promise me you'll keep Kip away from Rose."

"I plan to keep him for myself. He has good prospects."

"He'll be your cousin."

"Spice is nice but incest is best. Ouch! You meanie. I'll bet he's got stamina, too."

"My prospects are looking up, too. I won't need a business excuse to get my foot in the door at the Weider place anymore. Ouch! Alyx. She's hurting me."

72

Do you feel like a captain of industry? the Dead Man asked.

I waved a hand in a dismissive gesture he couldn't possibly see. "What I feel like is a guy dancing six inches above the ground because I have completely, thoroughly, irrevocably nailed Morley's mangy hide to the wall. I have hoisted him on his own petard. I've spent months and months and months trying to map out some absurdly complicated revenge scam to get even with him for the Goddamn Parrot. And in the end a better answer just dropped her bottom into my lap. I just had to introduce Morley to Evas, let Morley be Morley, let Evas be Evas, and let Deal Relway be his own suspicious self."

The Dead Man wasn't pleased. Once I'd decided to point Evas at my pal Morley, I'd launched a companion scheme which resulted in her wanting to keep the feathered clown with her.

Evas couldn't leave The Palms, now. There were too many watchers outside who reported to the Emergency Committee for Royal Security. It may be a long time before they tire of observing comings and goings at Morley's place.

Oh, me! Oh, my! I love it!

I wonder how long it'll take Morley to realize that he's reaped the whirlwind?

No more Mr. Big, trying to get me stoned on the streets, following me everywhere, keeping track, nagging me. No more . . . "Gah!"

A ferocious squabble had broken out inside the front wall.

Soundless, almost gloating laughter seemed to fill the atmosphere.

Well, hell! He might not miss a step.

Still, I could cherish thoughts of Morley's delicious plight.

Although Fasfir didn't approve.

She had managed to establish communications with the Dead Man. She found it painful to be completely alone. When Old Bones didn't make her feel better she joined me in my office. By means of notes, a few words spoken with difficulty, and my small ability to sense moods, she made it known how cruelly terrifying being alone and lonely was for her kind.

I told her, "Casey's here."

But Fasfir found Casey nearly as alien as she did me, and he was a lot less fun after dark. I could scramble her brains and push the fear away for a while.

"Huh? You worked hard enough but I never felt like you got much out of it."

She informed me that she was much more diverted when I was with Evas and she was in Evas' mind. Evas' flesh responded more readily, thoroughly, and willingly than did her own. Though her problem probably existed entirely within her own mind.

Odd. Though she believed she had mental hang-ups she admitted to being every bit as enthusiastic as Evas. Only she enjoyed it best at second hand.

Life gets stranger by the hour.

This is TunFaire. That would be the taproot iron law. Things get weirder.

Ask the Dead Man what it was like in the old days, when he was young and callow. He'll let you know that everything was normal and straightforward, way back then.

The written record, however, doesn't support him. There may be cycles of less and more but weird is with us always.

Company is coming. Another Visitor. He had concluded that our silver elves were identical to the strange people who had been called Visitors when he was a child. He'd found fragments in Casey's head to confirm his speculation. So from now on we were going to call them Visitors.

Fasfir whipped past me as I eased into the hallway. She

hurried to the front door, then stood there baffled by all the mechanisms. I nudged her aside, looked through the peephole.

A very small, scruffy, nervous brunette was on the stoop. Homely enough to be related to Dean, she was poised to knock but wasn't sure she was ready to commit. She looked around to see who might be watching.

She flickered.

I lifted Fasfir up so she could look. "Is that your other friend?"

Fasfir nodded.

I opened the door, which startled the Visitor because she hadn't yet announced herself.

Fasfir revealed herself, slithering around me as lithely as a cat, before the ill-favored little woman could run away.

I shut the door and left the ladies to their reunion.

I went to the Dead Man's room. "You been eavesdropping?"

I got the equivalent of a mental grunt in response. I noted that Casey, who seldom strayed from the Dead Man's room, was lapsing into sleep. Again. By the time he left my place Casey was going to be years ahead on his sleep.

"Finding anything interesting? Like why this one is running around loose when she ought to be a captive of the Masker contingent?"

Given fewer distractions I might exploit the present moment of emotional vulnerability to unearth those and further significant answers.

I pinched my lips closed.

We can call this woman Woderact. She seems to be what we would call a sorceress. She would be the most socially reserved of the female crew. She is not an adventuress. Yet there is about her that same intense suppressed hunger that characterized Evas. Some not so suppressed amusement. The Maskers kicked her out because she was of no use to them. She would not cooperate. Also, the Maskers may have thought she could lead them to Fasfir and Evas, either of whom might know something that would help them repair their ship.

These Maskers seem to be more hardened than are the other Visitors.

"Except for Casey."

Except for Casey. I do believe that it is just marginally possible that Casey could do direct, willful physical harm to another being. None of the other Visitors seem able to entertain the thought.

Ah! The excitement of the reunion has begun to ebb. Fasfir's thoughts are no longer accessible. And there goes the new mind. Ha!

A vast miasma of amusement wrapped itself around me. *My metaphysical side seems to be asserting itself. I have suffered a psychic episode. You are going to have to teach night school at least one more time.*

"I can lock my door."

But you will not.

No. Being an empathetic kind of guy, I probably wouldn't. Not for a night or two.

Please move the women out of the hallway, now. We are about to suffer another caller. It would be best that the Visitors are not seen.

73

I looked out the peephole as someone knocked. I saw a lean beanpole of a man all dressed in black. He had a black beard and wore a wide-brimmed black hat. I didn't recognize him.

Dean came into the hallway, started to go back when he saw that I'd reached the door first. I beckoned him forward, to answer while I eavesdropped and covered him from the small front room. The stillness and emptiness in there were sweet. With luck the parrot smell would fade away eventually.

Dean followed instructions but didn't fail to stomp and employ his full arsenal of disgusted expressions.

The man on the stoop asked, "Is this the home of the confidential operative known as Garrett?"

Sounded to me like he knew the answer already.

Dean thought so, too. "Yes. Why?"

"I have a message from Miss Contague." Sounded like he was talking about a living goddess, the way he said that. "For Mr. Garrett." Making sure.

He went away without saying anything more.

"That was strange," Dean told me, handing me a vellum document folded and sealed with a red wax seal as ornate as any used by the nobility. "That man had a voice like an embalmer."

"She chooses her henchmen to ornament her own epic. Which she rewrites as she goes along."

"It's a crying shame. Such a lovely young woman to be so twisted. I blame her father."

"So do I. But however cruel Chodo was, he never put a

knife to her throat and forced her to do evil. She made the choices." When first we'd met Belinda had been trying to kill herself by slutting it up down in the Tenderloin. At the time that had been fashionable amongst unhappy young women from wealthy families.

Even now Belinda seemed determined to bring about her own destruction. Except that these days she wanted to go out in a flashy orgy of violence. So her pain could be seen and shared by everyone.

The Dead Man once told me that monsters aren't born, they're made. That they are memorials which take years of cruelty to sculpt. And that while we should weep for the tortured child who served as raw material, we should permit no sentiment to impede us while we rid the world of the terror strewn by the finished work. It took me a while to figure out what he meant but I do understand him now.

You just need one intimate look at what a fully mature monster can do to achieve enlightenment.

He may have been the most wonderful pup you've ever known but you don't hesitate to strike the dog if he goes rabid.

What is it?

"Belinda found the flying ship that got away out in the wine country."

Dean said, "It took that much paper just to tell you that?" No wondering on his part about why she'd even been looking.

"There's some cry-on-the-shoulder stuff, too." Almost like a confession. Which made me wonder if I shouldn't be more pessimistic about my personal longevity. I might be scheduled to share her funeral pyre. "And her people have found the stable where Casey keeps his donkey." That for the Dead Man's benefit, not Dean's. Dean didn't care. "Things he told the people there led Belinda's agents to another apartment. It doesn't sound as fancy as Casey's Bic Gonlit place but the stuff she says they found there makes me wonder if half of TunFaire's population isn't our pal Casey in disguise."

Excellent. Will you want to relay any of this to Colonel Block?

"Not today. Because he'd pass it on." And the people he'd pass it to don't really need more power than they already have. "You think we can use this as leverage to work on Casey?" I wished we'd find something. I was way tired of having the Visitor underfoot. "Can we make him think we have him over a barrel, now?" He'd been around too long just to hand over to the Guard, now. Block and Relway would want to know why I hadn't bothered to mention him earlier.

Probably. And the point to doing that would be what?

"Oh. Yeah. He's on a mission."

I will discuss it with him. Meanwhile, it is time you stopped lollygagging and went back to work.

I'd begun to loathe the captain of industry gig.

All right. Yes. Everybody did warn me. But . . . I guess it's mostly because my partners don't have any patience with my relaxed attitude toward work. They're worse than tribe of dwarves trained by Dean.

There is supposed to be a lot of humorless, from under the roots of mountains, all work and no play, dwarfish blood up one of the branches of the Tate family tree. I can't provide any arguments against the allegation, of my own knowledge. Tinnie definitely finds it hard to step away from work for any extended length of time.

I was the only key member of the new company not having great fun with our venture. Kip haunted his vast new workshop twenty hours a day, and usually fell asleep there. Fawning Tate nephews and cousins rushed hither and yon, making sure Kip's genius remained unencumbered by scutwork. Experts from the discontinued military leather goods operations now stayed busy trying to determine the most efficient means of three-wheel production.

My own three-wheel, the only pay I'd yet received for any of my trouble, had been spirited in from Playmate's stable. It now resided in the Tate compound inner courtyard, where there were always folks lined up to take a short ride. The managers didn't want *their* several completed prototypes defiled by the unwashed. Even brother, sister, and cousin unwashed.

Though two-thirds of the shoe factory floor had been

turned over to new manufacture, the Tates weren't abandoning their traditional business base. They were just scaling back to the peacetime levels known by their great-grandfathers.

Shoes become a luxury when you have to pay for them yourself.

The Tates would remain the leading producers of fashionable women's footwear. They'd held that distinction since imperial times.

Though I was a rabid fan of the three-wheel and wasn't interested in much else, less than half the reassigned production space was intended for the manufacture of my vehicle. My associates were equally taken with several other Kip Prose inventions. His writing sticks were in production already, in three different colors. And orders were piling up.

The Guard and the Hill folk hadn't taken notice, perhaps because writing sticks don't fly.

Kip was having the time of his life. He was the center of everything. Everyone else was having a great time, meeting the challenges. Everyone but poor Garrett. There wasn't that much for him to do.

I'd used up my ration of genius.

There were no crooks here, trying to steal from the boss. I didn't have any other assets to kick in, except for knowing a lot of different people I can bring to bear on a difficulty. But the only bringing together I was getting done these days took place back at the house, nights. Woderact was proving to be a researcher every bit as dedicated as Evas had been. A tad more shy, initially, but Fasfir kept egging her on. And climbed right in there with us when the adventure called her.

TunFaire gets weirder by the hour. And my life marches in the van.

There wasn't much I could do but all my business associates seemed determined to have me right there at the factory not doing it.

I'm an old hand at skating out of the boring stuff. I acquired that skill in the harsh realm of war. I ducked out of the Tate compound. I recouped my spirit and recovered from my difficult nights by undertaking the promised visits to the troubled Weider satellite breweries.

That killed three days but didn't demand much genius. Like so many TunFairen villains, the various crooks were completely inept. They betrayed themselves immediately. My report named several managerial types who had to go when the thieves went because bad guys as incompetent as the ones I'd caught couldn't possibly have operated without their superiors turning a blind eye while extending a palm for a share of the proceeds.

74

Fasfir decided she had to try her luck in person, one more time. No man could've faulted her enthusiasm. But something was missing from her makeup. She just wasn't a Katie. Inevitably, direct participation left her disappointed. But she didn't have problems enjoying what Evas or Woderact shared with her, mind to mind.

Weirder by the minute.

This latest time Fasfir had a different motive for joining me.

Of late we had been refining our communication skills until, using gestures, grunts, a few spoken words, some writing, and what I could pull out of thin air, she could get ideas across. She had a big something on her mind this time.

"You want to get your whole crew back together?" I tried to appear distraught, though that very notion had been worming around in my head for two days. As things stood, my having sicced Evas on Morley hadn't changed anything for me. Except that I didn't have to listen to the Goddamn Parrot anymore. "Could I count on you three to stay out of mischief?"

Absolutely.

That came through almost as clearly as one of the Dead Man's messages. I didn't swallow it whole. The ladies hadn't lost their interest in going home.

"I'll see what I can do."

Fasfir became quite excited and grateful.

Moments later an equally excited and grateful Woderact joined us.

Weirder and weirder.

I hired a coach, grumbled about the expense the whole time, put the lady Visitors inside it. I let them reclaim some of the fetishes Woderact had brought along to the house. They would appear to be human if they were seen on the street.

Casey got aggravated because he wasn't allowed to come along. Neither of the ladies believed him when he told them that he'd help them get home.

"Lookit dis," Puddle enthused as I pushed inside The Palms. "Somebody done fergot ta lock da goddamn door again." Puddle wasn't doing anything but loafing in a chair. His was the only body in sight. I'd timed my visit perfectly.

"Morley around?"

"What was dat?"

"Huh?"

"T'ought I heard somet'in'." A huge grin drove suspicion off his face. "We ain't seen much a Morley da past few days, Garrett. What wit' him spendin' so much time takin' care a dat bird."

Sarge shoved out of the kitchen, clearly having been eavesdropping. "Poor boy is gettin' kinda pale, Garrett. I'm t'inkin' he mought oughta get out in the sunshine more. What da hell was dat?"

"What was what?" I asked, as innocent as the dawn itself.

"I t'ought I heared da stair creak." Sarge scratched his drought-stricken, failing crop of hair. He and Puddle both eyed me suspiciously.

"What?" I inquired.

Puddle demanded, "Whatcha up to, Garrett?"

"Actually, I just wanted to drop in to see if I had any good reason to gloat."

Both men nodded and smiled. They could understand that. Sarge told me, "I don' know where ya found dat little gel, Garrett, but I sure do wish dey was one or two like her aroun' back when I was 'bout sixteen."

Puddle nodded enthusiastic agreement. "Gloat yer heart out."

"I will," I said. "Well, if the man can't come down, then things are going just wonderfully. If you do see Morley, tell him I stopped by. And that I'm thinking of him. But don't let him know I'm having a hard time keeping a straight face when I do."

A feeble groan limped, stumbling, downstairs.

Everybody snickered.

Before Sarge and Puddle discovered my latest maneuver seemed like a good time to move myself along somewhere else. "Later, guys."

Both henchmen observed my retreat with abiding suspicion.

I set course for home, making plans for indulging in some serious rest and brew tasting. I kept breaking out in giggles, which inclined the streets to clear away around me.

75

My opinion of the legal profession seldom soars above ankle height. I believe that most troubles would settle out faster without lawyers stirring the pot. So it irks me to have to admit that Lister Tate and Congo Greve really did turn out to be useful.

Tate was a good idea man. Greve seemed to know everybody who was anybody. Well, he did know the legal beagles that everyone who was anyone paid to put words in their mouths. And he knew how to work them when they were just hanging around.

Tate told the rest of us, "We'll create a demand for three-wheels by having them seen underneath the most important people."

I didn't get it. I protested, "You're talking about giving them away! You don't make money giving things away."

"You have to consider promotion as a part of the investment process, Mr. Garrett. It's an investment in public exposure paralleling our investments in tools and materials. We'll only comp ten units, total. And those will be prototype and pilot units we put together while we're figuring out the most efficient way to build the three-wheels."

Congo Greve said, "I've placed all ten already, too. *Two* with the royal household! One with the Metropolitan. Thousands of the best people will see that old goof and his two acres of beard pedaling around the Dream Quarter. Every Orthodox heretic in town will want one to ride to church. Plus I got one placed in Westenrache House, with the imperial family. How about that? Just those four units should give us exposure enough to generate thousands of orders."

I never got a protest in because I couldn't get my jaw moving. Greve knew people inside Westenrache House? The remnants of the imperial family, with hangers-on, had been forted up, or under household arrest, there, for centuries. Ever since the ineptitude of generations of ancestors let the empire crumble into kingdoms and principalities and tiny quasi states, each of which paid lip service to the imperial crown while ignoring its wishes completely.

The sole function of the empire these days, insofar as Karenta is concerned, is to furnish somebody who can crown the king whenever a new monarch ascends Karenta's throne. Which occurs with some frequency, though we haven't had a coronation recently. Our present monarch is particularly adept at sidestepping assassins. With Deal Relway covering his back he'll probably live forever.

I croaked, "I think I understand." If the King's daughters happened to be seen larking around on our three-wheels, every young woman of substance would demand she be provided one of her own. And the herd instincts of their fathers would ensure that the girls remained indistinguishable from the princesses.

"Good, Mr. Garrett," Mr. Greve said. "Once we establish a list, and the social primacy of our product to the exclusion of all imitators, we'll have written ourselves a letter of marque allowing us to plunder the aristocracy."

I gave brother Greve the fish-eye. That sounded a whole lot like the true lawyer coming through.

Greve sighed, explained, "We *must* ensure that our three-wheel is the only three-wheel the elite find acceptable once the fad gets started. Imitations are certain to appear as soon as someone capable of building them lays hands on one he can tear apart. We have to make sure that anybody who actually buys a competing three-wheel is considered a second-rater. Or worse." His expression suggested that he had begun to rank me with the dimmer of the dimwit Tate cousins.

Lister said, "It's possible that I can work my royal household connections to wangle a decree of patent."

If the Crown so ordered, nobody would be allowed to build three-wheels but us. Until somebody able to offer a big enough bribe got the King to change his mind. Or got the people who made up the King's mind for him to do so. Likely, the King himself would never know about the decree of patent.

"I'm glad you guys are on our side." I thought I could see how Weider beers had become the choice of beer drinkers, now. Snob appeal, backed by suggestions that any tavern brewing its own beverages on premises was an outdated second-stringer, its product likely fit only for the meanest classes.

Which is true. In many cases. The uniformity and consistent quality of Weider brews exceeds anything produced by corner taverns. And I can claim a certain expertise in judging the quality of beers.

Greve continued to pontificate. "Obviously, our ability to produce three-wheels will be limited. Demand will exceed supply for as long as the fad runs. We want to sustain and exploit that situation. First, we'll set a publicly announced fixed unit price—exorbitant, of course—then we'll place our buyers' names on a list. Then Lister and I, being cheesy lawyers, will let those who want to do so bribe us to move their names up the list."

"Excellent thinking!" Lister Tate declared. He actually rubbed his hands together in washing motions and chuckled wickedly till he realized some of us were staring. He grinned, told us, "Sorry I don't have mustache ends to twirl. Here. Let's do this while we're at it. Publish the list by posting it outside the compound entrance. Update it daily. So the buyers will know where they stand. In case they feel an urgent need to move on up."

"Oh, yes! Excellent idea! Here's another idea. We'll put serial numbers on the three-wheels. The lower the serial number, the more exalted the status of the three-wheel."

I said, "I can see people falsifying serial numbers. . . ." Oh.

Both men gave me looks that said they wondered how a grown man could be so naive and still be here among the living.

More than one three-wheel would go out the door with the same low serial number.

Pure, raging, unbridled capitalism. Now, if they could just find ways to steal our raw materials, evade taxation, and not pay our workers their wages, our profit margin might begin to approach what those guys would consider minimally acceptable.

I was becoming increasingly certain that the best thing I could do for the company I had invented would be to stay away. I should just let them haul my share of the profits over to the house aboard a beer wagon.

My mind just wouldn't fall into a businesslike groove.

If I was building a business I'd do it as if everybody involved was a partner. Kind of the way I had things already.

Enough of that.

I saw Kip's family whenever I visited the Tate compound. Kayne was bored. Prosperity was all right with her but she wanted something to do. She was used to working, long and hard. I told her, "There's plenty of work around here. I'll pass the word. Cassie? Rhafi? How about you guys?"

Cassie was extremely adept at doing nothing useful and planned to keep right on doing what she did best. Rhafi was content to polish his loafing and consuming skills as well.

"So be it."

I was in the Tate compound when the workers completed our first presentation three-wheel, half of the pair of gaily painted monsters meant for the King's daughters. We drew lots to see who would pedal it away. I didn't win.

76

Sleepily, the Dead Man again asked, *How does it feel to be a captain of industry?* His inquiry had an amused, sharp, mocking edge to it. The sort of edge his thoughts take on when things go exactly according to his prognostications.

"I feel like a man wasting his life. Like the proverbial square peg."

Indeed? But if you were not working there you would be here either sleeping off hangovers or indulging yourself in some rakish indulgence.

"Yeah. That'd be great. Indulging in some indulgence."

He was feeling generous. He didn't mention the several Visitor women I'd finagled out of the house not that long ago.

Singe invited herself into the Dead Man's room, then into the conversation. Evidently the Dead Man had kept her posted. She took a sandwich out of her mouth long enough to ask, "Are you having problems with the red-haired woman again? I hope?"

"Absolutely. Always. That goes without saying. But not as many as usual." Mainly because Tinnie was too busy working. And I stayed out of her way.

"I am sorry."

"No, you're not. You've been polishing up your sarky, haven't you?"

"When you are lower than a ratman's dog you do have to try harder. John Stretch was here not long ago. He wanted us to know that he knows where the other Visitors are hiding. The ones we ran into out in the country." Singe still shivered when she recalled that adventure, though it made her the awe of all ratpeople who heard the tale. "They are here in the city, now. Their skyship is hidden inside a large, abandoned structure on the Embankment, a little ways north of the Landing."

Way up there in strange territory.

Coincidentally within a few hundred yards of the site where the ship belonging to Lastyr and Noodiss is suspected to have gone beneath the water.

I frowned, trying to picture such a fantasm as an abandoned building in TunFaire. I'd expect to bump snoots with a unicorn first. This city is awash in refugees from the former war zone. Nothing that remotely resembles shelter isn't infested with desperate, dangerous people.

Singe anticipated my question. "People lived there until ten days ago. Something scared them into moving out." Meaning maybe somebody more dangerous had moved in.

"What do you think, Old Bones? Worth a look? Or are we out of the thing since Kip doesn't seem to be in trouble anymore?" Though how could we be out while we still had Casey underfoot? I wished there was some way I could give him to Morley, too.

The Dead Man's response was the mental equivalent of a distracted grunt.

"Don't you dare go to sleep on me! Who'll keep Casey under control?"

The question elicited only a mental snort and the equivalent of "I was just resting my eyes."

"You don't keep him managed, Chuckles, I won't have any choice but to turn him over to the Guard. I can't handle him. We've already seen that."

Mental grumbles. Old Bones was getting testy, a sure sign he was headed for a long nap. He's predictable. Kind of like the weather is predictable. You look out the window and tell everybody a storm is on its way. No way you're ever wrong, given sufficient time.

What is your attitude toward unearthing Lastyr and Noodiss?

"Not quite obsessed but definitely still interested. Despite all logic. They planted that one deep, whoever did it."

He didn't tell me what I wanted to know.

"That was supposed to be a hint, Old Bones. Who messed with the inside of my head?"

I am inclined to suspect Casey but I do not know. I have not read direct responsibility in any Visitor mind yet. But the Visitors have been exceedingly adept at concealing specific items. Witness Evas and her sisters. Witness Casey himself. He has not yielded up a tenth of his secrets even though he has been in direct mental contact with me for ages now.

Also, it might be wise to consider the possibility that your urge is not of Visitor origin.

"What?"

We might do well to recollect, occasionally, Colonel Block's several subtle cautions about the intense interest in the Visitors being shown, behind the scenes, by several Hill personages. You have been rendered unconscious with some frequency of late. We might review your memories of those episodes with an eye toward the possibility that some of our own folk might have created an opportunity to implant a compulsion.

"Maybe who really isn't as important as what. Who wants the secrets of the Visitors' magic isn't truly critical to us. Who won't have much direct impact on our lives."

Perhaps. If you discount the moral dimension.

"Naturally."

And when the talking is over, you do want to meet the mysterious Lastyr and Noodiss yourself.

"I sure do. I know I'll be disappointed. I always am. But I'd definitely like to see who got the cauldron bubbling."

Then cease investing your time in the three-wheel business. There is nothing you can contribute there except exasperation for your associates.

I'd had the feeling that even Willard Tate was considering changing the locks on the compound doors. It isn't just that I ask too many questions, I ask questions that make people uncomfortable.

Even the bloodiest villains have to work hard at conscience management sometimes. Until they get their full arsenal of justifications filed, sanded, and polished to fit their shadowy needs.

Indeed you do. Also, you must stop juggling the women in your life. I understand that you are trying to live every young man's dream and are managing a twisted approximation. But there come moments when each of us must step away from the dreamtime.

Sometimes somebody besides me flops something uncomfortable onto the table.

Find Lastyr and Noodiss. Before they perish from old age.

I didn't contradict him. But Evas had told me that Visitors never grow old, nor do they die of old age. They live on until Fate finds a way to squash them with a falling boulder or until they do something really stupid, like going into a horse stall all alone, without a witness around anywhere.

Which sounds like some of those old, false legends about Morley's people.

"Singe, it ought to be safe out there now. You ready for another adventure?"

"Whither thou goest."

"Oh, that's rude. All right. First thing in the morning. Bright and early. For real. But for now, let's just hit the kitchen and tip a few mugs of Weider Select."

I *am* getting old. I thought about heading out to Grubb Gruber's to enjoy a few with the old jarheads. I thought about wandering over to serenade Katie, whom I hadn't seen in so long she might've forgotten her favorite little honey bunny. I thought about several other ways to fritter my evening. And, in the end, I just stayed in, sipping the dark and exchanging brew-born wisdom with my pal Singe. I hit the sack early, never suffering a thought about the feuding pixies.

77

Singe and I set out about a week before my normal getup time. We headed for the Casey digs Belinda's connections had discovered. We didn't learn a thing there except that the Guard had the place under surveillance—a fact that would interest Miss Contague a great deal. We also learned that thugs I assumed to be Relway's were keeping watch on us loyal subjects, by means of some very clever operatives and tactics.

The shiftiest operatives alive have trouble keeping up when the folks they're watching can step around a corner and vanish. Which Singe and I did a few times. Then I decided it wouldn't be smart to give away the fact that we really could slide around a corner and disappear.

That invisibility fetish was a wonderful device. I didn't want it taken away by some Bubba Dreadlock.

The pursuit did a hell of a job of hanging on. I'd have to congratulate Block and Relway. Someday.

I told Singe, "We can't shake them. Every time we give them the slip they get right back on track after a while." I hadn't been too obvious about trying to lose them yet, however. I was just pretending to take normal precautions. I didn't want them to know that we knew we were the object of a massive tail.

Singe stopped being talkative as the morning wore on. Her shoulders hunched. She seemed to shrink. Maybe I did a little, too. We had reached the Embankment, which is an ancient docking and warehousing district along the riverbank north of the Landing. It's rough country and I don't know my way around there. Nor do I know a soul amongst its denizens, which isn't true of the waterfront on the south side. The Embankment seemed a bleaker, harsher, less colorful district than its more familiar cousin.

The Embankment is the jumping-off point and home base for all trade along the navigable waterways, some of which reach a thousand miles beyond Karenta's borders, a thousand miles into the heart of the continent. The southside waterfront is the jumping-off point for what seems to me far more exotic destinations along the ocean coasts and overseas.

"What is that smell?" Singe asked.

"The sweet aroma of uncured animal hides." I was able to answer that one because of my intermittent association with the family Tate. "You won't believe this but there are men crazy enough to hunt thunder lizards and mammoths and saber-tithed toogers in the plains and mountains and forests back in places so far away they don't even have dwarves or elves there yet. Flatboats bring hides and teeth and horns and bones and ivory and fur and, sometimes, even meat down to TunFaire. And sometimes gold or silver or gemstones, or lumber or untaxed whiskey. It all gets unloaded right here on the Embankment." Where several of the bigger warehouses belong to the Contague family and store none of the mentioned goods except whiskey.

A broad range of herbs and spices grows wild in the interior, too.

But hunting is the thing.

A bold enough hunter, responding to the appropriate commercial demand, can set himself up for life by making a handful of the right kills. I expect a lot of bold veterans will toss the dice out there before long. And have enough success that the market for animal by-products will get shaky.

Perhaps the Crown ought to encourage homesteading. That would bleed off a lot of extra people.

Generally speaking, the quickest way to get dwarves to give up their silver and gold is to take it away, over their dead bodies. But if you can bring them the head of the right kind of thunder lizard—which they won't hunt themselves, no matter what—they'll throw gold dust at you like the bags are filled with sand. But that head has to come off an adult specimen of one of the major carnivores. Or off a three-horn or the rarer five-horn, because an infusion of powdered horn will scare impotence into the next continent.

I've never heard why dwarves covet the teeth of the great meat eaters, but who better than a lady dwarf to know, intimately, the meaning of rock hard?

Singe told me, "We must pass through this place that smells of old death."

"Huh?'

"The area where they make leather from those uncured animal hides."

"The tannery district." There were places which processed tallow and bone, too, though little of that would be imported. None of those places lacked their enthusiastic odors. "Why?"

"Someone is using ratman trackers to follow us. There can be no other explanation for their success. Yet few of my people have the courage to visit the fastnesses of death. Even if they forget that not many generations have passed since our own kind were killed and flayed to provide fashionable trousers for young dandies, the stench will overwhelm anything as subtle as traces left by you and me. Without leaving it obvious that we were trying to distort our backtrail."

"Ah, my friend, you continue to amaze me."

"A year from now you will be working for me."

There was a thought to rattle me.

Singe jumped up and down and clapped her paws. "I did it! I did it! You should see the look on your face."

"I believe I've created a monster."

Ratpeople aren't built to laugh but Singe sure did try. And she kept her mind on business while she was having fun. She led the way along a path a ratman tracker ought not to find suspicious, yet one that would overload any tracker's nose.

Singe was too naive to understand that anything not going his way would be suspicious to Director Relway.

I may have remained a little naive myself.

Not till after we had begun taking advantage of the district's natural odiferous cover did it occur to me that having Relway's fanatics on my backtrail might be a lesser evil.

78

Singe and I were on a holiday stroll, giddy because we had shaken free. Singe more so than I because she had a better appreciation of what she had accomplished—and of its cost. Her own olfactory abilities had been dampened hugely.

A sudden whir. The pixie Shakespear materialized above my right shoulder. He told me, "You must hide quickly. They will be here in a minute."

Another whirr as Shakespear went away. I glimpsed a second pixie, hovering, pointing in the direction of the threat. I heard the wings of several more.

Singe pulled me toward the nearest doorway. It was open. Beyond lay the noisome vats of a small tannery. I wondered how the flies stood the smell. I whispered, "Did you know that the wee folk were with us?"

"You did not know? You missed the sound of their wings?"

"You have better ears than I do. And you're starting to make me feel old. I should've been more aware of what was happening around me." Maybe my friends are right. Maybe I am getting too tied up inside my own head.

There wasn't anything in the tannery. There was no tanning going on, thought the place was still in business. It gave the impression that the entire workforce had slipped out just minutes before we arrived. Curious. It wasn't a major holy day that I knew of, though possibly the place employed only members of some lesser cult.

Still, there ought to be somebody around to keep opportunists from finders-keeping all those squirrel hides.

"Here."

Singe had located a low opening in the outer wall, placed so air could waft in and rise to roof vents, so the tannery could share its chief wonder with the city. The opening lay behind a heap of pelts from small animals. The majority had come off rodents but some were scaly. The odor off the pile guaranteed that no ratman tracker would find us here.

Singe had both paws clamped to her muzzle.

Gagging, I whispered, "Could you pick me out of this?"

Singe shook her head slightly, took a paw away from her muzzle long enough to tap her ear, reminding me that her people also had exceptional hearing. Then she dropped down so she could watch the street between bars that kept dogs, cats, and other sizable vermin from getting to the delicacies. They would have to stroll all the way down to the unlocked and open door if they wanted to compete with the bugs.

Singe beckoned me. I went for the fresh air.

I got down on the dirt floor, amongst the crud and the hair and the fleas off the pelts, and observed. And learned.

The first few hunters weren't unusual. They were just thugs. But they were extremely nervous, very alert thugs. They were thugs whose main task was to protect a brace of extremely unhappy ratmen. The trackers kept glancing over their shoulders. I didn't recognize anybody but wasn't surprised. I didn't know many members of the Guard. And Relway was enlisting fellow fanatics like harvesting dragons' teeth.

Then I saw white boots. With platform soles and cracked, fake jewels. Bic Gonlit was up on top of them. The real Bic Gonlit. And Bic wasn't alone. Nor was he in charge. His companion wore black as tattered as Bic's white but was a lot more intimidating. He looked like he was about nine feet tall. He wore a mask. Arcane symbols in gold and silver spattered something like a monk's hooded robe. An extremely threadbare robe. This particular stormwarden wasn't enjoying a great deal of prosperity.

That would make him especially dangerous.

Singe was even more careful than I was about not attracting attention by breathing. Her people have nurtured that skill since their creation.

I didn't recognize anybody but Bic.

My first inclination was to drop everything and head for home. Let Bic and the big boy play the game. Which is exactly what most people do and what all the big boys expect us to do. They count on that, up there on the Hill. They don't know how to react when ordinary folks refuse to fold and fade.

Usually that's followed by a lot of sound and fury and people getting hurt. Which explains the prevalent cowardly attitude.

Once they passed by, I whispered, "I've got Bic Gonlit figured out, now." He'd taken Casey's money. He'd underwritten his taste for high living by collecting books for Casey, but once things got real interesting the little pudgeball had made a fast connection up the Hill.

That being the case, why hadn't any Hill-type visitors come to the house?

Maybe Brother Bic hadn't made himself a deal so good that he felt like giving up everything he had, informationwise. Or, more likely, the Dead Man had revised his recollections before letting him leave the house.

You've got to keep an eye on the dead guy. He's sneaky. Old Bones has been getting slicker every day for a long time. He doesn't keep me adequately informed, though, I thought. I must have an unrecognized tendency to blab all over town.

Another pack of intense bruno types came along, following Bic and his buddy in black. They were alert. They were all armed, too, though that was against the law.

Once again, neither Singe nor I breathed.

I'd love to see Relway attempt to impose his idealistic, no exceptions, rule of law outlook on the lords of the Hill. Or even on their minions.

The resulting fireworks would make for great popular entertainment.

Bic's stride faltered. He stopped. He seemed uncertain.

He bent to caress his ragged magic boots. Frowning, he looked straight at me, though without seeing me. He frowned, shook his head, said nothing to the ragged wizard. The stormwarden beckoned two ratman trackers. A conference ensued.

The whole crew had become confused.

Nobody had the track now, by scent or by sorcery.

Singe pinched me.

79

I breathed, "This isn't the time," because she'd snuggled up like she wanted to get really friendly. It hadn't ever gotten this complicated when I was running with Morley. Then Singe proved that I had misjudged her again.

She pointed back past the heap of possum and muskrat hides.

Several Visitors were up to something back there. Singe had pressed against me to make sure the invisibility spell concealed us both.

I whispered, "What the hell are they doing? They're not supposed to be here." One of the Visitors had his arm in a sling. Another seemed to have a broken leg. Evidently the Maskers hadn't been able to work any medical magic.

Every Visitor carried at least one gray fetish and studied it intently.

I whispered, "There're too many of them." There were more here than the Masker four. I couldn't get them all in sight at once but I definitely counted at least five Visitors. Though it was hard to tell one from another, even when the Visitor hailed from Evas' crew. Unless you charmed them out of their silver suits.

I whispered, "We're still blocks away from where John Stretch said they're hiding."

Singe murmured, "Quit whispering so much," then added a thought I'd had already and didn't want to be true. "Maybe they were warned about us coming. Maybe they are here because they expected us to go to the place where we were told that they would be hiding."

Maybe. Because in TunFaire nothing ought to surprise you. The possible will happen. The impossible takes only a few minutes longer.

In this case the probabilities were apparent. Certain overly friendly Visitor ladies, desperate to get a ride home, had conned simple old Garrett into returning some Visitor fetishes they said they'd need in order to sneak in and join Evas in her adventures with Morley Dotes at The Palms. Taking advantage of simple old Garrett's understandable and righteous desire to rectify a near-cosmic injustice.

If they got away I hoped the girls were dim enough to take the Goddamn Parrot with them.

Smirk. I'd have to remember to call the place The Joy House next time I dropped in at Morley's. Smirk.

The extra Visitors lurking here had to be Lastyr and Noodiss, erstwhile missionaries. Just had to be. Because no Visitor would be going home if they couldn't all work together, and the Maskers would have been gone already if they'd gotten reinforcements from the old country. The women in particular had to be extremely cooperative with the others. They were at everyone's mercy.

Disdaining Singe's advice, I whispered. "You watch them. I'll keep an eye on the street." The confusion out there had begun to commence to begin to get ready to head on out somewhere else.

Bic and his pal resumed moving, though confusion didn't cease being their guiding spirit. They faded away.

I expected them back. You cast around a bit but you always return to the point where your track evaporated, to hunt for the one thing you missed the last time you looked.

Minutes later Singe murmured a grand understatement. "We should leave. Sooner or later they will stumble over us in spite of this invisibility amulet."

"Or they might have some way to tell if an invisibility spell is being used anywhere nearby." If I invented an invisibility-maker I'd sure try to come up with a way to tell if somebody else was using something like it around me.

"Or they might hear you whispering."

That, too.

We'd come to the Embankment to find Visitors. Although this wasn't quite the situation I'd hoped for. This wasn't good. This didn't fit in with my half-assed plans at all.

Singe was spot on about whispering. But she was a tad off when it came to who would do the eavesdropping.

Yikes! Here came Bic Gonlit and his threadbare stormwarden buddy, hustling like they were being driven by one of the wizard's spooky winds. Their trackers and henchmen scampered along behind them, confused and alert and able to keep up only because Bic had those stubby little pins.

The flotilla's course ran straight toward me.

I poked Singe, indicated that she should peek through the airhole. Once she'd done so we got up on our hind feet and, chest to chest, in careful lockstep, began to ease along the brick wall, toward the cover of another mound of hides. We found it necessary to freeze every few steps because the Visitors had become extremely nervous, suddenly. They were inclined to jump at the slightest sound.

They had to suspect that they had trouble in their hip pocket.

Several Visitors, fetishes extended before them, suddenly rushed the hide pile Singe and I had abandoned. Bic and his cohorts were causing a disturbance outside. And Singe and I hadn't gotten but a dozen feet away. So we froze. And shivered. And held our breaths. And hoped nobody stumbled into us.

The Visitor with his arm in a sling missed running into me by scant inches.

Tension mounted amongst the Visitors. The advent of danger reawakened the bad feelings between the Maskers and Kip's pals. I could sense just enough to tell that the Maskers blamed Lastyr and Noodiss for everything. Kip's friends blamed the Maskers for zipping all over the sky, thereby alerting the savages to their presence.

Lastyr and Noodiss had abandoned the altruism that had brought them to TunFaire. In fact, prolonged exposure to our fair flower of a city had turned them bitter and cynical.

Imagine that.

Singe and I continued to move, teensy baby steps, then with more vigor once we realized that the people outside intended to come inside.

Visitors began flying all over the place. Two quite literally. I didn't see any ropes or wires. "Keep moving," I told Singe, in what I thought would be an inaudible whisper.

Visitors froze.

Something had changed. The Visitors were alert in a whole different way.

The Visitors then unfroze, every man jack getting busy with fetish boxes.

Those guys needed bandoliers to carry all the fetishes they had. Evidently every task imaginable could be managed with the right gray box.

Two Visitors headed our way, weaving slow, serpentine courses, zeroing in.

Bic's gang poured through the open door.

Big surprises happened. For everybody.

The confusion attained an epic level.

At first it looked like it would be a walk for the startled Visitors. Thugs went down left and right, exactly as easily as I had in my first several encounters with Masker magic.

Then Bic came through the doorway.

The Visitor sorcery didn't affect Little Bitty Big Boy.

Bic selected a paddle meant for stirring the contents of a curing vat. He took a swing at the nearest silver figure, which happened to belong to the Masker with the broken leg.

The Visitor rewarded Bic with a beaten-sheep sort of bleat.

The shabby stormwarden stepped inside. And instantly called down some of that old-fashioned thunder and lightning, the ability to control which gave stormwardens their name.

Weather magic is the flashiest and most obviously destructive power possessed by our lords of the Hill—and the most common.

Hides flew. Vats exploded. People shrieked. Bic Gonlit rose ten feet into the air, spinning faster and faster as he

did so. The stormwarden followed, spinning himself. But
he threw off spells like the sparks coming off one of those
pinwheel fireworks.

I told Singe, "We *really* need to take ourselves somewhere else."

The game looked like it was just starting to get serious.

"I thought you wanted to find the Visitors. . . ."

"We found them. Now let's take advantage of the fact
that nobody here has us at the head of their to-do list
right now."

80

Pixies flitted around us, giggling and squabbling, more annoying than a flock of starving mosquitoes. Not a single one had anything useful to say. Their presence didn't help anything. Singe and I weren't invisible anymore. There was no need.

Nobody was interested in us. But the squawking bugs threatened to attract attention.

For the gawkers, trying to figure out what was happening in the slowly collapsing tannery, a guy hanging out with a ratwoman bold enough to walk the streets by daylight was a secondary spectacle.

Threads of blue light as thin as spider silk crawled over the ruins. The entire heap of rubble hurled itself skyward. Everything inside went up with the building itself. People and debris alike floated on the surface of an expanding, invisible bubble.

More time seemed to pass than actually did.

The bubble popped. And collapsed.

A raindrop smacked me in the cheek. I noted that a cold breeze had begun blowing. The change in weather wasn't unseasonable or unlikely, it was just a surprise because I hadn't been paying attention.

Vigorous lightning pranced over the remains of the tannery. One bolt struck something explosive, probably chemicals used for treating leather. The explosion scattered brick and broken timbers for a hundred yards around. A spinning sliver sixteen inches long flew between Singe and me, narrowly missing us both.

Singe said, "We have found them. Do we really need to stay so close, now?"

"I don't know. You may have a point." I spied a dirty white behind wagging as somebody struggled to back his way out of the mess. When the pile finally finished birthing Bic it developed that he had hold of his employer by the ankle. He strove to drag the wizard out by main strength.

I said, "I think we might move a little farther away."

Lightning bolts, like swift left and right jabs, rained down on the ruins, starting small fires, flinging debris around. Despite his discomfiture and the inelegance of his situation the stormwarden was still in there punching.

Other things were happening at the same time. They were less intensely visual. I credited them to the Visitors because Bic's gang were the people being inconvenienced.

Damn! We'd dropped the invisibility spell and were trying to fade into the onlookers but Bic spotted us almost immediately. But he didn't get the chance to report us. A Visitor floated up out of the ruins, jabbed one of those gray fetishes in his direction. And he fell down, sound asleep. I wasn't feeling real charitable. I hoped he woke up with a headache as ferocious as the worst I'd enjoyed back when they were knocking me out all day long.

I told Singe, "It'll be a week before they get their stuff together back there. Let's use the time."

We did. To no avail whatsoever. Not only were the Maskers not hiding where John Stretch said, there was no sign of their skyship. I'd hoped it would be right there where I could sabotage it. Or whatever seemed appropriate at the moment of discovery.

Why would I want to keep them from going away? The longer they hung around the more likely they would fall into the hands of somebody off the Hill. Which would make times just that much more interesting for those of us who couldn't fly away.

"Singe? You smell anything that might be the Masker skyship?"

She strained valiantly. And told me, "I can tell nothing. What happened back there has blinded my nose."

Poor baby. "Follow me." It was time to get the hell away from the Embankment.

Our line of retreat took us back past the ruined tannery.

Raindrops continued to strike randomly, scattered but getting fatter all the time. And colder. One smacked me squarely atop the bean. It contained a core of ice. It stung. I regretted my prejudice against hats.

"Look," Singe said. We were slinking through the crowd of onlookers, which had swollen to scores, most of them tickled to see a stormwarden looking like he had a firm grip on the dirty end of the stick.

A groggy Bic was back up on one knee, a black-clad ankle still in hand, glaring at the mob, not a man of whom offered a hand. He spied somebody he thought he recognized, that somebody being Mama Garrett's favorite boy. He croaked out, "Garrett!"

Garrett kept on rolling. Maybe a little faster. Garrett's sidekick puffed and hustled to keep up.

Bic yelled as loud as he could. His excitement didn't do him any good at all. The one response he did get was a growing hum that sounded like a swarm of bumblebees moving in for the kill. It came from within the rubble. Masker sorcery. Bic slapped another hand onto his boss' ankle and went back to pulling.

"Look!" Singe gasped again.

The rubble had begun shifting and sliding as though restless giants were awakening underneath.

The bubble was coming up again. And now the bumblebees were singing their little bug hearts out.

The bubble got a lot bigger this time. Bricks and broken boards, ratmen and squealing henchmen all slid off. Bic forgot about me and Singe. He forgot his manners entirely. He yanked the mask off the stormwarden, slapped his face. I caught a glimpse of pallor disfigured by indigo tattoos. A real heartbreaker of a face. It must drive the hookers wild.

Something began rising up inside the bubble. Something shiny, like freshly polished sword steel.

The bumblebees lost the thread of their hearty marching song and began to whine. The bubble began to shrink and the steel to sink. But the bees picked up the beat after a few false notes.

The Masker skyship emerged from the ruins.

The addled stormwarden popped it with his best lightning bolt.

The skyship popped him back. Enthusiastically. He flew twenty yards, ricocheted off a brick wall, barely twitched once before an incoming Bic Gonlit, tumbling ass over appetite, crash-landed on top of him.

The Masker vessel lumbered into the sky and headed south, the bumblebees occasionally stumbling, the ship itself wobbling.

"A little faster with the feet, I think," Singe said when I slowed to watch. "I am developing a strong need to find myself somewhere far away from here." The crowd seemed to agree with her. Everybody thought it was time to be somewhere else.

"Yes, indeed, girl. Yes, indeed. Before old Bic wakes up and decides to blame us for everything."

We did go somewhere else. But we weren't much happier there than we'd been on the Embankment.

81

"I've got a bad feeling about this, Singe," I said, puffing as I headed south, the knees beginning to ache. "I'm willing to bet I know exactly where that thing was headed."

No dummy she, Singe opined, "Mr. Dotes' establishment."

"Yeah."

Yeah.

The skyship was long gone by the time we reached The Palms but people were still hanging around in the street, telling each other about it. There'd been enough excitement for the visitation to become a neighborhood forty-day wonder. I noted a couple of familiar faces among the gossipers, guys asking only occasional questions and doing a lot of listening.

Some snooty galoot got his heart broken when I didn't even slow down going past him at the door—with a rat in tow, for the gods' sake! For a moment I thought I'd finally get me a chance to witness a genuine sputtering fit of apoplexy.

Snooty galoot disappointed me.

People so often do.

"I smells, wit' my little smeller, somet'in' what a man ought not ta got ta smell," Puddle announced from the shadows at the other end of the room.

Sarge hollered from the kitchen, "Dat mean dat Garrett's here?"

"Dat it does indeed."

"Ha! So pay up! I told ya da man don't got a ounce a shame an' he'd turn up before da dust settled."

"Sounds like we guessed right," I told Singe. "They did come here."

"Hey, Greenwall," Puddle yelled. "Ya need more help talkin' people outa comin' in da door?"

The snooty character gobbled some air. It was obvious that Morley had hired him for his upthrust honker, not for his ability to intimidate hard men.

I said, "Don't be too rough on the guy, Puddle." I intended to explain how he naturally went spineless when he saw Singe and me bearing down, but Puddle interrupted.

"Yer right, Garrett. It's his secont day on da job. Ain't every day ya look out da door an' dere's one a dem flyin' disk kinda t'in's landin' in da street out front, wit' goofy-lookin' silvery elf guys jumpin' down an' whippin' up on everybody."

I took a second glance at Greenwall. He did look like a man nursing a ferocious headache. So did Puddle, for that matter. "So the girls all got away."

Puddle stared at me with narrowed eye for several seconds. "Yeah. Dey went. But one a dem had ta be dragged kickin' and da udder two cried all da way 'cause dey didn't want ta go."

"Wow! Your boss is quite the man. He'll be heartbroken, I'm sure."

"Morley's gonna be singin' hosannas, soon as he gets enough strengt' back." Puddle's grin slid away. His face turned serious. "I hate ta be da one what gives ya da bad news, Garrett, but dem sluts, dey stole Mr. Big when dey went."

"Oh, that is awful." What an actor. I know what racket I ought to be in, now. Not involved in inventing and manufacture. I ought to be on the stage. I managed to be convincing in my loss. "O Cruel Asp of Fortune, thou wicked serpent, how painful thy sting . . ."

"Gods, Garrett, you aren't just a ham, you're the whole stinking pig." Morley had managed to get most of the way downstairs. He looked like a guy fighting a big headache, too.

Once again I brought my acting skills to bear and concealed my amusement. "You look like death warmed over. You been playing with the vampires?"

"Of a sort. Right now I don't think I ever want to see another woman."

"Oh, I suspect you'll change your mind. After you recover from the fantasy come true." Given a few days I'd found myself thinking of Katie and Tinnie in a nonplatonic fashion again. But I am a very resilient fellow.

"They stole Mr. Big, Garrett."

"You sound like that bothers you."

Morley's eyes narrowed suspiciously. Like why wouldn't that bother the gods themselves?

"It's no secret that I wasn't fond of the ugly moth. But if you miss obnoxiousness fluttering around you I'll send over some of the swarm of pixies that're living in my walls, now."

"No need. Mr. Big will be back," Morley predicted. He sounded so confident I wondered if I ought to be worried.

"You sound sure. And glum at the same time."

"Evas and her friends are going to come back with him."

"Heh-heh-heh." I pulled my most evil laugh out of my bag of attitudes for special occasions. "You sure they won't just wring his neck when they get tired of him?"

"You'll be laughing out the other side of your mouth when they get here, Garrett."

"I'll move. I'll go into hiding."

"You're marked, buddy. You're special. You started something and now you're marked for their special attention."

"I started nothing. It was all Evas' idea."

"You gave her the idea for her new idea, Mr. Entrepreneur. She's going to get hold of a bigger skyship and start bringing silver elf women to TunFaire for very special vacation getaways. And she sees you as a whole lot better partner in her enterprise than she sees me. She told me so." A bit of wickedness lurked in the corners of his eyes. He just might have had something to do with the lady Visitor's attitude.

Telling stories on me again, probably. I have to break him of that habit.

"Their government will never let them do that." Stopping adventurers was Casey's business. His whole purpose in life was to prevent contacts between his people and ours.

"You really think? It's beyond corruption?"

"Glad to see you're all right," I said. "Get plenty of rest. And get some meat in your diet. You'll need to beef up if you want to make it in the gigolo racket." I began to sidle toward the door.

"I plan to maintain my amateur status. But you being a businessman now, you might want to exploit the opportunity."

Maybe I could recruit Kip and Rhafi and a dozen of their friends. What they lacked in experience they could make up in enthusiasm.

I sidled some more, noting that Singe was enjoying my discomfiture entirely too much.

"What's your rush, Garrett?" my old pal asked.

"I've got to see a Dead Man about a horse."

Morley took his turn chuckling. Chances were he had a fair notion what was going on in my head. But he said only, "You be careful on the street. There are some ratfolk out there who resent what the Guard did to Reliance. And they think you and Singe might have had something to do with that. Your friend John Stretch is having trouble setting himself up as Reliance's replacement."

"My friend John Stretch is going to get some grief from me, too." I'd concluded that John Stretch had given me completely bum information about where to find the Maskers. That Singe and I had stumbled into the right place at the wrong time almost entirely by chance. That we never would have found the Visitors if Bic and his sorcerer friend hadn't been dogging us.

Dotes got in a final gouge as we stepped into the street. "See you at Chodo's birthday bash. I think you could sell your gigolo franchise to the Outfit."

Chodo's birthday party. That bucket of ice water put everything else into a more favorable perspective. The return of the insatiable Visitor girls sounded positively attractive by comparison.

82

"What the hell do you mean, he got away?" I yelled at Dean. "Between you and Old Bones in there you couldn't manage one guy four feet tall and only about fifty pounds soaking wet?"

"You exaggerate, Mr. Garrett," Dean replied with cold dignity. "That creature has Powers. And the thing in the other room went to sleep." He jabbed a thumb in the direction of the Dead Man. "If you insist on pillorying someone for dereliction, I suggest your candidate be the thing actually capable of having exercised control over the foreigner."

"But he's asleep. I can't vent my frustrations by yelling at him."

Dean shrugged. My need to yell was a matter of indifference to him. Unless I showed the slack-witted judgment to zero in on him personally. "I expect you're starved, Mr. Garrett. What do you say to stuffed peppers?"

That was blackmail in its rawest form.

Dean's smile was wicked, even demonic. He'd do it. He'd really make the whole house reek of that foul fruit.

"You watch out I don't change the locks next time you go out of the house."

Dean smiled. It's his firmly held conviction that I can't get along without him.

The man is mad.

"I'm going to go into my office. I'm going to put on my thinking cap. Singe, how about you grab us a pitcher and a couple of mugs?" I really wanted to go pummel the Dead Man but knew I'd just end up driving myself crazy. If he was soundly enough asleep to let Casey get away there'd be no waking him up anytime soon.

Because beer was involved Singe overlooked my treating her more like an employee than a partner, which is what she figured she was.

I didn't give Eleanor more than a passing glance because I knew what I'd find if I bothered to consult the woman in the painting. No help at all and a whole lot of amusement at my predicament.

Singe materialized with the beer. Not one pitcher but two, one in each paw, with mugs. We went to work sipping, nobody saying much. After a while she returned to the kitchen for refills. We sipped some more. I began to relax. Then Dean stuck his head in to tell me that Colonel Block was at the door and wanted to see me.

I hadn't heard him pounding.

Singe hadn't either, apparently. She said, "Just when I was about to seduce you."

"Life's a bitch. There's always a Westman Block ready to jump in and ruin the moment. Colonel! How good to see you. To what do we owe the pleasure?" Singe moved her special chair aside so Block could plant himself in the guest seat.

Block nodded his head sagely. "All right, Garrett. You got me fooled. You're thrilled to see me. I just wanted to share some news. We caught one of those silver elves that have been terrorizing the city."

"Terrorizing?" Being the superb actor I am, I kept a straight face and said, "Really? Congratulations."

"Don't waste the effort."

"Huh?"

"I know what's been going on, Garrett. Lucky for you, most of the time I buy into Deal's concept of the rule of law."

"I'm glad to hear it."

"Your attitude, however, frequently makes it hard to cut you any slack."

"So my best friends keep telling me. I had a rough childhood. My daddy got killed in the war."

Which wasn't the smartest choice of wiseass comments. But the good colonel set me straight.

"Don't be a dickhead, Garrett. Everybody's daddy got killed in the war. That's the way they did it in those days. They waited till a guy created a family before they conscripted him. That way they could be sure there'd be more soldiers coming up."

"Easy. Sorry." This was an aspect of Wes Block I hadn't seen before. "So let's be serious. You've caught one of the silver elves."

"And he isn't talking. We're not entirely sure that he can. The people who've examined him say it might not be possible to make him talk because we don't have the technical expertise."

Clever, clever Casey. He was selling his strangeness. "And?"

"And there have been suggestions, from some quarters, that your partner might be able to fill the communications gap."

Ah. Now we came to the reason for the friendly visit. "There's an idea that hasn't found its time. Assuming there was any way at all he could be talked into underwriting the delinquencies of the people you're fronting, there's still one problem. He's sound asleep. Based on grim experience, I'd say there's a cruel chance he'll stay that way for a long time. Because he's had to stay awake a lot, lately."

"I'm trying to save you some grief, Garrett."

"And I appreciate it. But no amount of good intentions on your part, or of anybody else's wishful thinking, can change the facts. Come on. I'll show you." Like there's anything visibly different about how the Dead Man looks when he's sleeping. "Stick a pin in him if you want. He wouldn't feel it anyway but if he was awake he'd respond to the insult. Or you could say something revolting but true about the Loghyr."

"I'll take your word for it." But his tone wasn't that reassuring. "The trouble is, I have people pressing me who don't really care about such problems."

"You have people pressing you who're stupid enough to risk offending a dead Loghyr?"

"In a word, yes. There really are people who don't know any better."

"People that survived the Cantard?"

"We have a crop of apprentices coming up who didn't get a chance to experience the worst the war had to offer before the Venageti collapse. They don't know they're not invulnerable. They have no grasp whatsoever on their true limitations. And they're in a hurry now."

"You don't say. And you don't know any older, cooler heads who might rein them in?"

Block shrugged. He looked grim. He shuddered. I asked, "What?"

"I never expected it would be easy. But I did hope."

"Which means?"

"Which means that I'm going to have to find a hole and pull it in after me because Relway's gotten a big head lately, too. He insists that if any of those spook-chaser pups do step very far outside the law, he'll nail them the same as if they were muggers on the street."

"Oh, boy. That'll bring their daddies out." I took a huge breath, let it go in a grand sigh. "I didn't think he'd move this soon."

"That little man is crazy, Garrett. But crazy like the proverbial fox. I'd bet he's a lot more ready for a showdown than you or I think he could be. If he does go down he'll make sure it's in a conflagration so dramatic that not just TunFaire but all Karenta will be changed forever."

I sighed me another one of those huge sighs. "All right. I don't want to do this. I hate to get noticed by those people. But there's a slim chance I can get through to your guy. If he's the one we called Casey. I assume he is because all the rest of them seem to have gone aboard the skyship that was terrorizing the city earlier today."

Block gave me one of his squinty looks. He knew that skyship had made an up close and personal appearance at the digs of my friend Morley Dotes. But he didn't press the matter.

I offered him a brief, thoroughly edited version of events on the Embankment, claiming I'd been there in the interest of my client Kip Prose, who still felt threatened. "The point is, I'm still finding myself up to my ankles in Bic Gonlit. Nothing I do gets that guy to go away. He's started to make me wonder if it isn't personal after all."

"Bic Gonlit. With a stormwarden, eh?"

"A thoroughly shabby stormwarden. You'd figure him for a fake, just looking at him. Nobody off the Hill ought to be that scruffy. But he sure brewed up the lightning when the time came to show his stuff."

"I haven't gotten the reports on that incident yet. I'll look into it when I get back." He asked several questions evidently meant to give him clues to the sorcerer's identity. I don't think I helped.

Singe decided to go refill our pitchers.

Block said, "That's creepy, Garrett."

"What is?"

"That rat running around here just like she was people."

"Oh." I didn't start an argument. "You get used to it. You are holding the silver elf at the al-Khar, aren't you?"

"Yes."

Good. It would've been bad—for me—if they'd decided to question Casey in the cellar of one of those ugly stone piles on the Hill. "Well, let me tie up a few loose ends here, then I'll wander over there with you and take a shot at seeing what I can do with your guy."

Colonel Black was suspicious, right away and right down to the bone. And he was right to be. "What're you up to, Garrett?"

"I'm trying to keep my life from getting infested with parasitic wizards. I've had run-ins with Casey before. If it's him you've got and not some other elf none of us knows about, I might be able to communicate with him. I managed once before. But he's stubborn. And he isn't afraid of anything."

Block's suspicions were allayed only slightly. I don't know why. I'm a trustworthy kind of guy.

"I'm going to go help Singe. If Dean's not there to do it for her she gets beer all over drawing it out of the cold well." I went to the kitchen. "Singe, I need the invisibility fetish."

Somebody trusted me. She handed the thing over without a question.

"You know if we have any more of these things squirreled away anywhere?"

She shook her head. "You gave all the rest back to the women or to that man in there. He's afraid of me, isn't he?"

"In a way. Yes. He'll get over it. Say a prayer for me to the gods of the ratfolk."

"Or maybe I will not. Our gods are all cruel and treacherous. Reflecting the world itself. We just try to trick them into looking the other way."

A philosophy I could embrace wholeheartedly.

83

My interview with Casey took place in the same big room where I'd gotten interviewed earlier. The same main players seemed to be on hand. Block was there. Three quiet wizards were there, none in costume, and none of them the one who ran with Bic Gonlit. I'm confident that Director Relway was there as well, back in the shadows, though I never actually heard or saw him.

Casey was there, seated in a hard chair at a bare table when I arrived. They hadn't bothered to restrain him. He was no physical threat. As I settled opposite him one of Colonel Black's men dumped a sack of nine fetish devices in front of me. I said, "Casey, old buddy, we're in the really deep shit here, now. You've been around TunFaire long enough to have a pretty good idea of the kind of people who have hold of you. You have a pretty good idea what they want. And you know they're not real good at taking no for an answer. You have to understand that some things are inevitable and that all you can do is make it easier on all of us." Lines of a sort everyone in that room, probably including Casey himself, would have used numerous times. I took out the fetish I'd brought from home, added it to the pile while staring straight into Casey's strange eyes.

Could he read me at all?

"What's that?" Block demanded.

"One of those amulet boxes of theirs. Singe found it today. When things were blowing up on the Embankment. Figured I ought to bring it over. Casey. Do you understand anything I've said? Do you know what these people want?"

After a long, long pause Casey nodded.

Of course he knew. It was his mission to make sure they didn't get it, from him or the Maskers or, especially, the Brotherhood of Light. I hoped he would keep his mission in mind. Because I was counting on him to get us all out of this mess.

"All right. Look here, Colonel. We're getting somewhere already. Told you I could get through to him. Whoa there, Casey. Slowly and carefully. We aren't sure which ones of those things are weapons."

Casey took such offense that his indignance was plain to everyone. "We do not . . . make weapons!"

That caused a stir, more because he'd spoken than because of what he'd said.

"Is that true? But I've been knocked unconscious over and over again by something that left me with the worst headaches of my life."

I believe Casey would have laughed if Visitors had the capacity for laughter. "What you experienced . . . was an effect . . . of a device used . . . for the removal of . . . the parasites common to . . . the bodies of most . . . of your animals . . . and races. Lice and . . . fleas in particular. With the device set . . . at its strongest . . . power. We do not . . . make weapons."

"I'll take your word for that. Which one of these doohickeys is a flea getter ridder ofer?"

Casey extended one spider leg finger slowly.

"Good. Sergeant, you want to take that one away?"

Excellent. Now I knew that Casey could tell these devices apart. Hopefully. Which would mean that he should know what kind of fetish I had placed on the table.

Maybe he was smart enough to understand what needed doing.

"So. Let's go over the rest of these, one by one. Tell me what they're supposed to do. Start with this one here."

Casey did that. And after we'd reviewed a couple of fetishes I realized that he couldn't really make me understand what he was talking about. I didn't have the vocabulary. Then his voice gave out.

I asked Block, "Can we get him some water in here? He's obviously not used to talking."

Block said something. One of his men moved. I glanced over. And when I looked back Casey wasn't there anymore. Neither were any of the fetishes. An instant later, as the shouting began, the hammer of darkness fell. Again.

84

"What happened?" I mumbled. I was the last one to wake up. The delouser's effects were cumulative for sure.

"How about you tell me," Block growled, dragging me into a seated position with my back against a wall.

"I've got a notion I don't have a lot of fleas anymore. Gods, my head is killing me! Hit me and put me out again." I meant it at the moment.

"No. I want you to get up. I want you hurting while you explain what just happened. You won't be able to concentrate enough to bullshit me."

"I don't know what just happened. You were here. You were paying attention. You probably got a better look than I did."

"Maybe I did. Maybe I didn't. I can't shake the feeling that there wasn't a pea under any of the shells."

Nausea overcame me as I tried to stand. Beer and my last meal beat me to the floor.

"Godsdammit! That just tops my whole day off, Garrett!"

I tried to climb the nearest chair. It was occupied. I gasped, "Get me some water. Wasn't somebody supposed to go after water?" And, "What happened to him?"

The man in the chair was one of the sorcerers. His eyes were open but nobody seemed to be at home behind them.

The look was worse than the thousand-yard stare. With that you knew your guy would probably come back someday. Seeing this, you knew he wouldn't, ever.

"I don't know, Garrett. He seems to have turned into a vegetable. They all have. But nobody else was hurt." He stepped carefully, avoiding my mess.

Wow. Casey must've done that deliberately. He wasn't a nice guy after all. Unless he hadn't been aware what they were and this was a by-product of them owning their talent in the wrong place at the wrong time.

Block declared, "I think their intelligence was deliberately and systematically destroyed."

"That would make our Casey a vindictive little bastard, wouldn't it? Completely without a sense of humor about being misused. Why do you suppose he let you and me and the rest of these guys slide? Because we're like him, just battling the darkness the best we know how?"

"Gift horses, eh? You could be right." He didn't say anything for a while. I seized the opportunity to concentrate on feeling sorry for myself. I wondered if Lastyr and Noodiss had gotten away before they gave Kip an idea for a miracle headache cure. I'd better check. Then Block told me, "I'd better have you taken home. I want you to stay inside your house until I get this sorted out. There'll be questions. Some of you men want to get this mess cleaned up? Can't anybody around here do something without waiting to be told?"

It didn't seem likely. Not when everybody was preoccupied with a killer headache.

"This is bad shit, Garrett," Block whined. "This's real bad shit. I'll be lucky to get out of this just losing my job."

"Aren't you being a little too pessimistic?" I clamped down and pushed the pain back. But not very far. "Man, you let yourself get way too impressed by people off the Hill. Did Hill people give you your job? I thought Prince Rupert did that. And what were these guys trying to pull, anyway? They were trying to cut the rest of those witch doctors up there out of the jackpot. You watch. The rest of their kind will take one quick look at the facts and figure they had it coming."

"You do have a knack for looking on the bright side, Garrett. I sure hope it's as easy as all that."

First I'd heard of me being a brightside kind of guy. But what the hell, eh? If I played to that maybe Block would forget to nag me about Casey's getaway.

I reminded the good colonel of his obligations. "I thought you were going to take me home."

85

Colonel Block's coach was still a block from my house when it bogged down in traffic. Macunado Street was clogged with bodies, most of them human and only remotely acquainted with personal hygiene, but with plenty of odds and ends and mixtures in the crowd, too. Everybody wanted to see the glowing blob in the sky that seemed so interested in our neighborhood.

This blob wasn't a flying disk. Nor was it like those things that Evas and her friends had flown. This was more of a cylinder with gently tapered ends, with nothing protruding outside. To hear the crowd tell it, the cylinder had descended to ground level several times but was now just hovering, like it was confused. Or just waiting.

I told Block, "I'm telling you right now, flying around up in the air isn't one-tenth as much fun as you might think."

"And you'd know what you're talking about?"

"Hasn't been that long since I took a few rides on a pegasus."

"Garrett, you ought to write all your adventures down. Being mindful not to leave out any of the bullshit you're always laying on people you know."

"I'd do that if there was any way to make a few coppers out of it. But even I have trouble believing some of the stuff that's happened to me."

"You're right. You'd have a credibility problem. I don't believe some of it—and I was there when it happened."

The crowd oohed and aahed as the skyship suddenly dropped down almost to touching level, just about where

the Garrett homestead stood. It hovered there only briefly.
Colonel Block was looking out the other side of the coach
at the time. He might not have noticed.

He did say, "All these weird things going on in the sky
lately have had their positive side effects."

"For instance?" I wasn't paying close attention. I was
worrying about Casey's stubborn streak. Was he going to
get after Kip again, now?

"Such as the political shenanigans have quieted down for
a while. We haven't had anybody march for days. And it's
been at least a week since there was a significant race riot."

"People get tired of the same old entertainment."

Casey's skyship rose up against the backdrop of the
night, dwindled till it was a point lost among the stars. I
wondered just how strange his home country could really
be. Presumably those of his people that I'd met were
amongst the most bizarre specimens. The normal people
would stay home, content to do normal things.

Colonel Block dropped me in front of the house, the
street having emptied quickly once the show came to an
end. "Hang on, Garrett." He made me wait. "What do you
intend to do about Bic Gonlit?"

I hadn't given that much thought. It didn't need much.
"Ignore him and hope he goes away, I suppose. He's just
been doing his job. He can go on doing it. I don't see how
that could involve me anymore."

Block grunted, said, "I do want to know which stormwarden he's running with, if you happen to stumble across that
bit of information."

"You got it." I started up the steps to the house.

A moment later I was surrounded by a cloud of pixies,
every one of them squeaking, all of them determined to
have me adjudicate countless disputes and quarrels. I was
rude to them all, whether or not I knew them.

Singe opened the front door. She held a big, cold mug
of beer. Ah, the little woman, welcoming me home.

As I started to extend my drinking hand Singe tossed
back half the mug. Then she told me, "The Dead Man said
you were coming."

"He's awake again?"

"That Casey woke him up. He said."

"Damn! That's a trick I wish he'd taught me before he went away."

Garrett.

"All present and accounted for, near as I can tell. Headache and everything. What's up, Big Guy? What'd the Visitor have to say?"

Just no hard feelings and farewell and thank you and do not be too concerned about reactions to his report. He does not believe that his superiors will insist upon any follow-up. The damage done by the Brotherhood of Light was slight and should damp itself out within a generation. Apparently it did the same last time around.

"That's good to know. Whatever it means. I'm going to go sleep off this headache." After I drank some beer and chased it with headache powders.

86

Deal Relway himself came to the house. He never made it quite clear why. The little man has trouble articulating sometimes. He did hint that he was convinced that I'd collaborated in the escape of a particular royal prisoner and that I had been an accessory to the total moronification of three already-subhuman subjects of the Karentine Crown. Not that that was necessarily a bad thing in the case of those particular subjects.

As far as he was concerned, justice had been served.

"What was that all about?" I asked the Dead Man after the director took his leave.

The only response I got was the psychic equivalent of a snore. I wanted to scream. I'd counted on the Dead Man to pluck Relway's psychic bones.

87

Karenta's current monarch has been so deft at survival that most of his subjects have had the opportunity to learn his birth date. They have begun taking advantage of the fact that the King's Birthday is, traditionally, a Karentine holiday.

This year the people of substance had chosen to collect in the reservoir park. There they would show off their new seasonal outfits and their participation in the latest fad, the wonderful world of inventions called three-wheels.

Any family that showed up without being able to claim at least one three-wheel on order might as well resign itself to being the butt of condescending gossip for at least as long as it took for us to develop a grander, bigger, more expensive model.

I had to attend with my business partners, who brought most of their families. Which meant there were beautiful women in every direction I looked, be they Tate, Weider, or Prose. I didn't get much chance to exercise my eyes, though. Tinnie had decided I was back on her A list. Which, apparently, awarded her complete custody of where I directed my vision.

Alyx Weider was too busy scooting around, showing off her own custom three-wheel, to afford her usual distraction.

I steered myself toward Tinnie's Uncle Willard. "This is an amazing show, sir." Every damned three-wheel we'd built was here somewhere. So it seemed. "When are we supposed to do the judging?" A huge part of the festivities was a contest to see which young lady could dress up her three-wheel the prettiest.

Our end users, so far, were almost all girls and young women of extremely considerable substance. A demographic I'd have found particularly interesting if I hadn't been claimed. For the moment.

"Ha!" I told the redhead. "I *am* supposed to be looking." Then, "Why aren't you out there outshining Alyx and Rose?"

Pout. "One of my wheels broke when we were leaving. They wouldn't let me get it fixed. That would make us late."

Two painfully homely young women, paced by four fierce-looking, thoroughly well armed characters on foot, passed us, leisurely following the bridle path. "Ugh!" I said.

Willard Tate cautioned me. "Those are the royal daughters, Garrett."

"Guaranteed to be winners in the contest," Tinnie added, because I would be too obtuse and democratic to figure that out for myself.

I tried to remember how to do the tug at the forelock thing. I was out of practice. I asked, "How are we doing, businesswise?"

"Overall? We couldn't be plundering the rich more effectively if we were a barbarian horde. And we're doing it without any bloodshed. You hit this one square on the nose. You're a wealthy young man, now. Or you will be before much longer. Have you been giving any thought to your future?"

Beyond maybe getting a bigger cold well installed so we could keep up with Singe's added demands on the beer supply, no.

I said, "Uh-oh."

"What?"

"Sounds like I'm about to be offered an investment opportunity."

Willard laughed, something he didn't do very often. Normally, he was as sour and serious as an accountant. "You might say that, Garrett. Deal of a lifetime. What I'm wondering about is, what are you and Tinnie thinking about?"

"Uncle Willard!"

Uncle Willard ignored Tinnie completely. "You've been

playing cat and mouse with each other for several years, now. You're both getting a little long in the tooth to keep it up."

"I'm thinking you might want to address your questions to the cat. The mouse don't get much say." Which observation earned me an enthusiastic dig in the ribs.

"You planning to go on the way you've always done?"

I checked Tate's expression for a clue to how he meant that. I thought I got it. "It's what I do. I find things. I find things out. I try to help people who are in trouble. It's what I'm good at. I'm not good at managing a big manufacturing thing. Hell, I have trouble managing the everyday business side of what I do now. Dean does most of that. So if you need me to fill in as the son you no longer have, well, I can try to play the role, but I don't think you'd be happy with the results." Deciding maybe I wasn't quite as great an actor as had seemed the case the other day.

"I understand that. Come. It's time for the formal judging. I hope you brought enough prize ribbons, Tinnie. Because everybody who's anybody has to get some kind of award."

"I brought one for every unit we've sold, plus a few extras."

"Isn't having been born into the aristocracy wonderful?" Tate asked. "You don't *really* have to compete. You're a winner automatically."

I agreed. "Beats hard work and study all to hell."

"You know what they say. Work like a dog and what do you get? Dog tired."

Tinnie hurried off to one of the Tate family carriages, of which there were several present. She came back with a sheaf of ribbons. I let her slide back in under my right arm, thinking it *was*, maybe, time to start putting the boy's life behind. If *she* maybe thought so, too. The only other candidate I'd ever honestly considered was a young woman named Maya, who hadn't been patient enough to wait for me. And Eleanor, of course, but that would've been a little too ethereal a relationship for me.

Just then a half dozen shimmering objects streaked across the northern sky in a tight formation, low, in the far distance. Three seemed sizable, sausage-shaped vehicles. The rest were exactly like the odd little skyships that Evas and her henchwomen preferred. The Masker ship must have flown home very fast indeed. And Evas' secret hunger must be one she shared with a lot of Visitor women—if this was what Morley had predicted and not some kind of raid.

Dotes might've made the whole thing up.

Still, maybe I ought to get into the entrepreneurial spirit and . . .

Tinnie made herself at home under my right wing again. I was still on her A list. After all these minutes. Despite Uncle Willard. She asked, "Aren't you done with those people?"

"I guess. As long as they're done with Kip." I did worry about the Goddamn Parrot, though. But I wouldn't tell anybody.

I shook the unsettling notion that those larger vessels might be troopships. They were hovering over the Embankment now. Up to something.

Within minutes they headed back the way they had come. With an extra, disklike vehicle floating amongst them.

I tried to concentrate on the three-wheel festival. And spied Harvester Temisk immediately. Riding a three-wheel of his very own. He was headed my way. Looking altogether too serious for my time of life.

Chodo's party was drawing close.

For us heroes party time is never done.